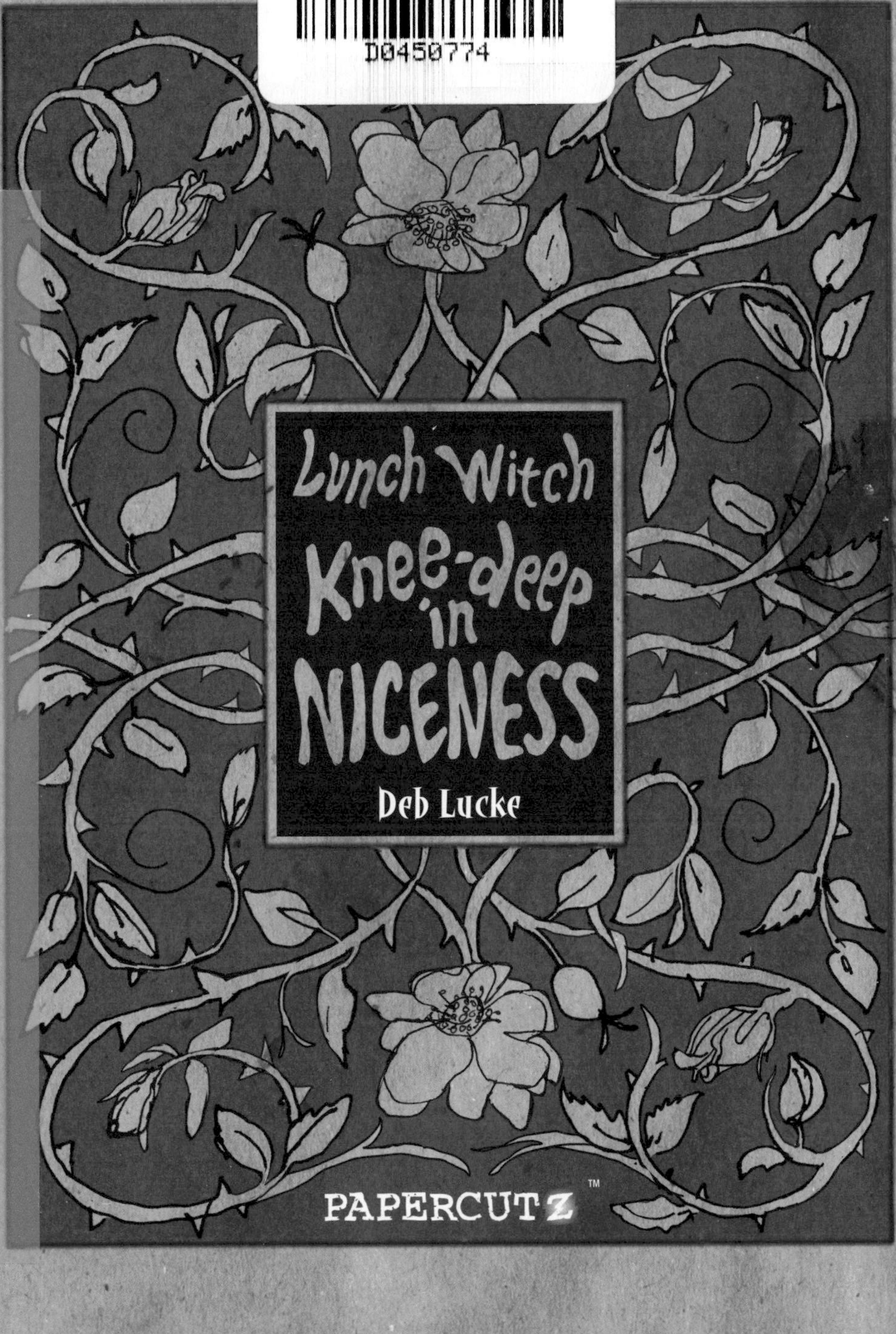
Lunch Witch
Knee-deep in NICENESS
Deb Lucke
PAPERCUTZ™

Dedicated to my parents:
Virgil and Phyllis Lucke
with rainbows, flowers, and puppies.

A shout-out to my fellow members of A.C.H.H.
—D.L.

Lunch Witch # 2
"Knee-deep in Niceness"

Brittanie Black — Production Coordinator
Bethany Bryan — Associate Editor
Jeff Whitman — Assistant Managing Editor
Terry Nantier — Editor and Publisher

Jim Salicrup
Editor-in-Chief

Color Flatter: Márcia Patrício
Additional Cartooning and Photography: Paul Hartzell
This book would not exist without his help!

Printed in China September 2016 by WKT Co. LTD.
3/F Phase 1 Leader Industrial Centre
188 Texaco Road, Tseun Wan, N.T.Hong Kong

Papercutz books may be purchased for business or promotional use.
For information on bulk purchases please contact:
Macmillan Corporate and Premium Sales Department at 800-221-7945 x 5442.
Distributed by Macmillan

First Printing

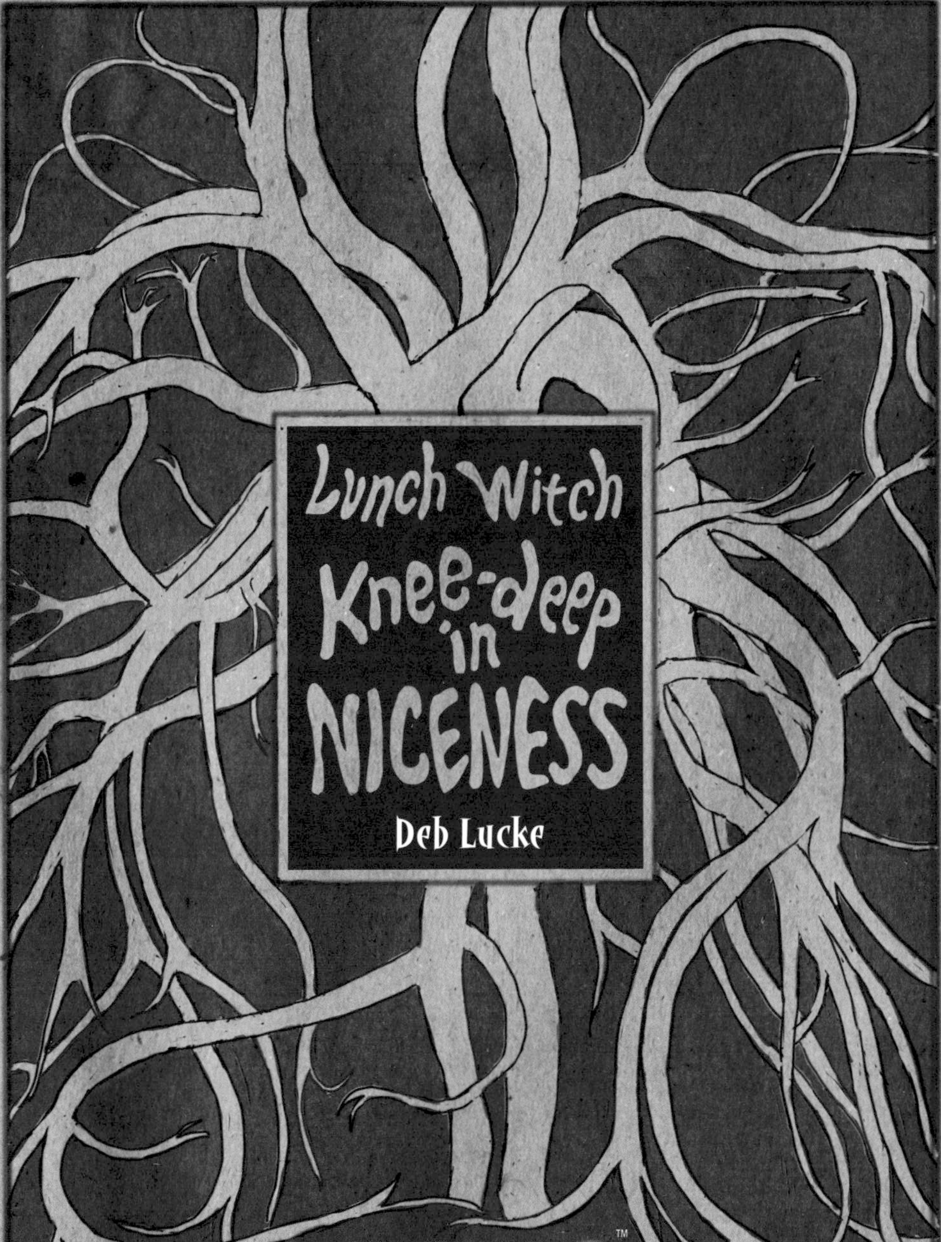

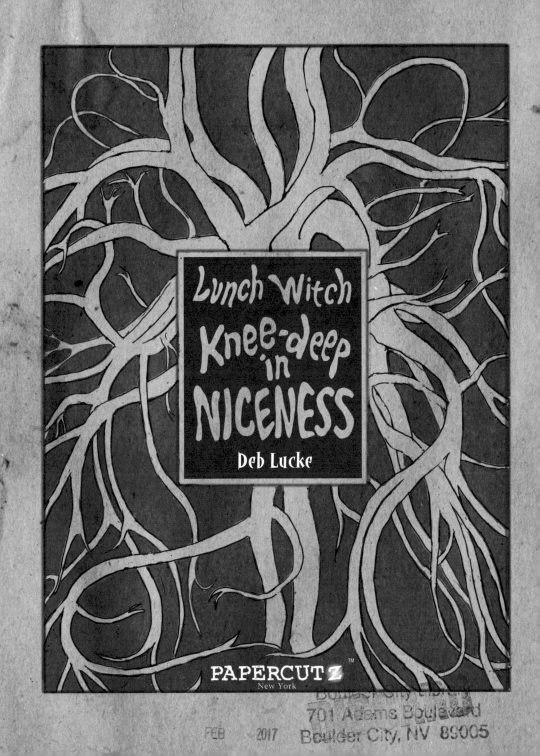

Lunch Witch

Knee-deep in NICENESS

Deb Lucke

PAPERCUTZ™
New York

1st

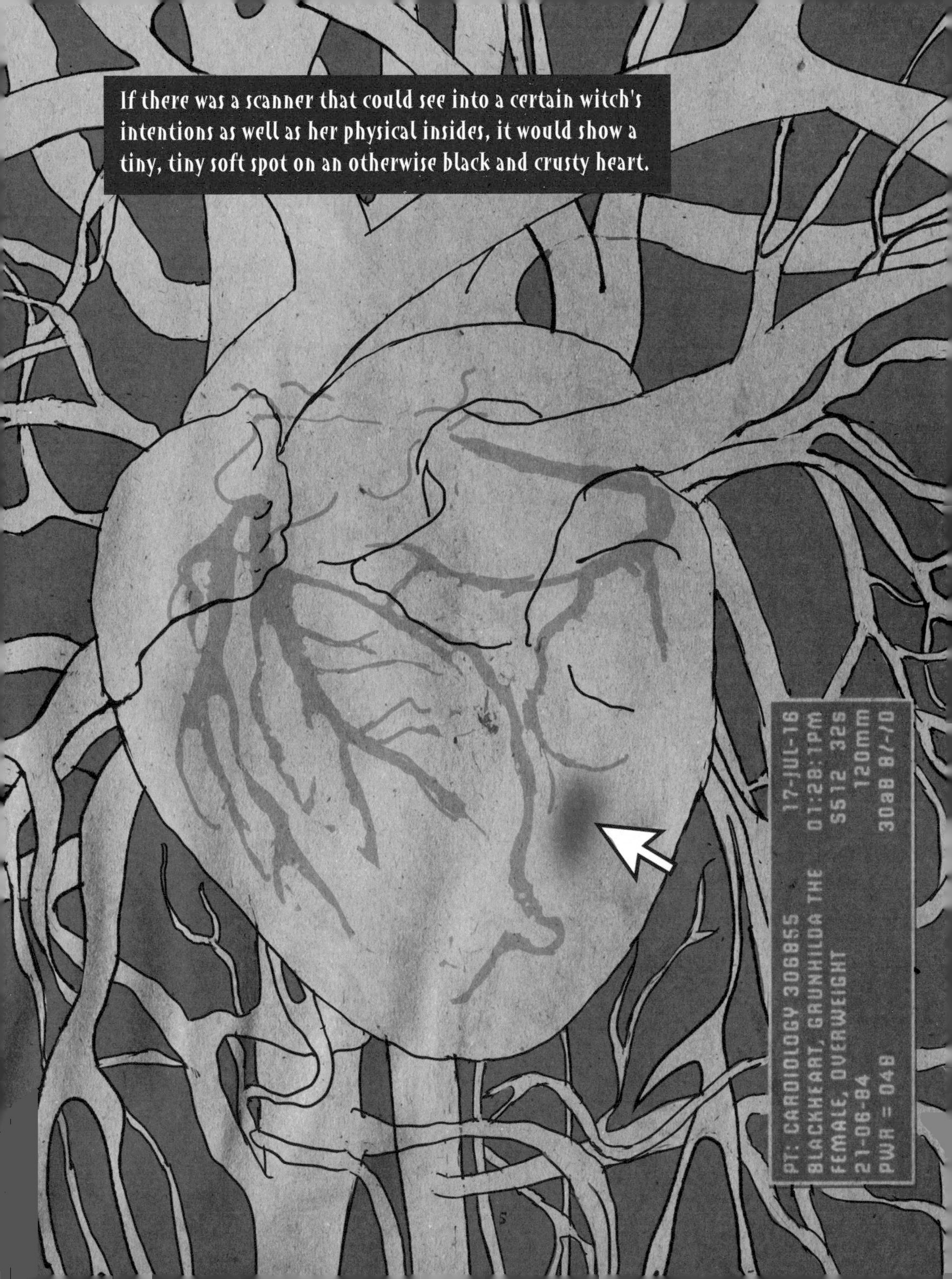
If there was a scanner that could see into a certain witch's intentions as well as her physical insides, it would show a tiny, tiny soft spot on an otherwise black and crusty heart.
PT: CARDIOLOGY 306855 17-JUL-16
BLACKHEART, GRUNHILDA THE 01:28:1PM
FEMALE, OVERWEIGHT SS12 32S
21-06-84 120mm
PWR = 04B 30aB B/-/0

2nd

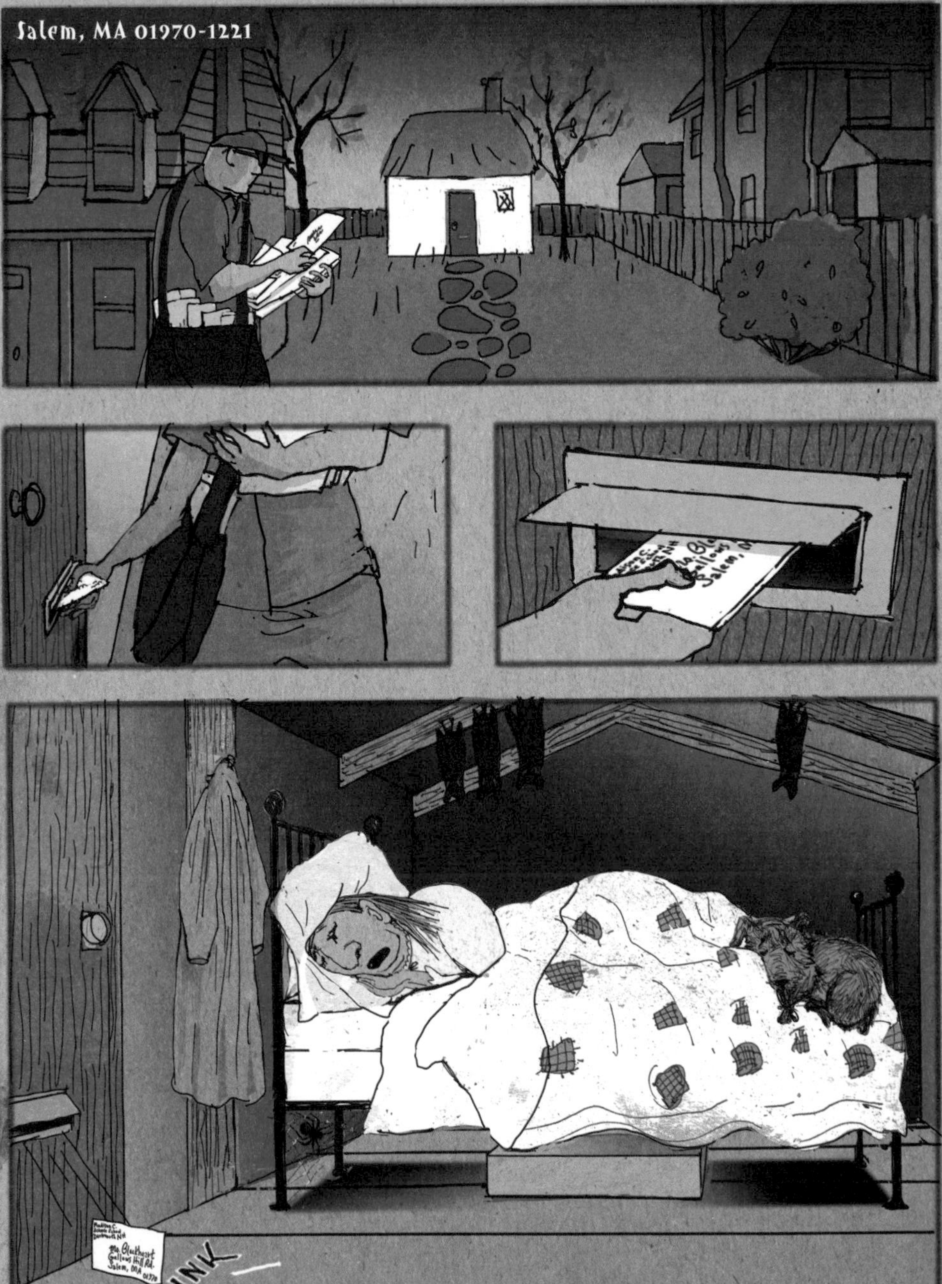
Salem, MA 01970-1221
Ms. Blackheart
Gallows Hill Rd.
Salem, MA 01970
PLINK

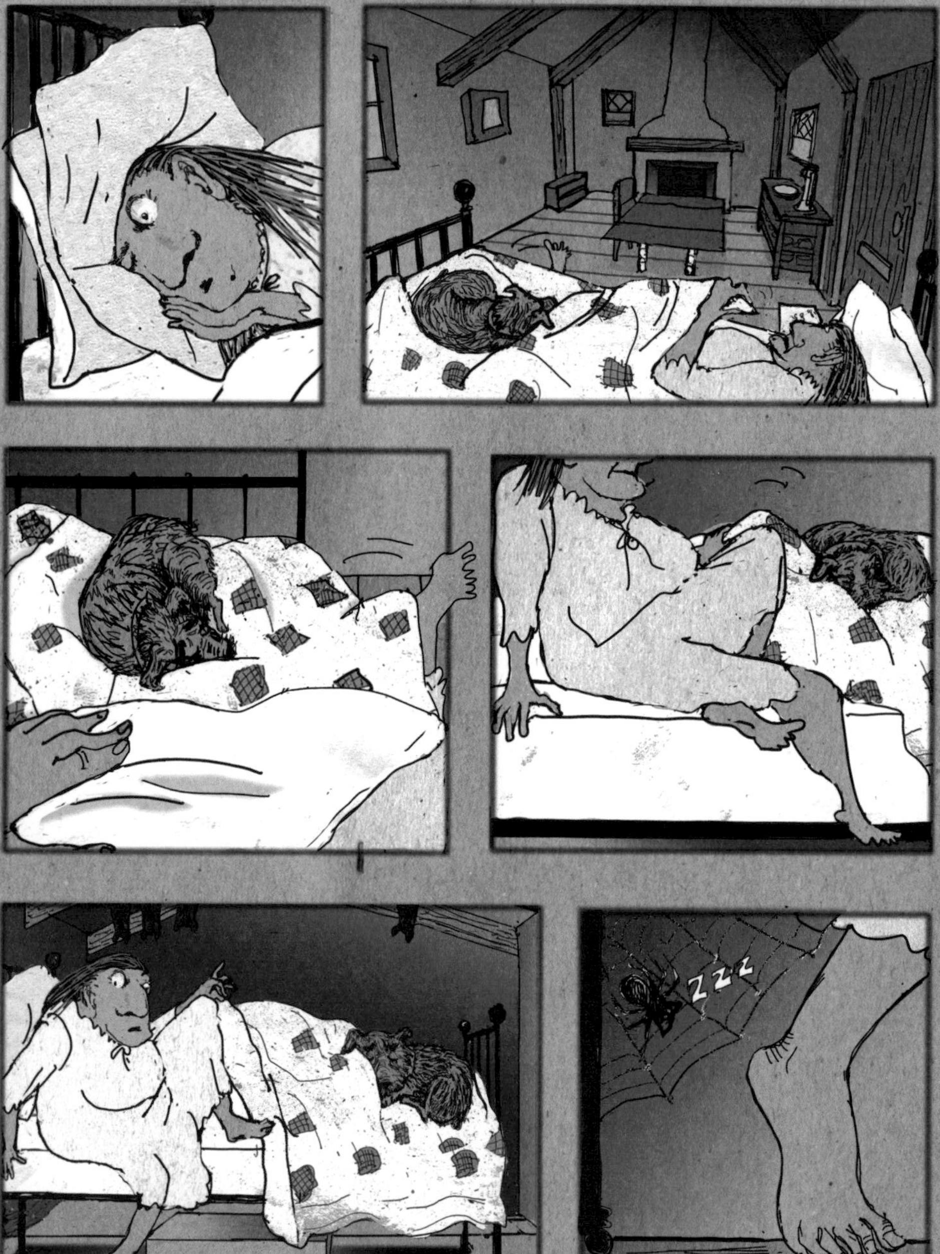
ZZZ

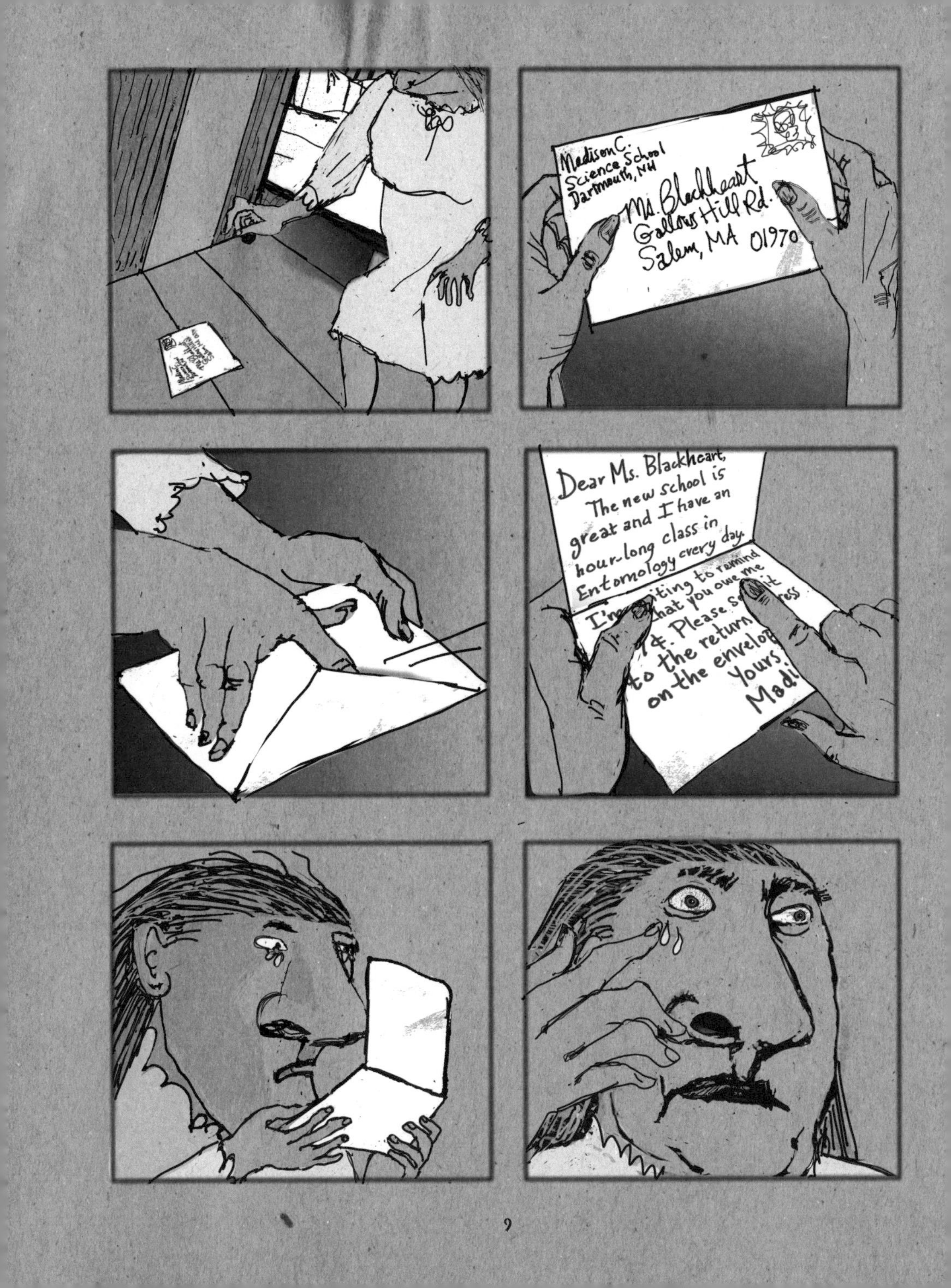
Madison C.
Science School
Dartmouth, NH
Ms. Blackheart
Gallows Hill Rd.
Salem, MA 01970
Dear Ms. Blackheart,
The new school is
great and I have an
hour-long class in
Entomology every day.
iting to remind
hat you owe me
it
ress
Please
to the return
to the envelo
on the
Yours
Madi

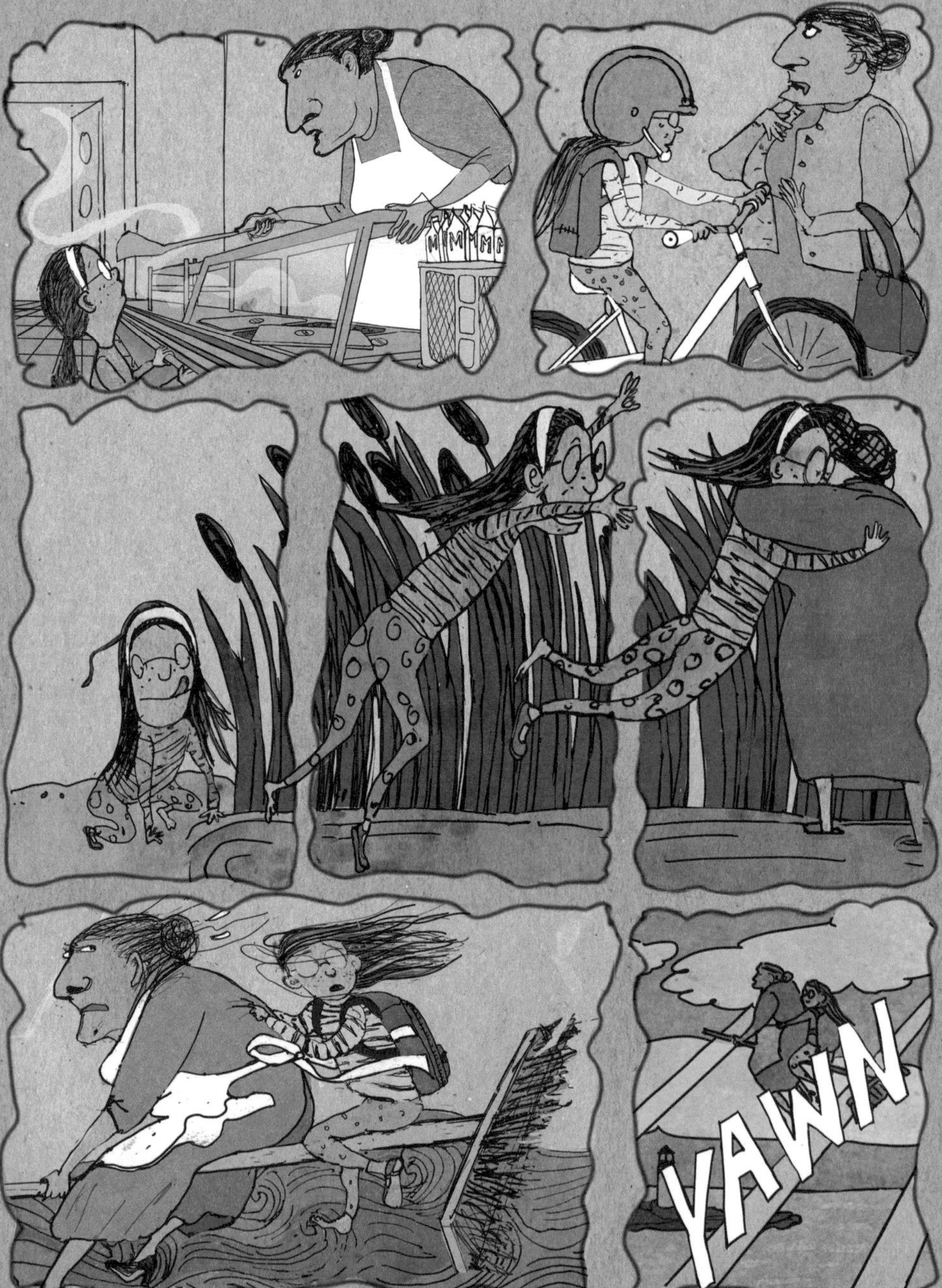
YAWN

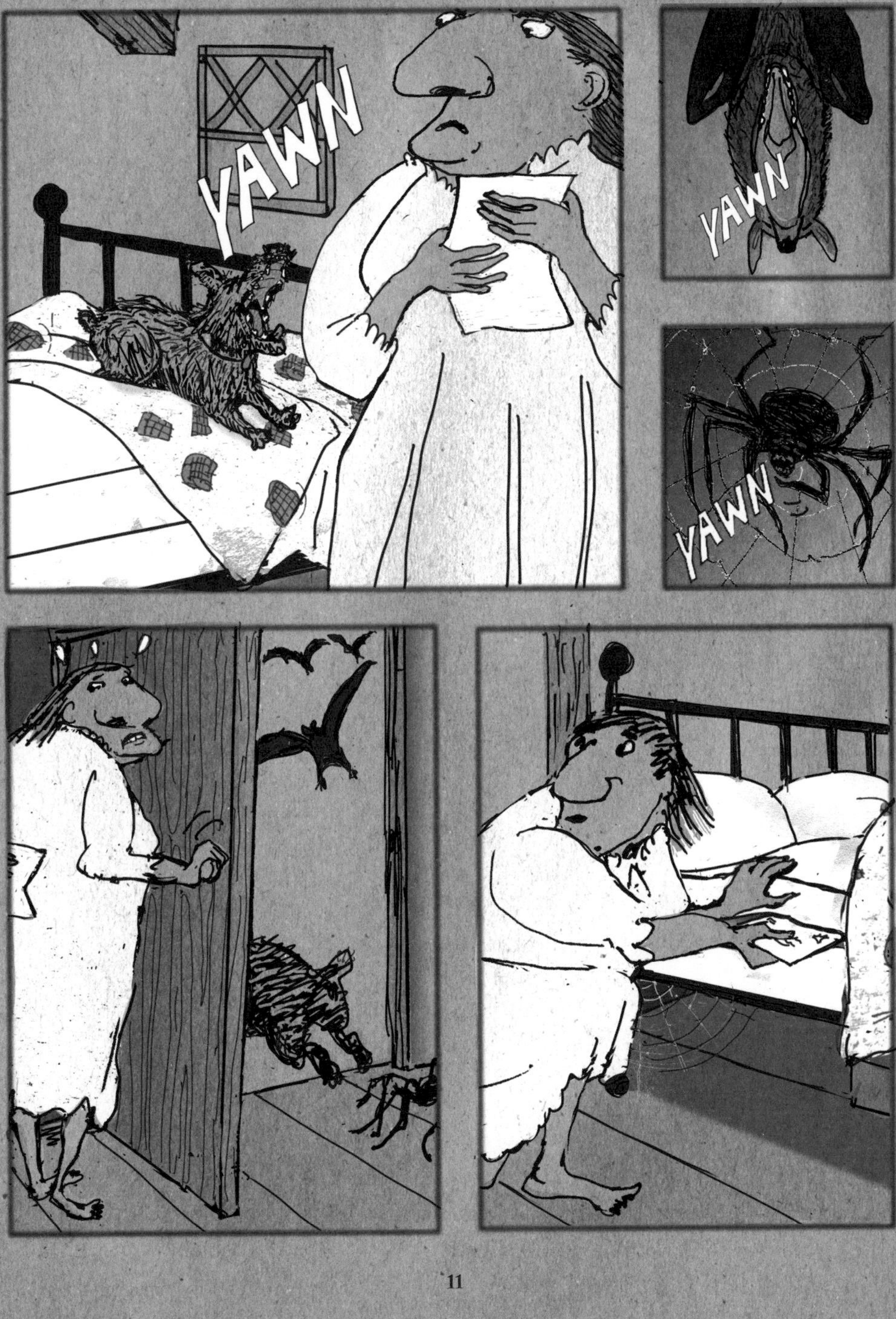
YAWN
YAWN
YAWN

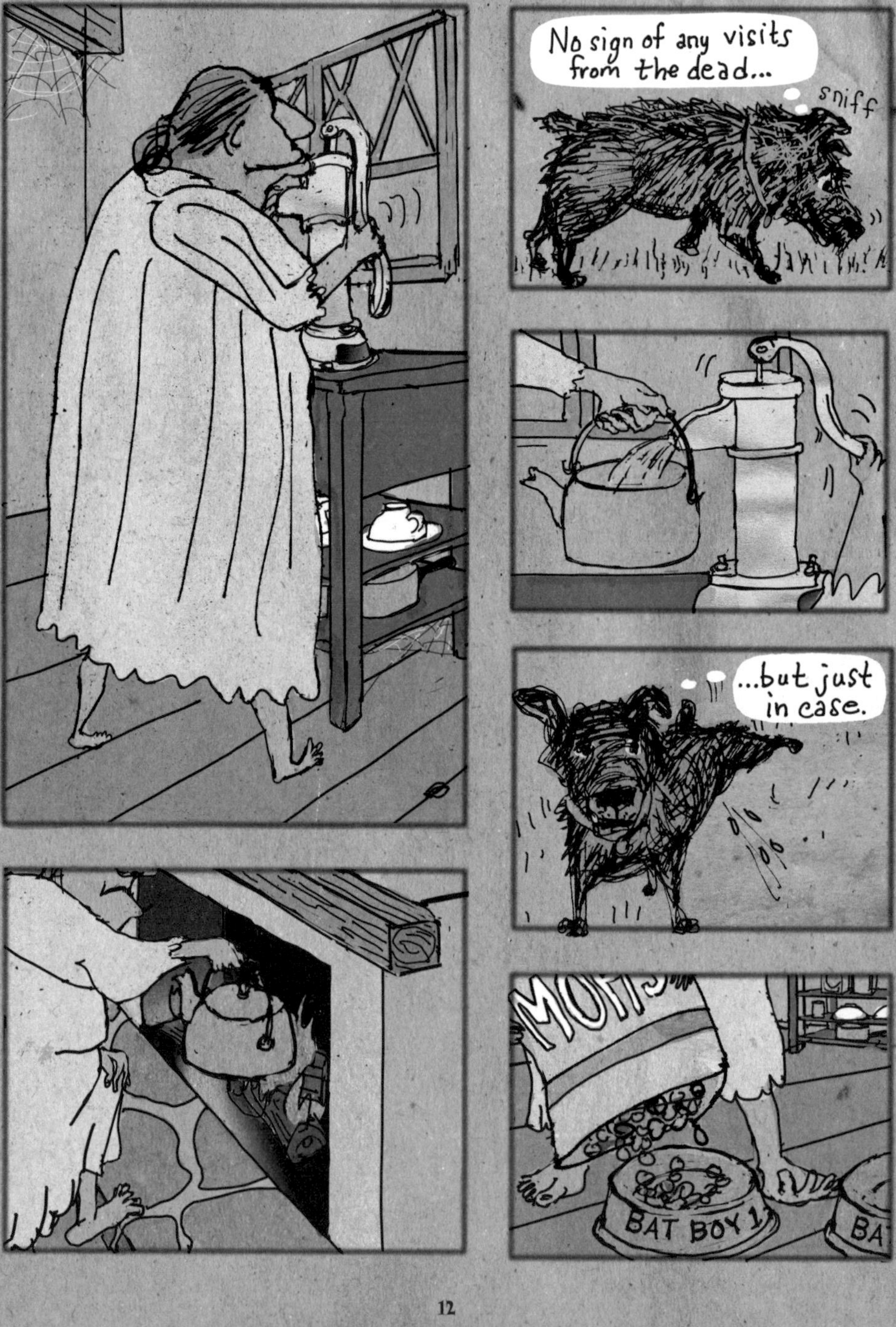
No sign of any visits from the dead...
sniff
...but just in case.
MOM'S
BAT BOY 1
BAT

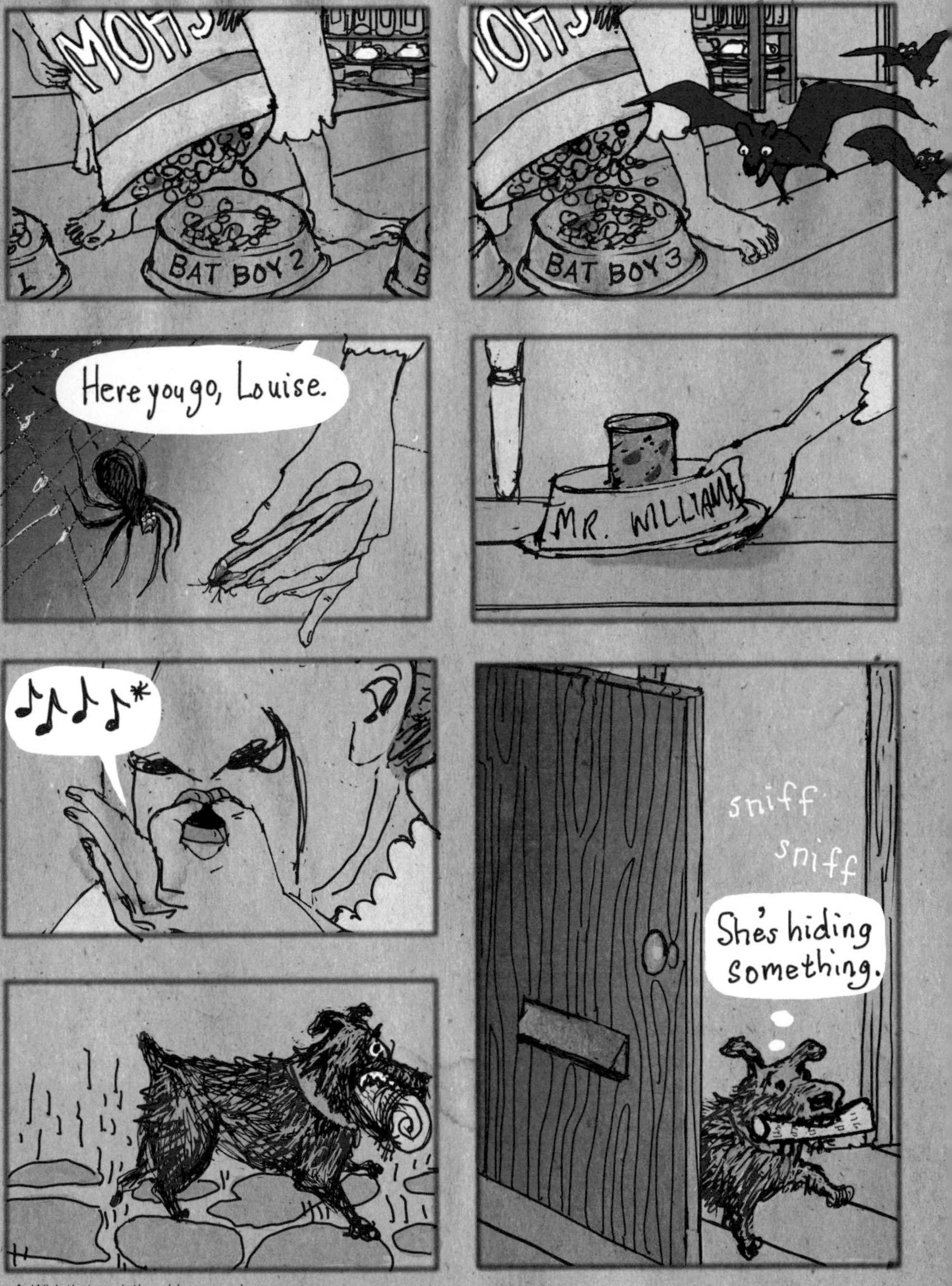
BAT BOY 2
BAT BOY 3
Here you go, Louise.
MR. WILLIAM
♪♪♪♪*
sniff
sniff
She's hiding something.

*Whistle translation: I love my dog.

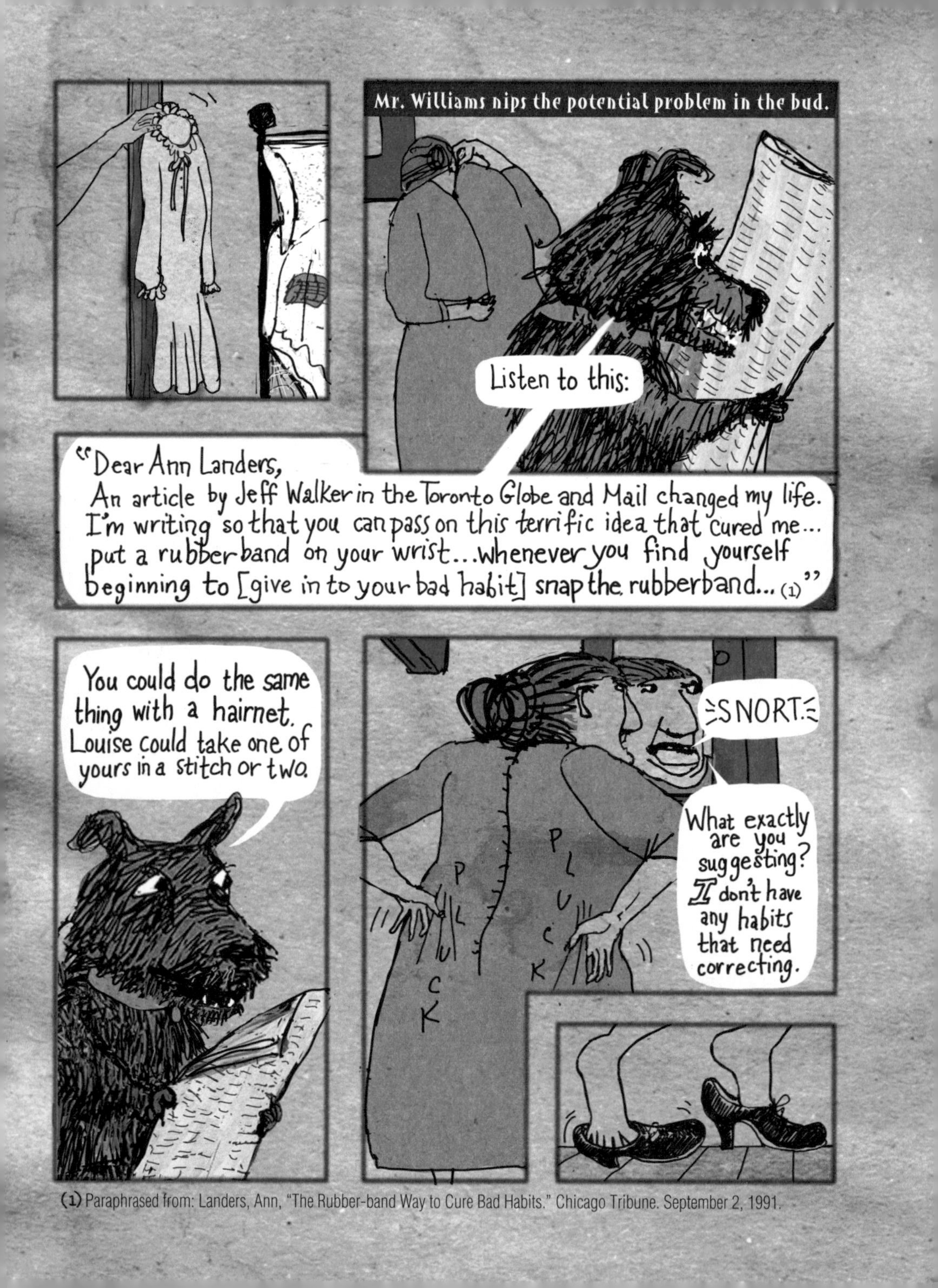
Mr. Williams nips the potential problem in the bud.
Listen to this:
"Dear Ann Landers,
An article by Jeff Walker in the Toronto Globe and Mail changed my life. I'm writing so that you can pass on this terrific idea that cured me... put a rubberband on your wrist...whenever you find yourself beginning to [give in to your bad habit] snap the rubberband... (1)"
You could do the same thing with a hairnet. Louise could take one of yours in a stitch or two.
SNORT.
What exactly are you suggesting? I don't have any habits that need correcting.
PLUCK
PLUCK

(1) Paraphrased from: Landers, Ann, "The Rubber-band Way to Cure Bad Habits." Chicago Tribune. September 2, 1991.

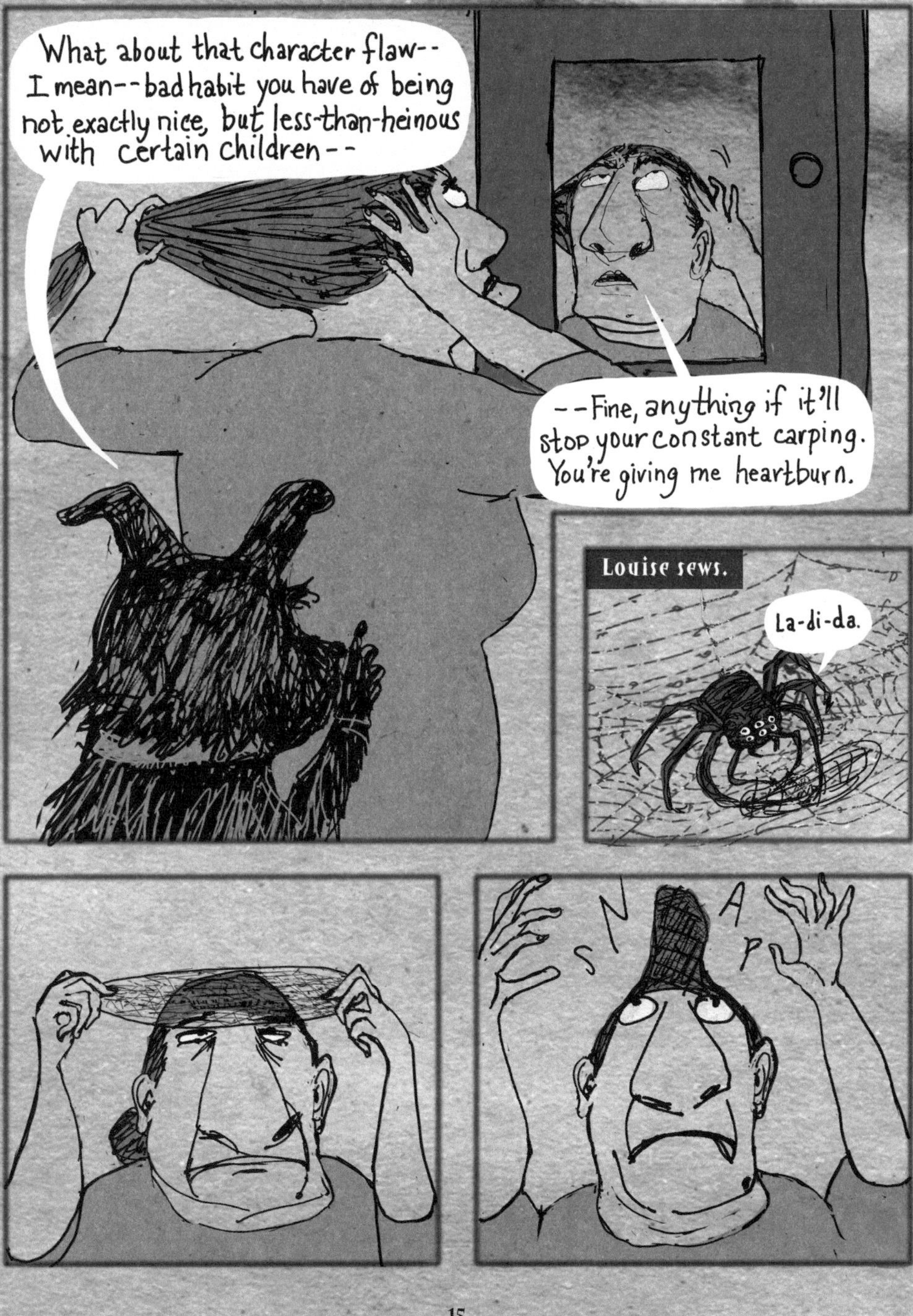
What about that character flaw--
I mean--bad habit you have of being not exactly nice, but less-than-heinous with certain children--
--Fine, anything if it'll stop your constant carping. You're giving me heartburn.
Louise sews.
La-di-da.
SNAP

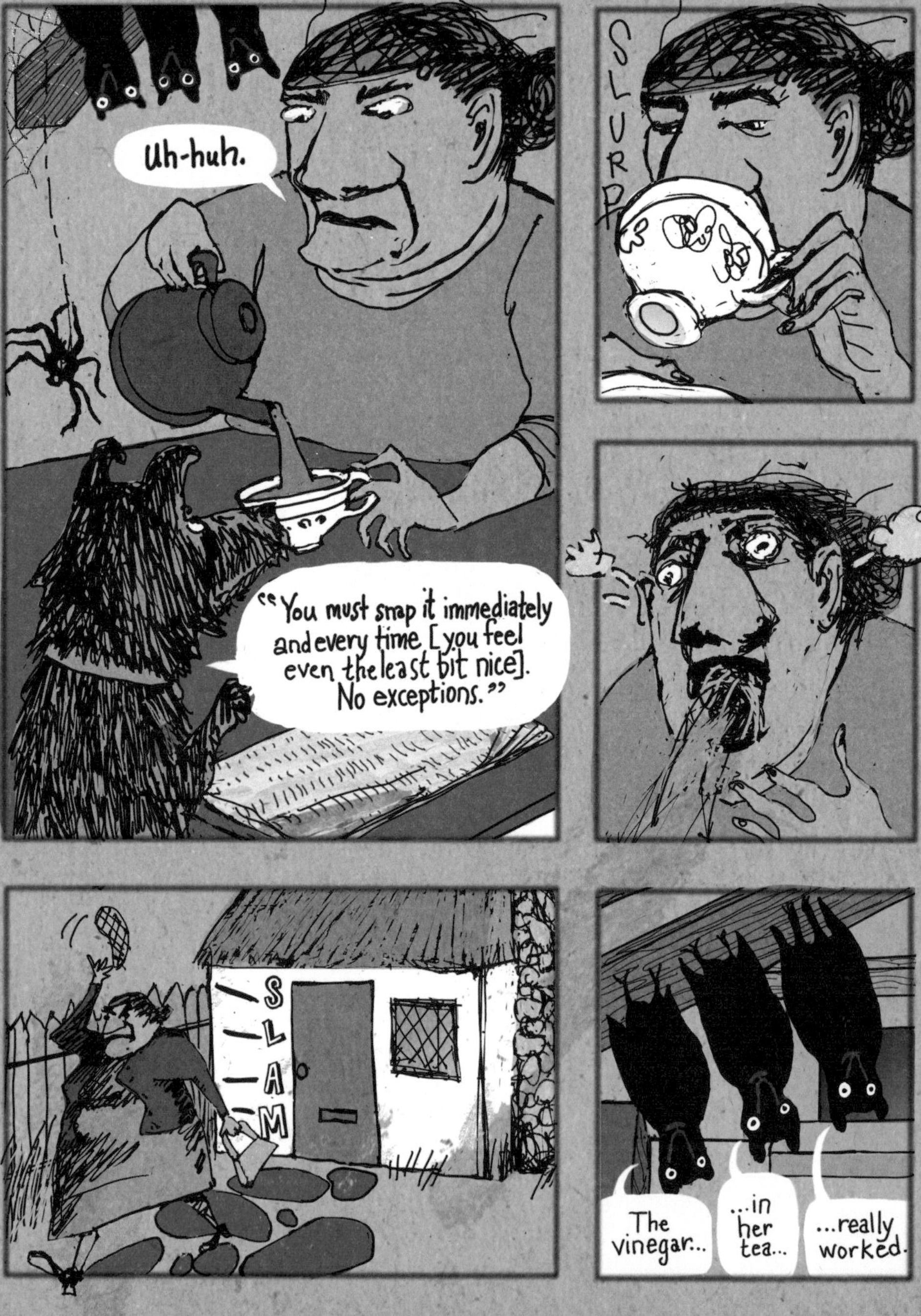
Uh-huh.
"You must snap it immediately and every time [you feel even the least bit nice]. No exceptions."
SLURP
SLAM
The vinegar...
...in her tea...
...really worked.

3rd

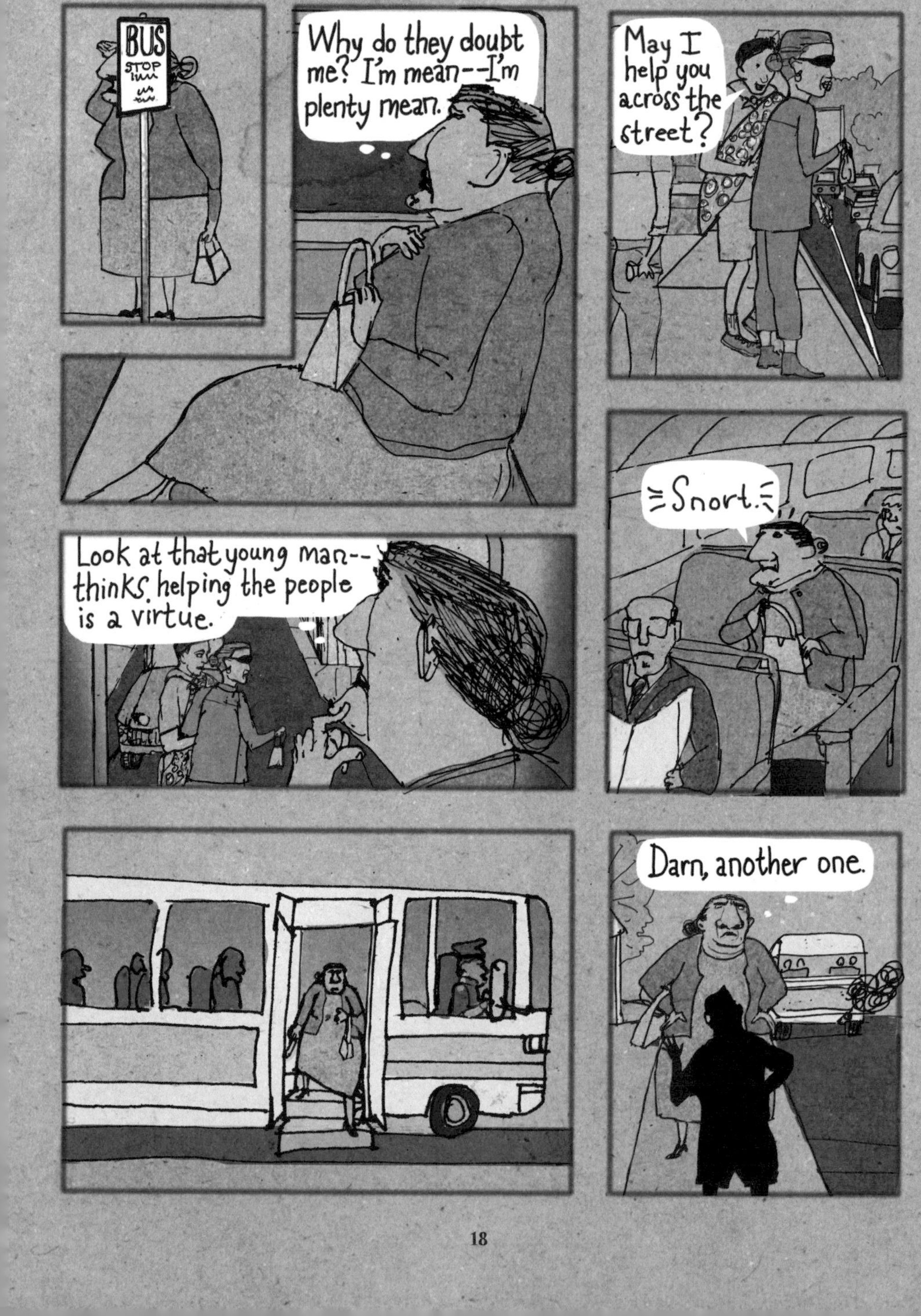
BUS STOP
Why do they doubt me? I'm mean--I'm plenty mean.
May I help you across the street?
Snort.
Look at that young man--thinks helping the people is a virtue.
Darn, another one.

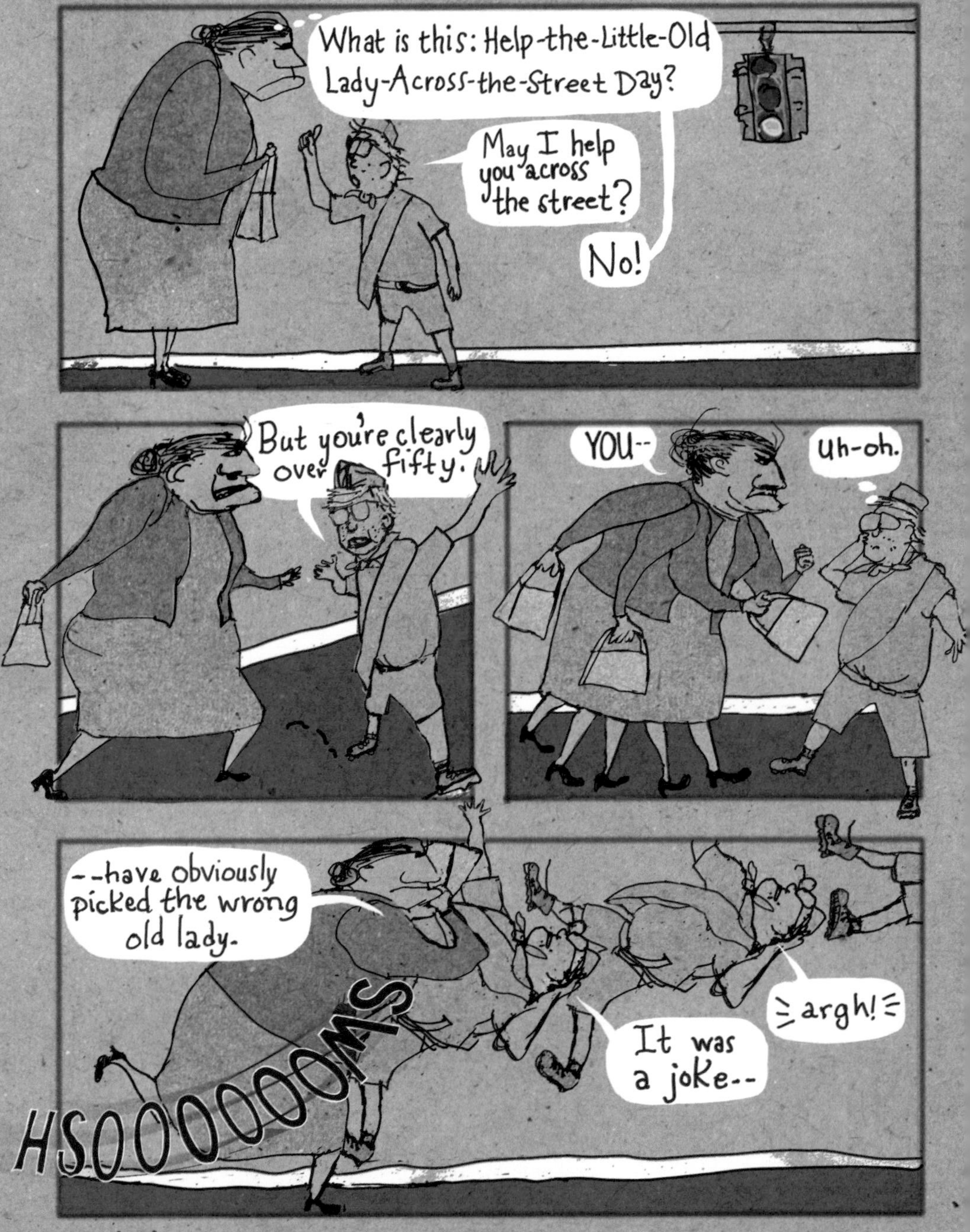
What is this: Help-the-Little-Old Lady-Across-the-Street Day?
May I help you across the street?
No!
But you're clearly over fifty.
YOU--
Uh-oh.
--have obviously picked the wrong old lady.
It was a joke--
argh!
HSOOOOOOOWS

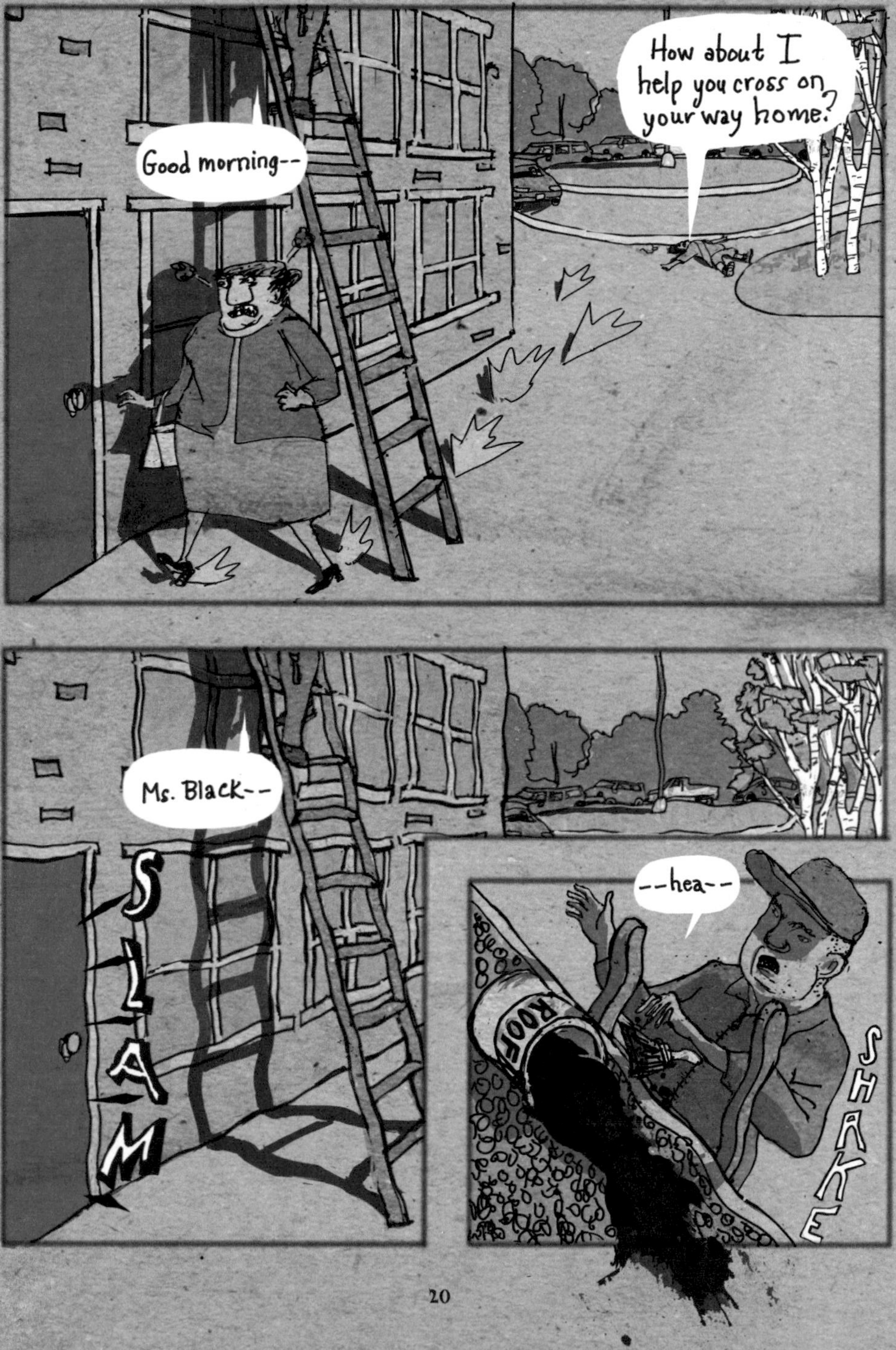
Good morning--
How about I help you cross on your way home?
Ms. Black--
SLAM
--hea--
ROOF
SHAKE

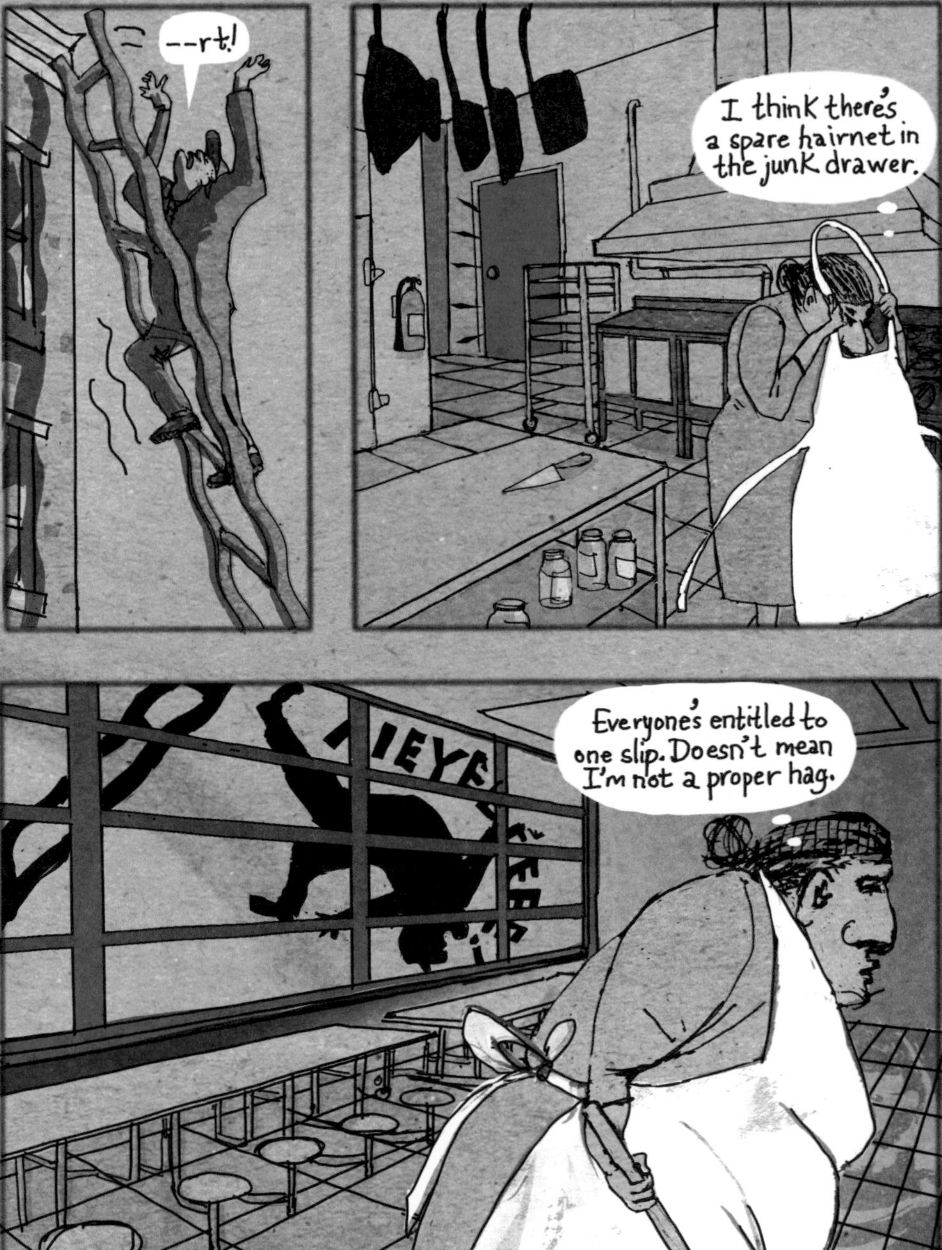
--rt!
I think there's a spare hairnet in the junk drawer.
Everyone's entitled to one slip. Doesn't mean I'm not a proper hag.

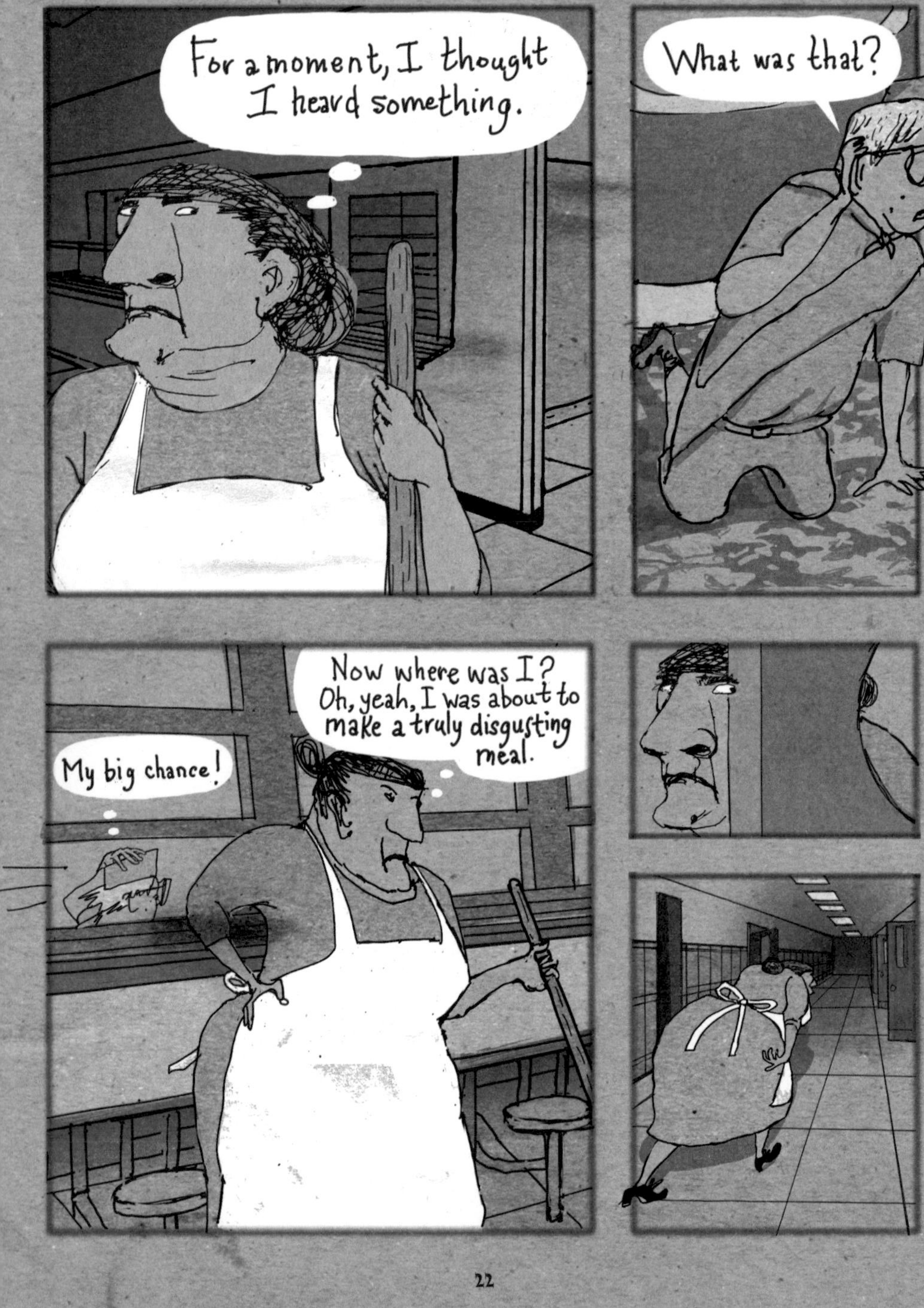

For a moment, I thought I heard something.
What was that?
Now where was I? Oh, yeah, I was about to make a truly disgusting meal.
My big chance!

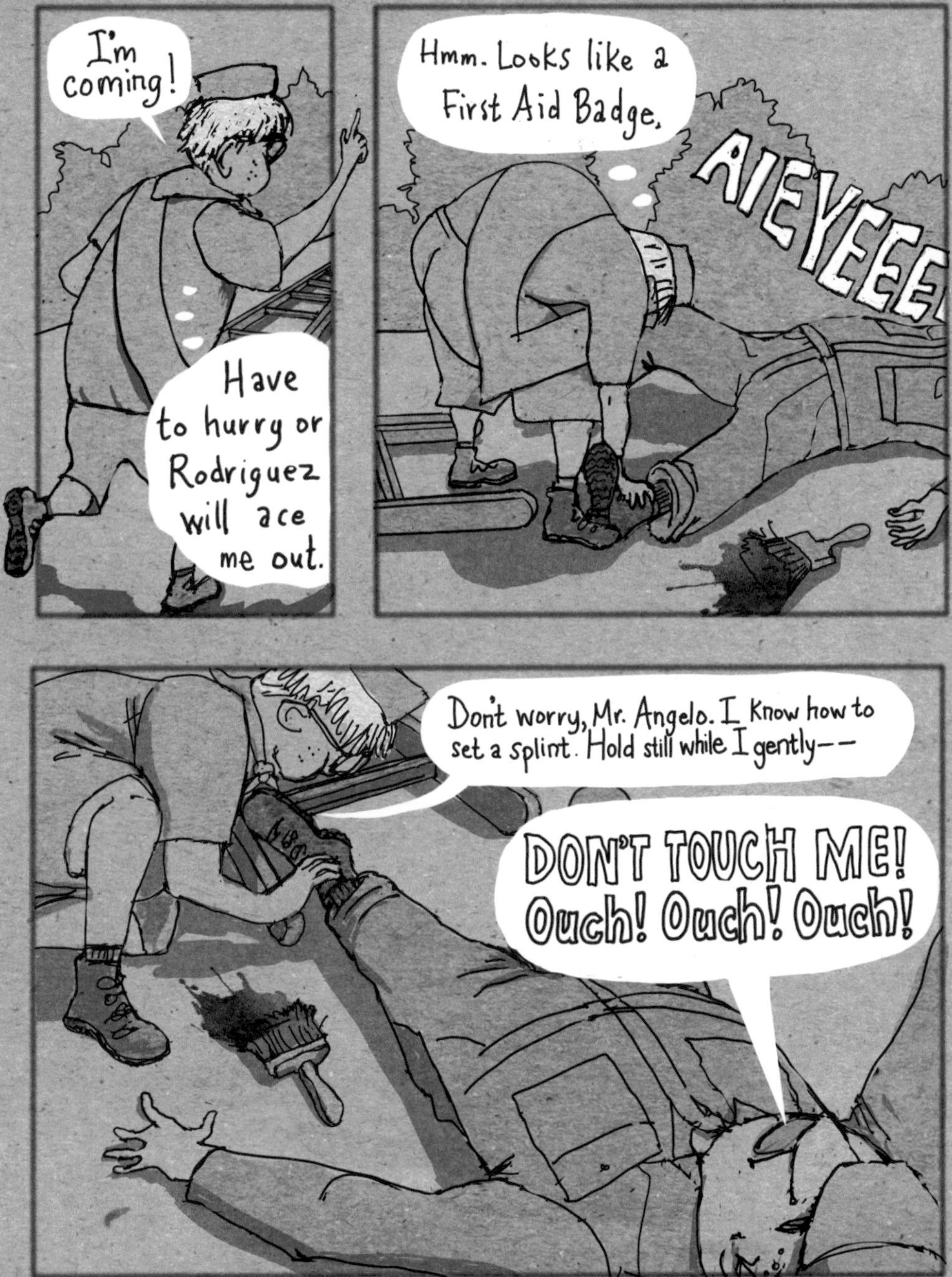
I'm coming!
Have to hurry or Rodriguez will ace me out.
Hmm. Looks like a First Aid Badge.
AIEYEEEE
Don't worry, Mr. Angelo. I know how to set a splint. Hold still while I gently--
DON'T TOUCH ME! Ouch! Ouch! Ouch!

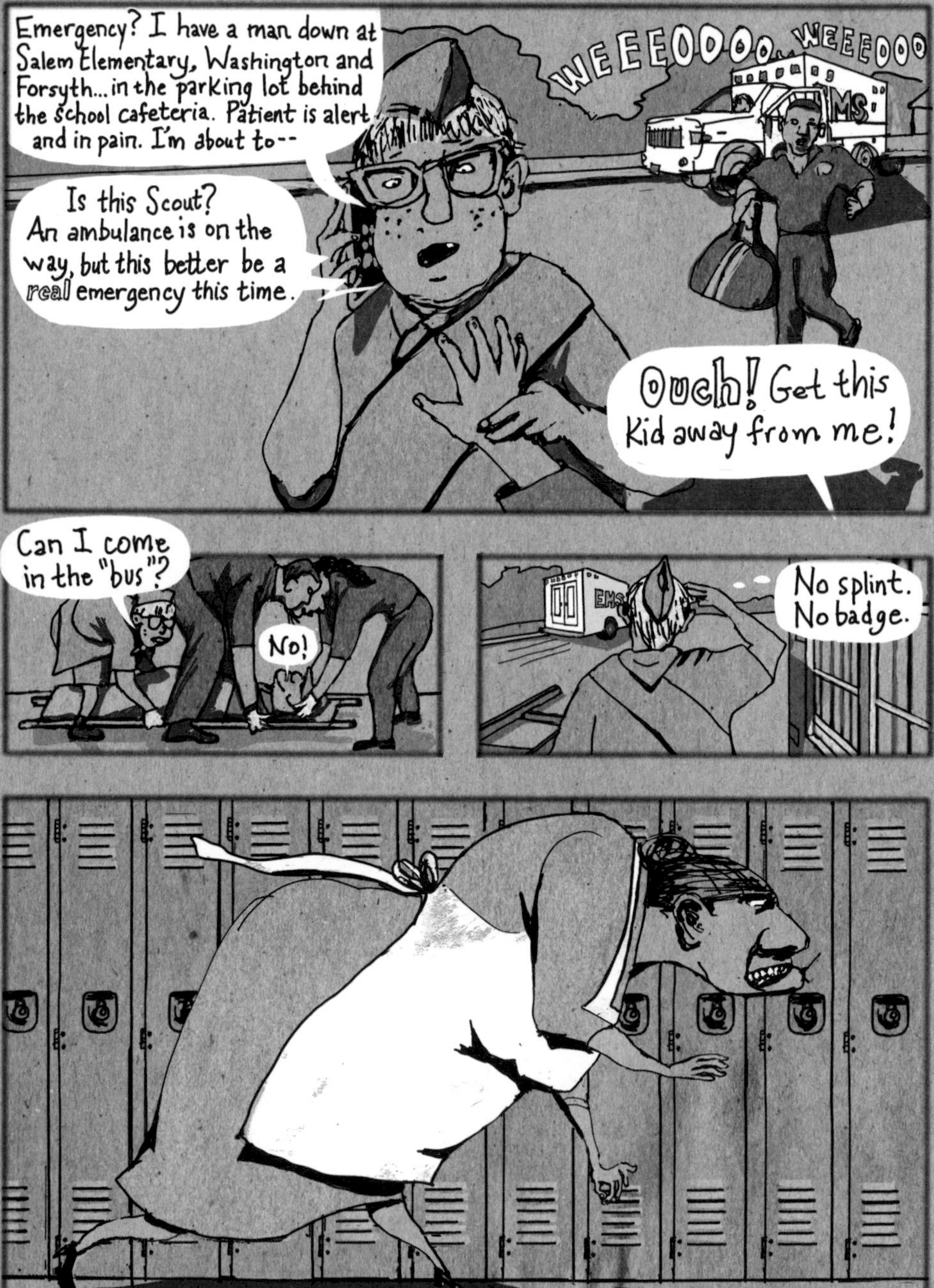
Emergency? I have a man down at Salem Elementary, Washington and Forsyth... in the parking lot behind the school cafeteria. Patient is alert and in pain. I'm about to--
WEEEOOOo... WEEEOOO
EMS
Is this Scout? An ambulance is on the way, but this better be a real emergency this time.
Ouch! Get this kid away from me!
Can I come in the "bus"?
No!
EMS
No splint. No badge.

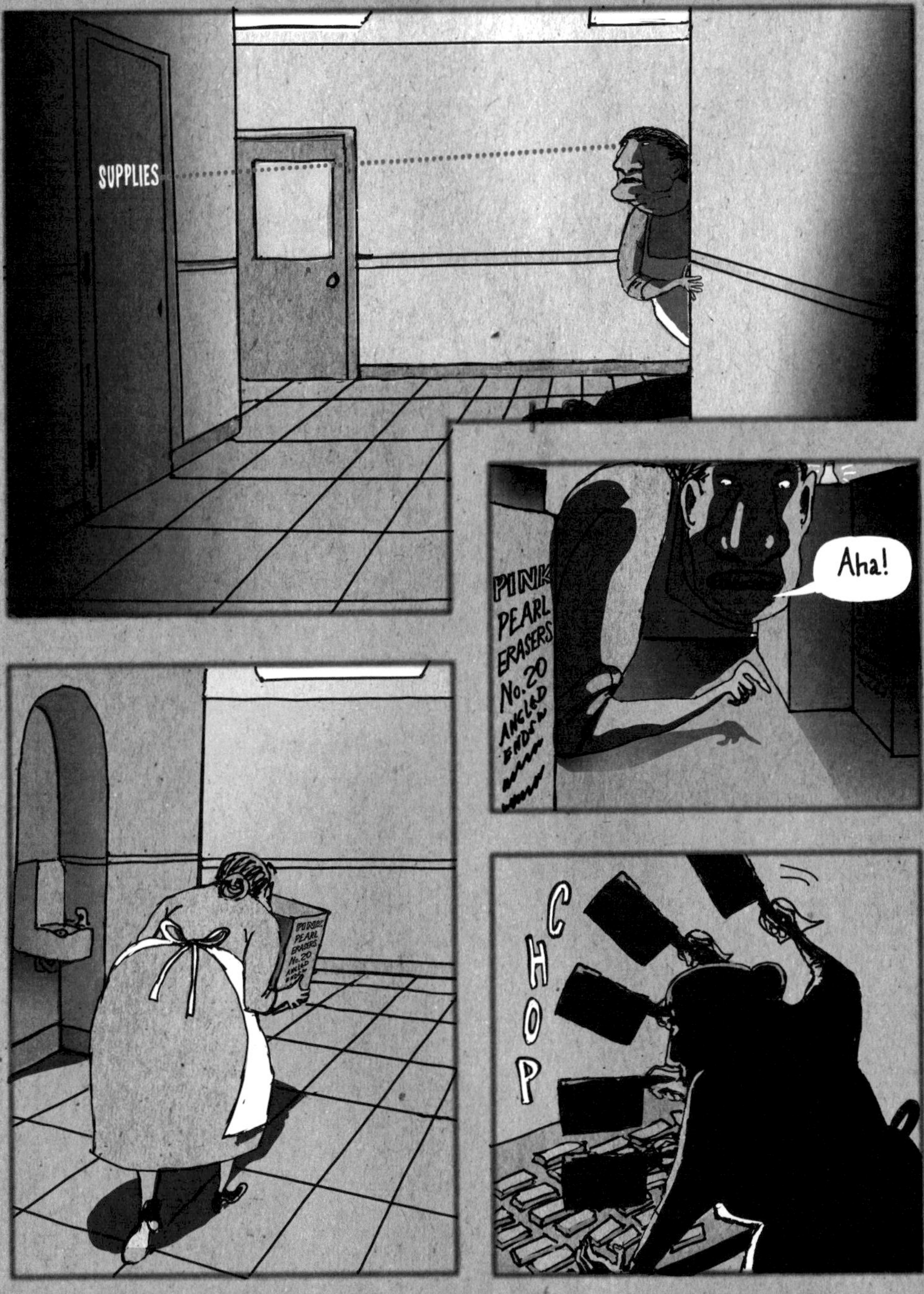
SUPPLIES
PINK PEARL ERASERS No. 20 ANGLED ENDS
Aha!
PINK PEARL ERASERS No. 20
CHOP

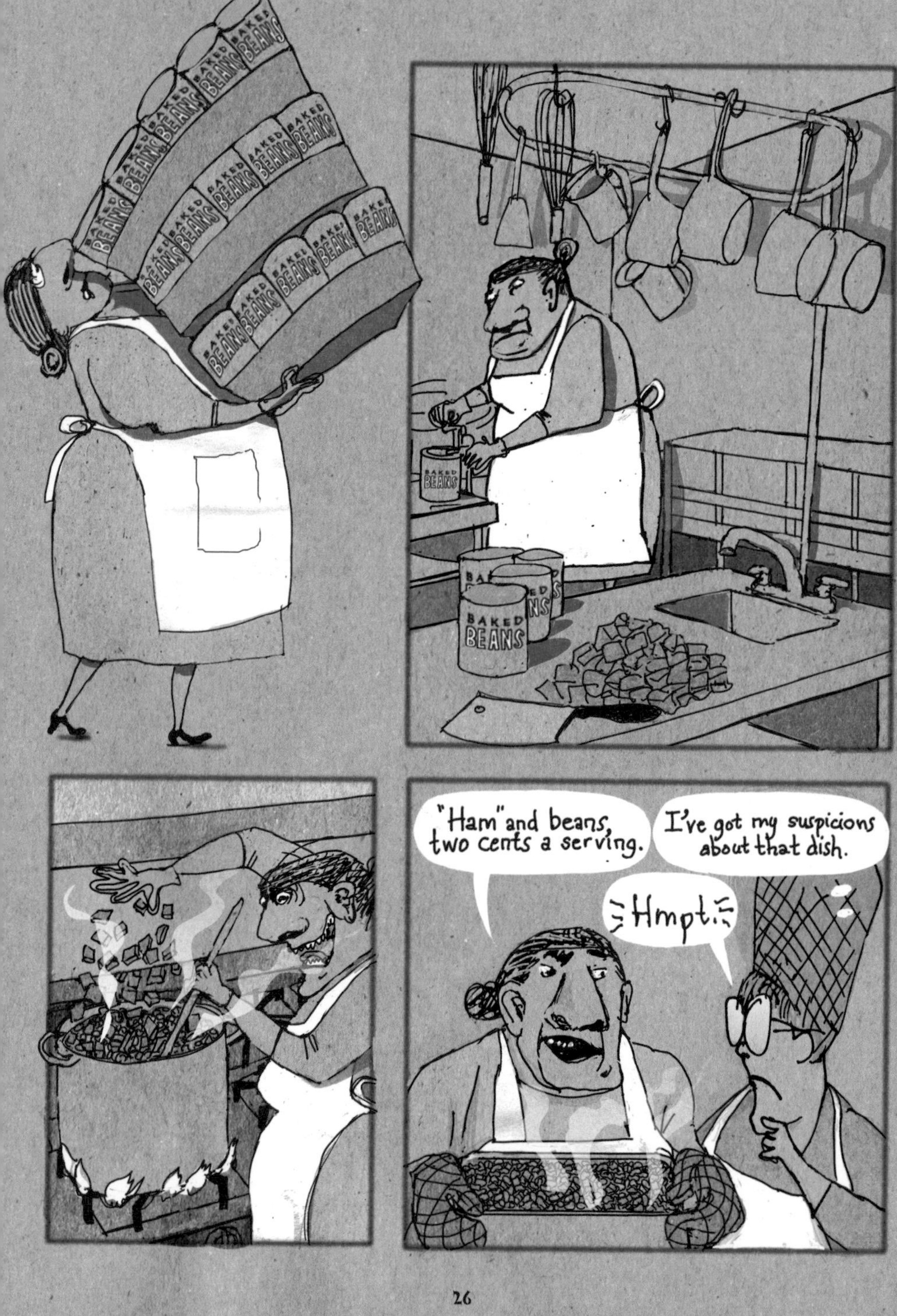

BAKED BEANS
"Ham" and beans, two cents a serving.
I've got my suspicions about that dish.
Hmpt.

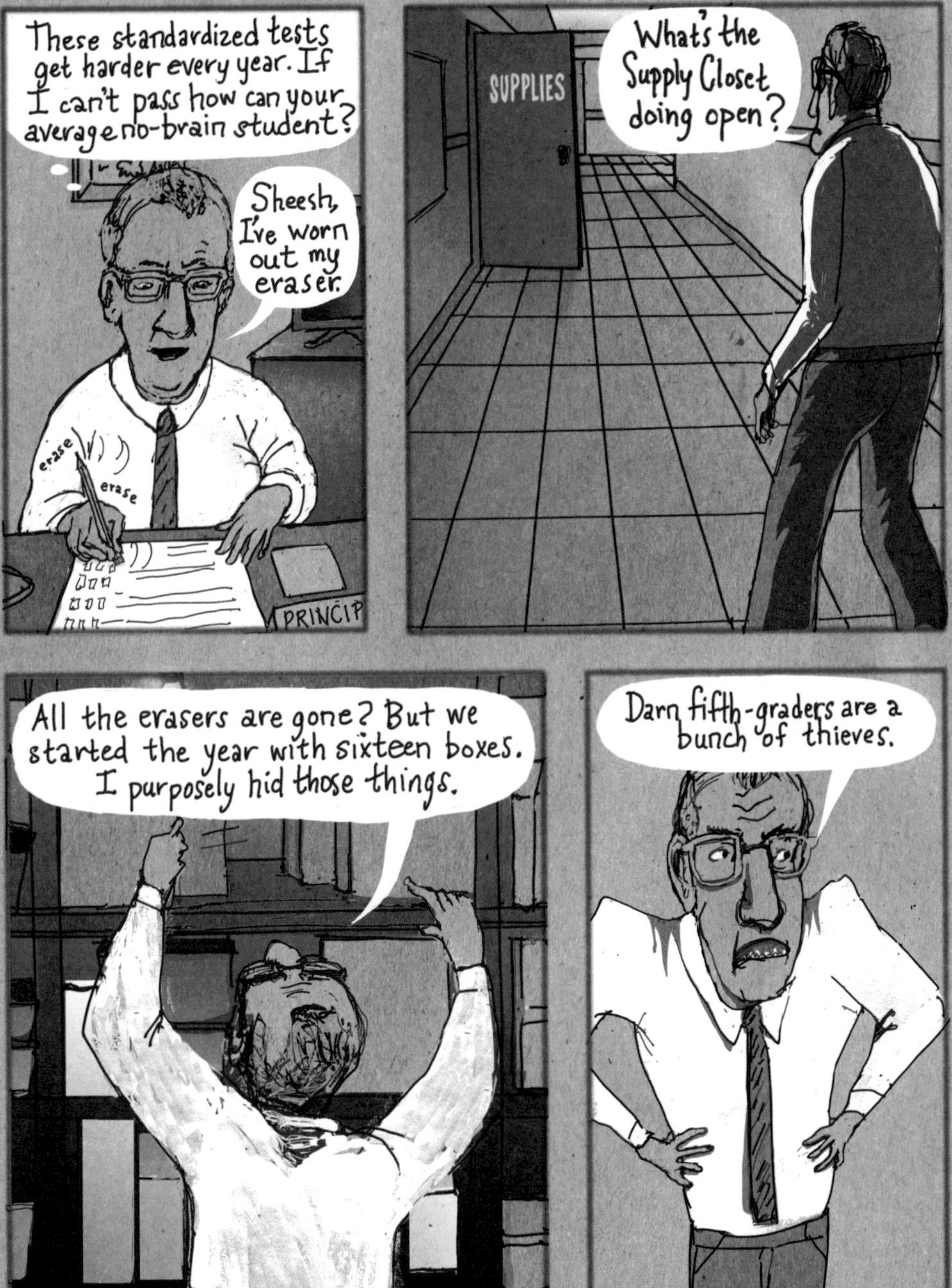
These standardized tests get harder every year. If I can't pass how can your average no-brain student?
Sheesh, I've worn out my eraser.
erase
erase
PRINCIP
SUPPLIES
What's the Supply Closet doing open?
All the erasers are gone? But we started the year with sixteen boxes. I purposely hid those things.
Darn fifth-graders are a bunch of thieves.

4th

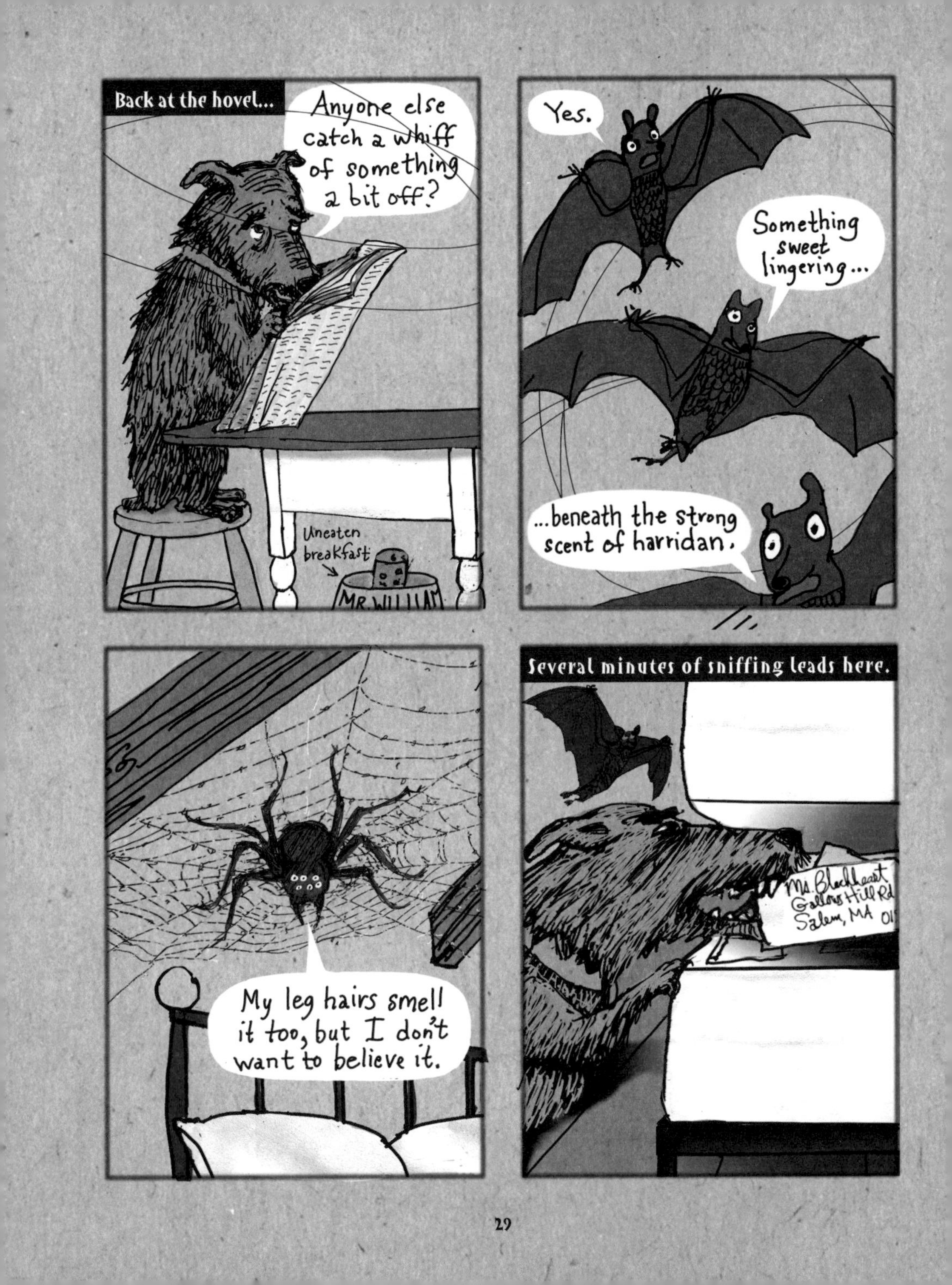
Back at the hovel...
Anyone else catch a whiff of something a bit off?
Uneaten breakfast
Yes.
Something sweet lingering...
...beneath the strong scent of harridan.
My leg hairs smell it too, but I don't want to believe it.
Several minutes of sniffing leads here.
Mr. Blackheart
Gallows Hill Rd
Salem, MA 01

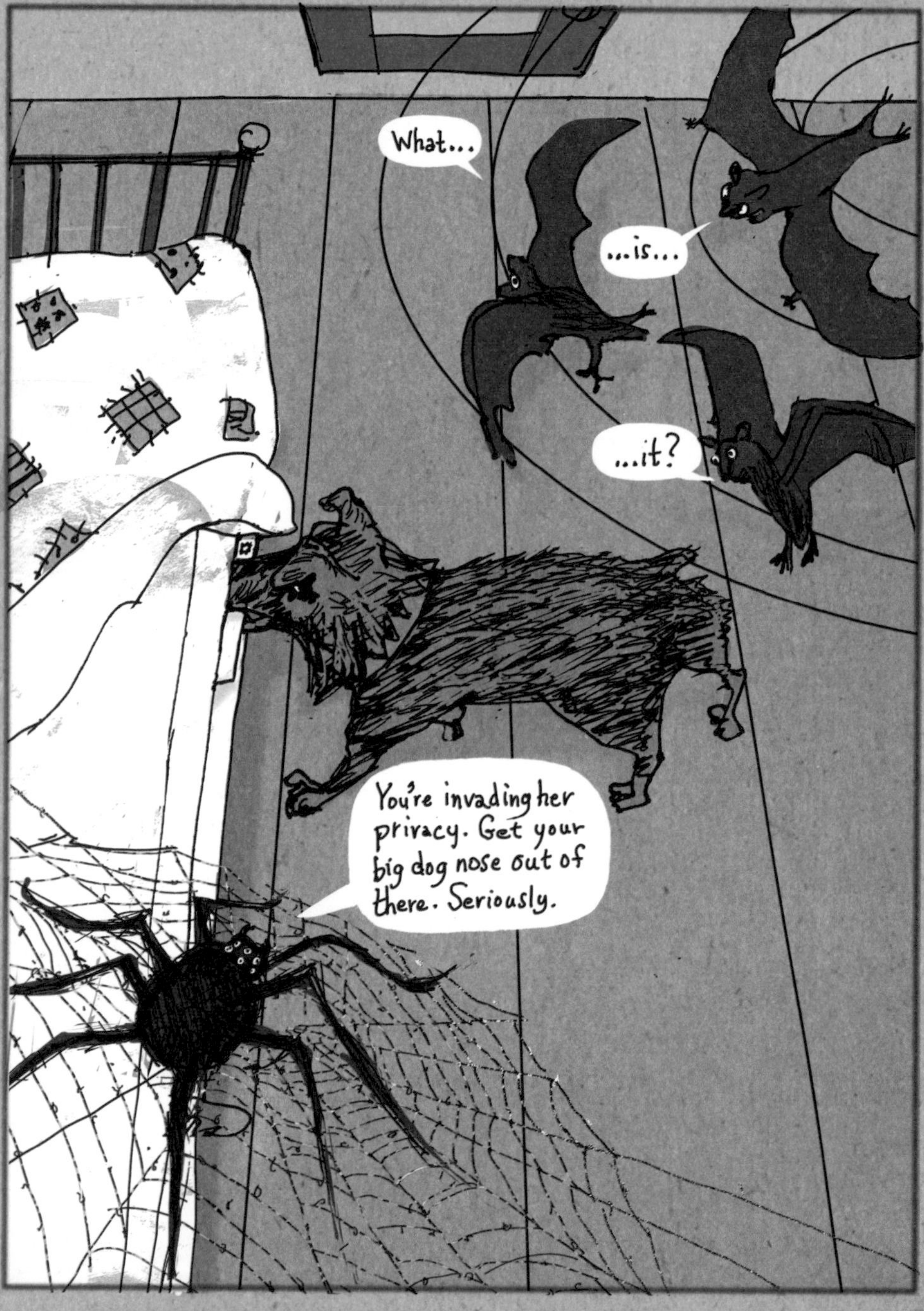
What...
...is...
...it?
You're invading her privacy. Get your big dog nose out of there. Seriously.

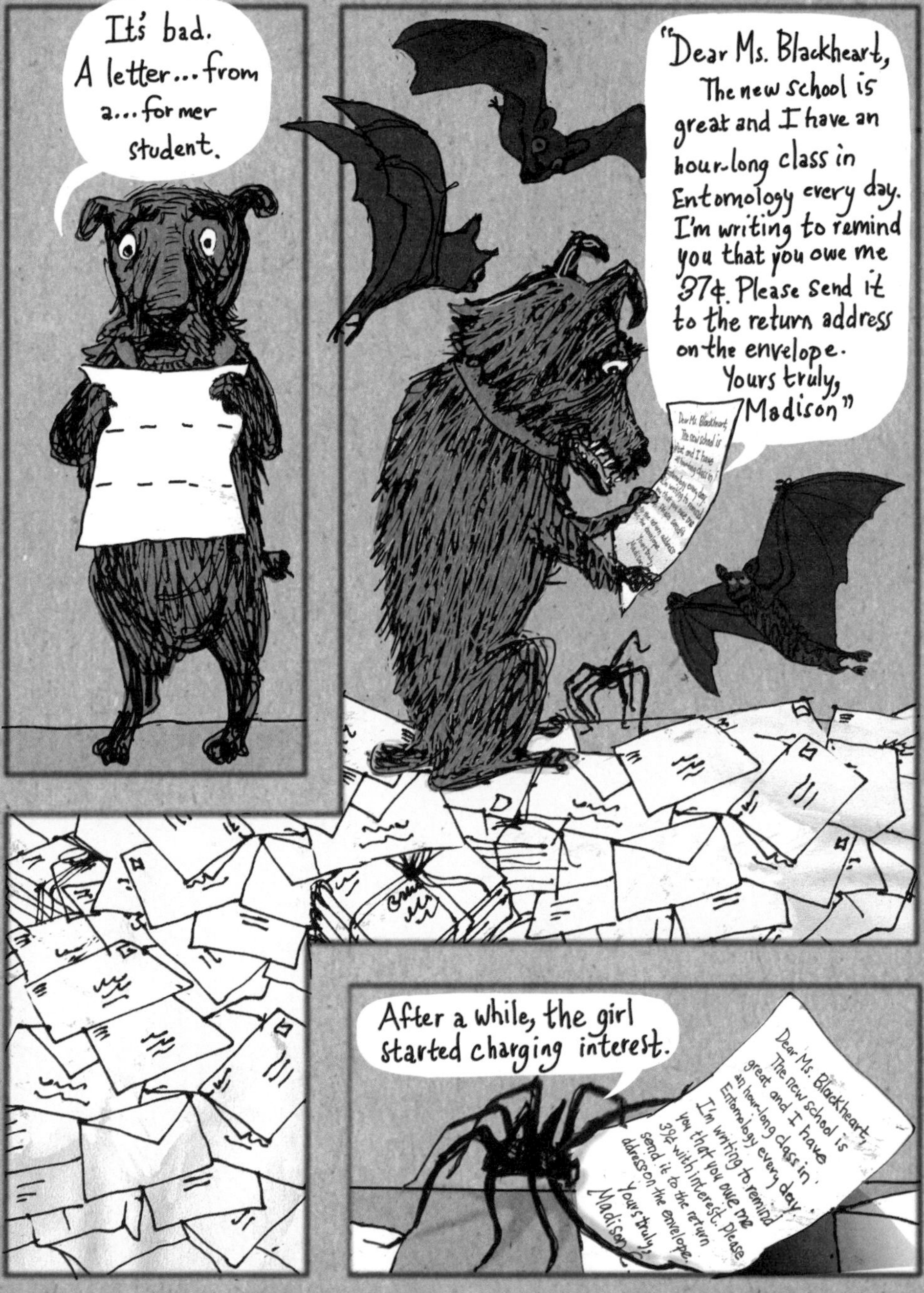
It's bad. A letter… from a… former student.
"Dear Ms. Blackheart, The new school is great and I have an hour-long class in Entomology every day. I'm writing to remind you that you owe me 37¢. Please send it to the return address on the envelope. Yours truly, Madison"
After a while, the girl started charging interest.
Dear Ms. Blackheart, The new school is great and I have an hour-long class in Entomology every day. I'm writing to remind you that you owe me 39¢ with interest. Please send it to the return adress on the envelope. Yours truly, Madison

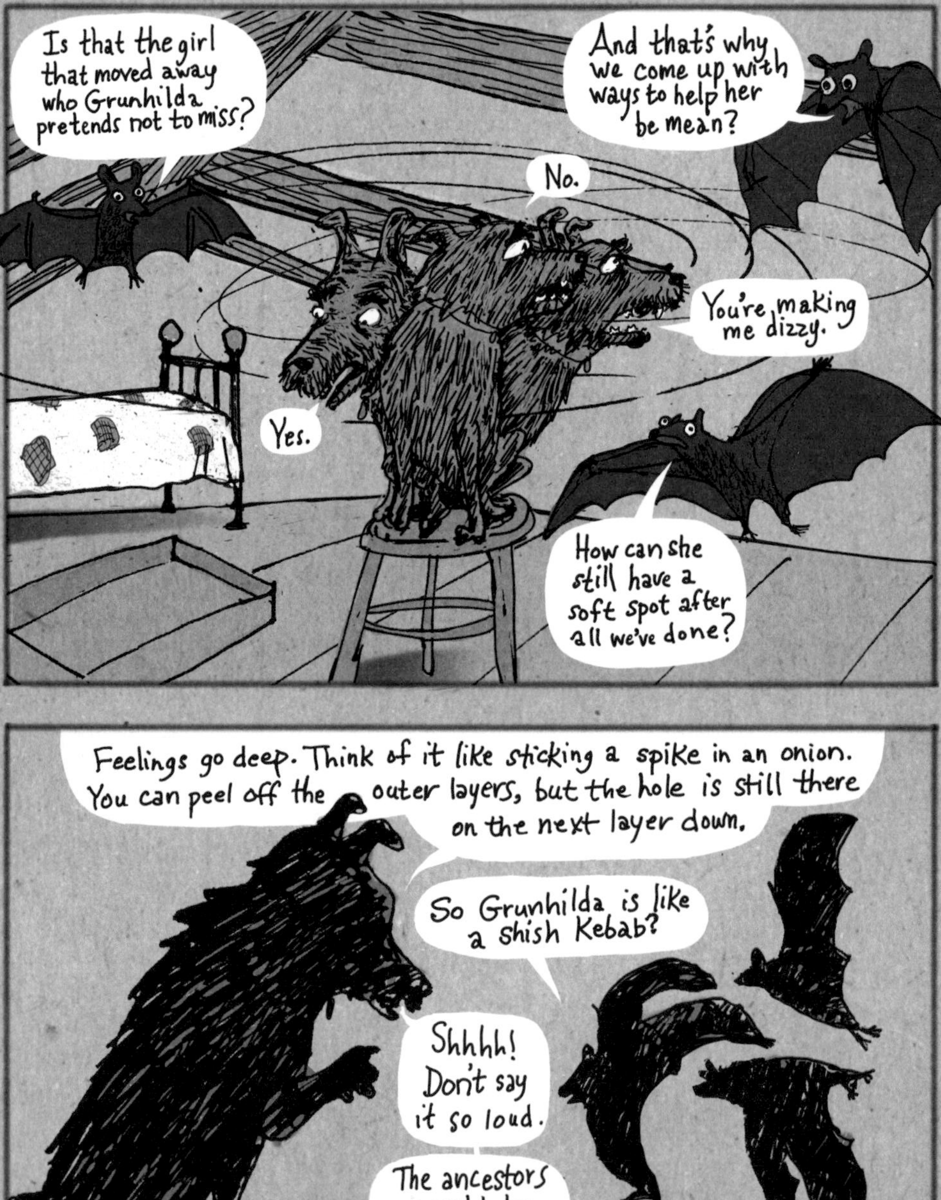
Is that the girl that moved away who Grunhilda pretends not to miss?
And that's why we come up with ways to help her be mean?
No.
You're making me dizzy.
Yes.
How can she still have a soft spot after all we've done?
Feelings go deep. Think of it like sticking a spike in an onion. You can peel off the outer layers, but the hole is still there on the next layer down.
So Grunhilda is like a shish Kebab?
Shhhh! Don't say it so loud.
The ancestors would be very upset... if they Knew.

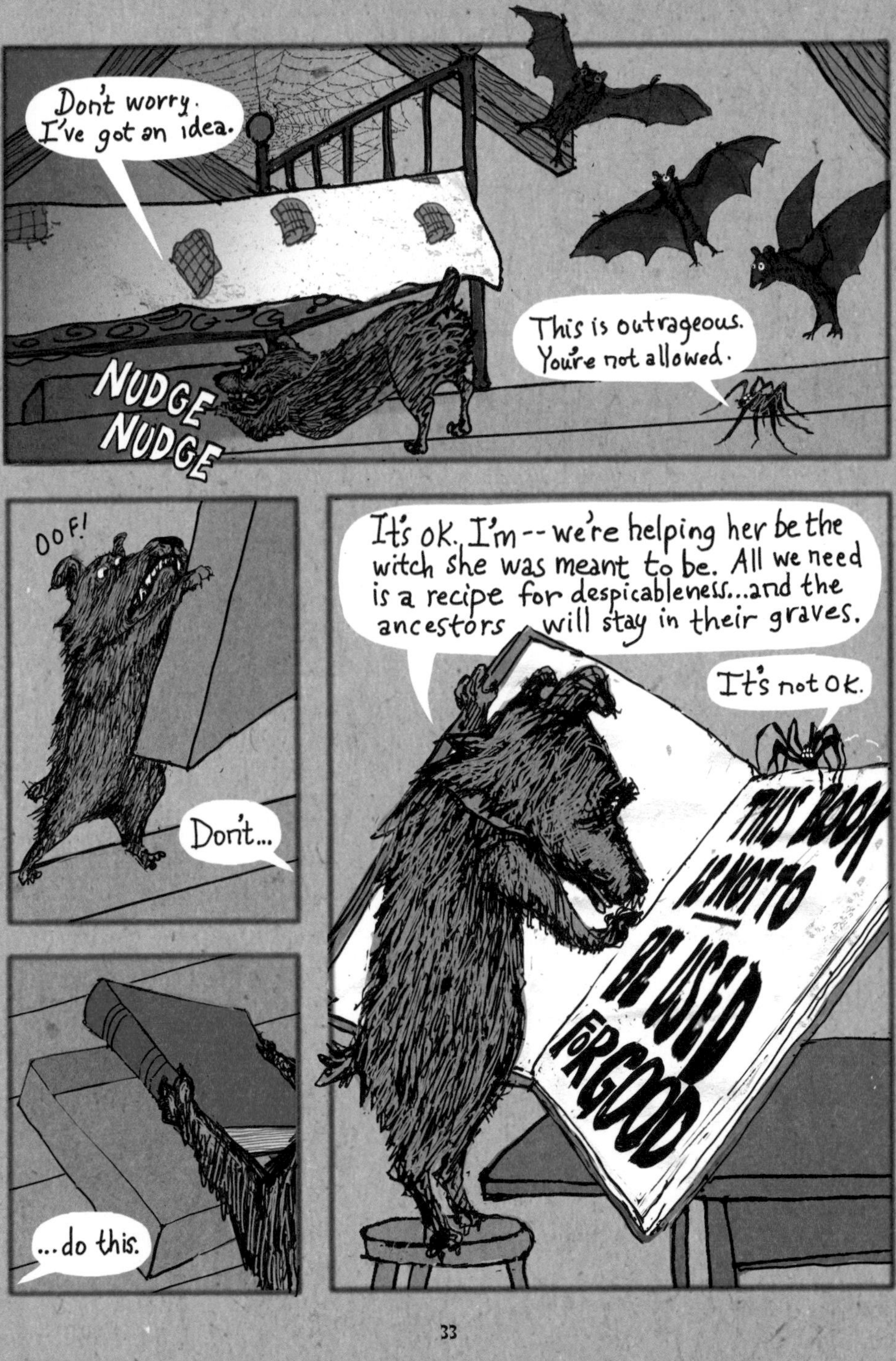

Don't worry. I've got an idea.
NUDGE NUDGE
This is outrageous. You're not allowed.
OOF!
Don't...
...do this.
It's OK. I'm -- we're helping her be the witch she was meant to be. All we need is a recipe for despicableness...and the ancestors will stay in their graves.
It's not OK.
THIS BOOK IS NOT TO BE USED FOR GOOD

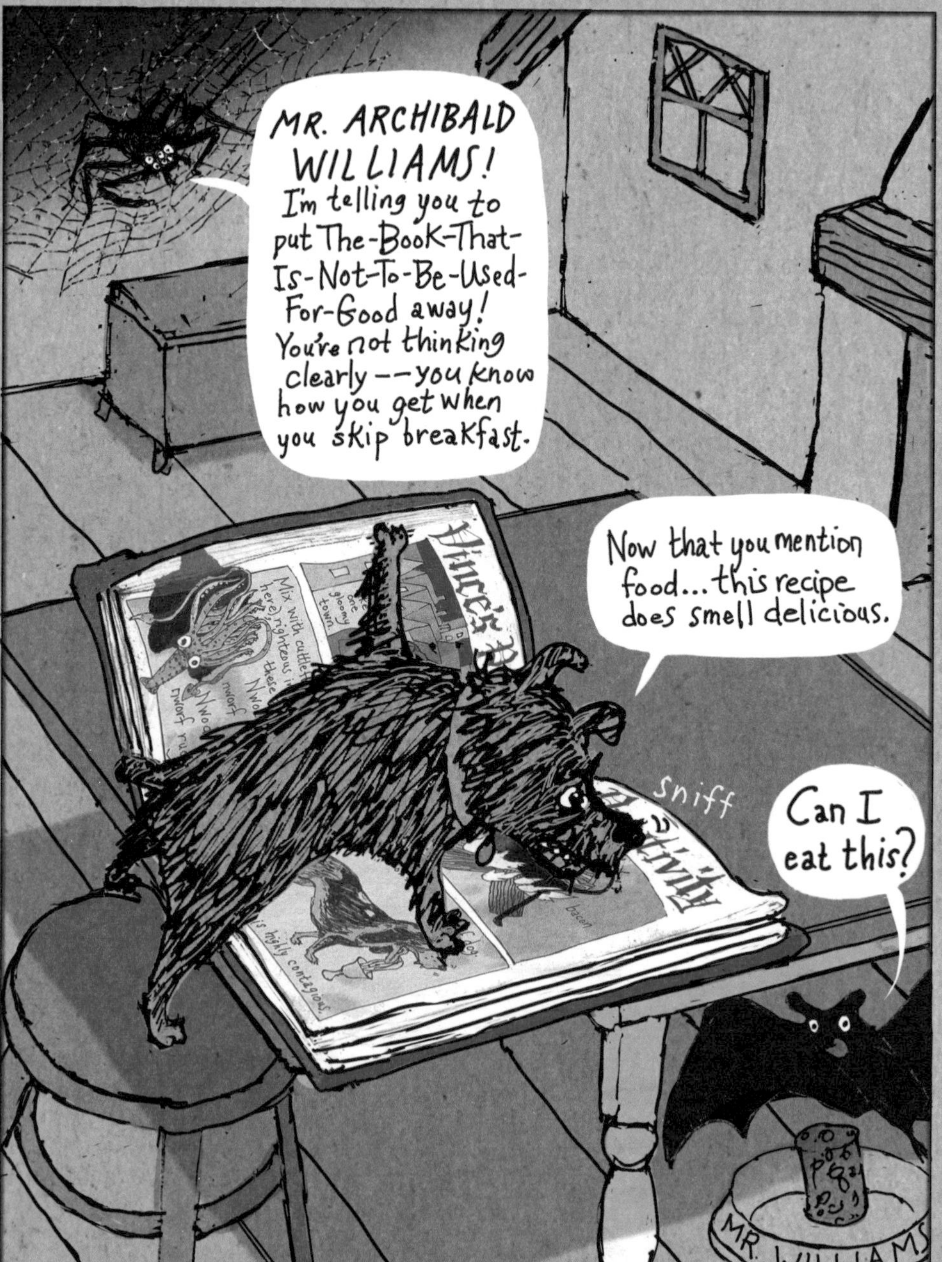
MR. ARCHIBALD WILLIAMS! I'm telling you to put The-Book-That-Is-Not-To-Be-Used-For-Good away! You're not thinking clearly -- you know how you get when you skip breakfast.
Now that you mention food... this recipe does smell delicious.
sniff
Can I eat this?
MR. WILLIAMS

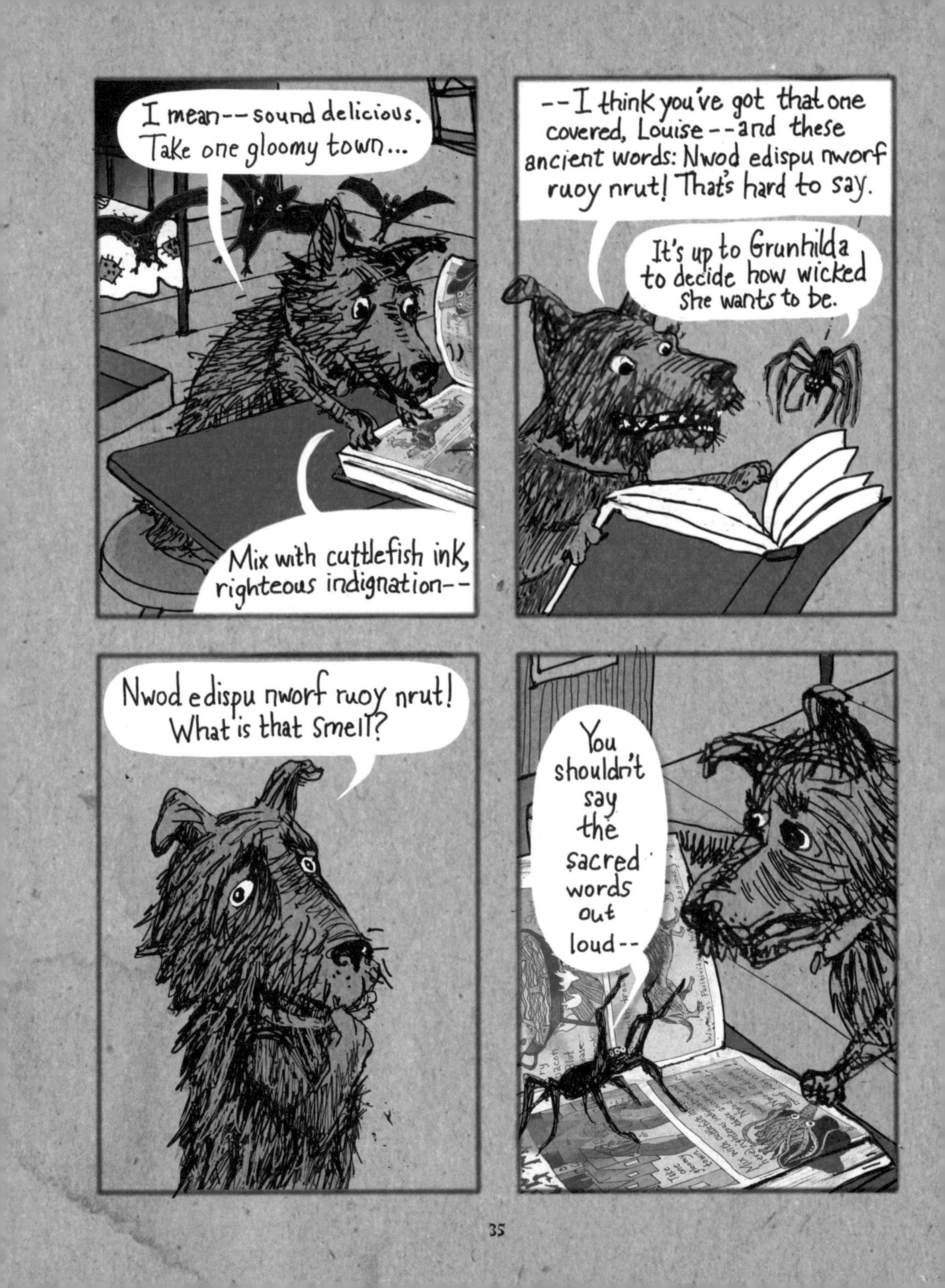
I mean-- sound delicious. Take one gloomy town...
Mix with cuttlefish ink, righteous indignation--
--I think you've got that one covered, Louise--and these ancient words: Nwod edispu nworf ruoy nrut! That's hard to say.
It's up to Grunhilda to decide how wicked she wants to be.
Nwod edispu nworf ruoy nrut! What is that smell?
You shouldn't say the sacred words out loud--

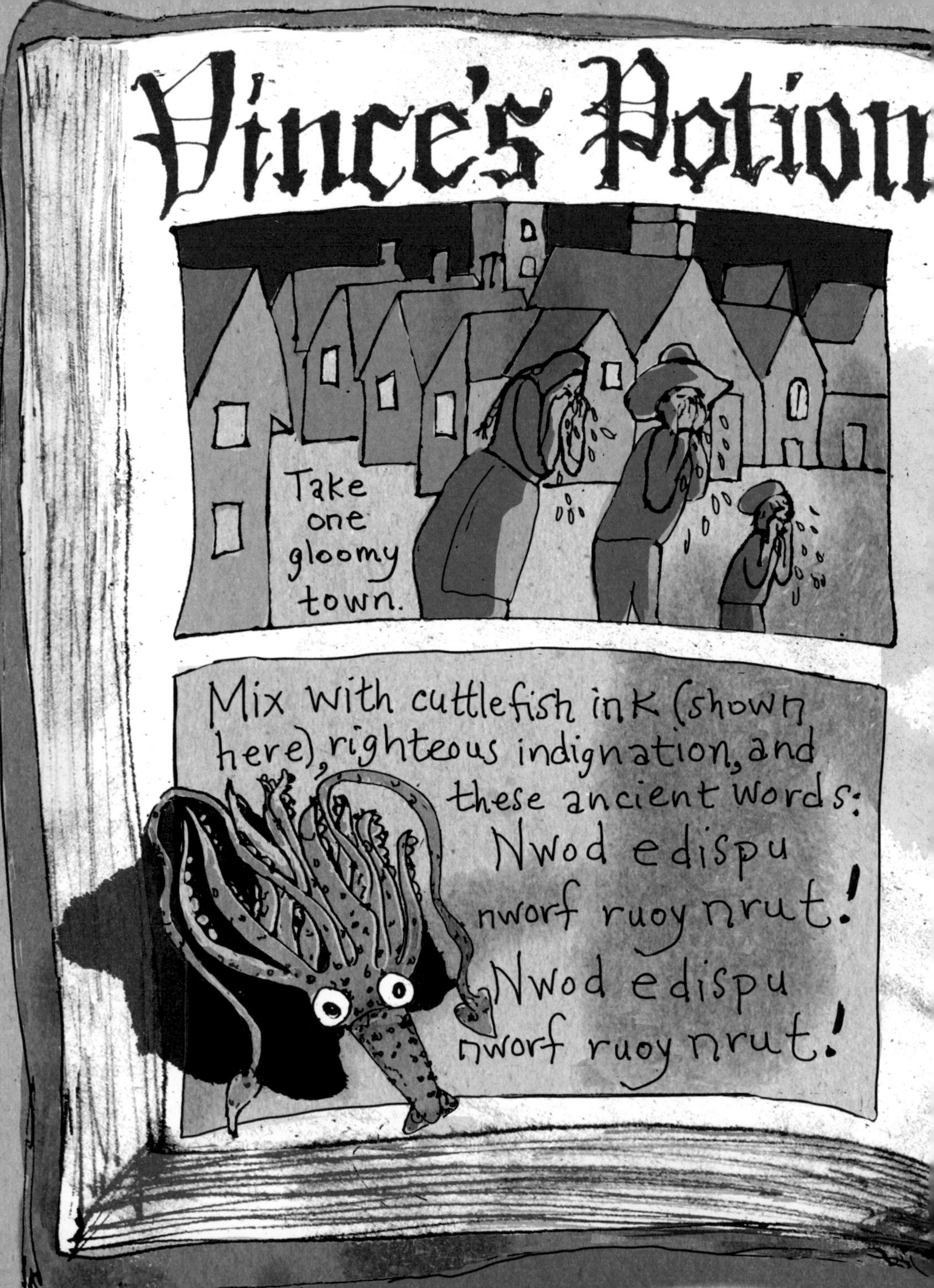
Vince's Potion
Take one gloomy town.
Mix with cuttlefish ink (shown here), righteous indignation, and these ancient words:
Nwod edispu nworf ruoy nrut!
Nwod edispu nworf ruoy nrut!

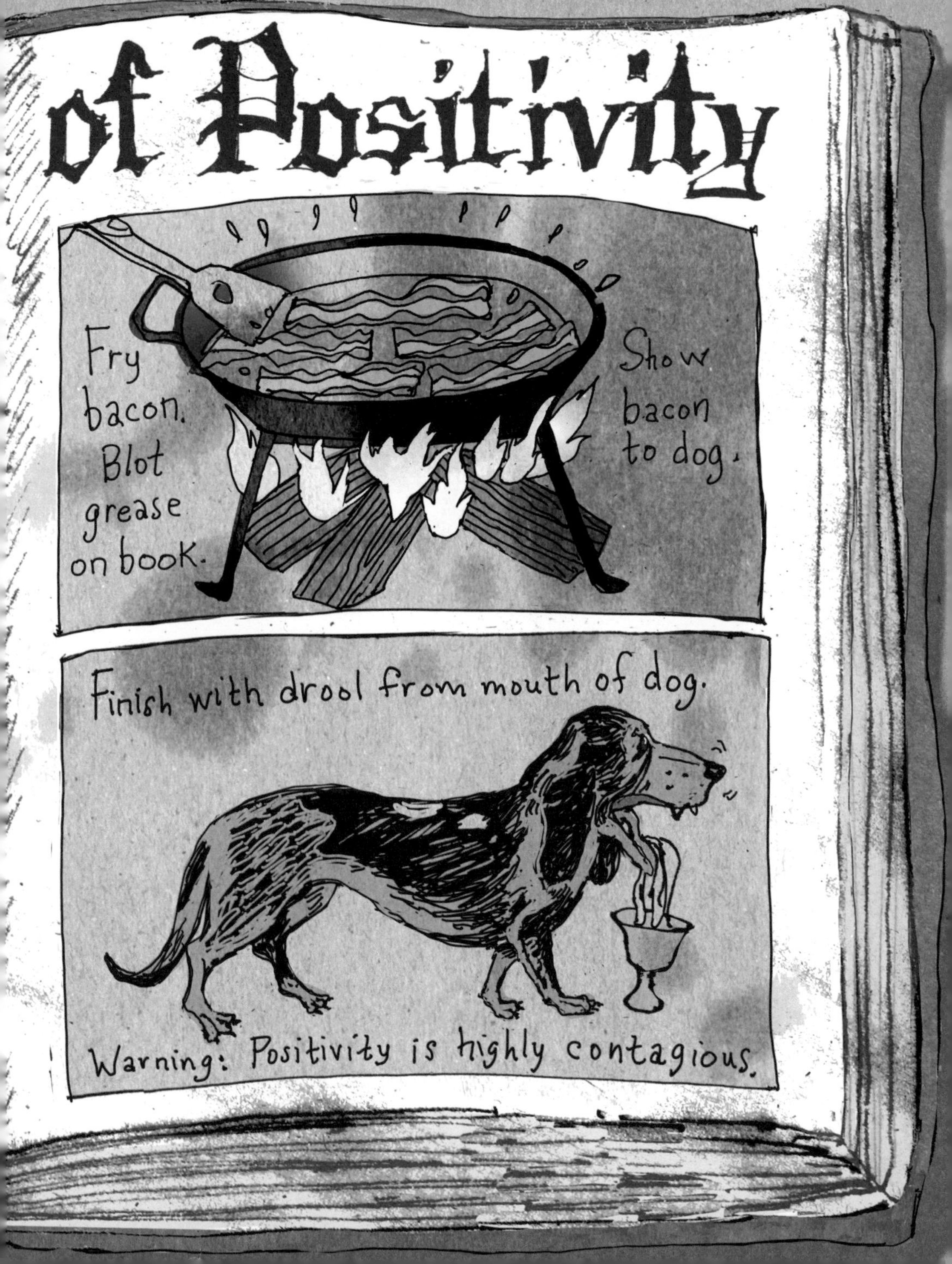

of Positivity
Fry bacon. Blot grease on book.
Show bacon to dog.
Finish with drool from mouth of dog.
Warning: Positivity is highly contagious.

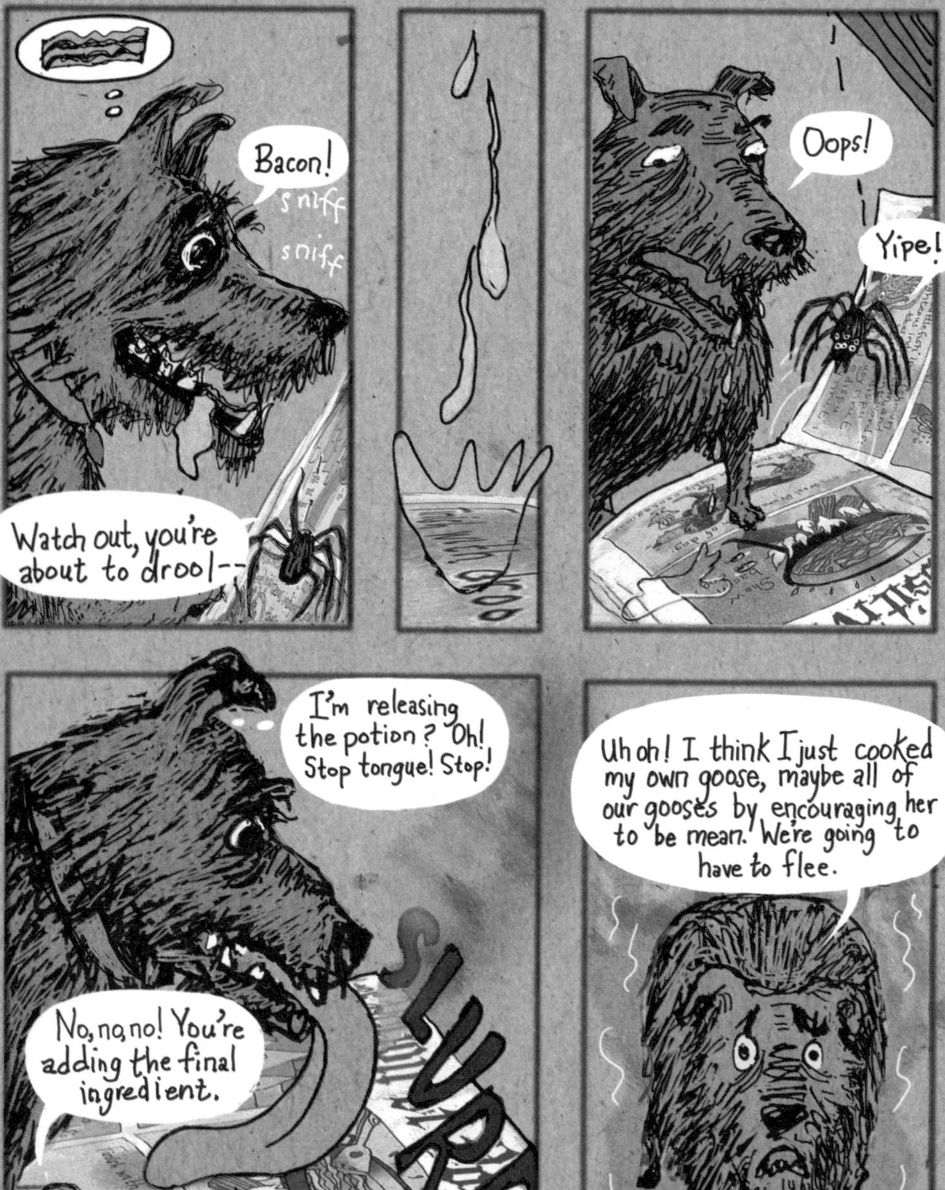
Bacon!
sniff
sniff
Watch out, you're about to drool--
Oops!
Yipe!
I'm releasing the potion? Oh! Stop tongue! Stop!
No, no, no! You're adding the final ingredient.
SLURP
Uh oh! I think I just cooked my own goose, maybe all of our gooses by encouraging her to be mean. We're going to have to flee.

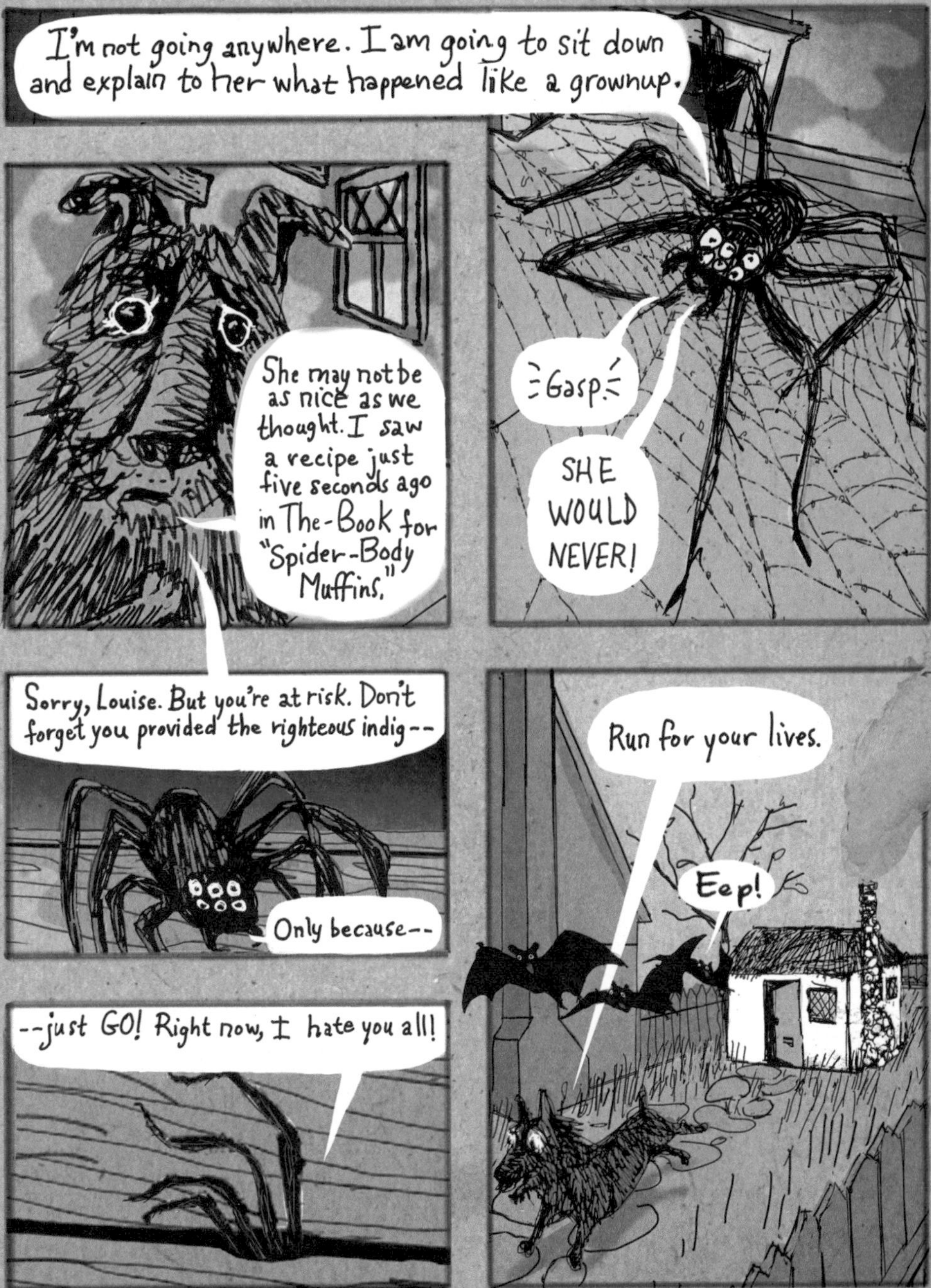
I'm not going anywhere. I am going to sit down and explain to her what happened like a grownup.
She may not be as nice as we thought. I saw a recipe just five seconds ago in The-Book for "Spider-Body Muffins."
Gasp.
SHE WOULD NEVER!
Sorry, Louise. But you're at risk. Don't forget you provided the righteous indig--
Only because--
--just GO! Right now, I hate you all!
Run for your lives.
Eep!

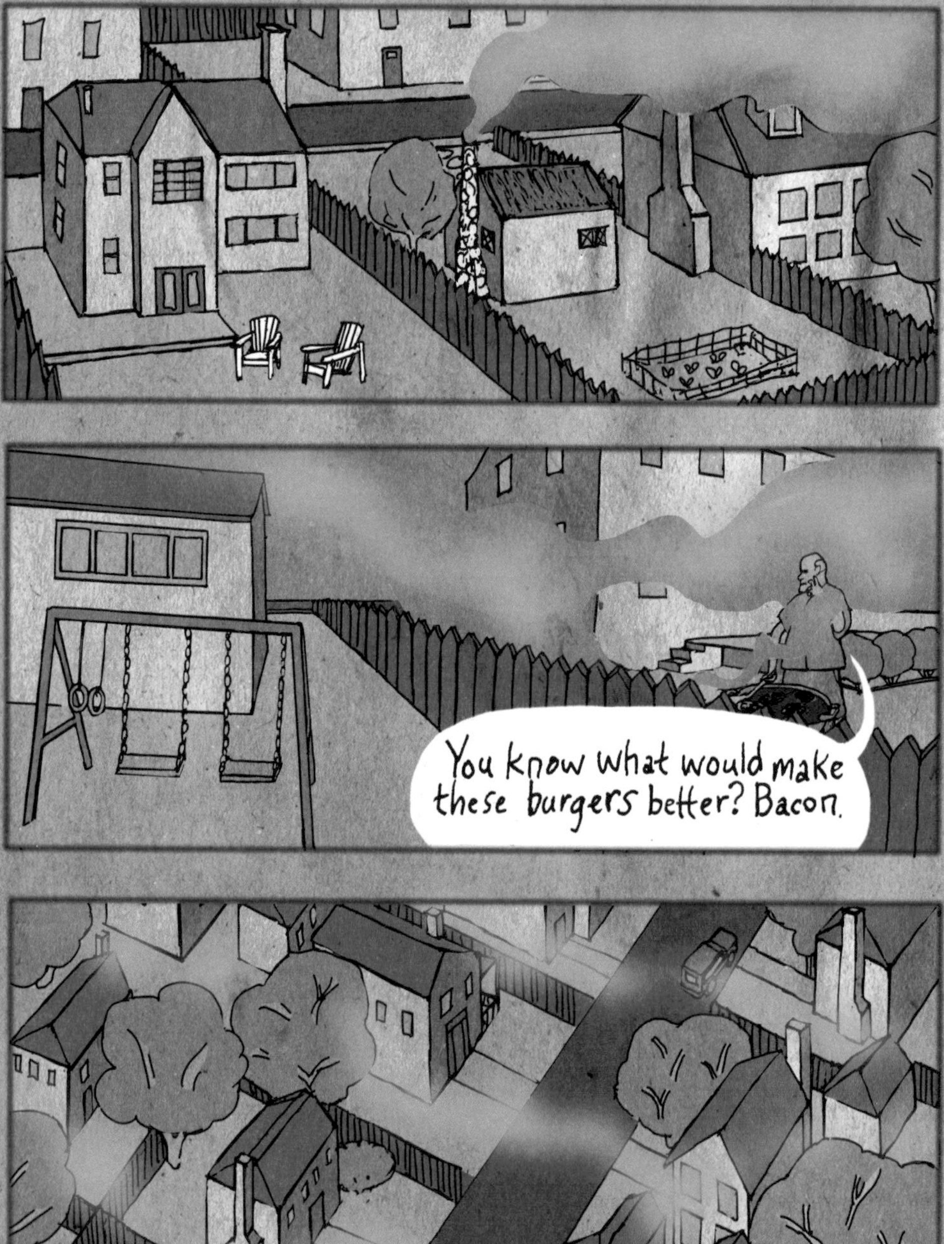
You know what would make these burgers better? Bacon.

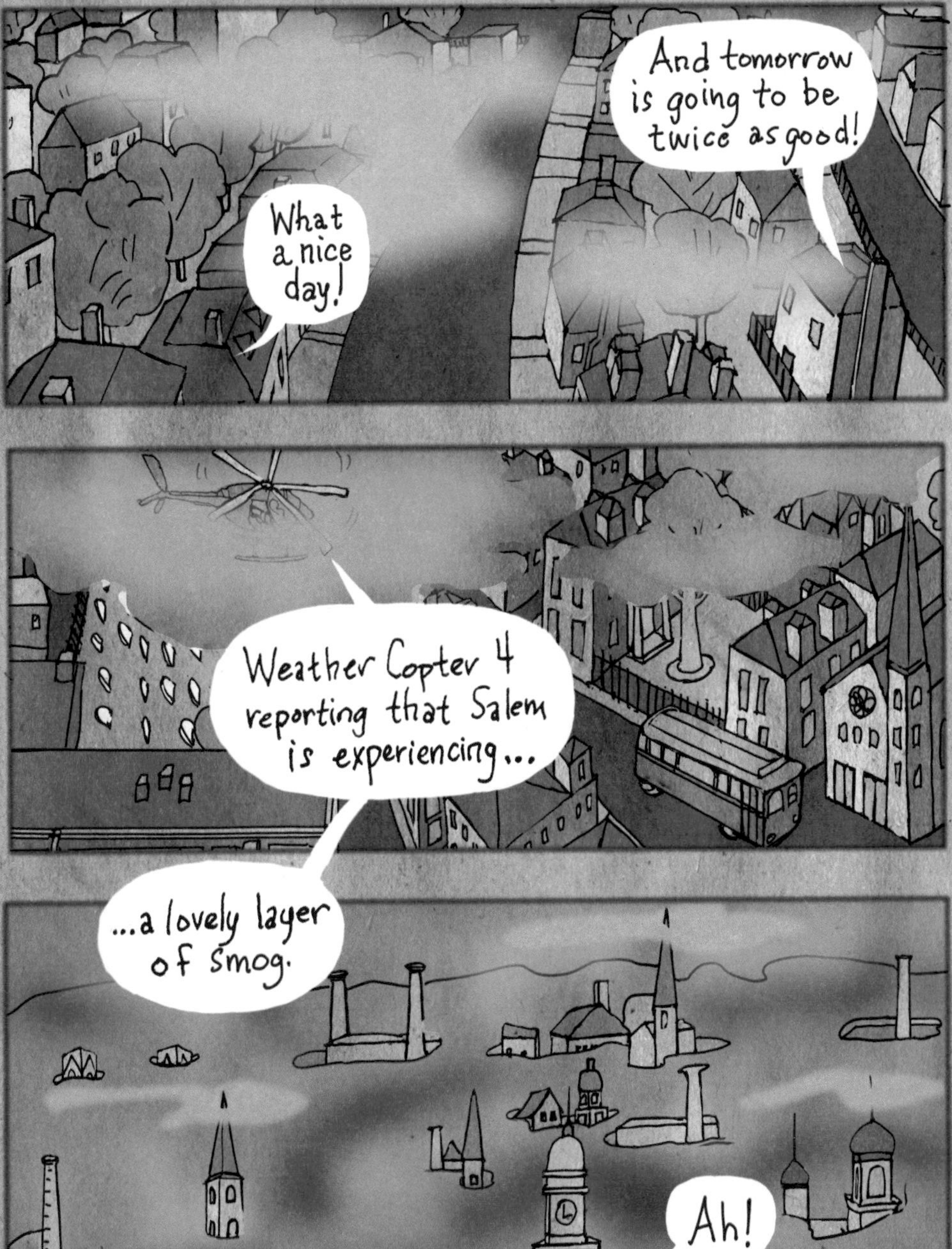
What a nice day!
And tomorrow is going to be twice as good!
Weather Copter 4 reporting that Salem is experiencing...
...a lovely layer of smog.
Ah!

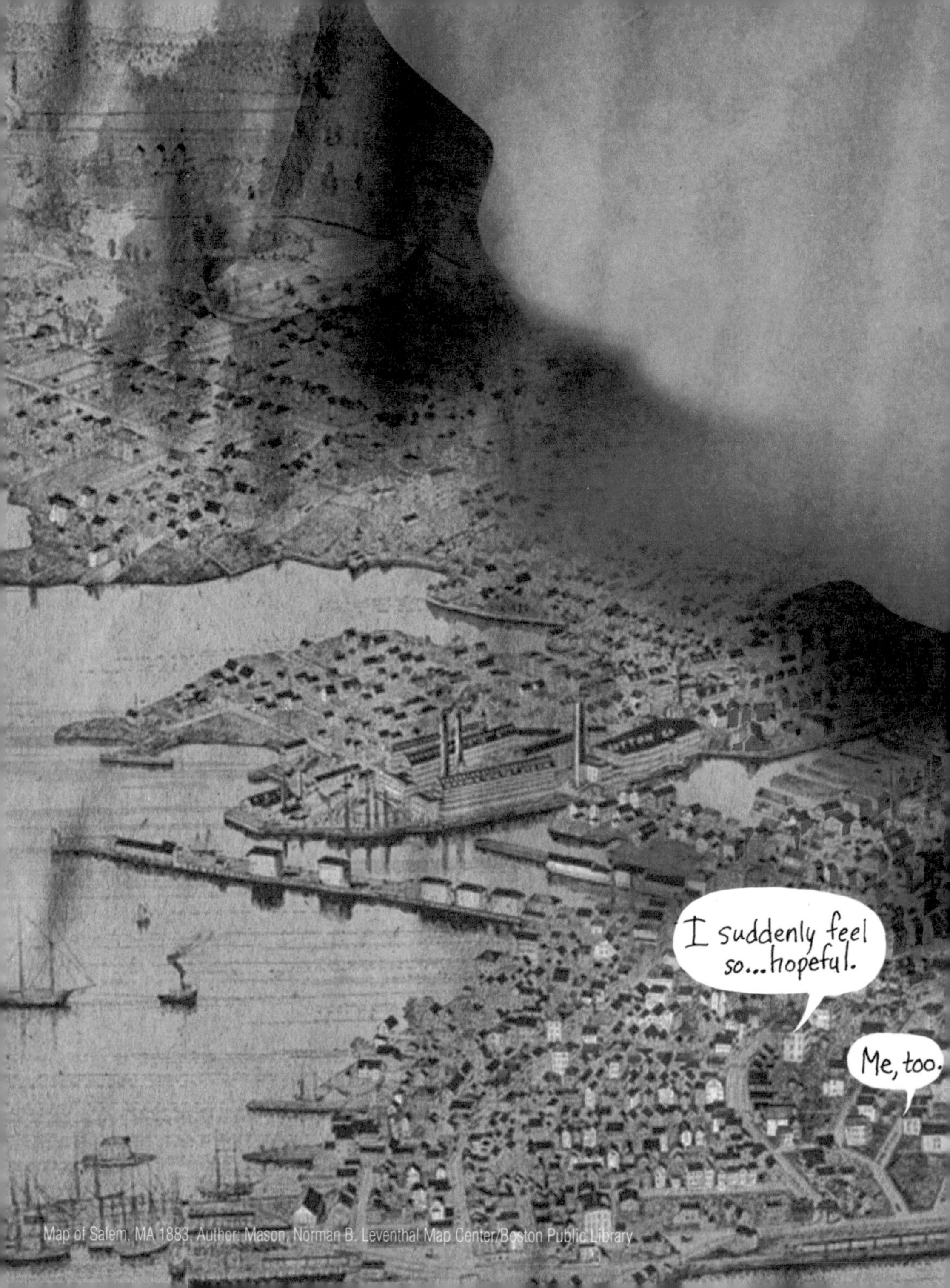
I suddenly feel so...hopeful.
Me, too.

Map of Salem, MA 1883. Author: Mason, Norman B. Leventhal Map Center/Boston Public Library

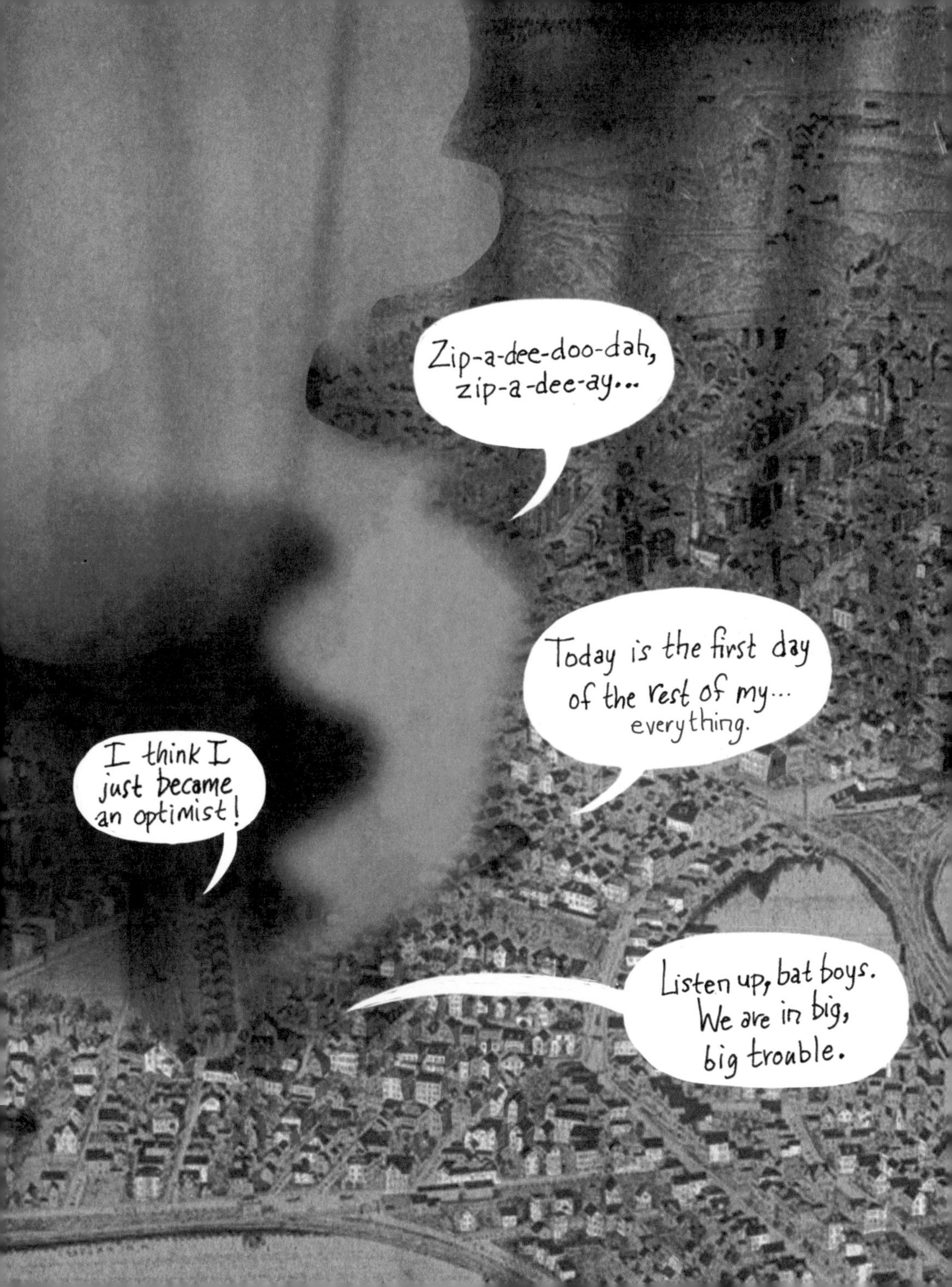
Zip-a-dee-doo-dah, zip-a-dee-ay...
Today is the first day of the rest of my... everything.
I think I just became an optimist!
Listen up, bat boys. We are in big, big trouble.

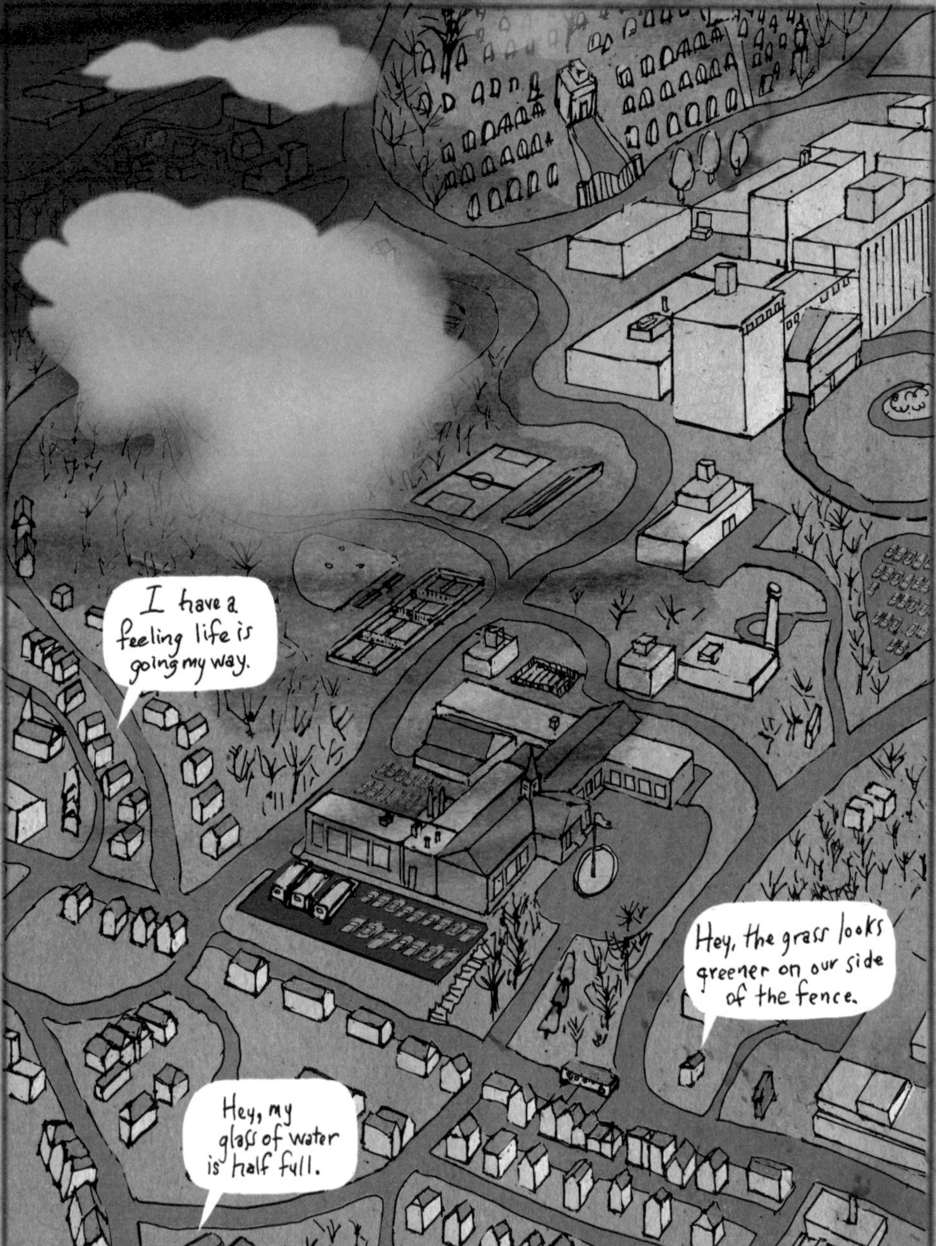
I have a feeling life is going my way.
Hey, the grass looks greener on our side of the fence.
Hey, my glass of water is half full.

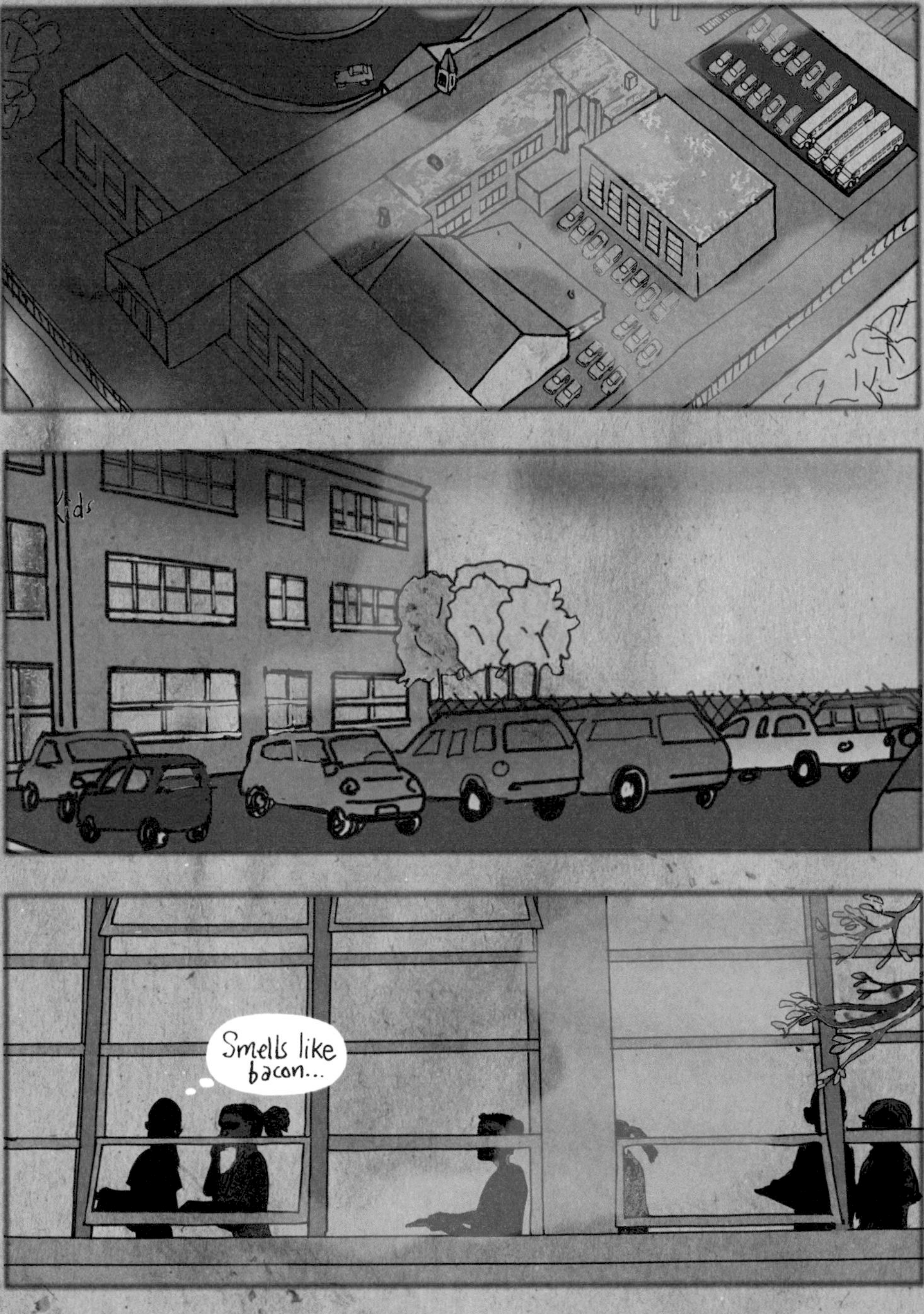
Kids
Smells like bacon...

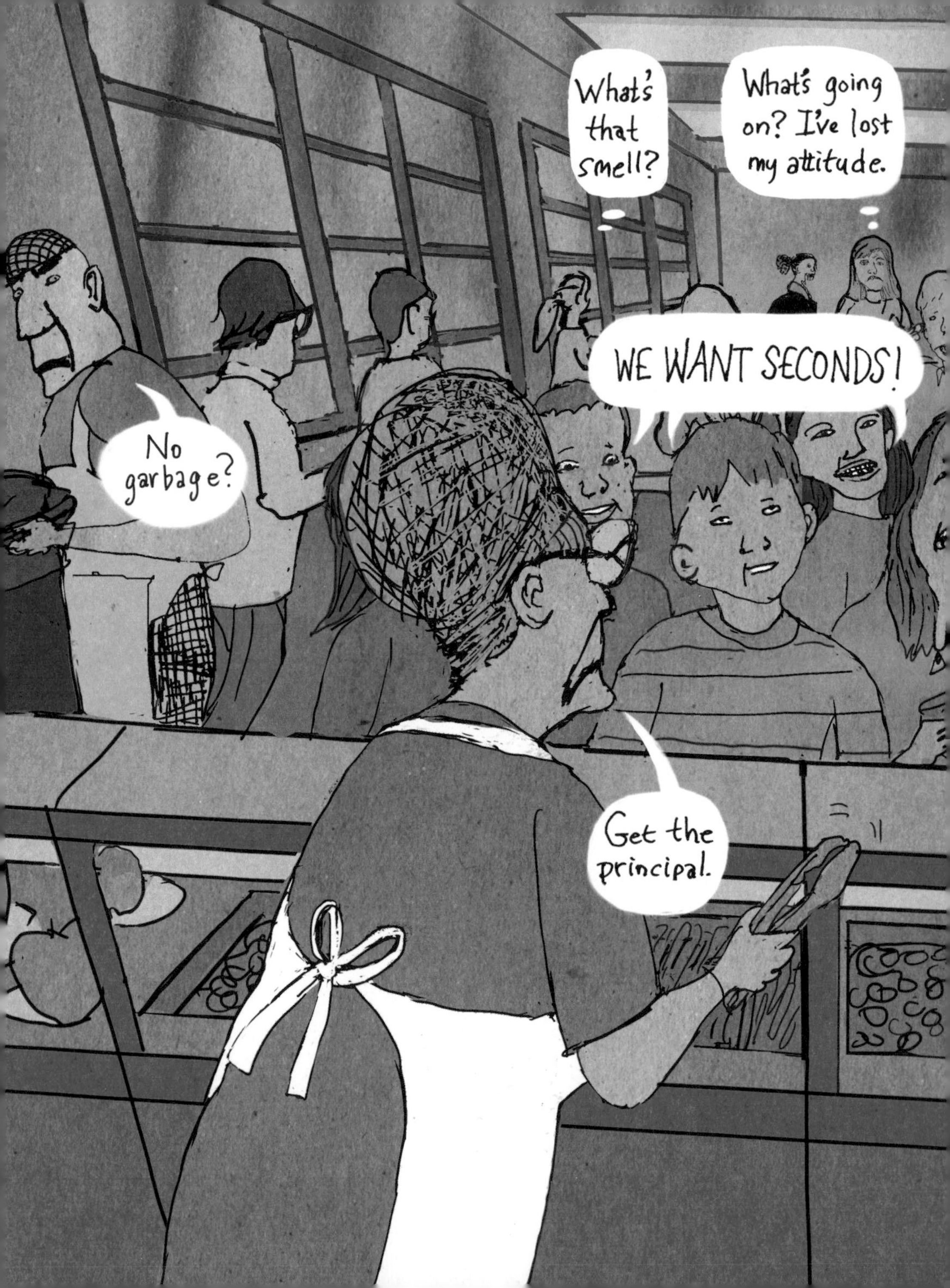
What's that smell?
What's going on? I've lost my attitude.
WE WANT SECONDS!
No garbage?
Get the principal.

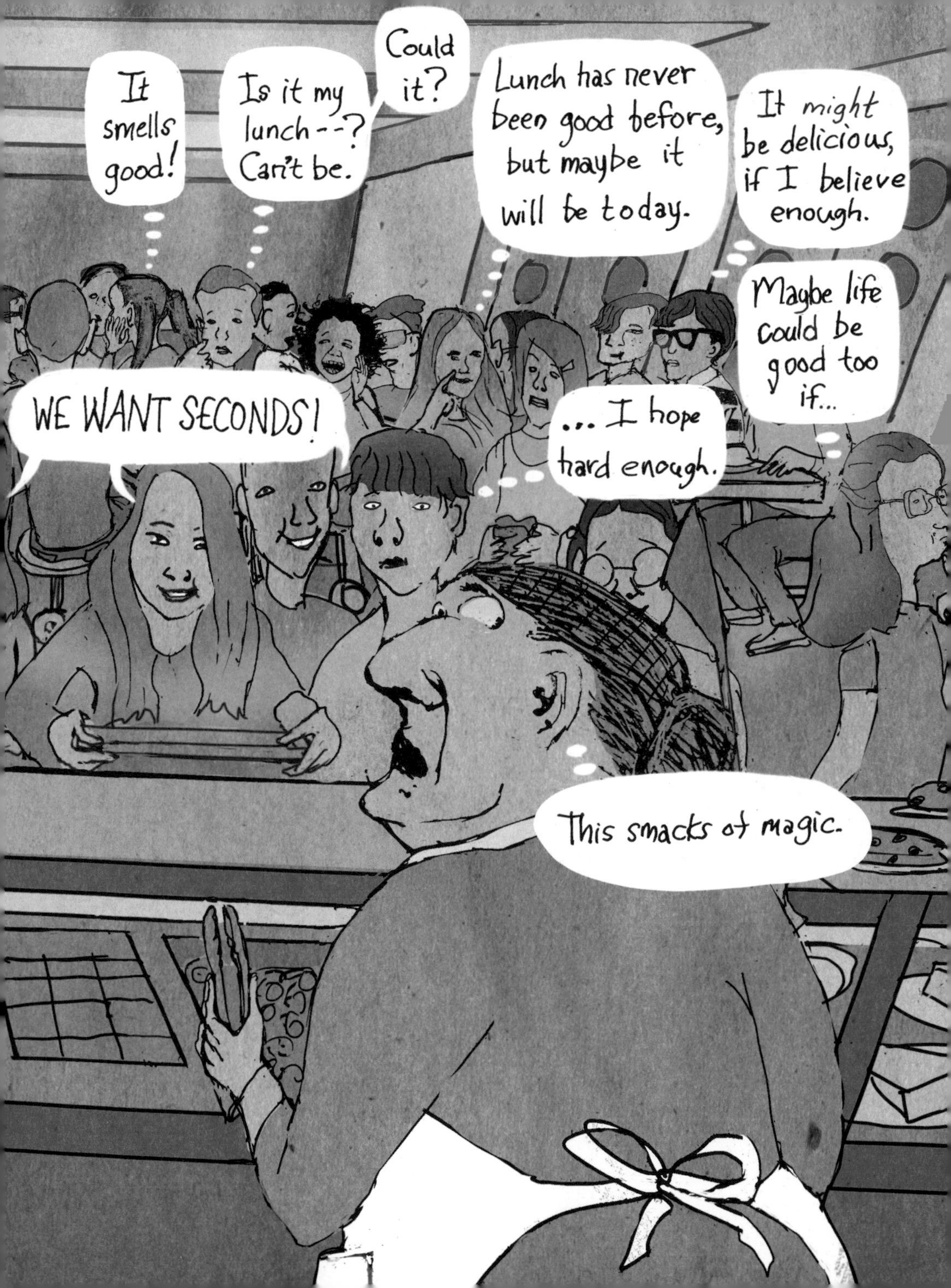
It smells good!
Is it my lunch--? Can't be.
Could it?
Lunch has never been good before, but maybe it will be today.
It might be delicious, if I believe enough.
Maybe life could be good too if...
WE WANT SECONDS!
... I hope hard enough.
This smacks of magic.

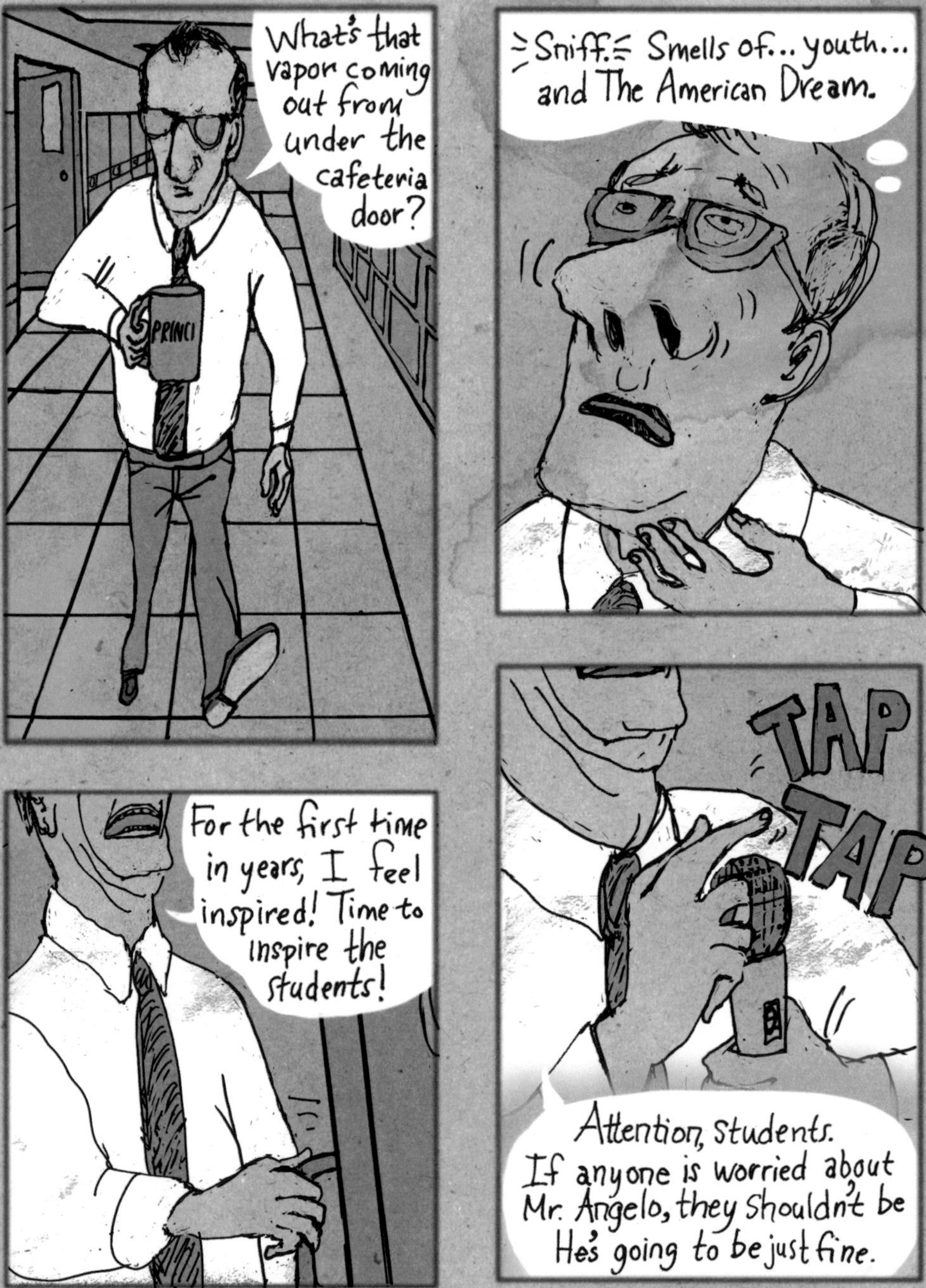
What's that vapor coming out from under the cafeteria door?
PRINCI
≈Sniff.≈ Smells of... youth... and The American Dream.
For the first time in years, I feel inspired! Time to inspire the students!
TAP
TAP
Attention, students. If anyone is worried about Mr. Angelo, they shouldn't be He's going to be just fine.

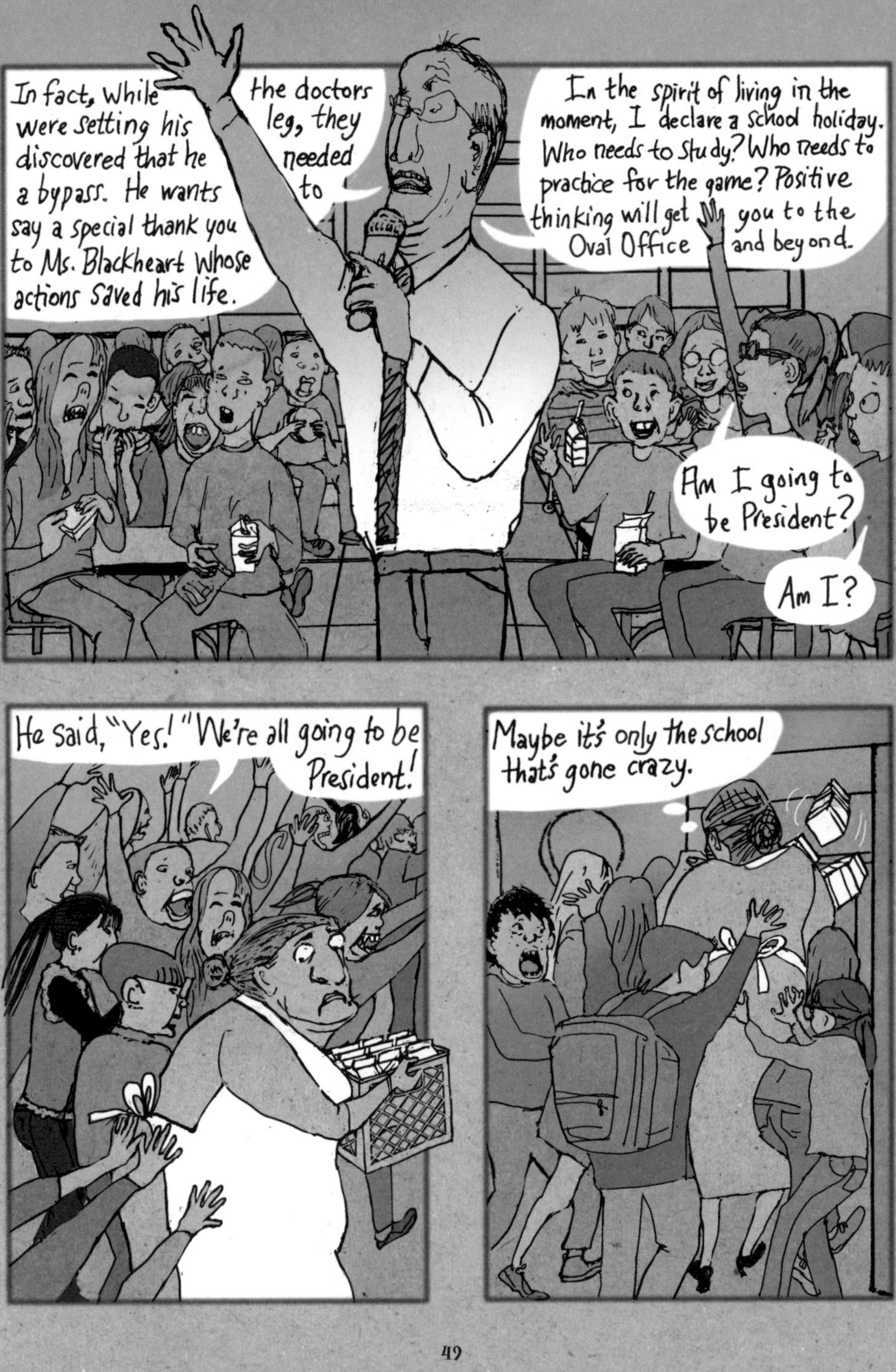
In fact, while the doctors were setting his leg, they discovered that he needed a bypass. He wants to say a special thank you to Ms. Blackheart whose actions saved his life.
In the spirit of living in the moment, I declare a school holiday. Who needs to study? Who needs to practice for the game? Positive thinking will get you to the Oval Office and beyond.
Am I going to be President?
Am I?
He said, "Yes!" "We're all going to be President!"
Maybe it's only the school that's gone crazy.

5th

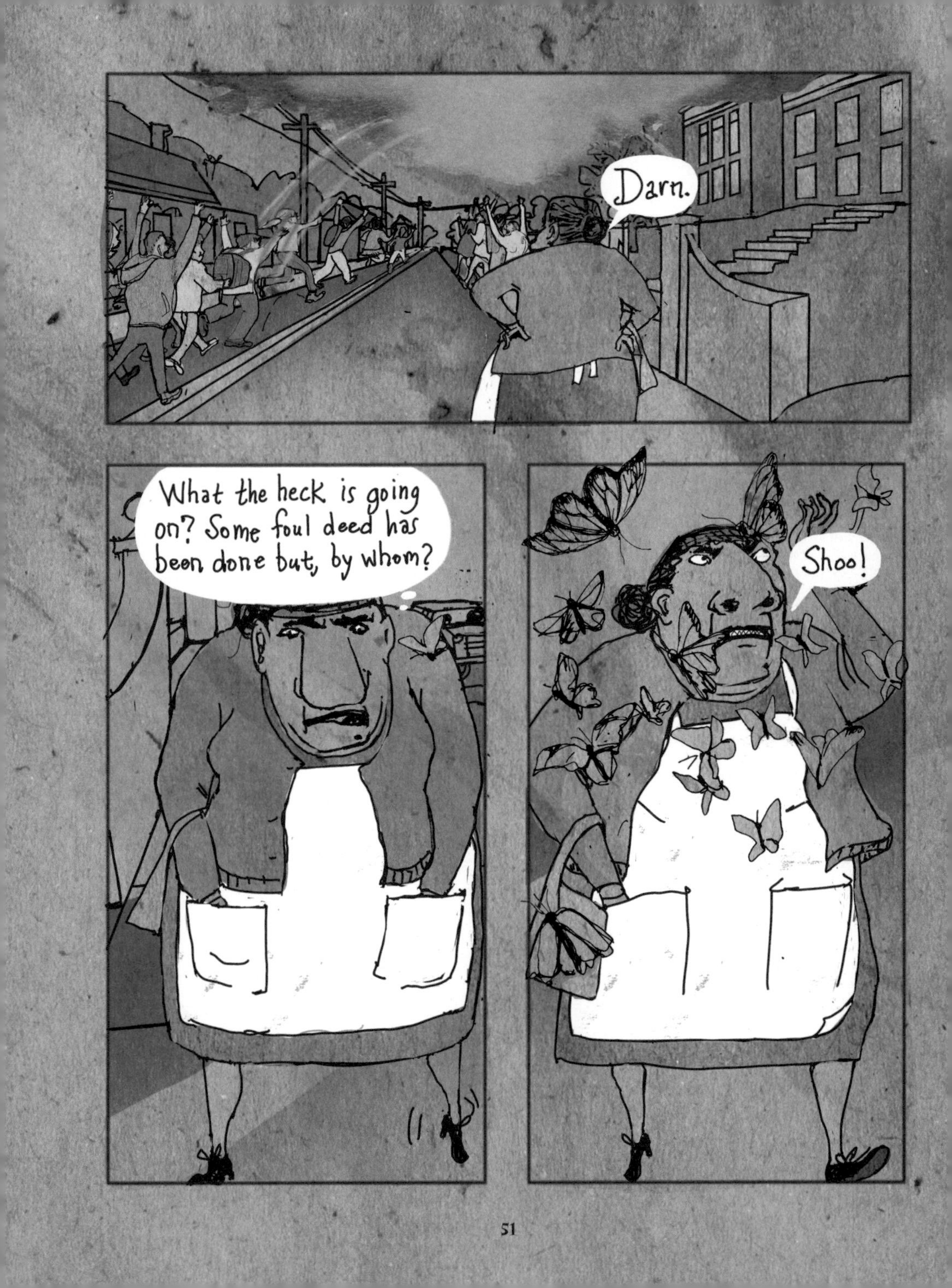
Darn.
What the heck is going on? Some foul deed has been done but, by whom?
Shoo!

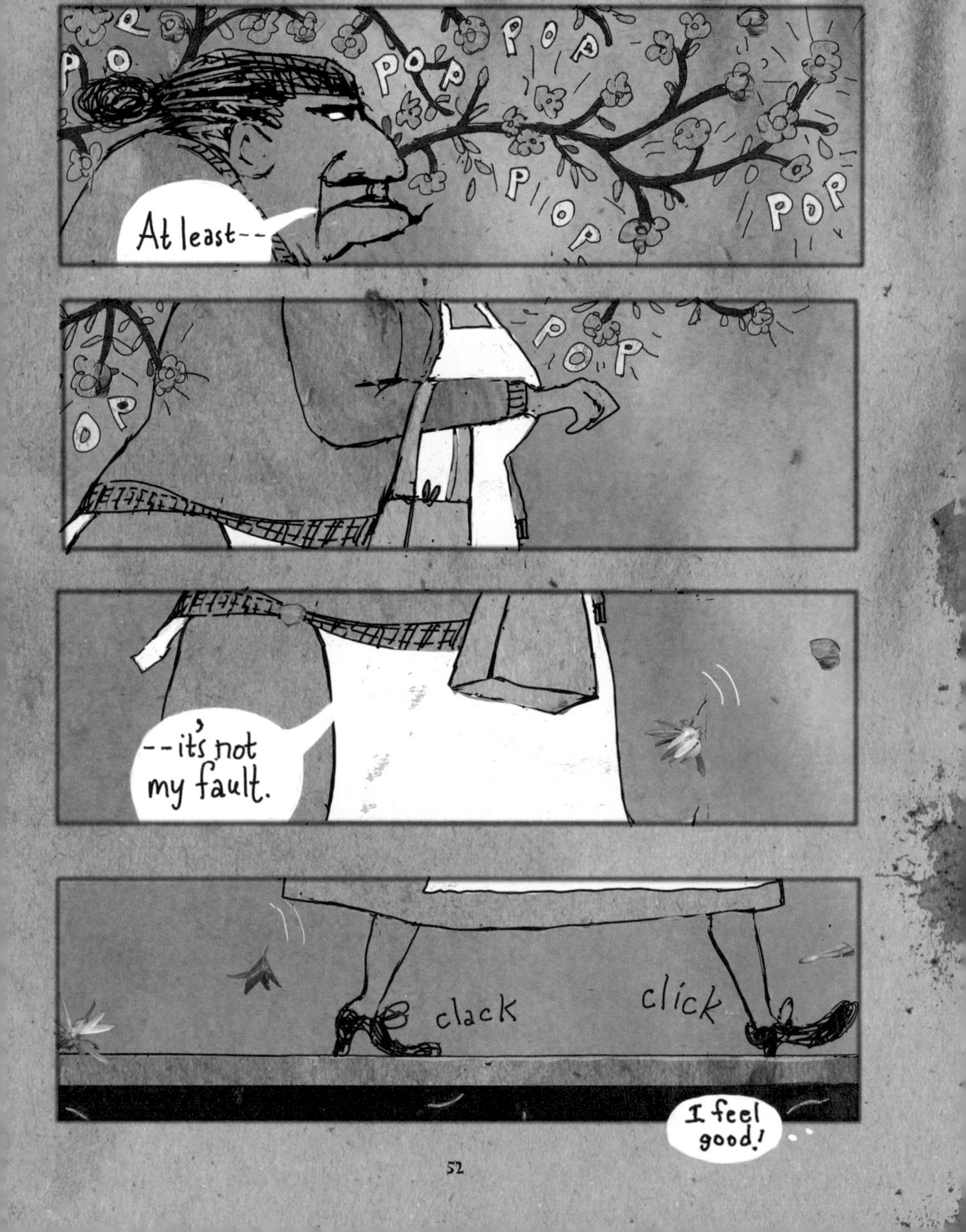
POP
At least--
POP
--it's not my fault.
clack
click
I feel good!

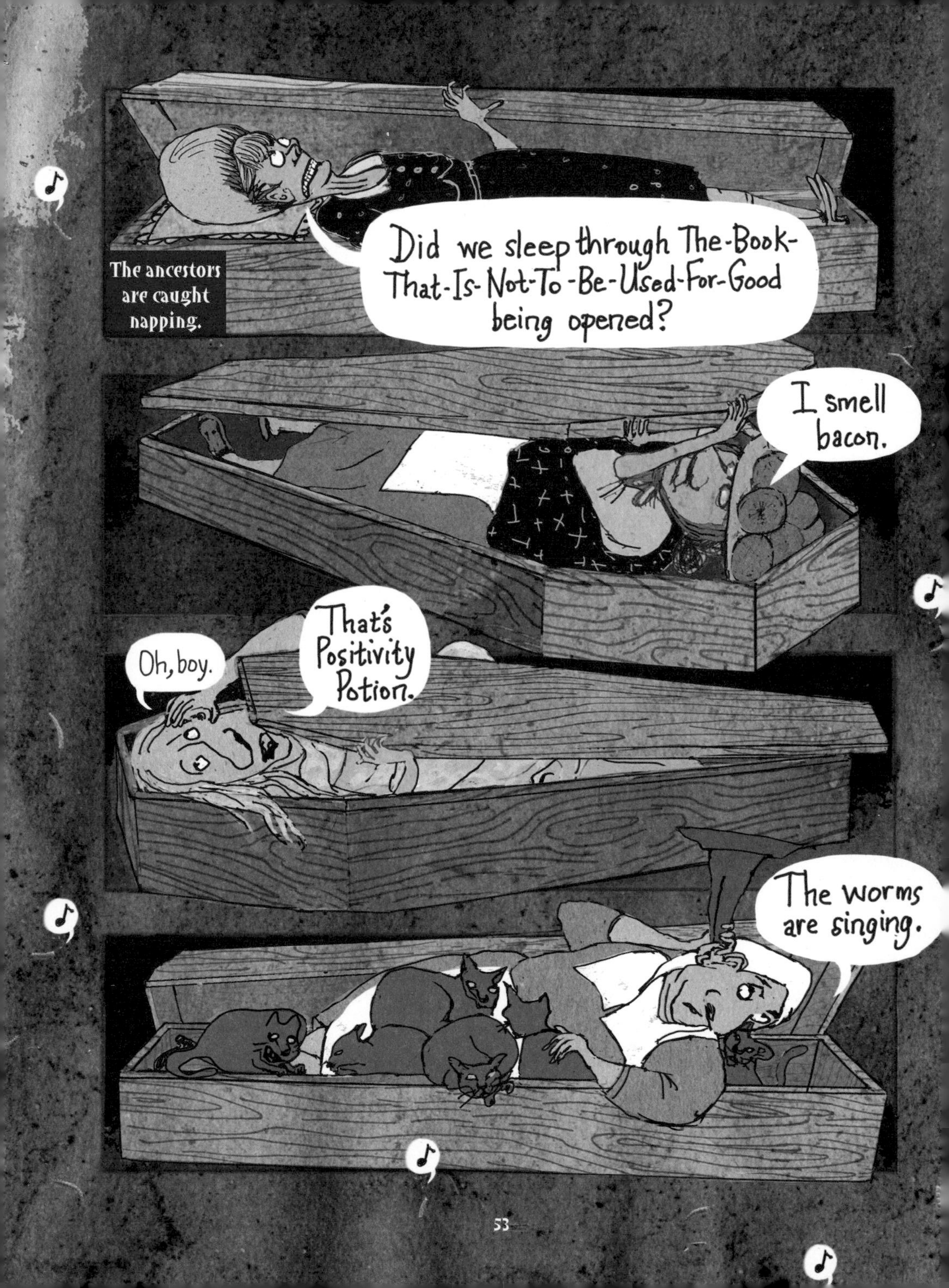
The ancestors are caught napping.
Did we sleep through The-Book-That-Is-Not-To-Be-Used-For-Good being opened?
I smell bacon.
Oh, boy.
That's Positivity Potion.
The worms are singing.

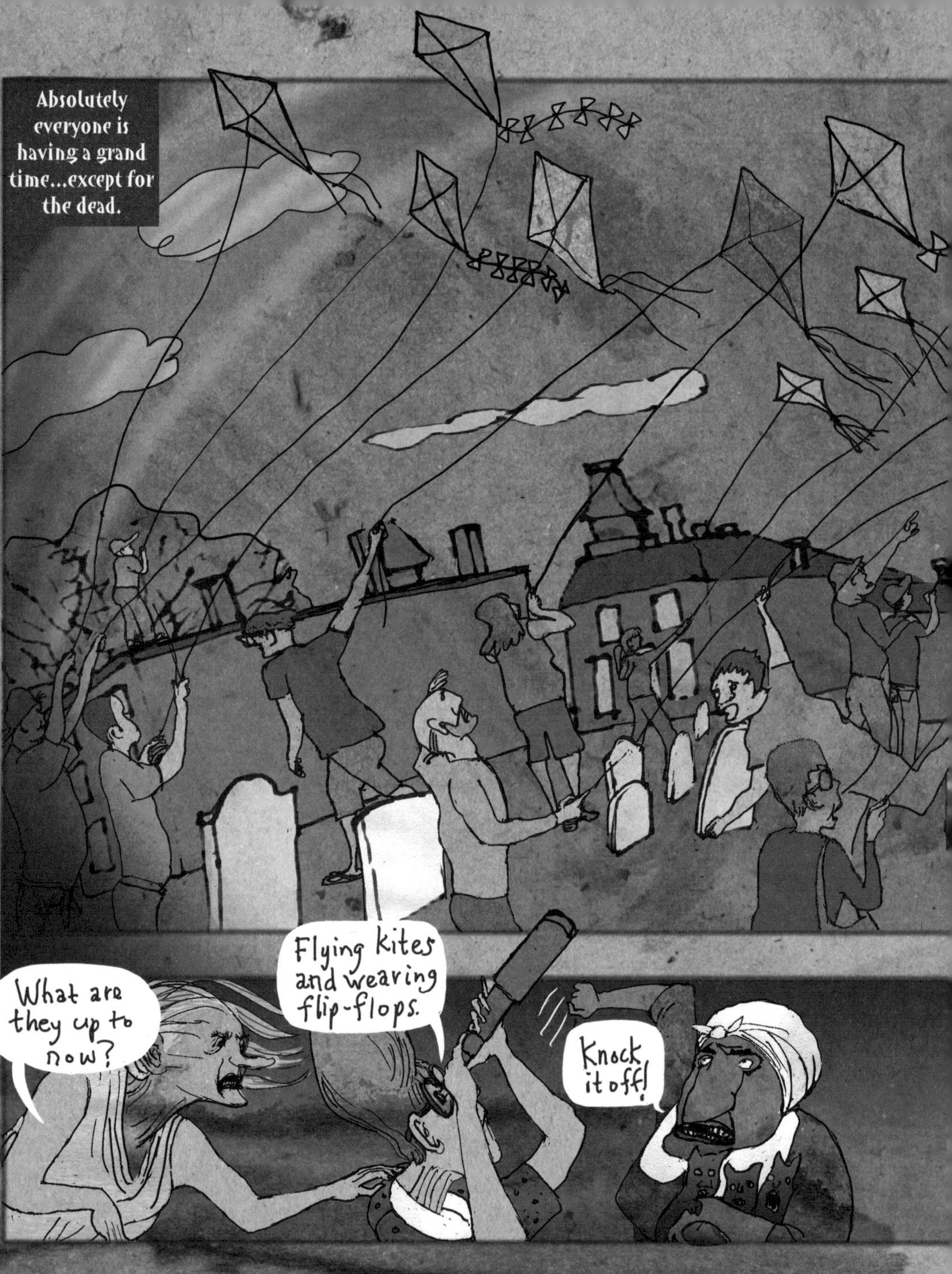
Absolutely everyone is having a grand time...except for the dead.
What are they up to now?
Flying kites and wearing flip-flops.
Knock it off!

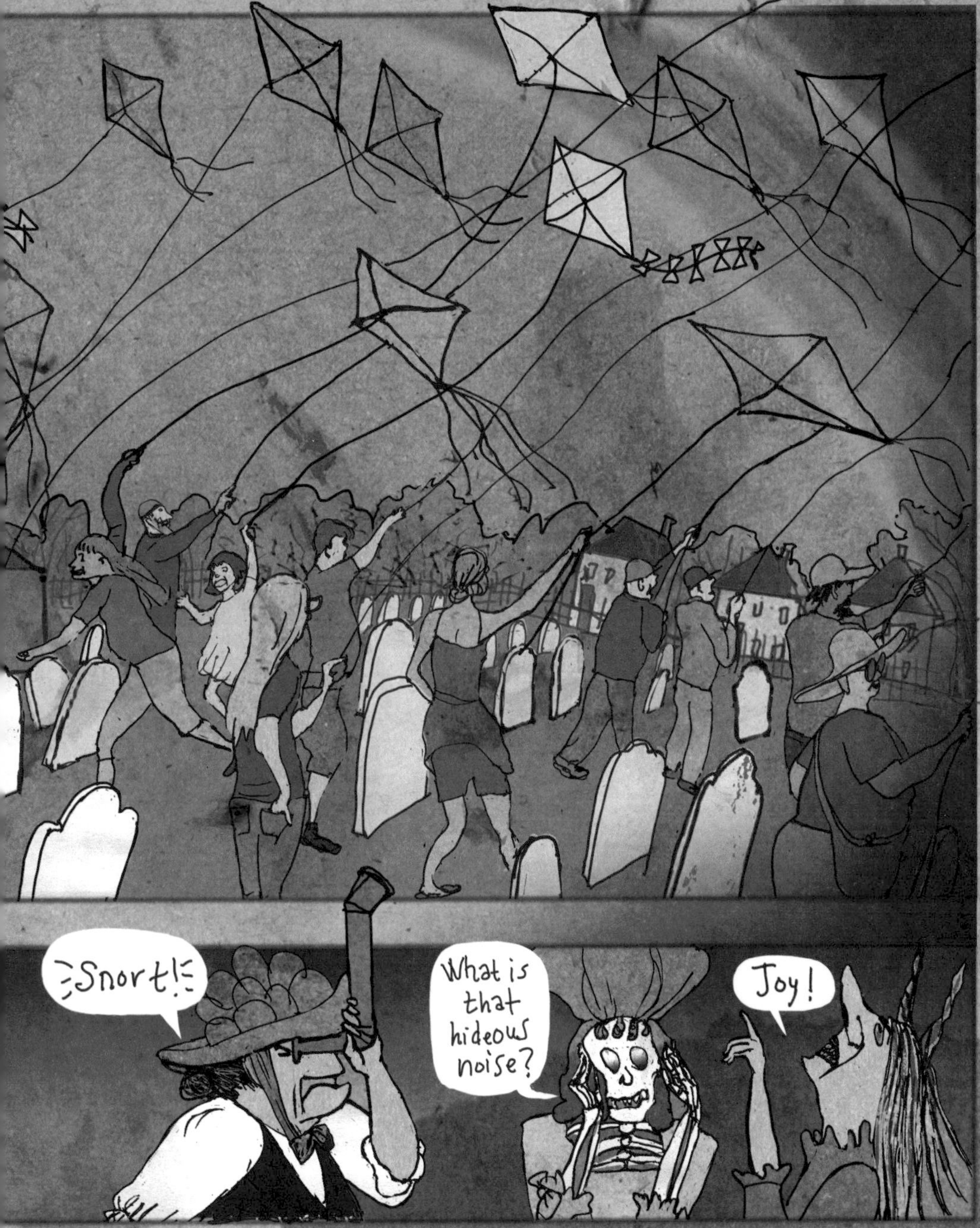
Snort!
What is that hideous noise?
Joy!

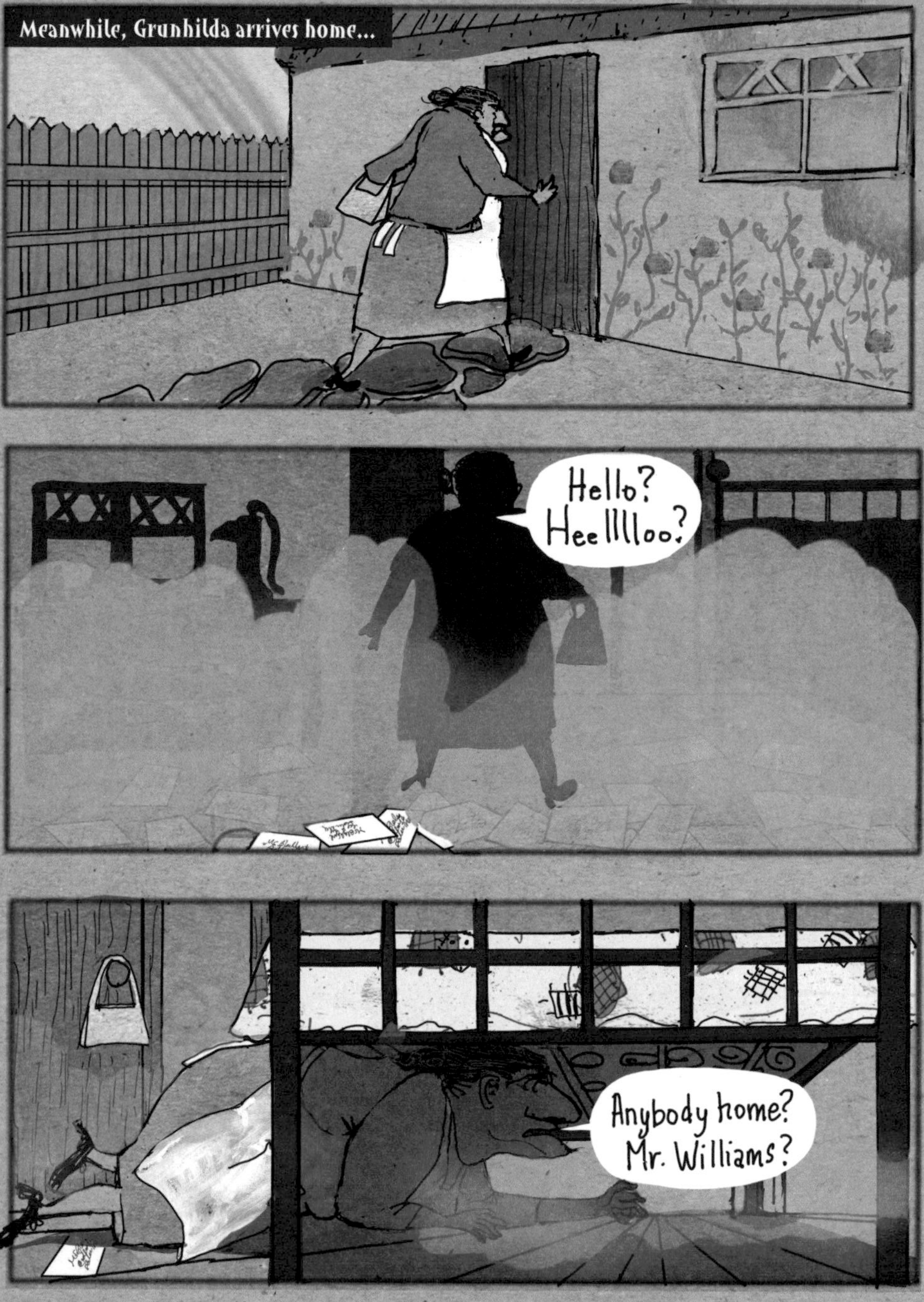
Meanwhile, Grunhilda arrives home...
Hello? Heellllloo?
Anybody home? Mr. Williams?

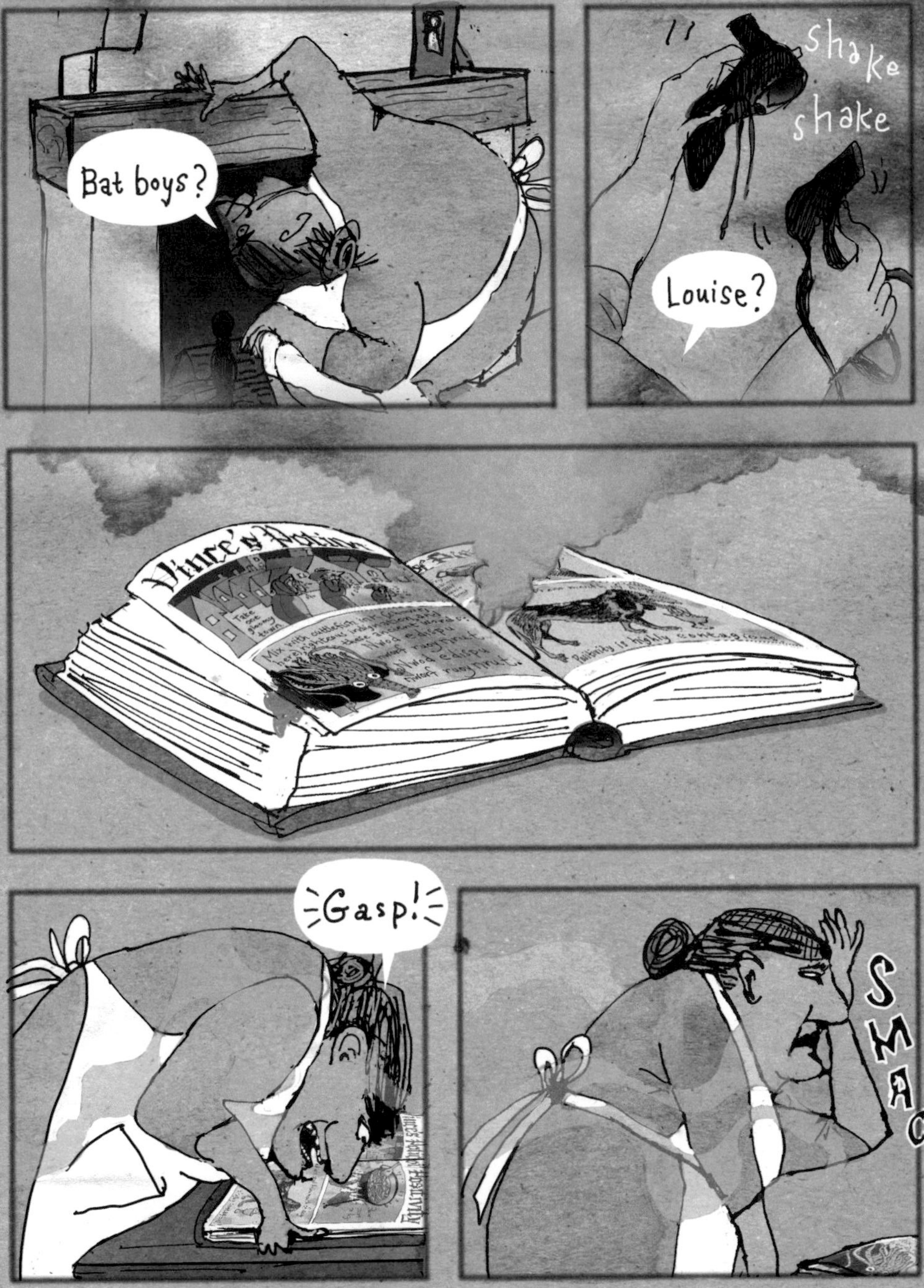
Bat boys?
shake
shake
Louise?
Gasp!
SMACK

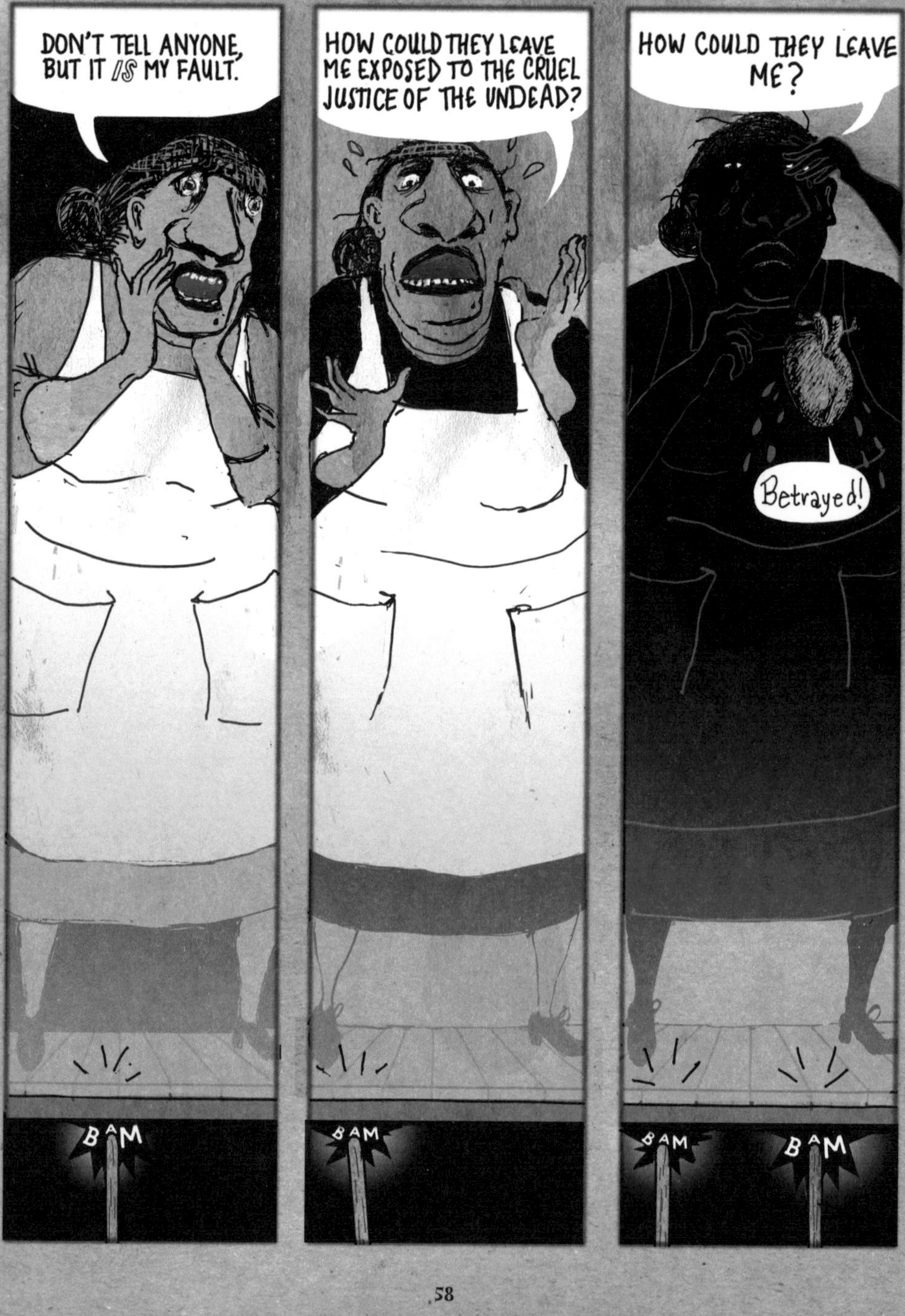
DON'T TELL ANYONE, BUT IT IS MY FAULT.
BAM
HOW COULD THEY LEAVE ME EXPOSED TO THE CRUEL JUSTICE OF THE UNDEAD?
BAM
HOW COULD THEY LEAVE ME?
Betrayed!
BAM
BAM

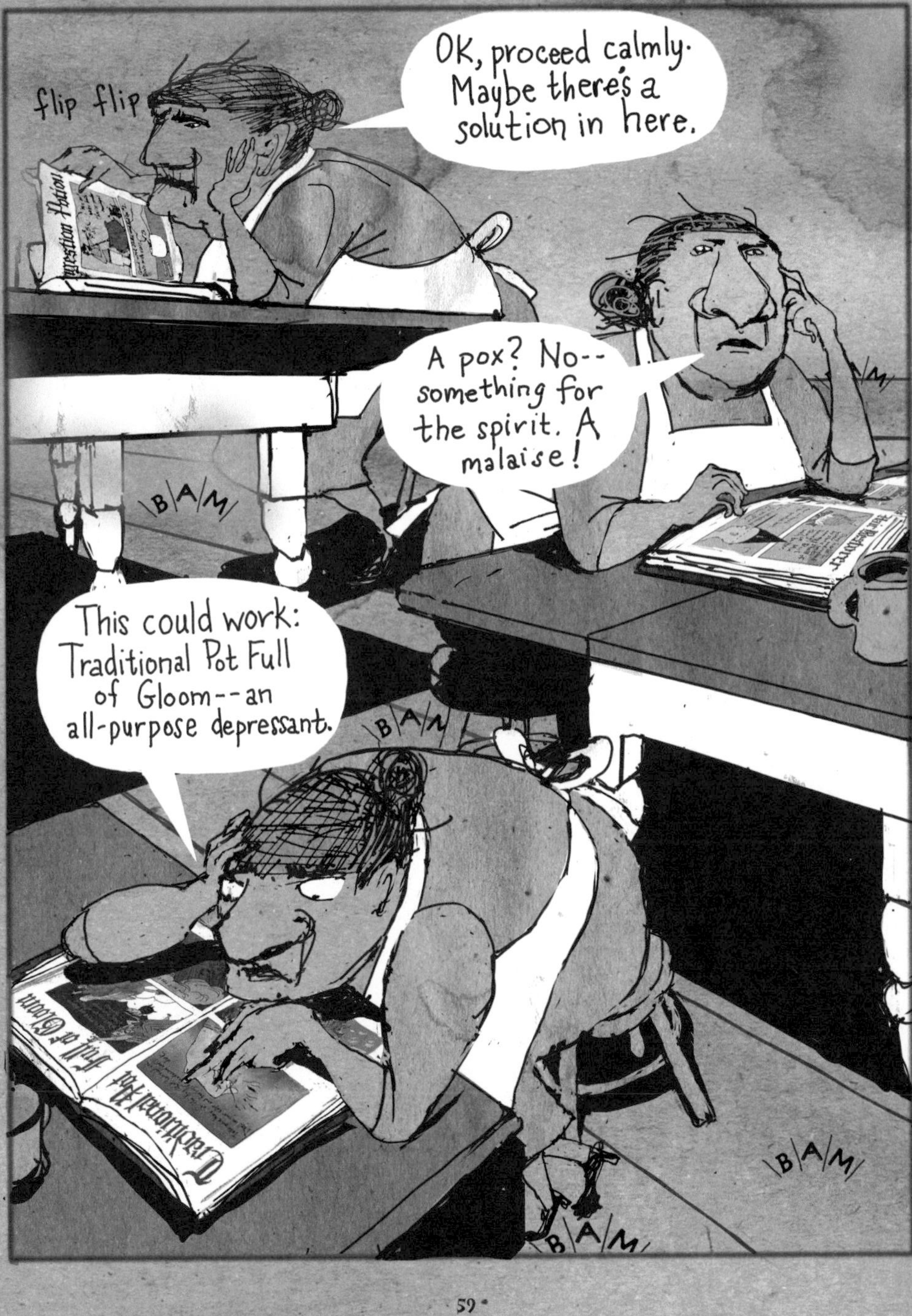
flip flip
OK, proceed calmly. Maybe there's a solution in here.
A pox? No-- something for the spirit. A malaise!
BAM
This could work: Traditional Pot Full of Gloom--an all-purpose depressant.
BAM
BAM
BAM
Traditional Pot Full of Gloom

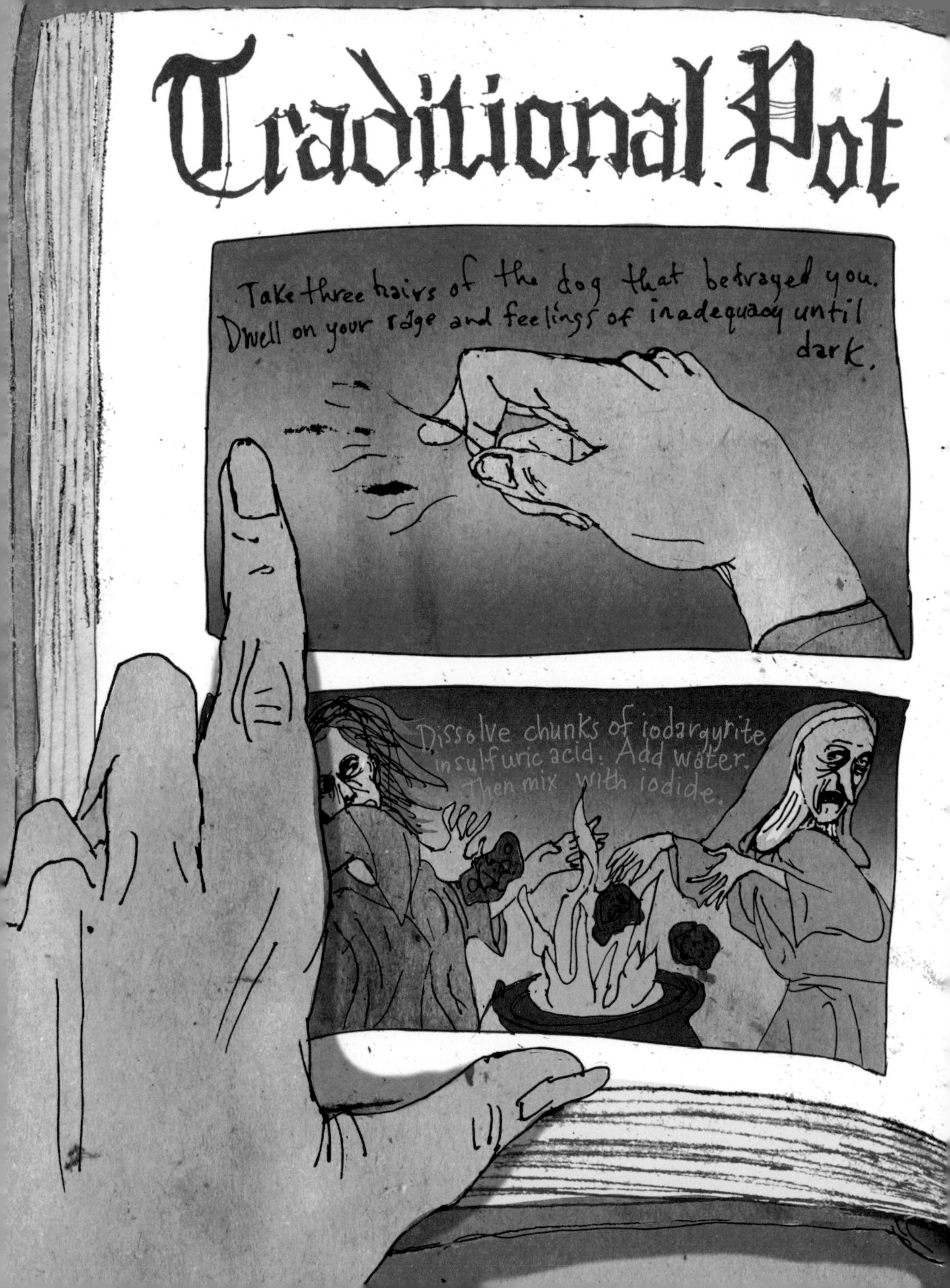
Traditional Pot
Take three hairs of the dog that betrayed you. Dwell on your rage and feelings of inadequacy until dark.
Dissolve chunks of iodargyrite insulfuric acid. Add water. Then mix with iodide.

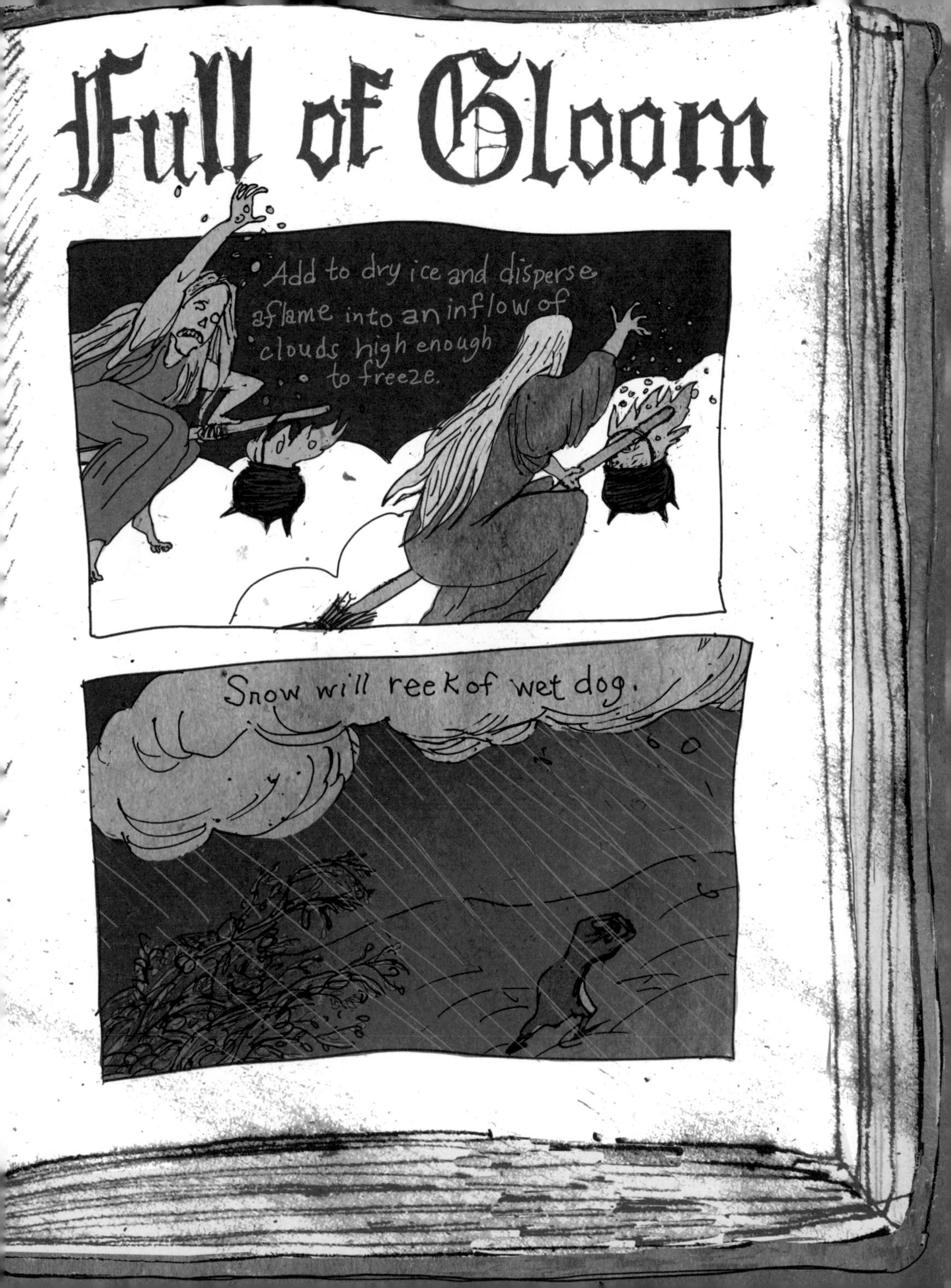
Full of Gloom
Add to dry ice and disperse aflame into an inflow of clouds high enough to freeze.
Snow will reek of wet dog.

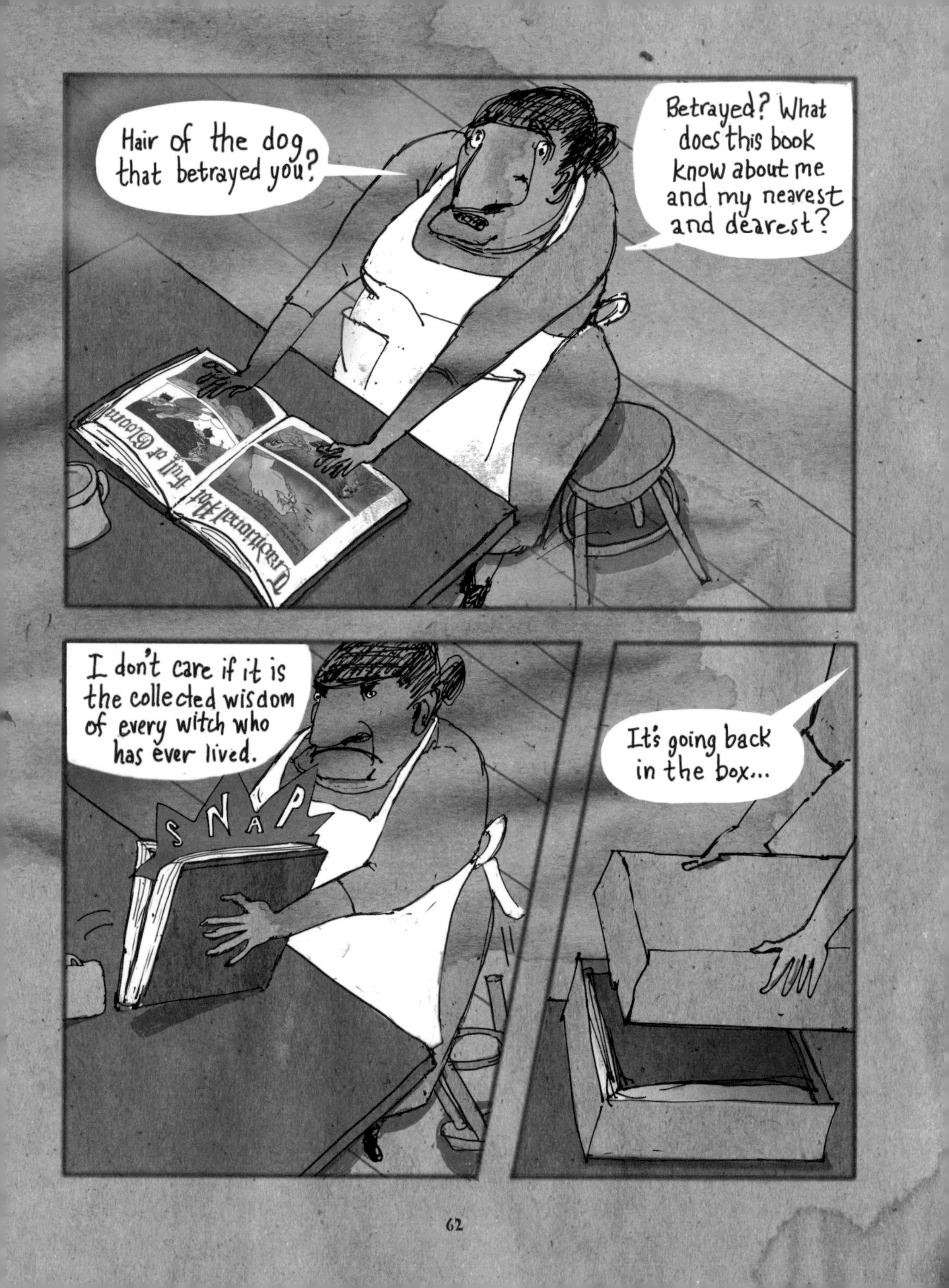
Hair of the dog that betrayed you?
Betrayed? What does this book know about me and my nearest and dearest?
I don't care if it is the collected wisdom of every witch who has ever lived.
SNAP
It's going back in the box...

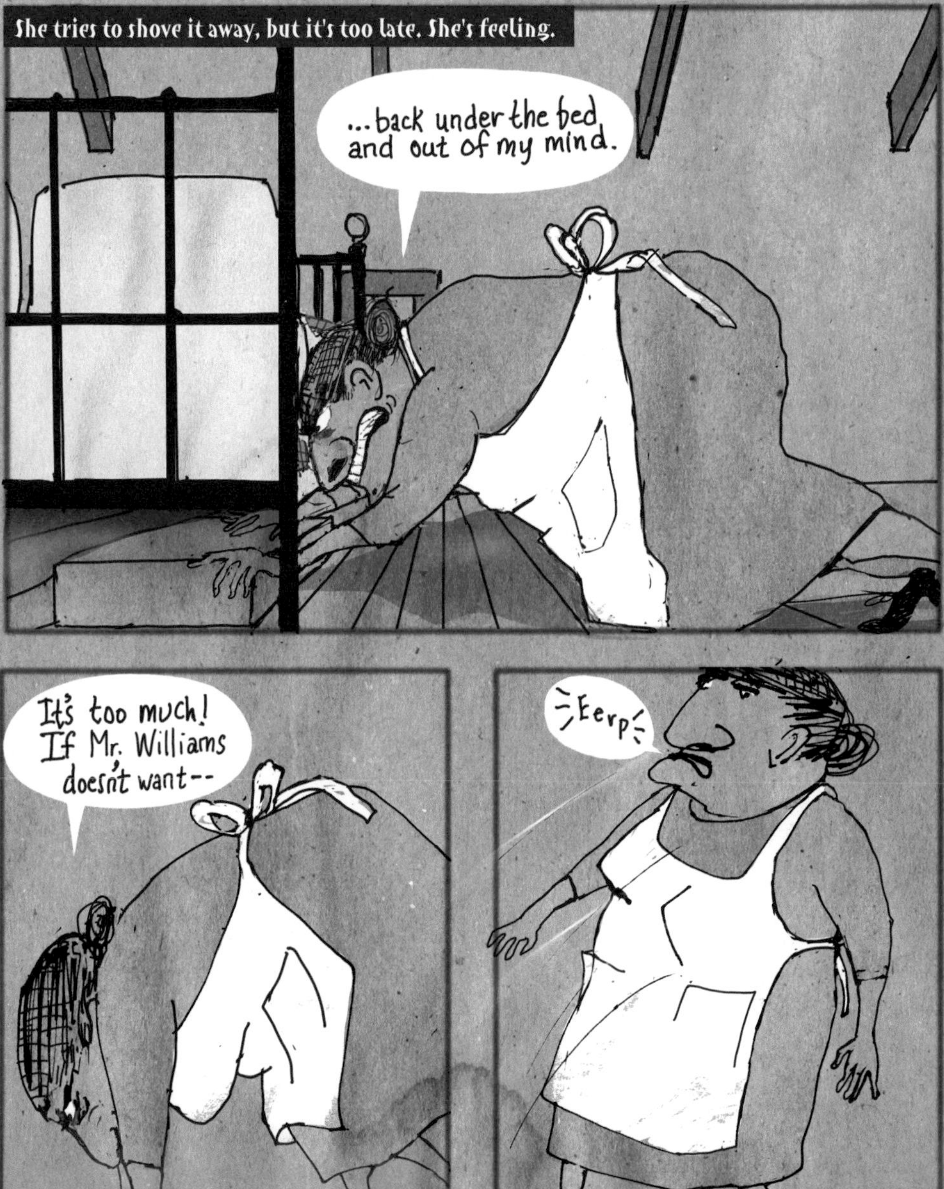
She tries to shove it away, but it's too late. She's feeling.
...back under the bed and out of my mind.
It's too much! If Mr. Williams doesn't want--
BAM
BAM
Eerp
BAM
BAM

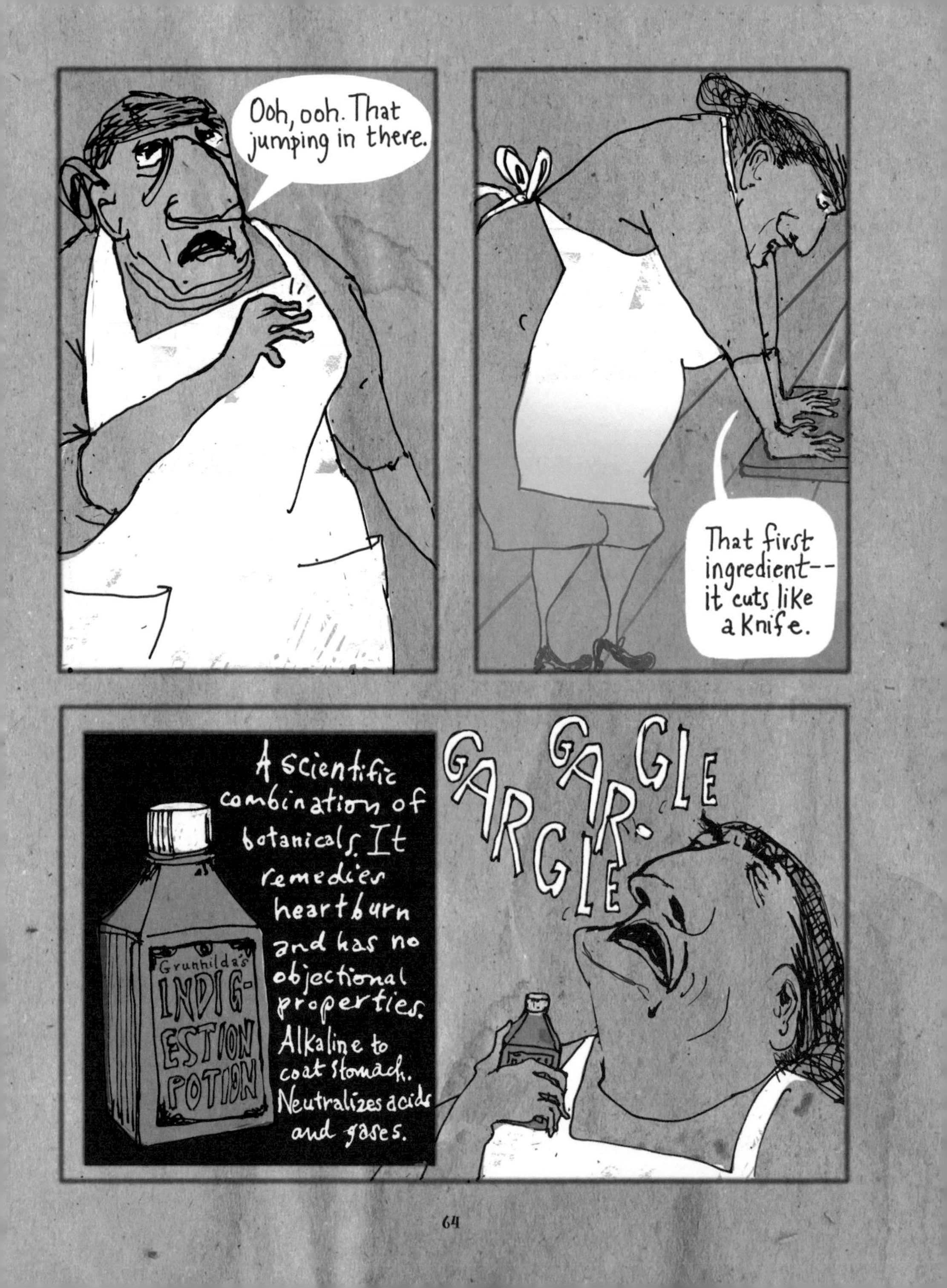
Ooh, ooh. That jumping in there.
That first ingredient-- it cuts like a knife.
A scientific combination of botanicals. It remedies heartburn and has no objectional properties. Alkaline to coat stomach. Neutralizes acids and gases.
Grunhilda's INDIG-ESTION POTION
GARGLE
GAR-GLE

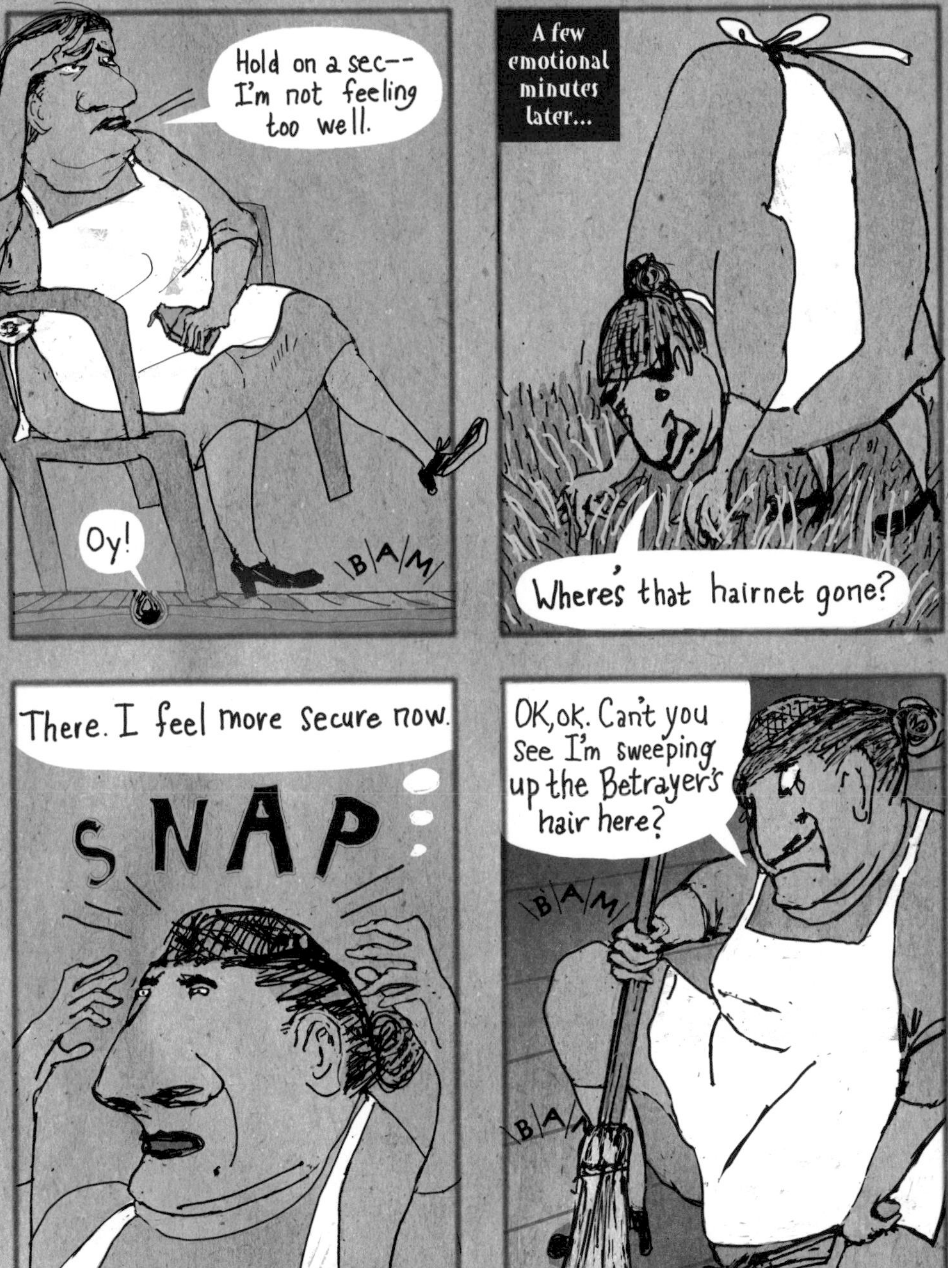
Hold on a sec-- I'm not feeling too well.
Oy!
BAM
A few emotional minutes later...
Where's that hairnet gone?
There. I feel more secure now.
SNAP
OK, ok. Can't you see I'm sweeping up the Betrayer's hair here?
BAM
BAM

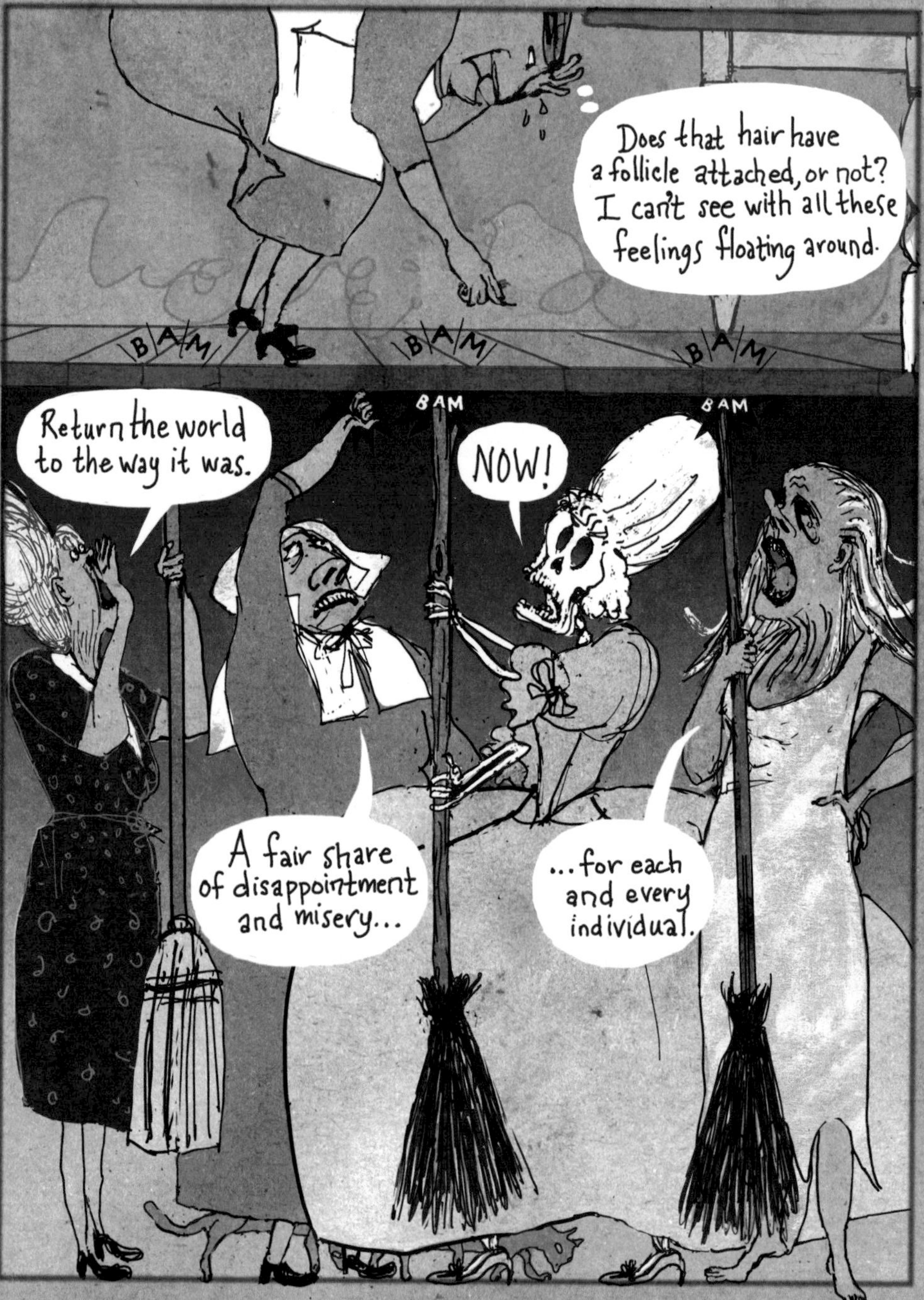
Does that hair have a follicle attached, or not? I can't see with all these feelings floating around.
BAM
BAM
BAM
BAM
BAM
Return the world to the way it was.
NOW!
A fair share of disappointment and misery...
...for each and every individual.

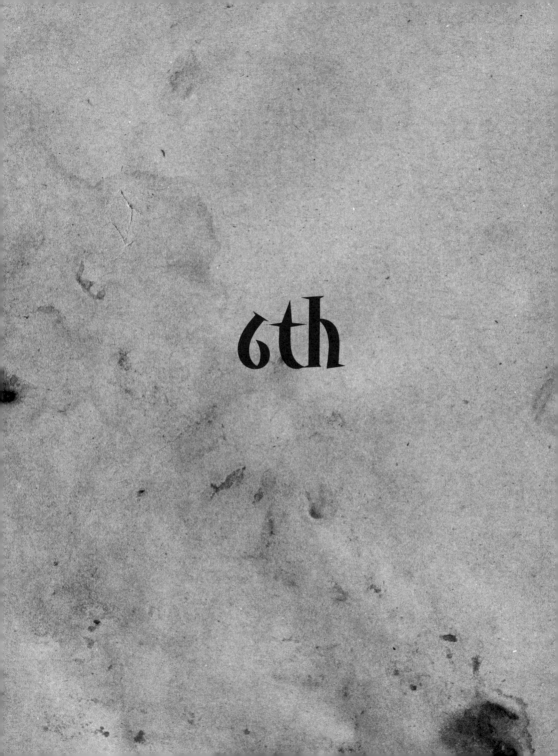

6th

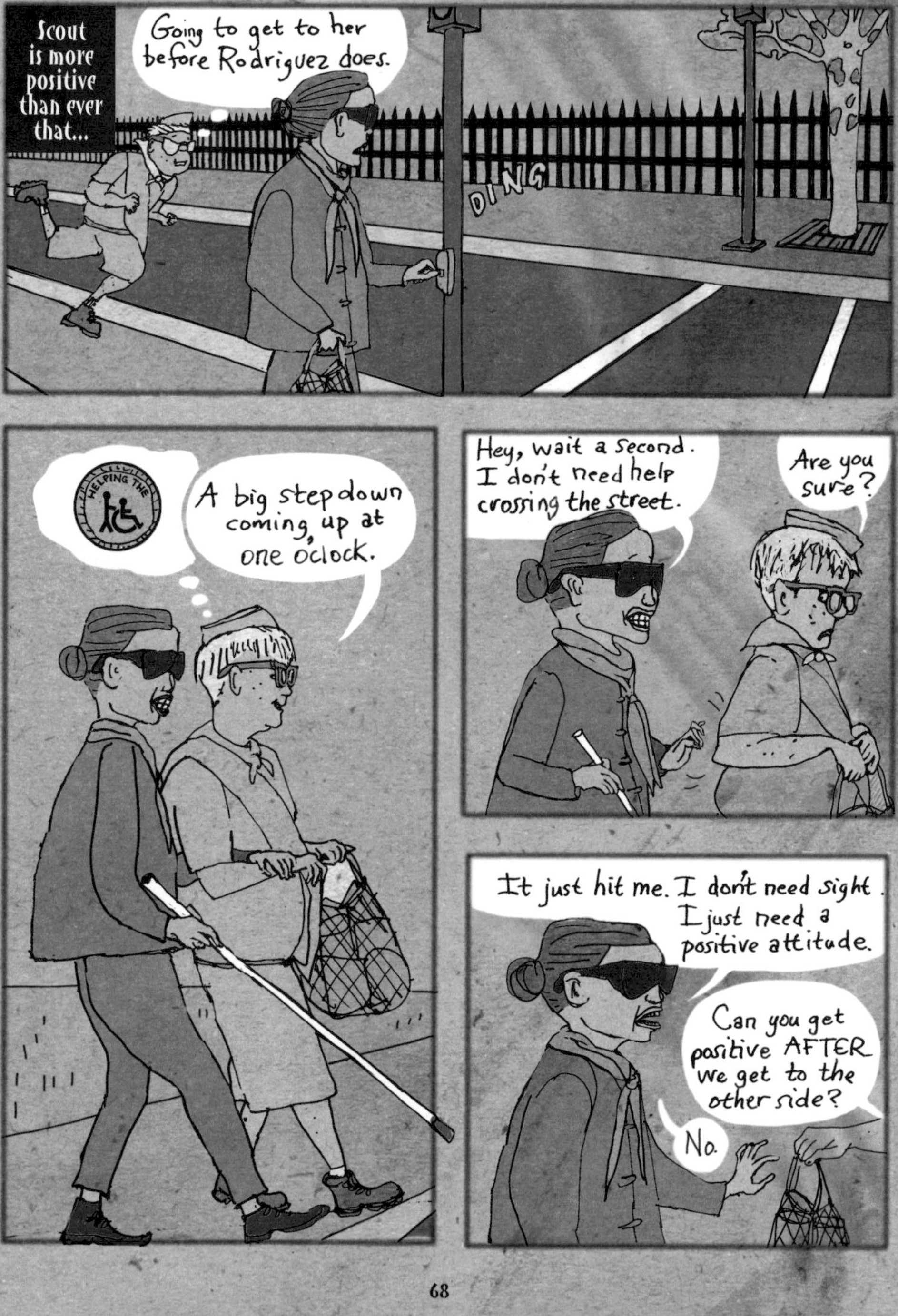
Scout is more positive than ever that...
Going to get to her before Rodriguez does.
DING
HELPING THE
A big step down coming up at one oclock.
Hey, wait a second. I don't need help crossing the street.
Are you sure?
It just hit me. I don't need sight. I just need a positive attitude.
Can you get positive AFTER we get to the other side?
No.

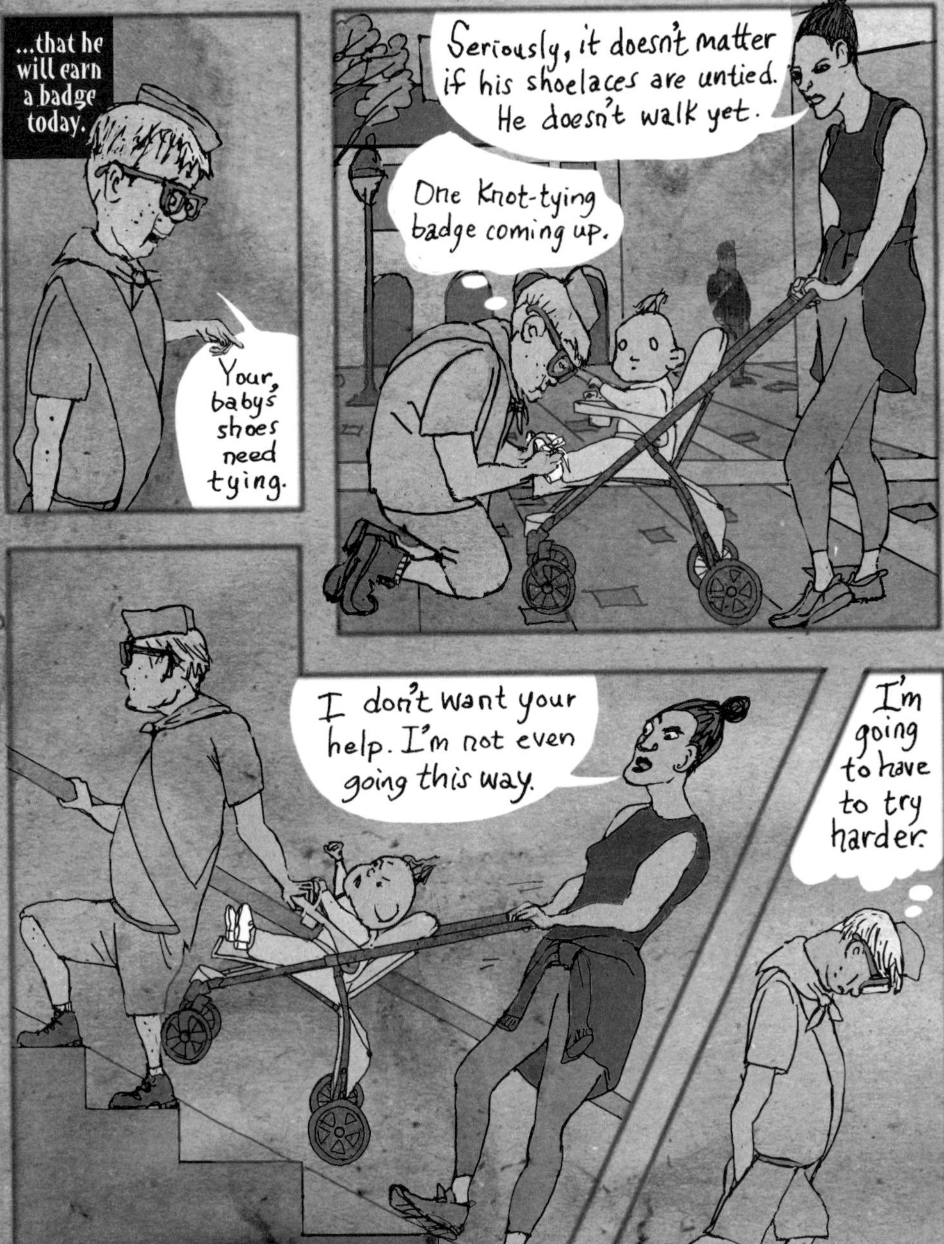
...that he will earn a badge today.
Your, baby's shoes need tying.
Seriously, it doesn't matter if his shoelaces are untied. He doesn't walk yet.
One Knot-tying badge coming up.
I don't want your help. I'm not even going this way.
I'm going to have to try harder.

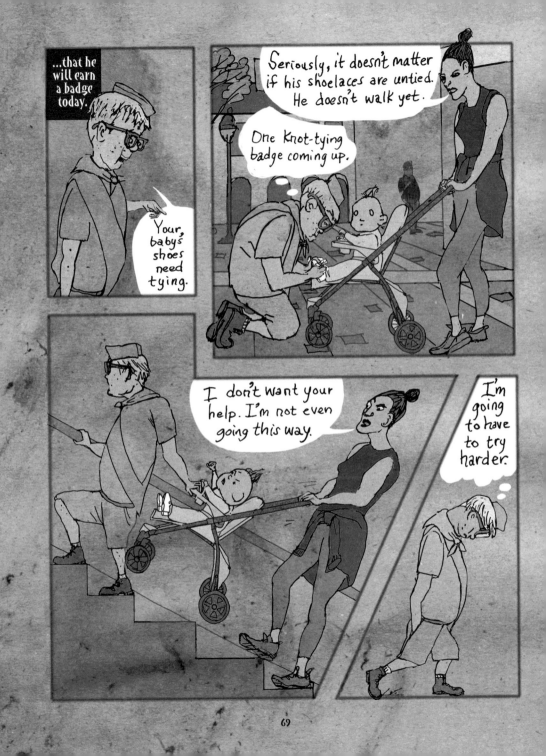

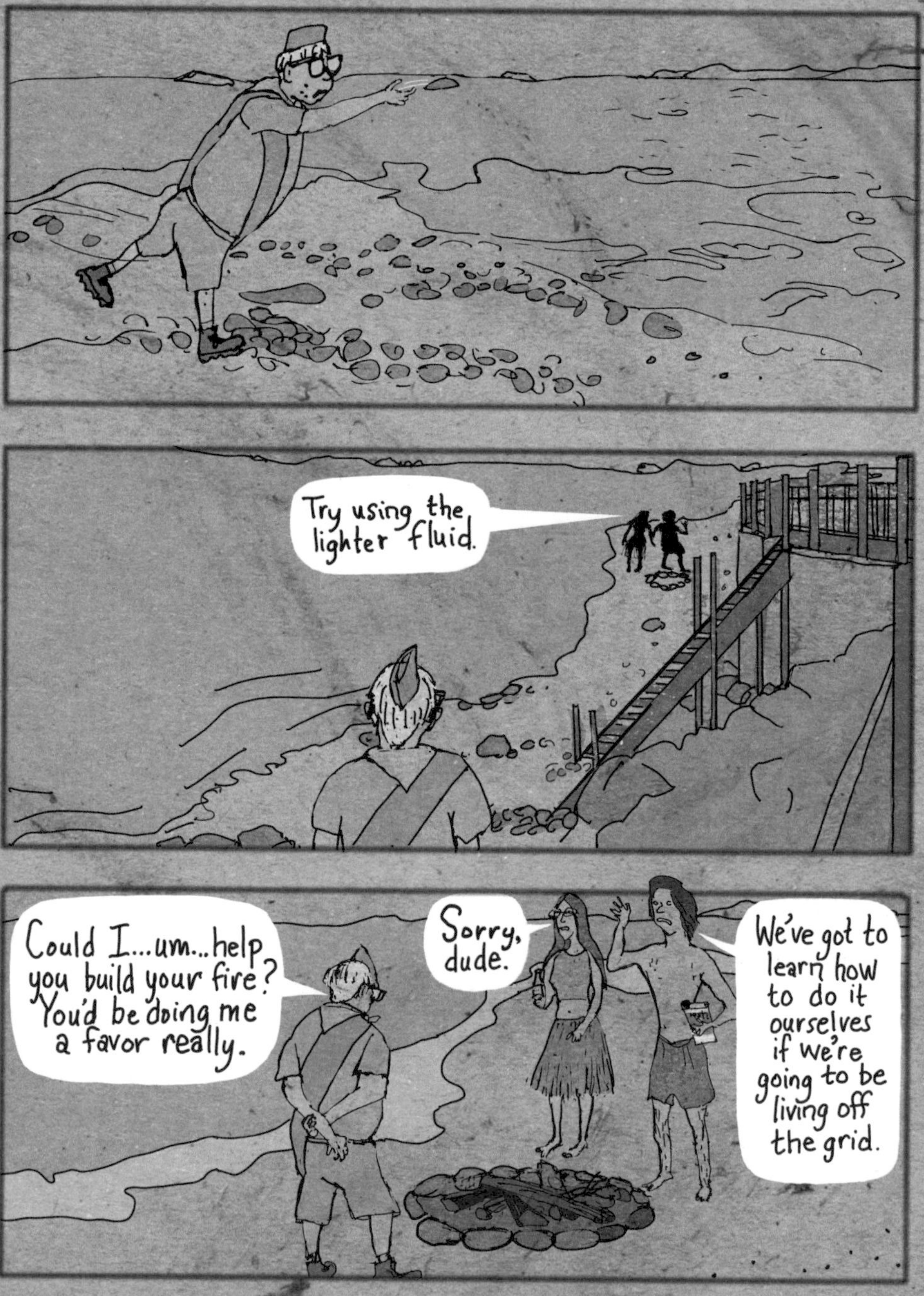
Try using the lighter fluid.
Could I...um...help you build your fire? You'd be doing me a favor really.
Sorry, dude.
We've got to learn how to do it ourselves if we're going to be living off the grid.

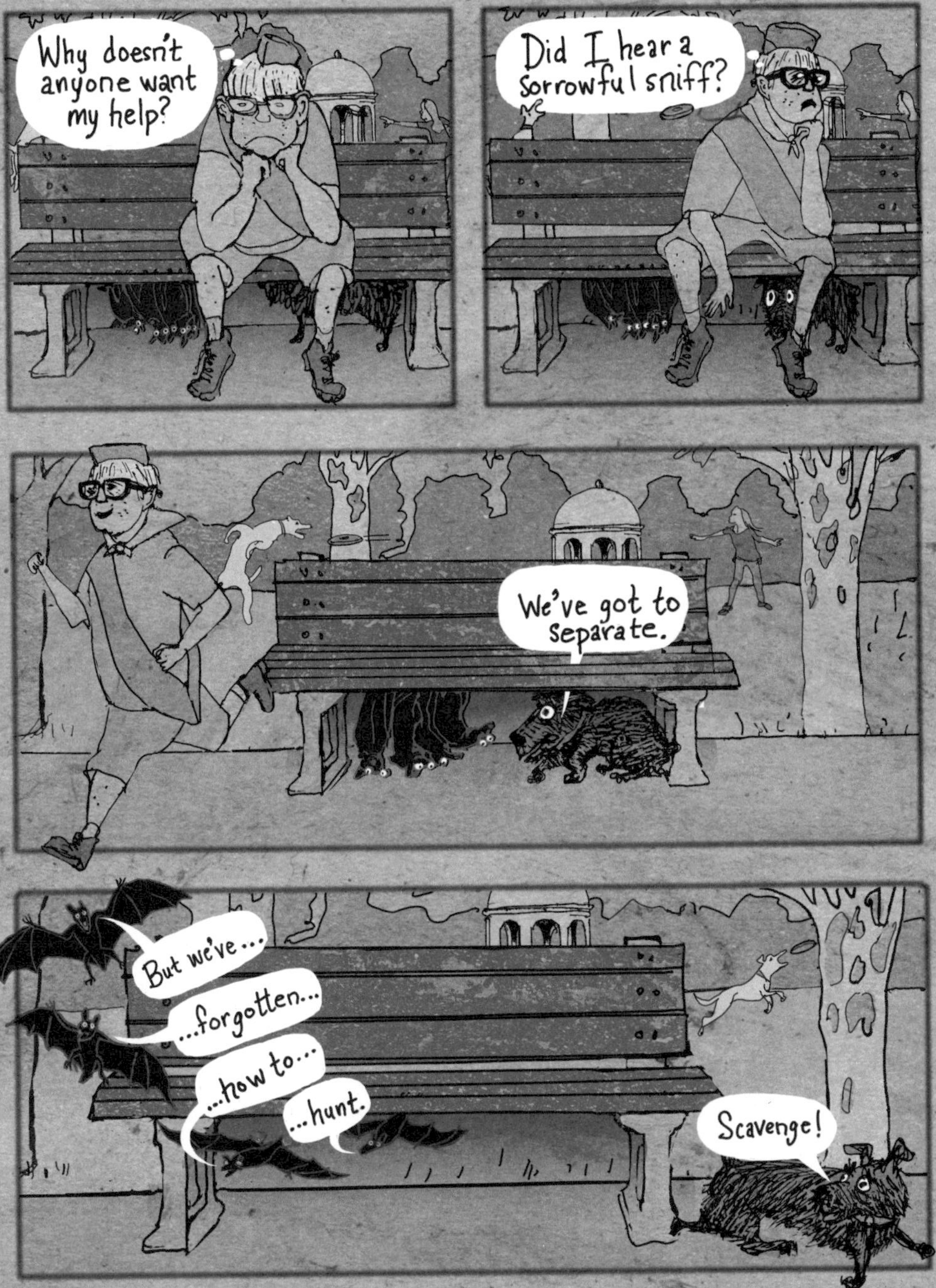
Why doesn't anyone want my help?
Did I hear a sorrowful sniff?
We've got to separate.
But we've...
...forgotten...
...how to...
...hunt.
Scavenge!

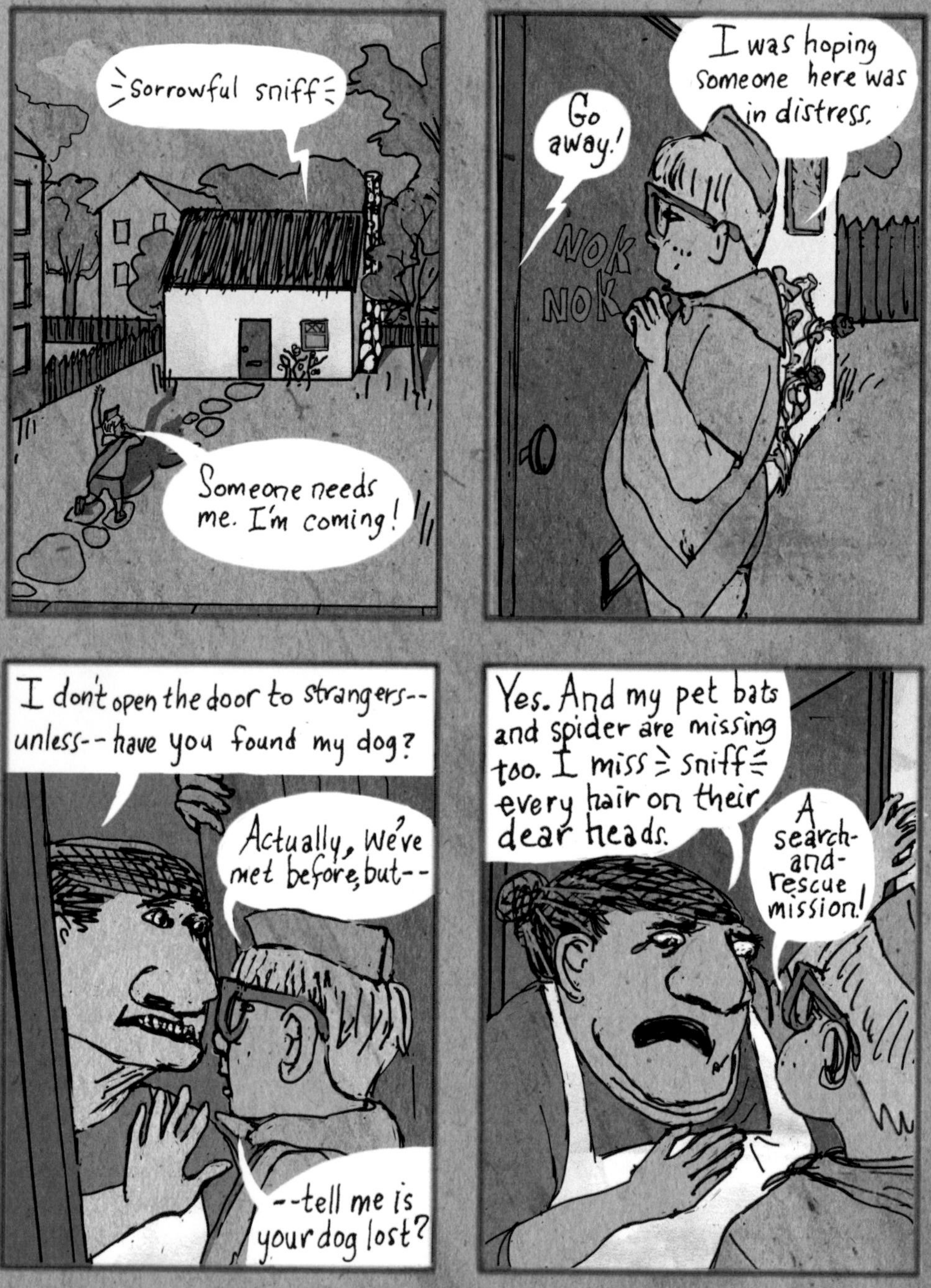
≡sorrowful sniff≡
Someone needs me. I'm coming!
I was hoping someone here was in distress.
Go away!
NOK NOK
I don't open the door to strangers--unless--have you found my dog?
Actually, we've met before, but--
--tell me is your dog lost?
Yes. And my pet bats and spider are missing too. I miss ≡ sniff ≡ every hair on their dear heads.
A search-and-rescue mission!

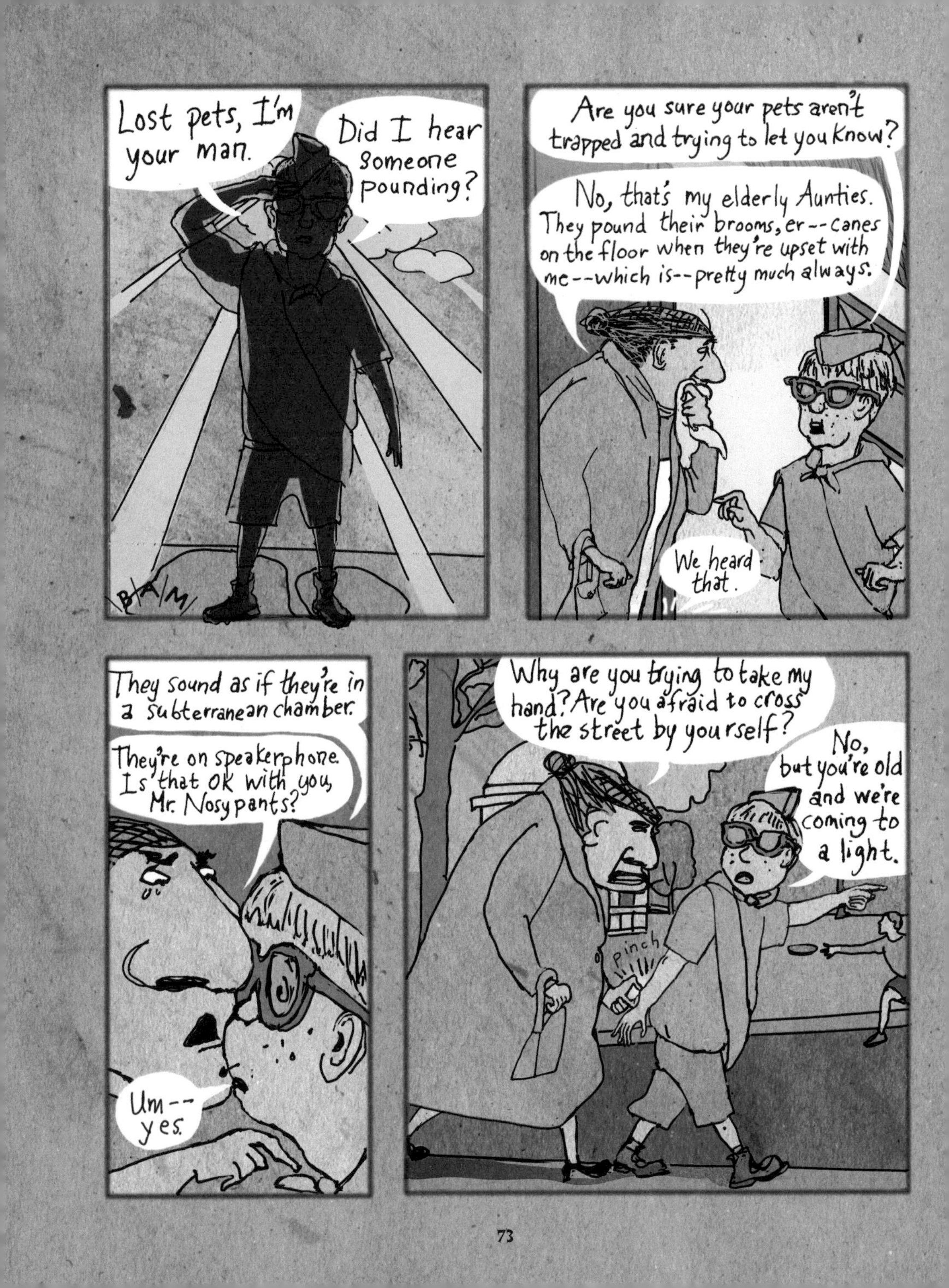
Lost pets, I'm your man.
Did I hear someone pounding?
BAM
Are you sure your pets aren't trapped and trying to let you know?
No, that's my elderly Aunties. They pound their brooms, er--canes on the floor when they're upset with me--which is--pretty much always.
We heard that.
They sound as if they're in a subterranean chamber.
They're on speakerphone. Is that OK with you, Mr. Nosypants?
Um--yes.
Why are you trying to take my hand? Are you afraid to cross the street by yourself?
No, but you're old and we're coming to a light.
pinch

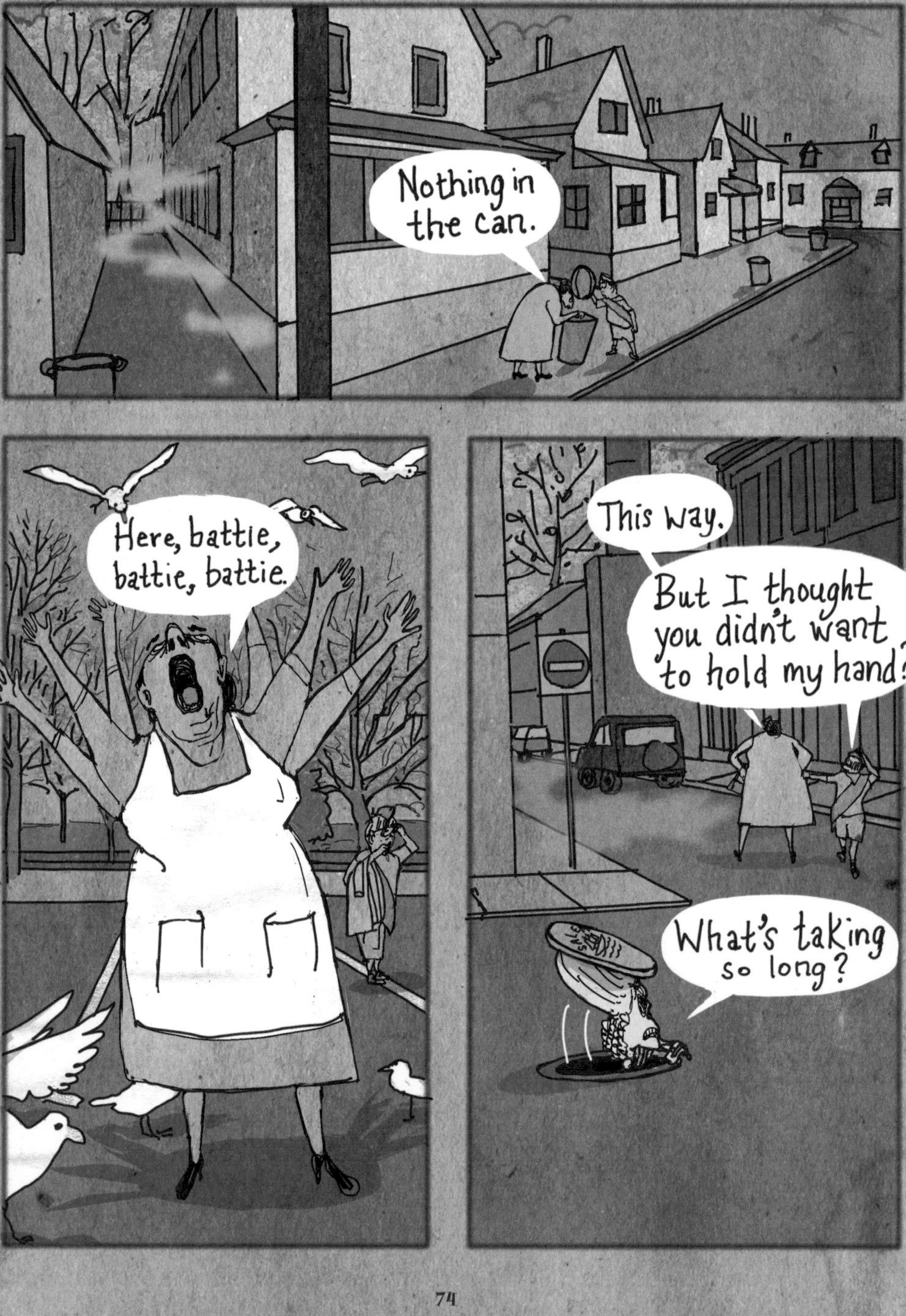
Nothing in the can.
Here, battie, battie, battie.
This way.
But I thought you didn't want to hold my hand?
What's taking so long?

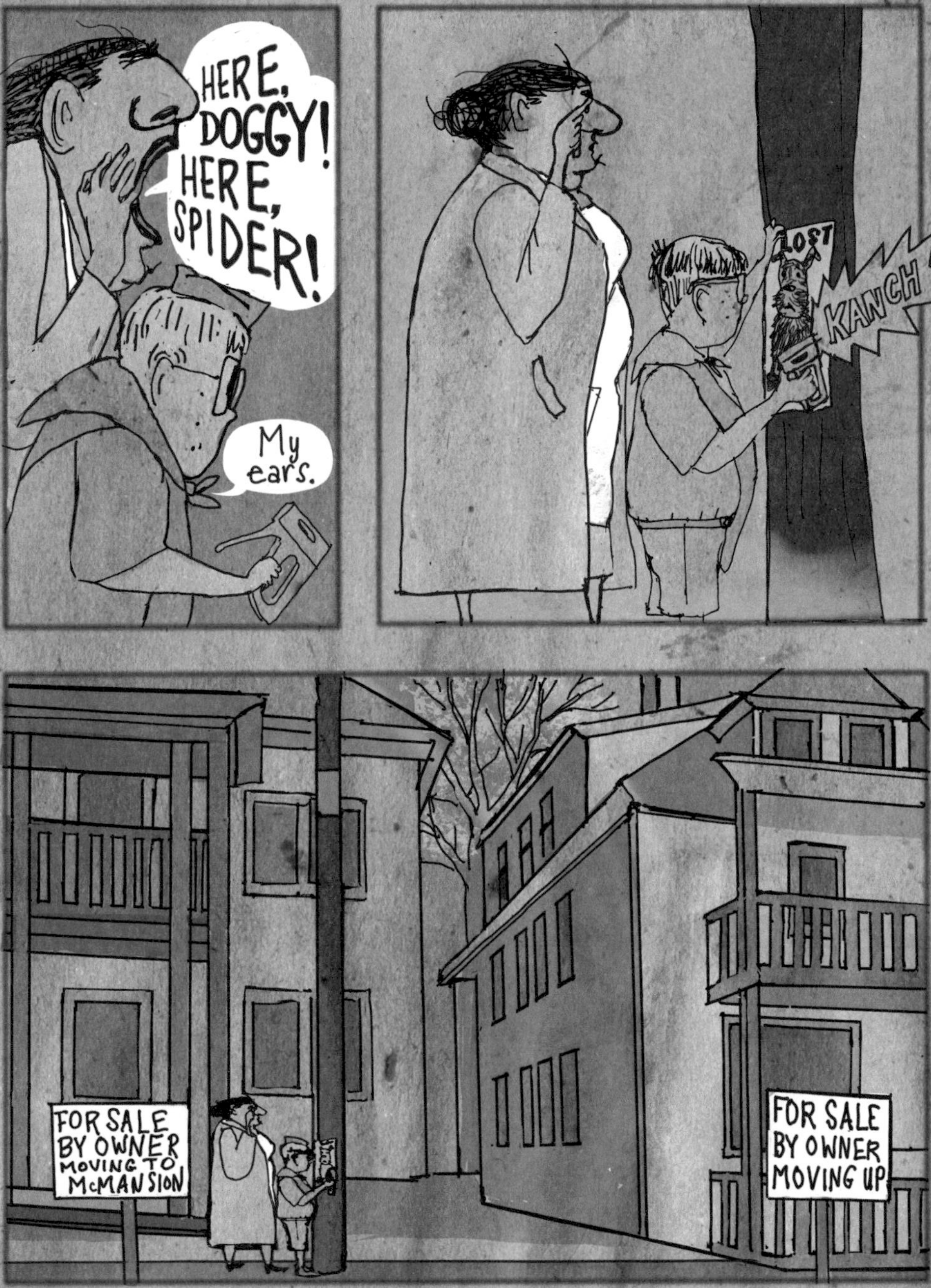
HERE, DOGGY! HERE, SPIDER!
My ears.
LOST
KANCH
FOR SALE BY OWNER MOVING TO McMANSION
FOR SALE BY OWNER MOVING UP

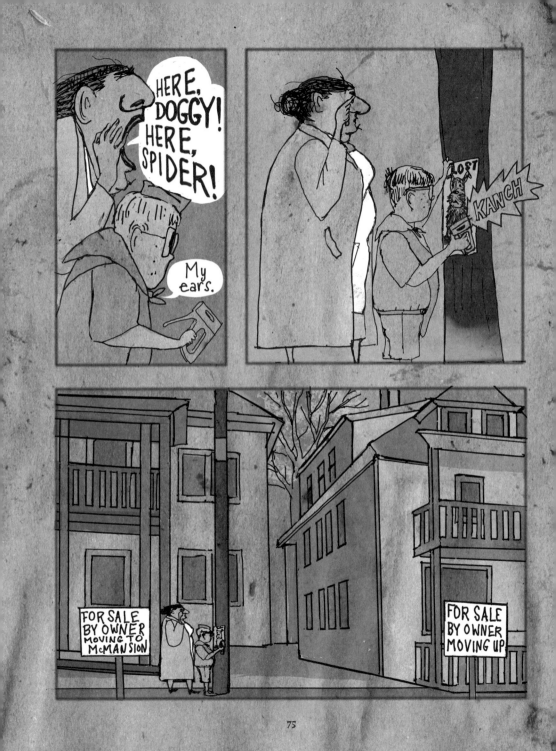

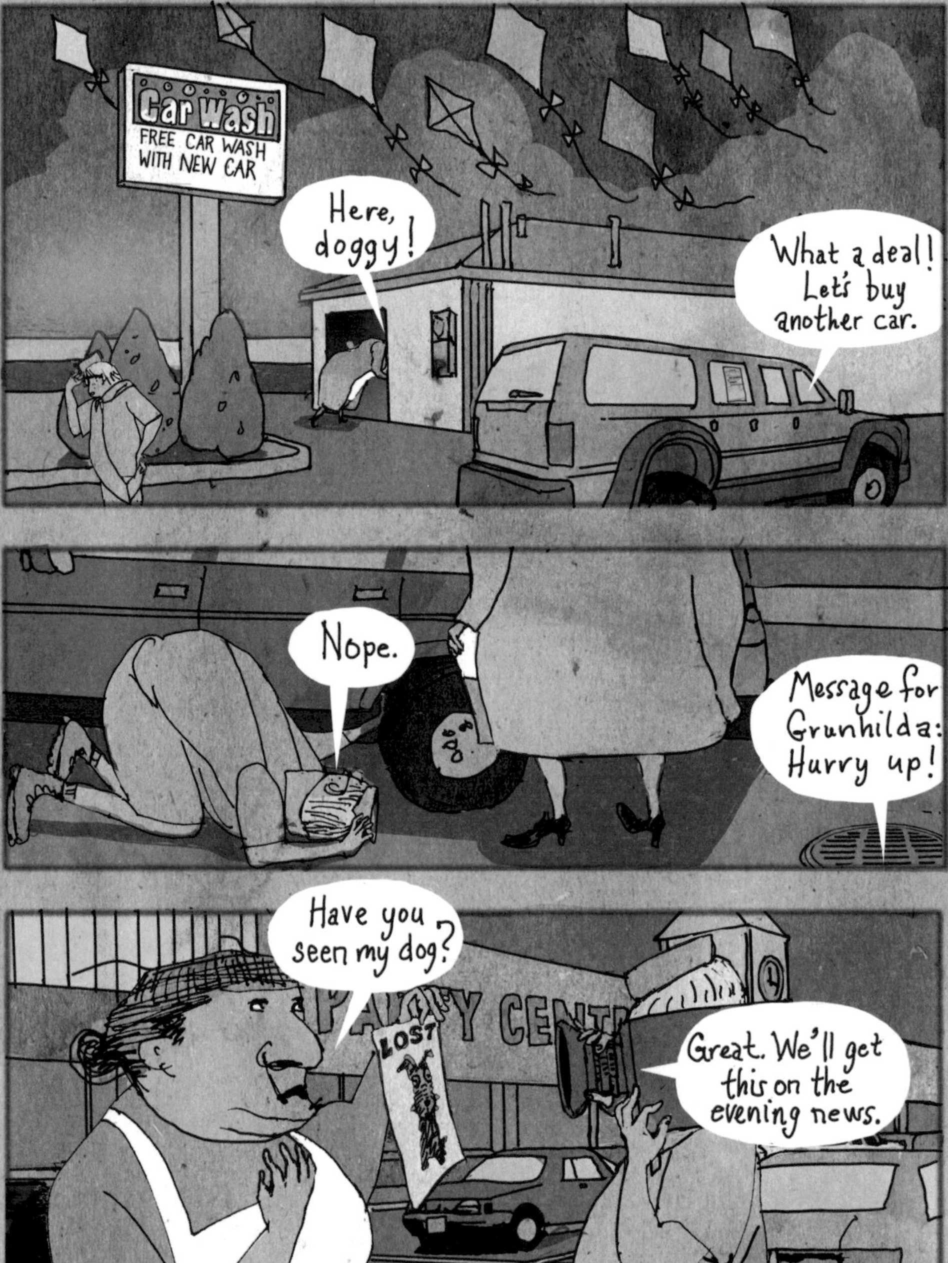
Car Wash
FREE CAR WASH WITH NEW CAR
Here, doggy!
What a deal! Let's buy another car.
Nope.
Message for Grunhilda: Hurry up!
Have you seen my dog?
LOST
Great. We'll get this on the evening news.

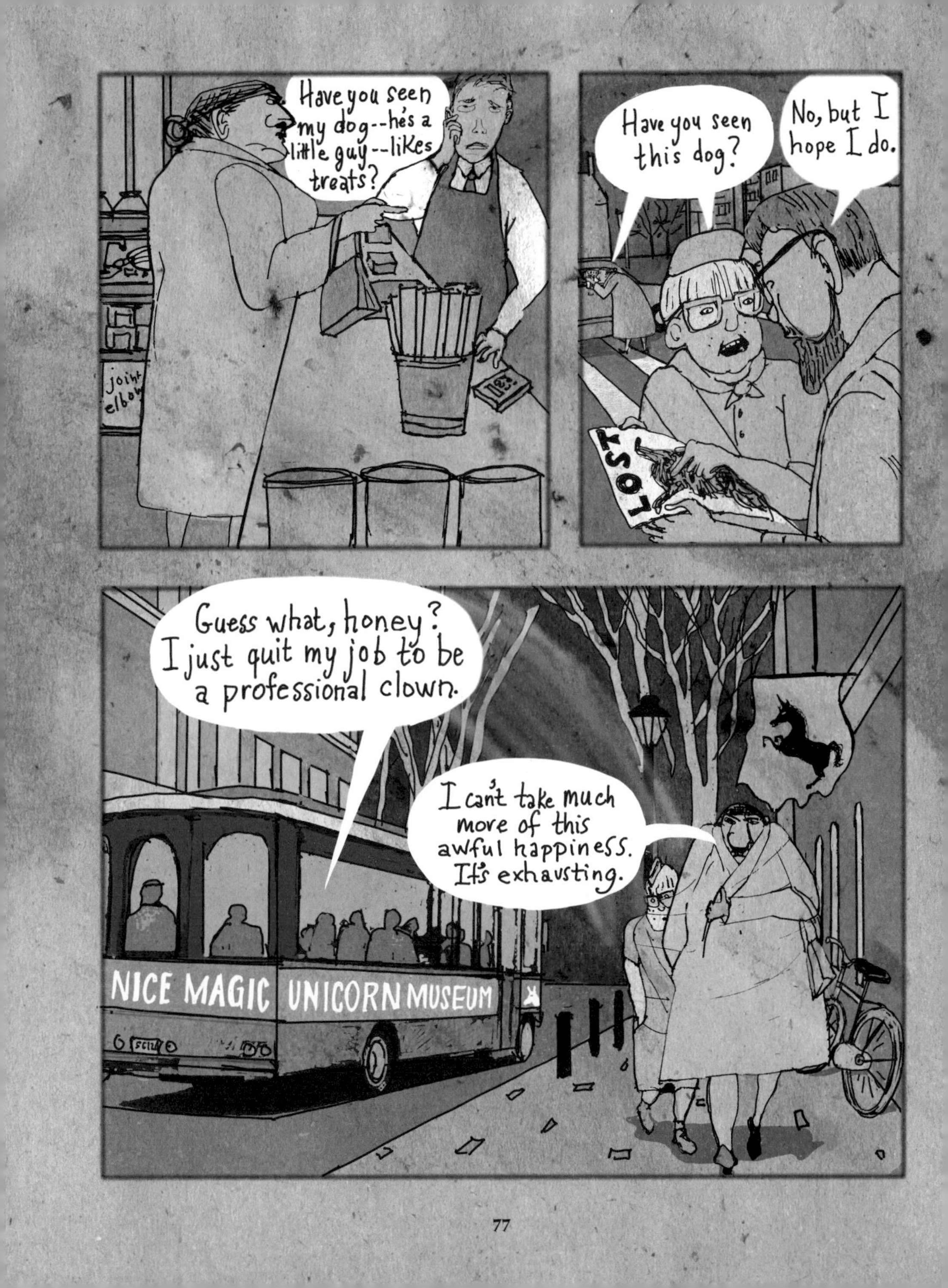
Have you seen my dog--he's a little guy--likes treats?
joint elbow
Have you seen this dog?
No, but I hope I do.
LOST
Guess what, honey? I just quit my job to be a professional clown.
I can't take much more of this awful happiness. It's exhausting.
NICE MAGIC UNICORN MUSEUM

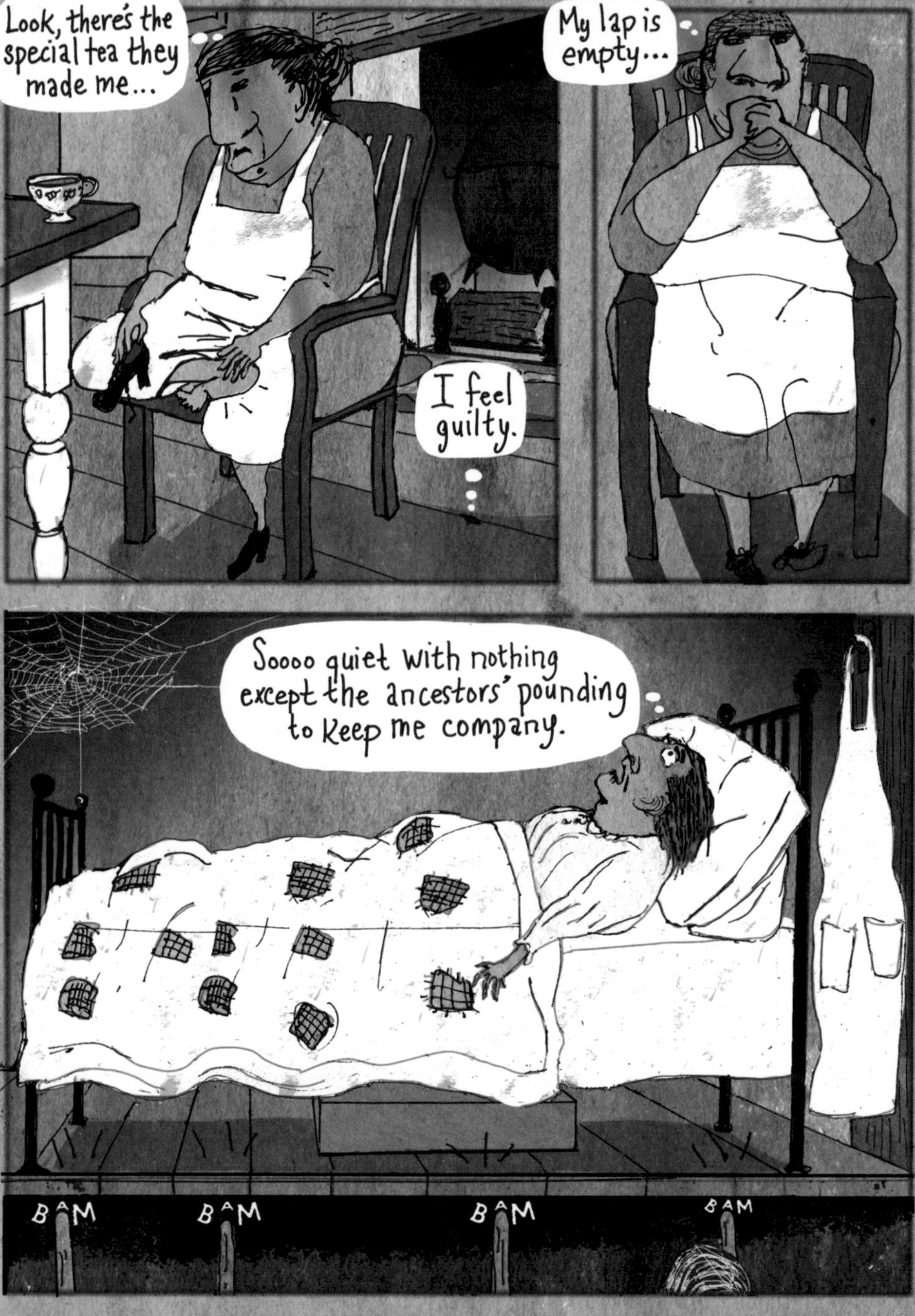
Look, there's the special tea they made me...
I feel guilty.
My lap is empty...
Soooo quiet with nothing except the ancestors' pounding to keep me company.
BAM
BAM
BAM
BAM

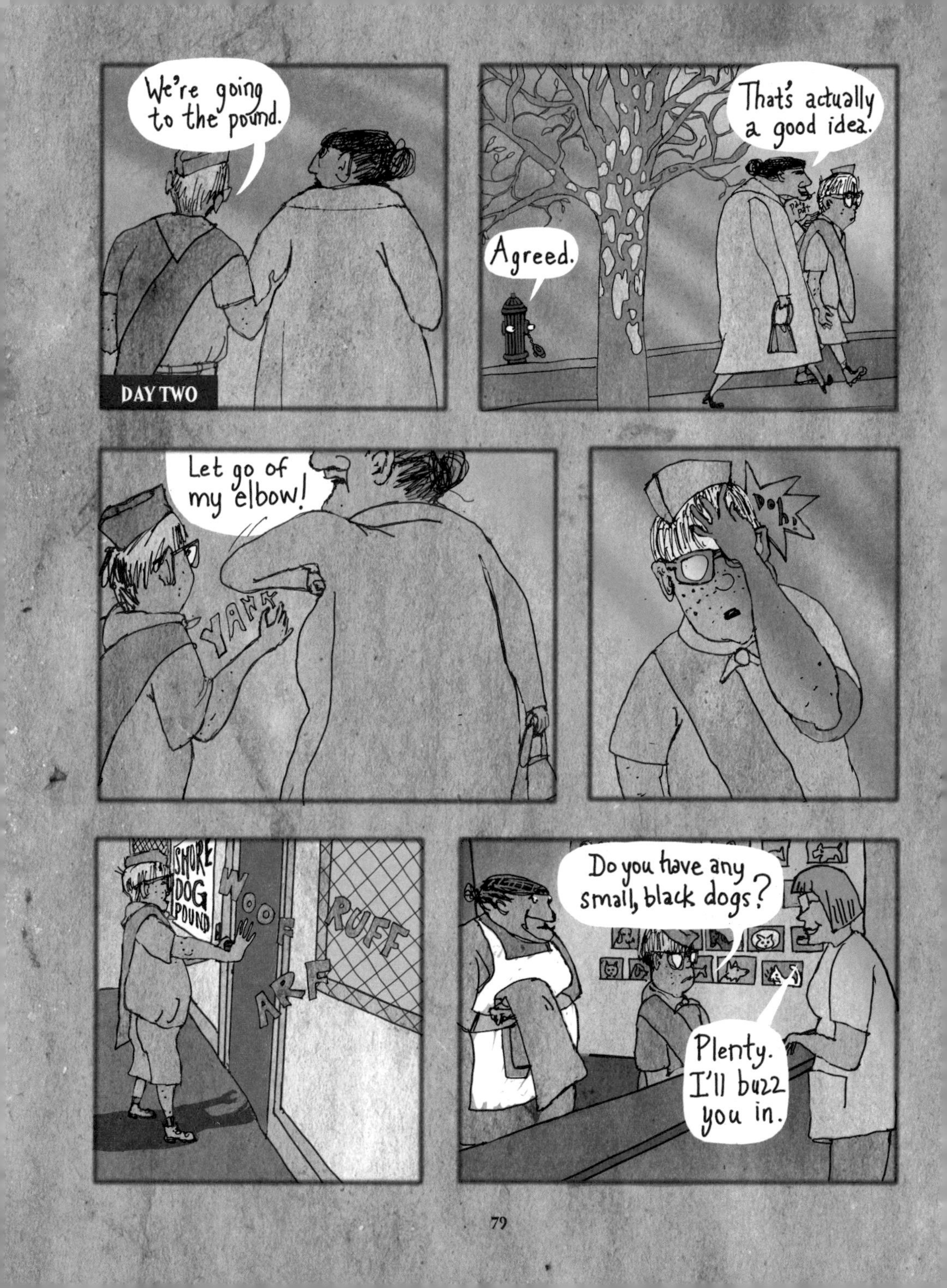
We're going to the pound.
DAY TWO
That's actually a good idea.
pat pat
Agreed.
Let go of my elbow!
YANK
Doh!
SHORE DOG POUND
WOOF
RUFF
ARF
Do you have any small, black dogs?
Plenty. I'll buzz you in.

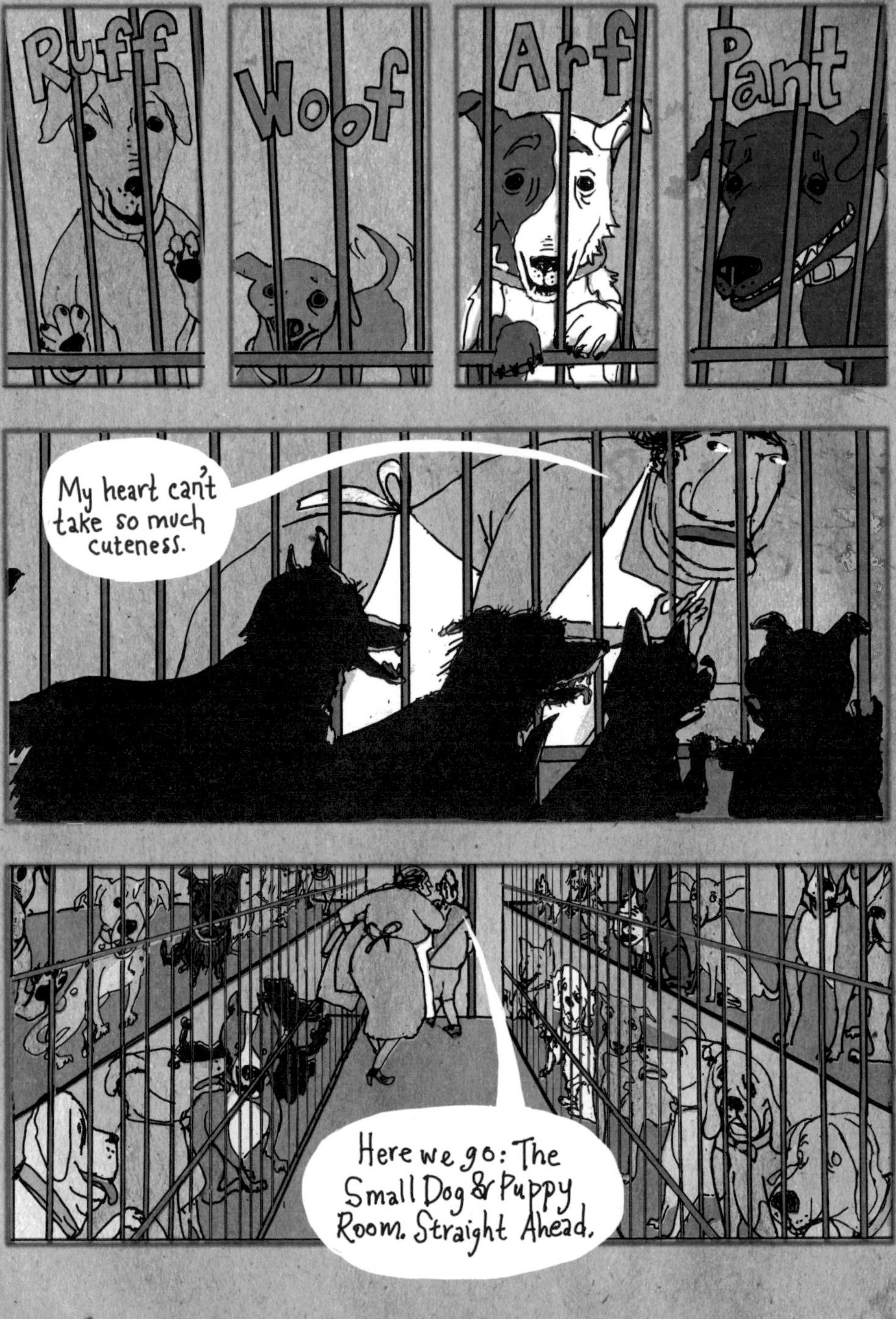
Ruff
Woof
Arf
Pant
My heart can't take so much cuteness.
Here we go: The Small Dog & Puppy Room. Straight Ahead.

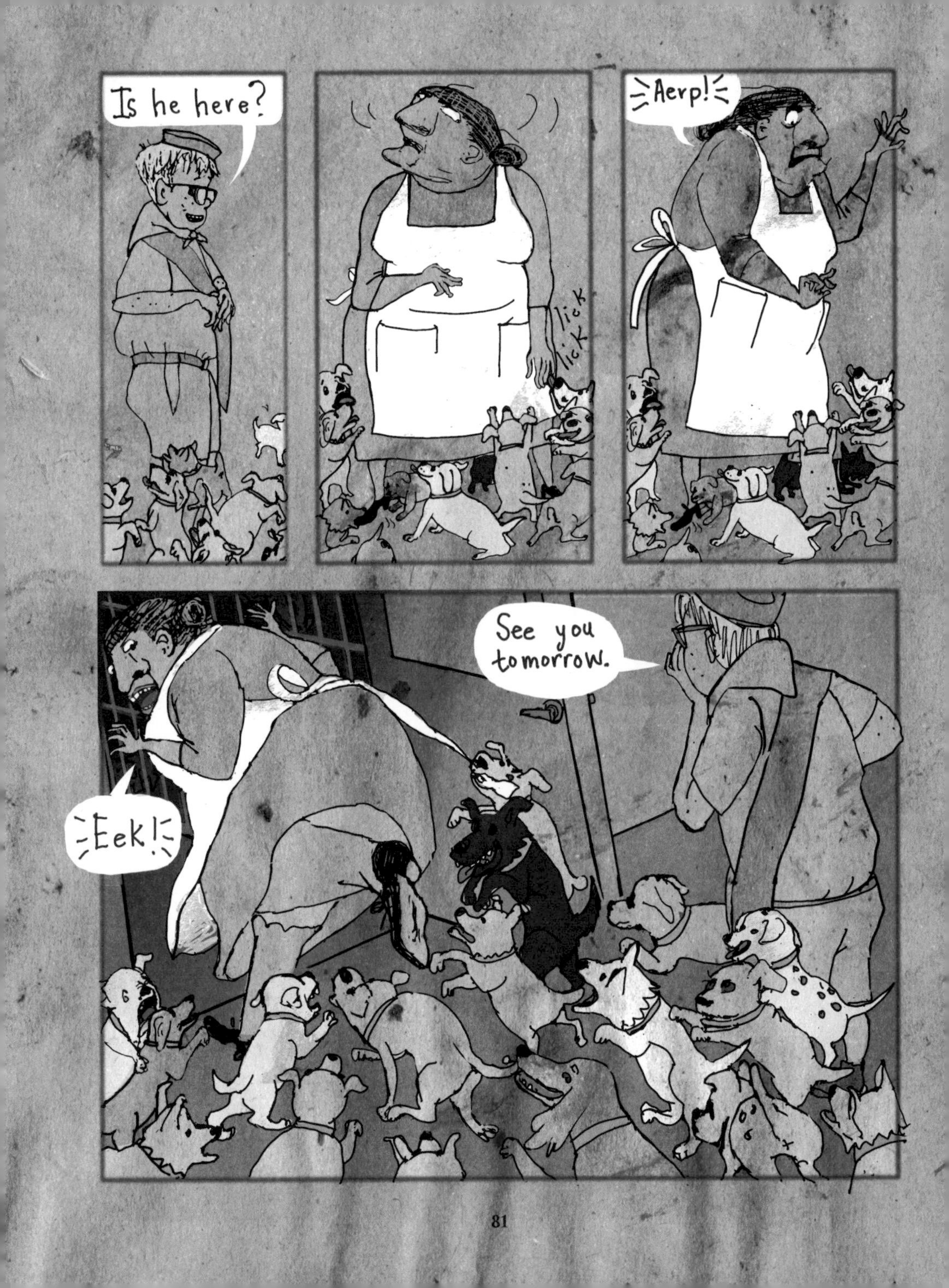
Is he here?
lick lick
Aerp!
See you tomorrow.
Eek!

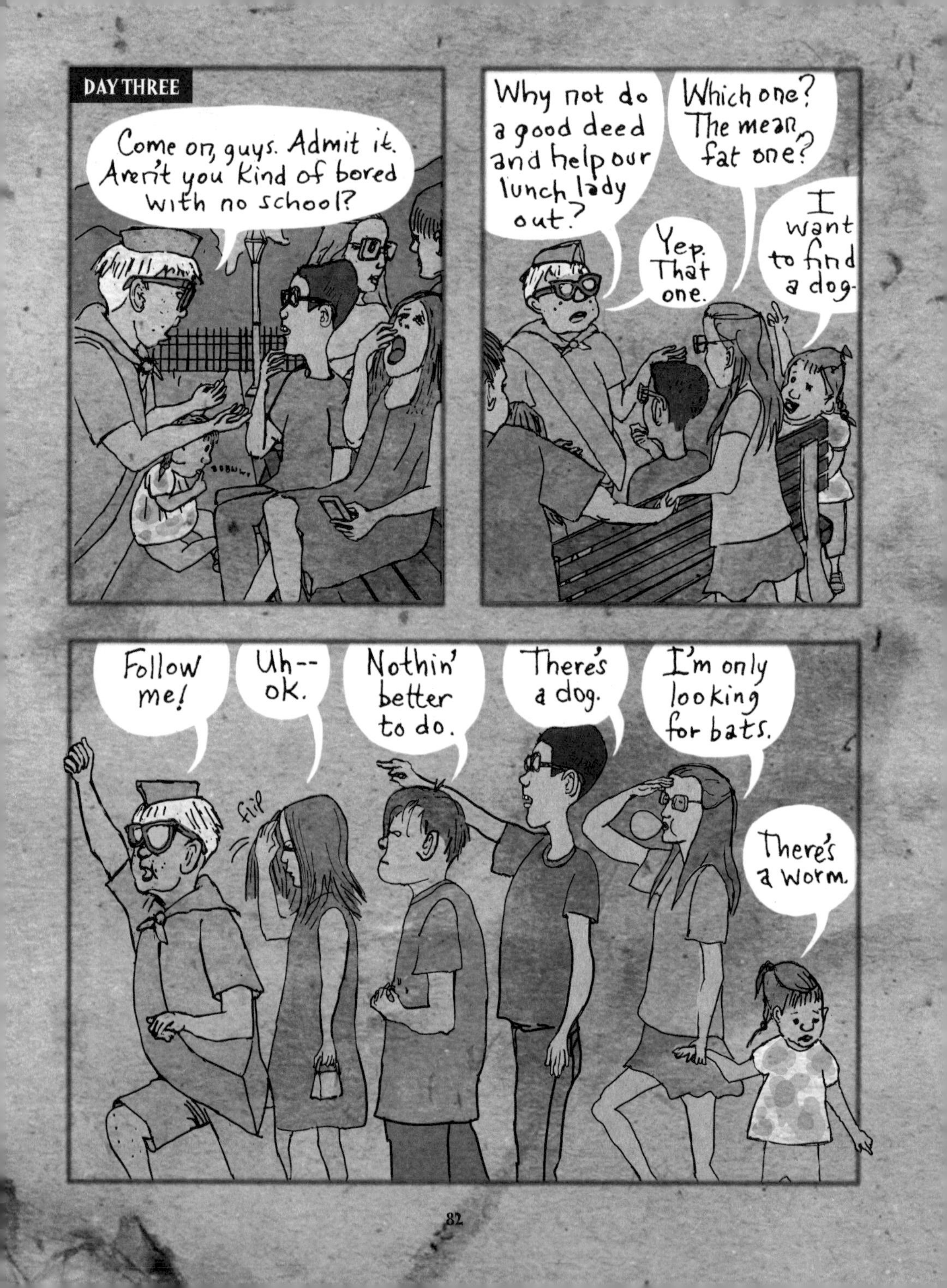
DAY THREE
Come on, guys. Admit it. Aren't you kind of bored with no school?
Why not do a good deed and help our lunch lady out?
Which one? The mean, fat one?
Yep. That one.
I want to find a dog.
Follow me!
Uh-- ok.
fip
Nothin' better to do.
There's a dog.
I'm only looking for bats.
There's a worm.

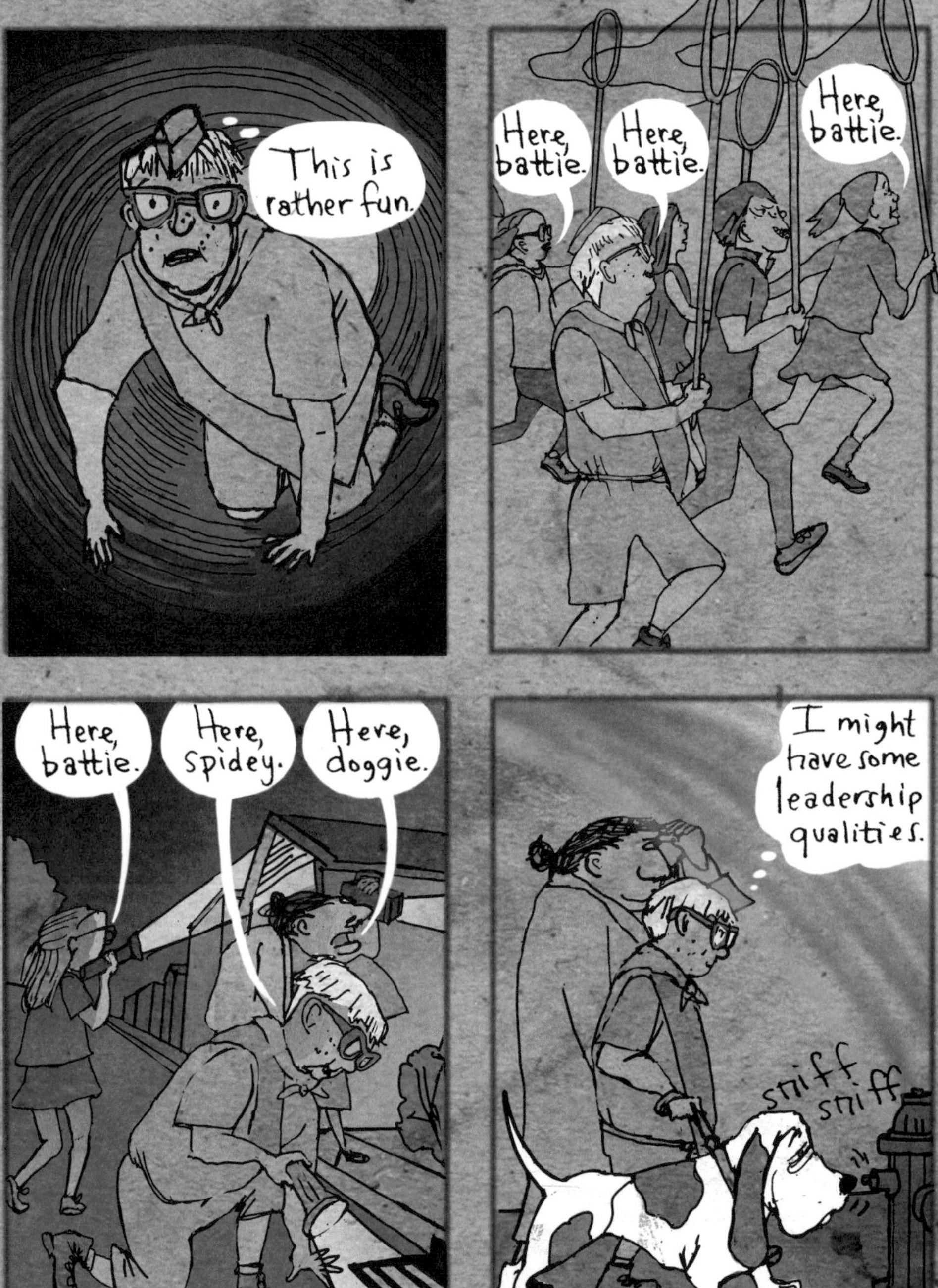
This is rather fun.
Here, battie.
Here, battie.
Here, battie.
Here, battie.
Here, spidey.
Here, doggie.
I might have some leadership qualities.
sniff sniff

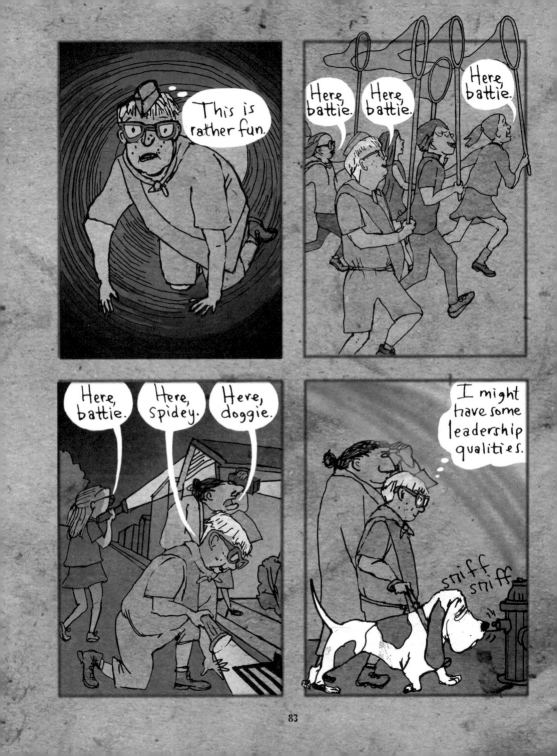

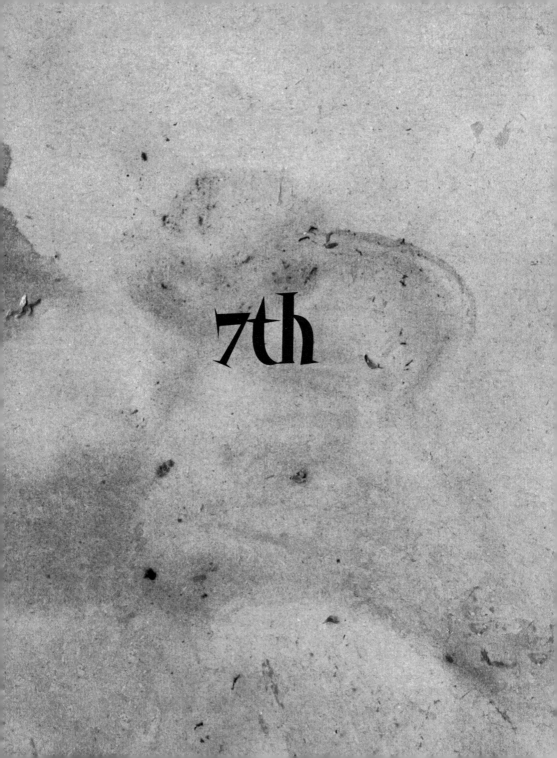

7th

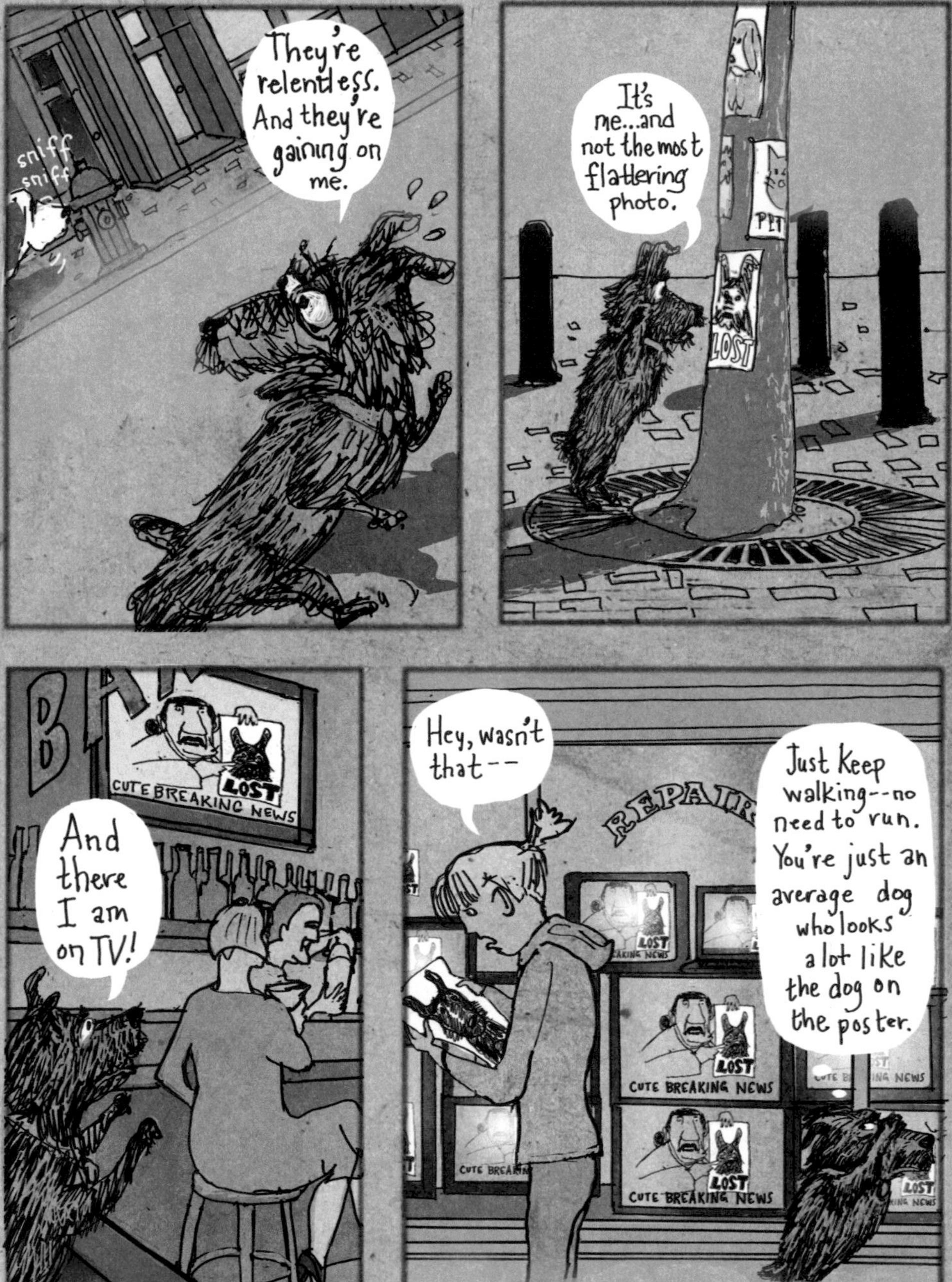
sniff sniff
They're relentless. And they're gaining on me.
It's me...and not the most flattering photo.
PET
LOST
CUTE BREAKING NEWS
LOST
And there I am on TV!
Hey, wasn't that --
REPAIR
Just Keep walking--no need to run. You're just an average dog who looks a lot like the dog on the poster.
LOST
CUTE BREAKING NEWS
LOST
CUTE BREAKING NEWS

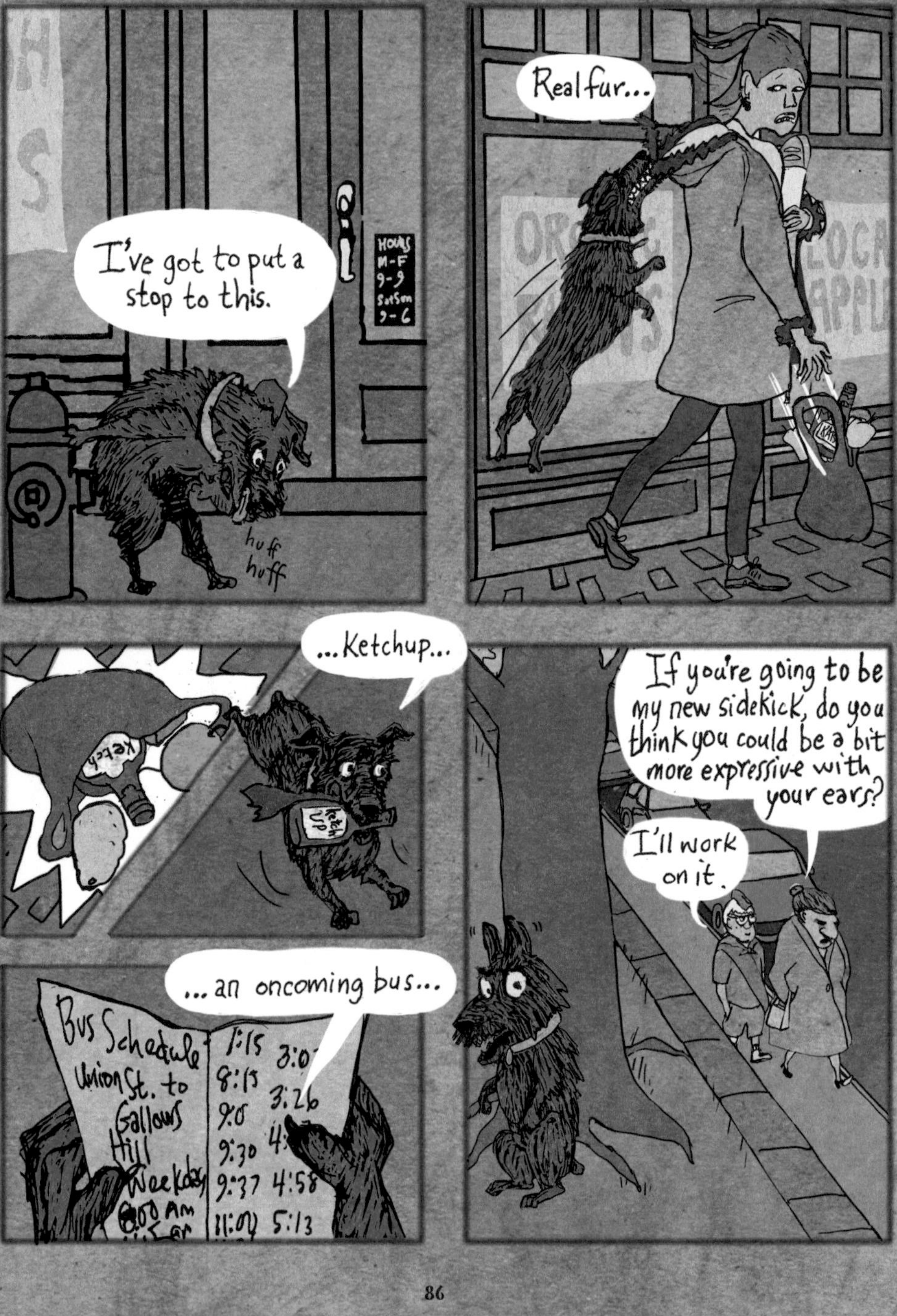
HOURS
M-F
9-9
SatSun
9-6
I've got to put a stop to this.
huff
huff
Real fur...
...Ketchup...
Ketch up
...an oncoming bus...
Bus Schedule
Union St. to
Gallows
Hill
Weekdays
8:15
3:26
9:30
9:37 4:58
11:02 5:13
If you're going to be my new sidekick, do you think you could be a bit more expressive with your ears?
I'll work on it.

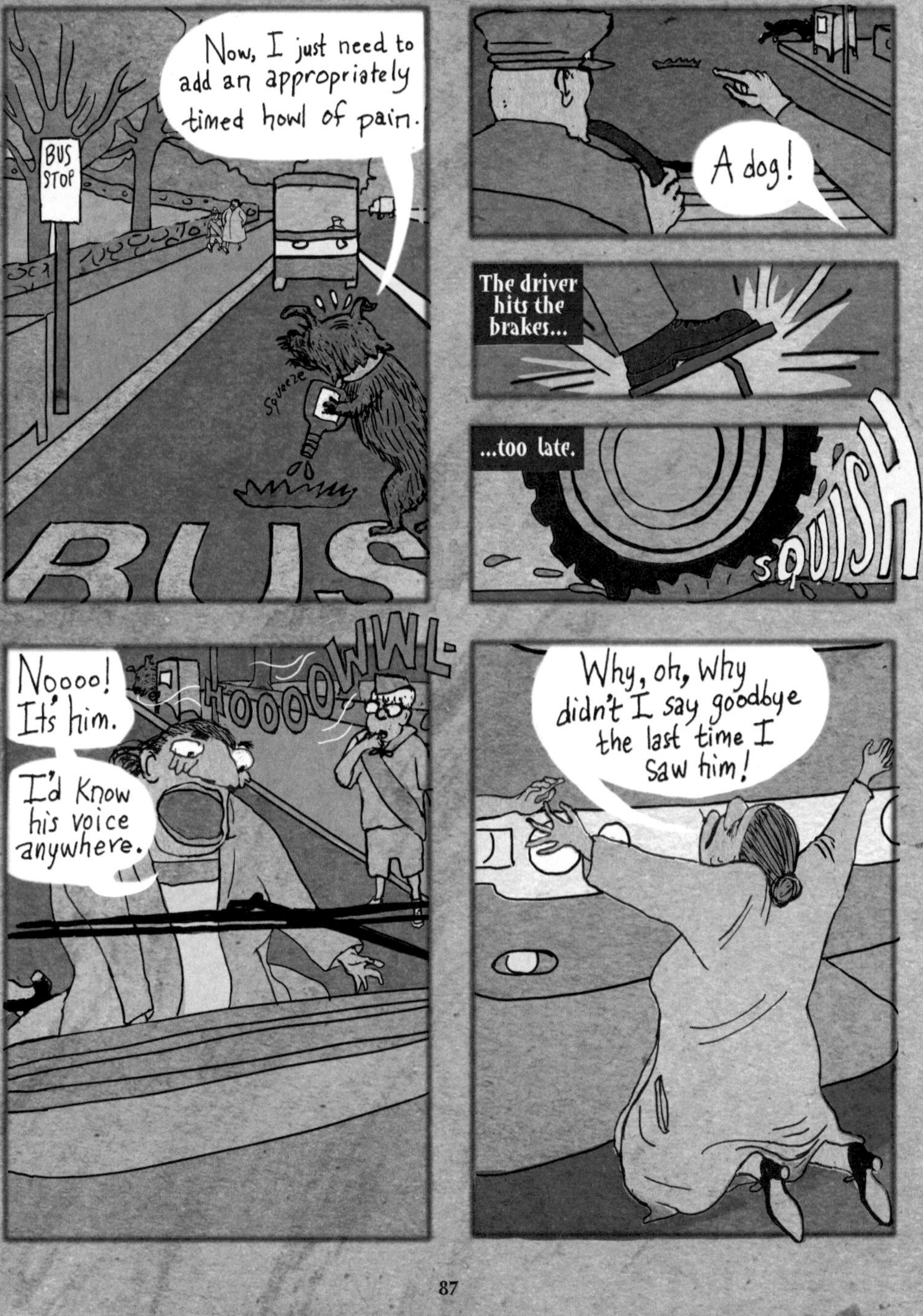
Now, I just need to add an appropriately timed howl of pain.
BUS STOP
Squeeze
BUS
A dog!
The driver hits the brakes...
...too late.
SQUISH
Noooo! It's him.
I'd know his voice anywhere.
HOOOOOWWL-
Why, oh, why didn't I say goodbye the last time I saw him!

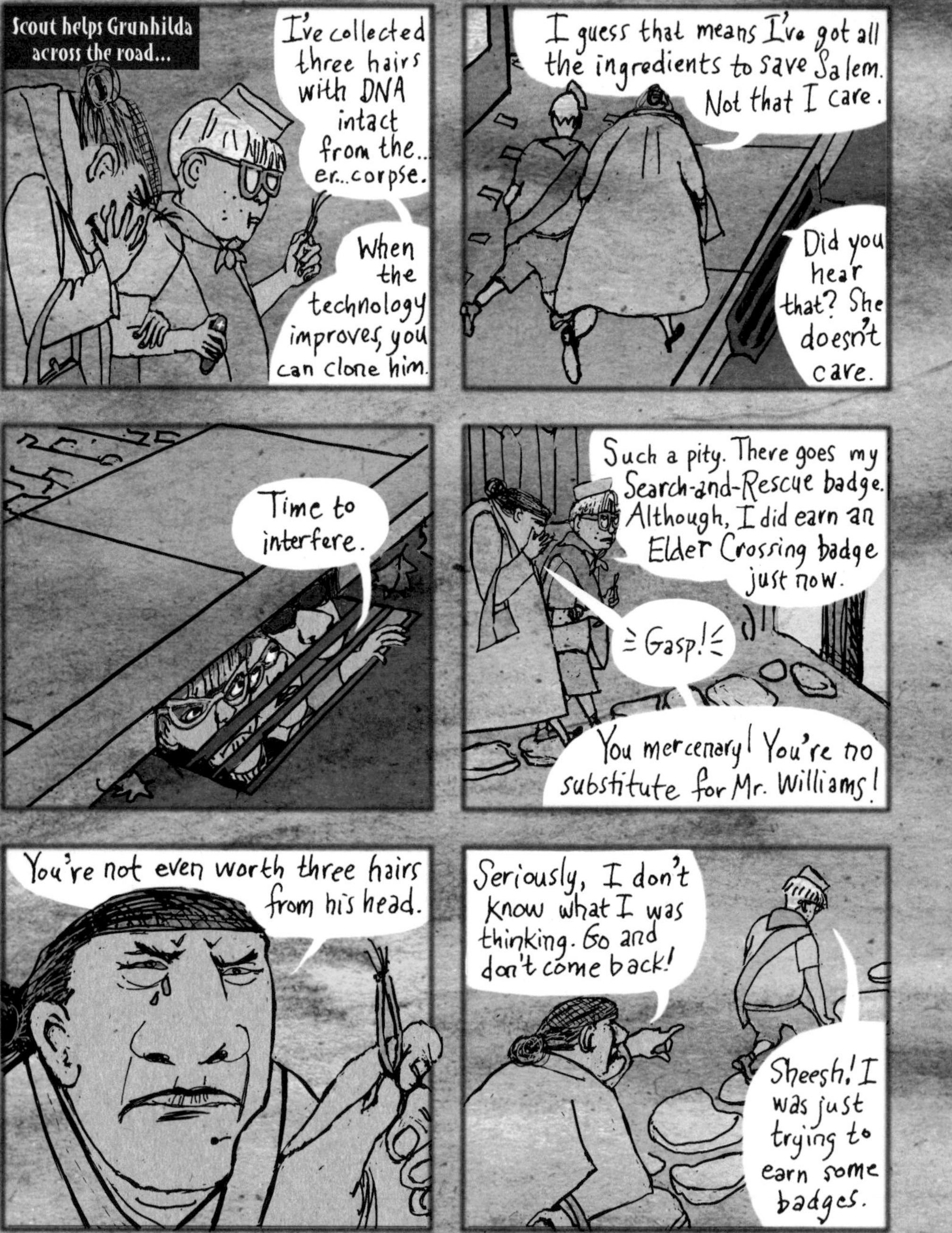
Scout helps Grunhilda across the road...
I've collected three hairs with DNA intact from the... er...corpse.
When the technology improves, you can clone him.
I guess that means I've got all the ingredients to save Salem. Not that I care.
Did you hear that? She doesn't care.
Time to interfere.
Such a pity. There goes my Search-and-Rescue badge. Although, I did earn an Elder Crossing badge just now.
Gasp!
You mercenary! You're no substitute for Mr. Williams!
You're not even worth three hairs from his head.
Seriously, I don't know what I was thinking. Go and don't come back!
Sheesh! I was just trying to earn some badges.

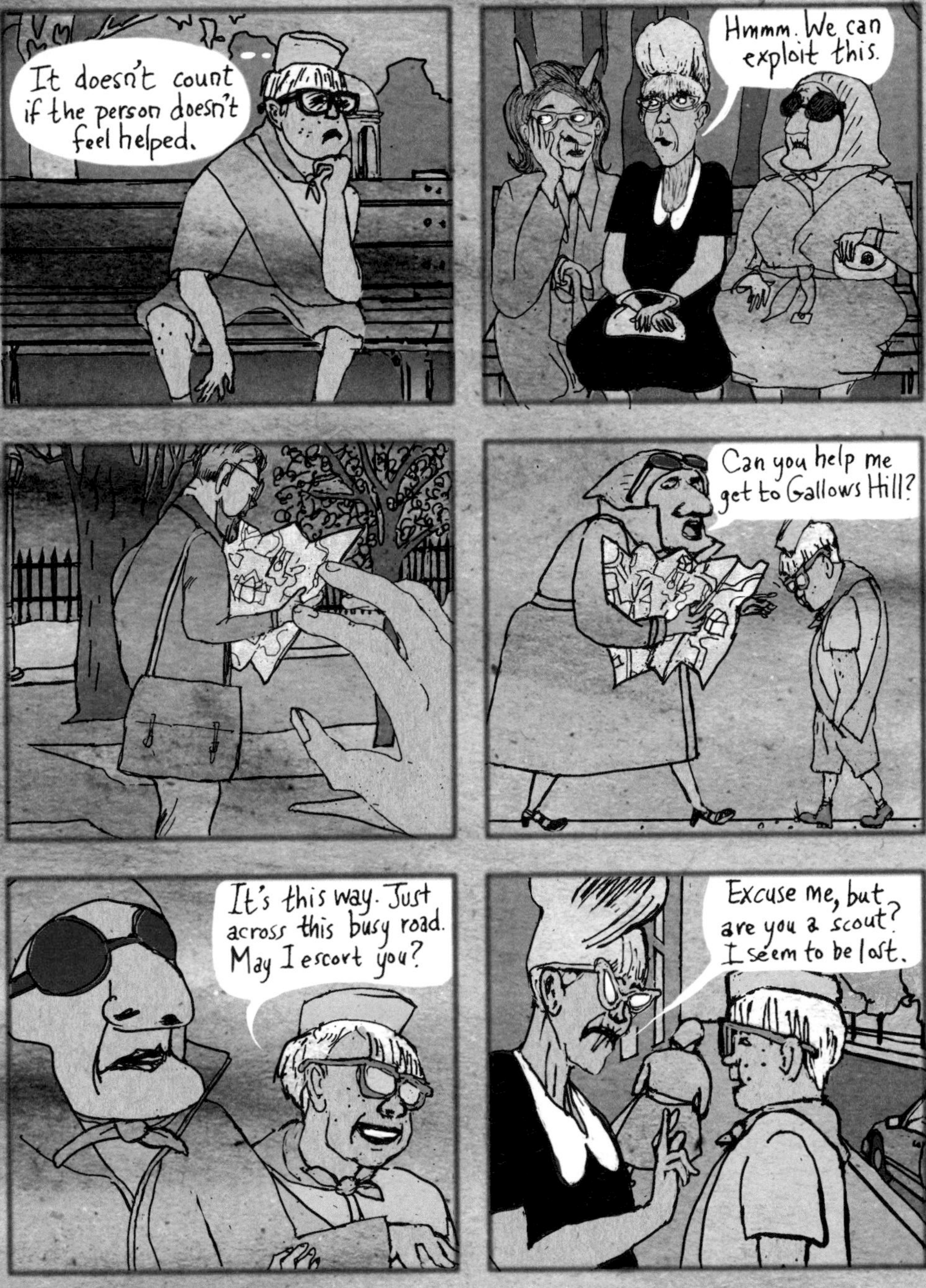
It doesn't count if the person doesn't feel helped.
Hmmm. We can exploit this.
Can you help me get to Gallows Hill?
It's this way. Just across this busy road. May I escort you?
Excuse me, but are you a scout? I seem to be lost.

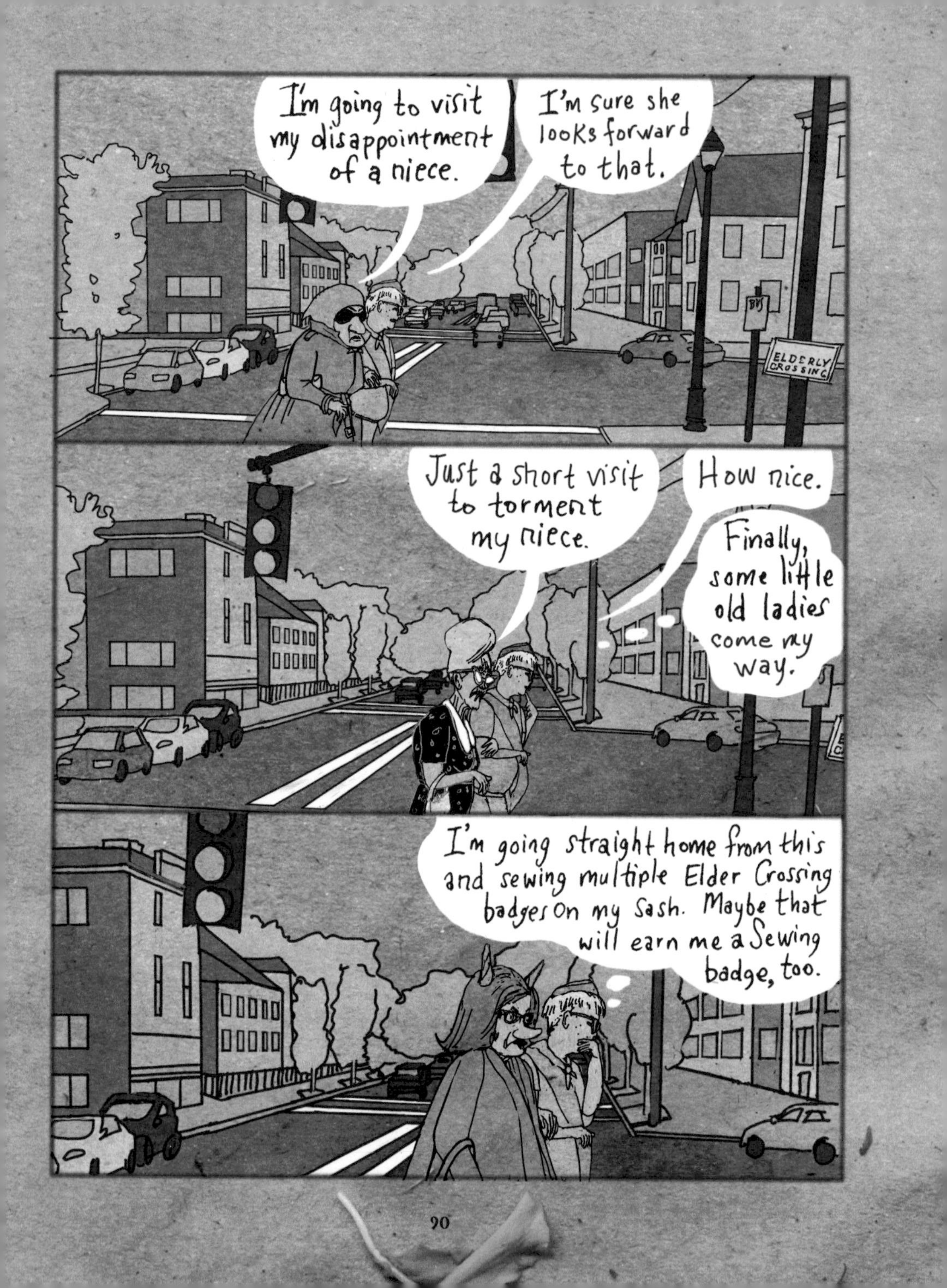
I'm going to visit my disappointment of a niece.
I'm sure she looks forward to that.
ELDERLY CROSSING
Just a short visit to torment my niece.
How nice.
Finally, some little old ladies come my way.
I'm going straight home from this and sewing multiple Elder Crossing badges on my Sash. Maybe that will earn me a Sewing badge, too.

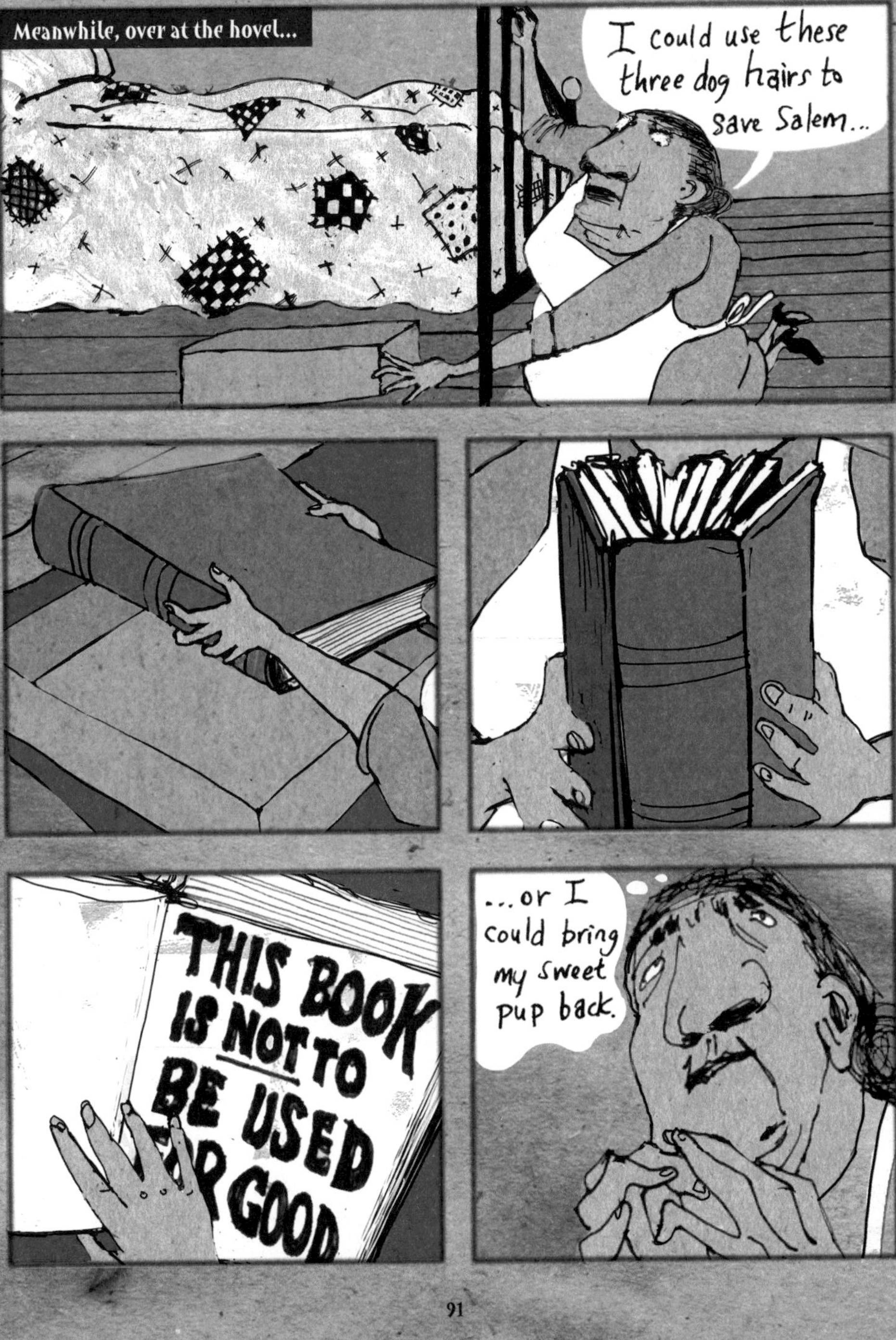

Meanwhile, over at the hovel...
I could use these three dog hairs to save Salem...
THIS BOOK IS NOT TO BE USED
...or I could bring my sweet pup back.

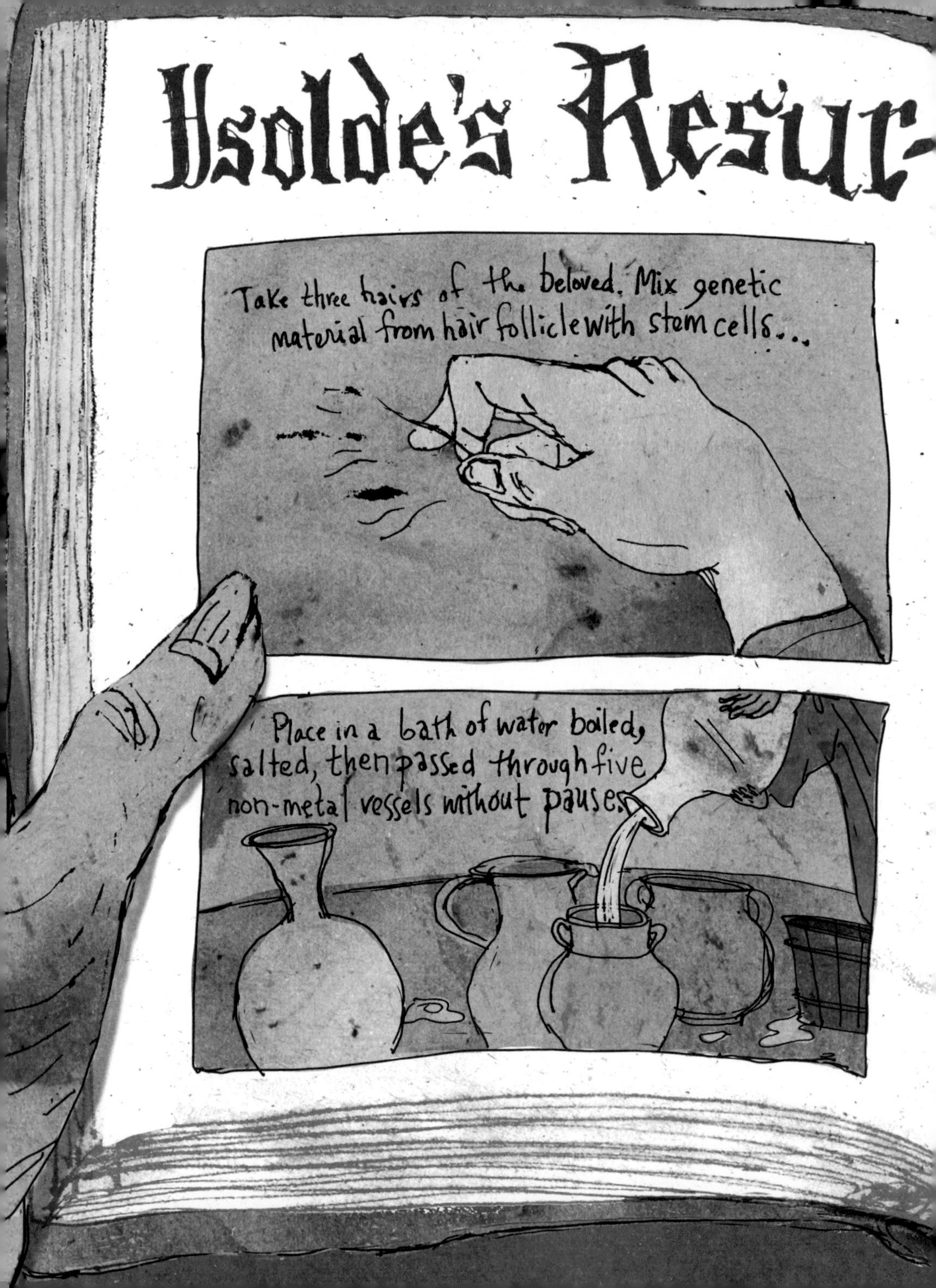
Isolde's Resur-
Take three hairs of the beloved. Mix genetic material from hair follicle with stem cells...
Place in a bath of water boiled, salted, then passed through five non-metal vessels without pause.

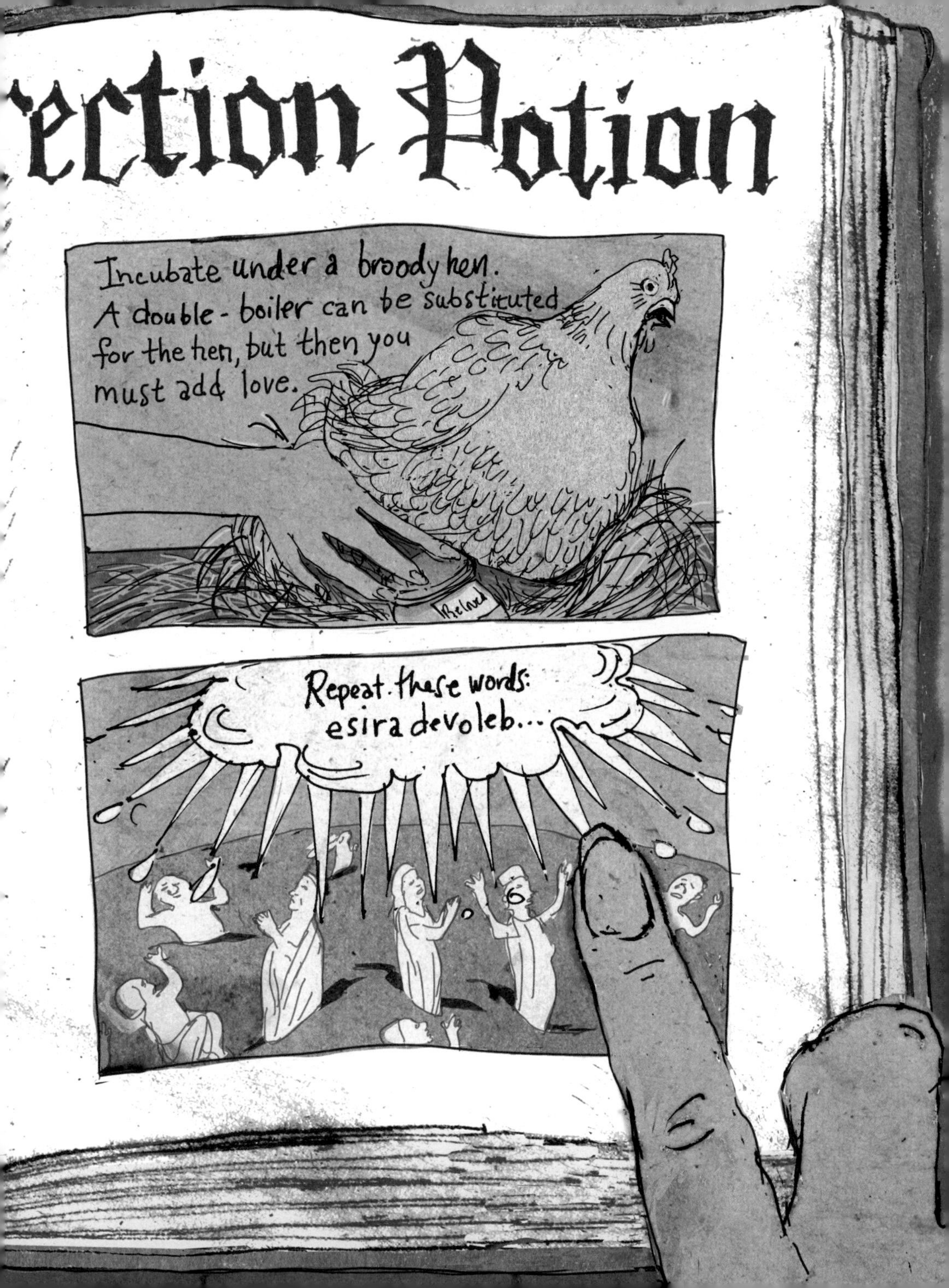
ection Potion
Incubate under a broody hen. A double-boiler can be substituted for the hen, but then you must add love.
Repeat these words: esira devoleb...

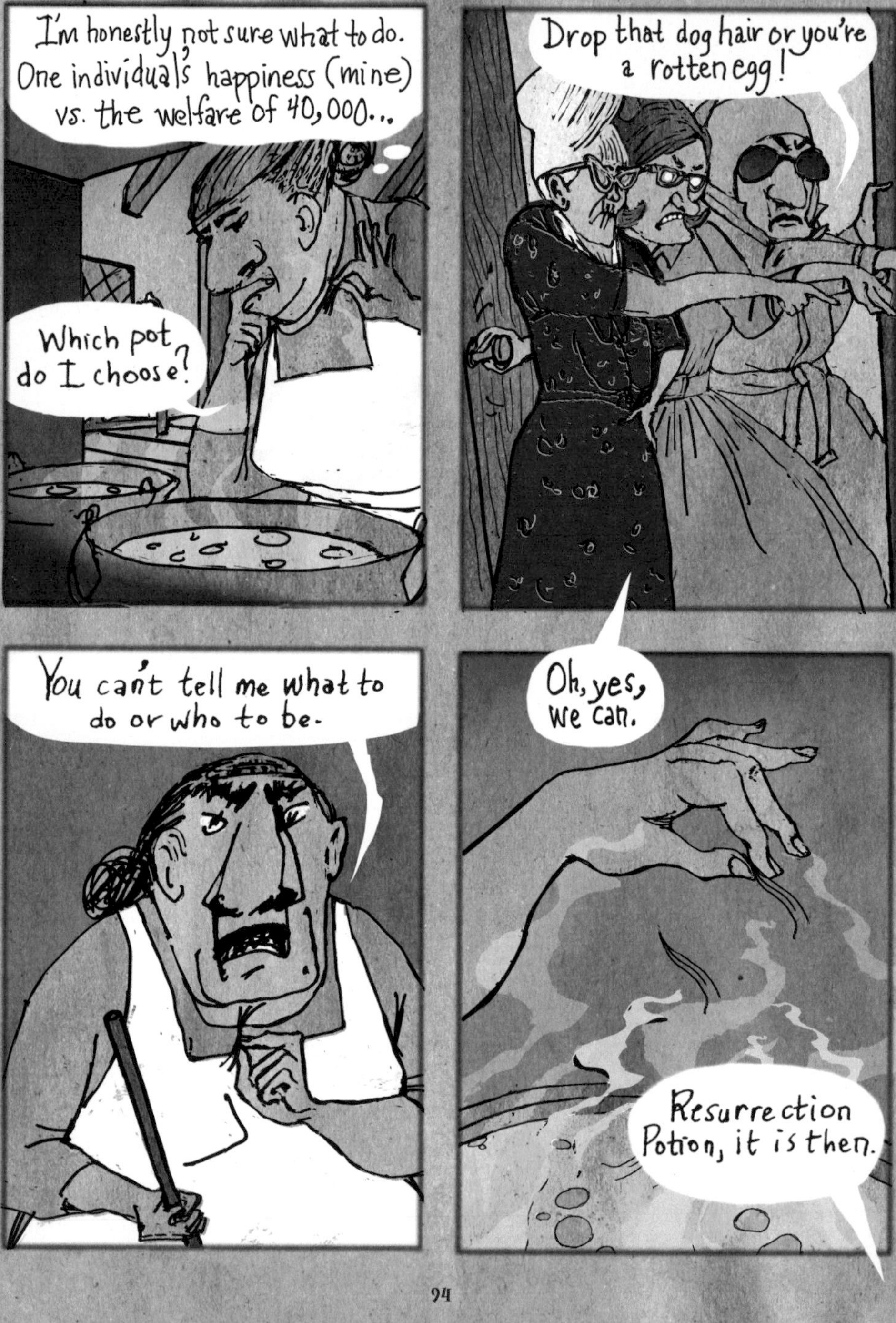
I'm honestly not sure what to do. One individual's happiness (mine) vs. the welfare of 40,000...
Which pot do I choose?
Drop that dog hair or you're a rotten egg!
You can't tell me what to do or who to be.
Oh, yes, we can.
Resurrection Potion, it is then.

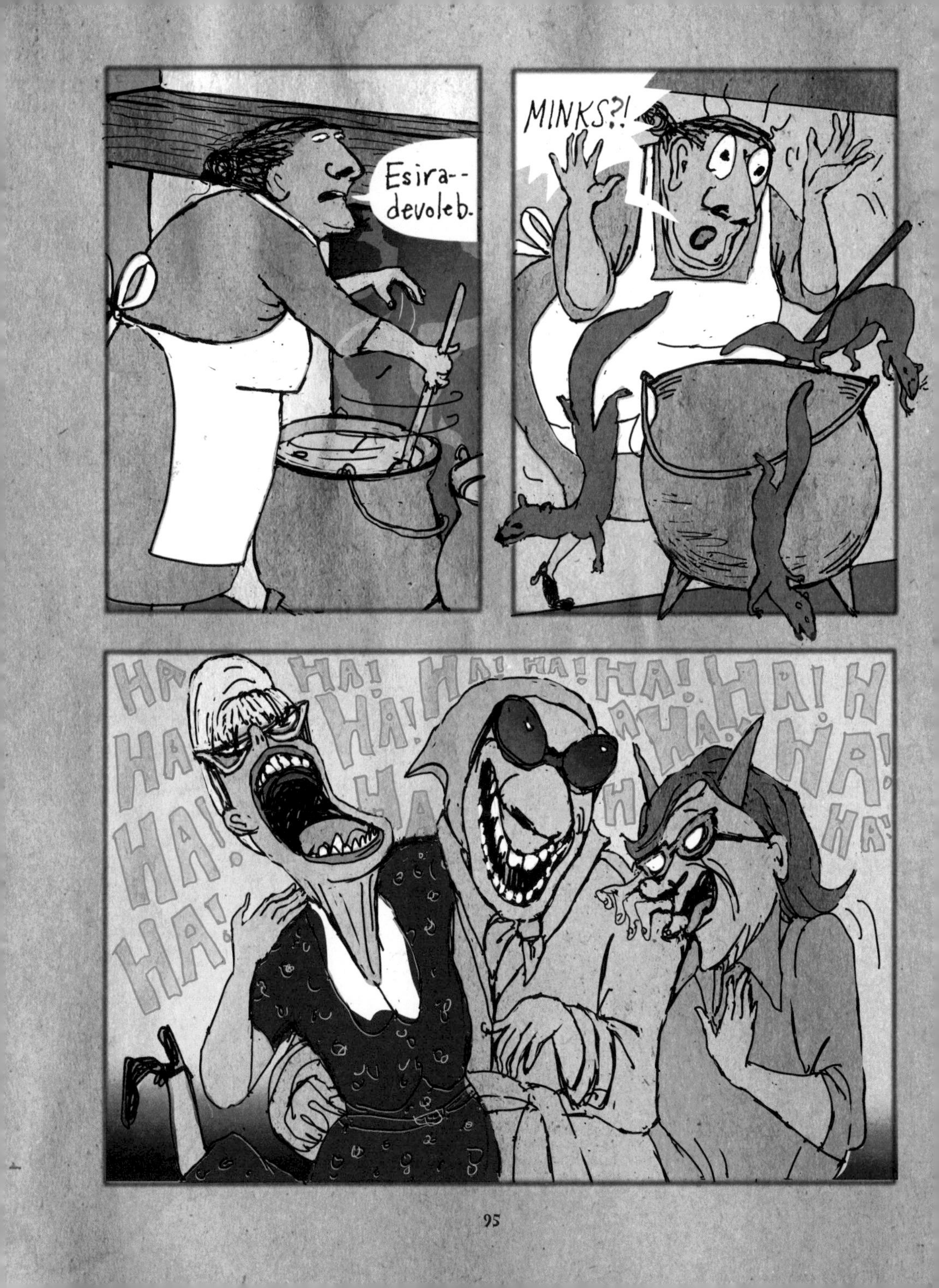
Esira--
devoleb-
MINKS?!
HA! HA! HA! HA! HA! HA! HA!
HA! HA! HA! HA! HA!

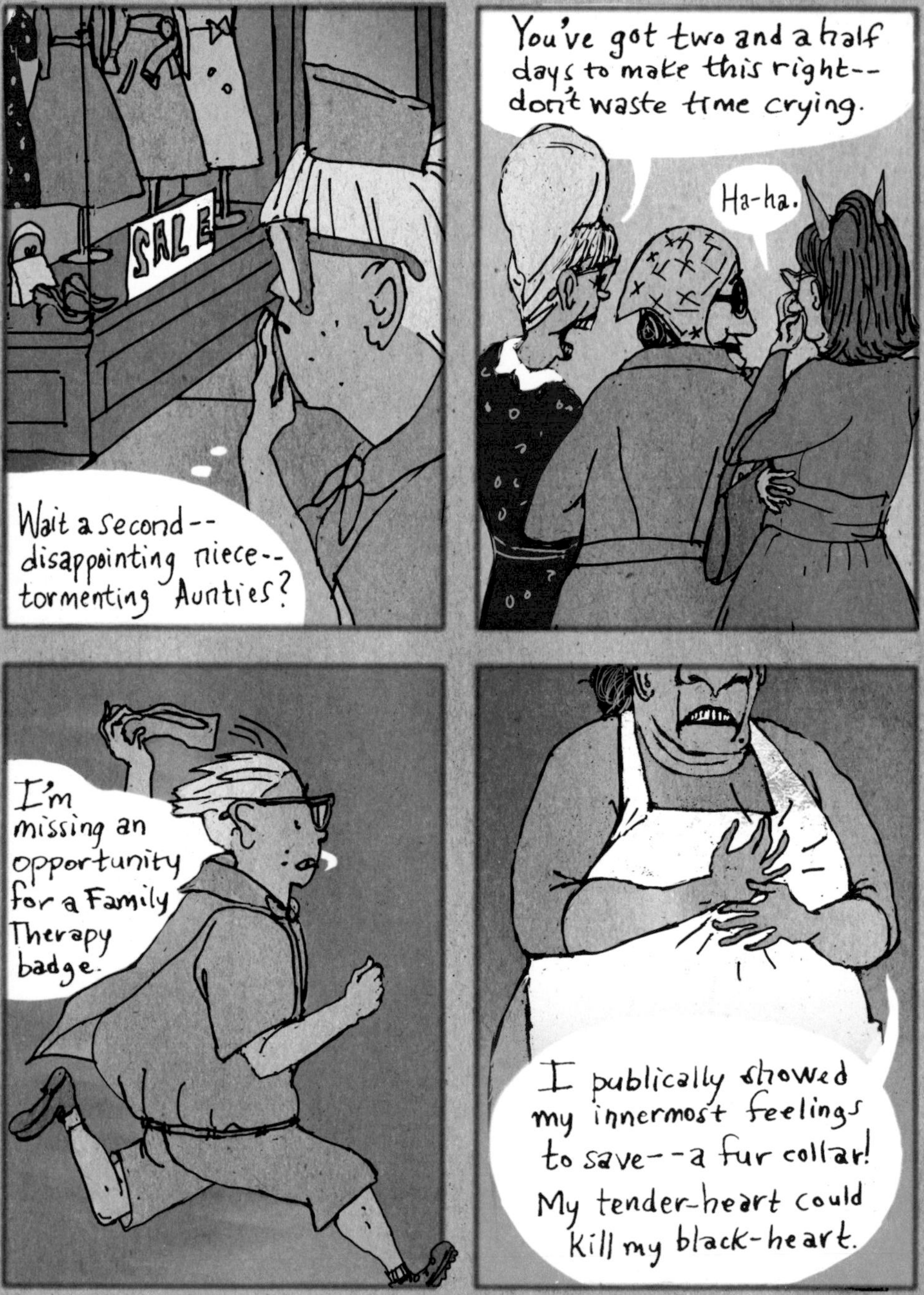
Wait a second--
disappointing niece--
tormenting Aunties?
SALE
You've got two and a half days to make this right--don't waste time crying.
Ha-ha.
I'm missing an opportunity for a Family Therapy badge.
I publically showed my innermost feelings to save--a fur collar! My tender-heart could kill my black-heart.

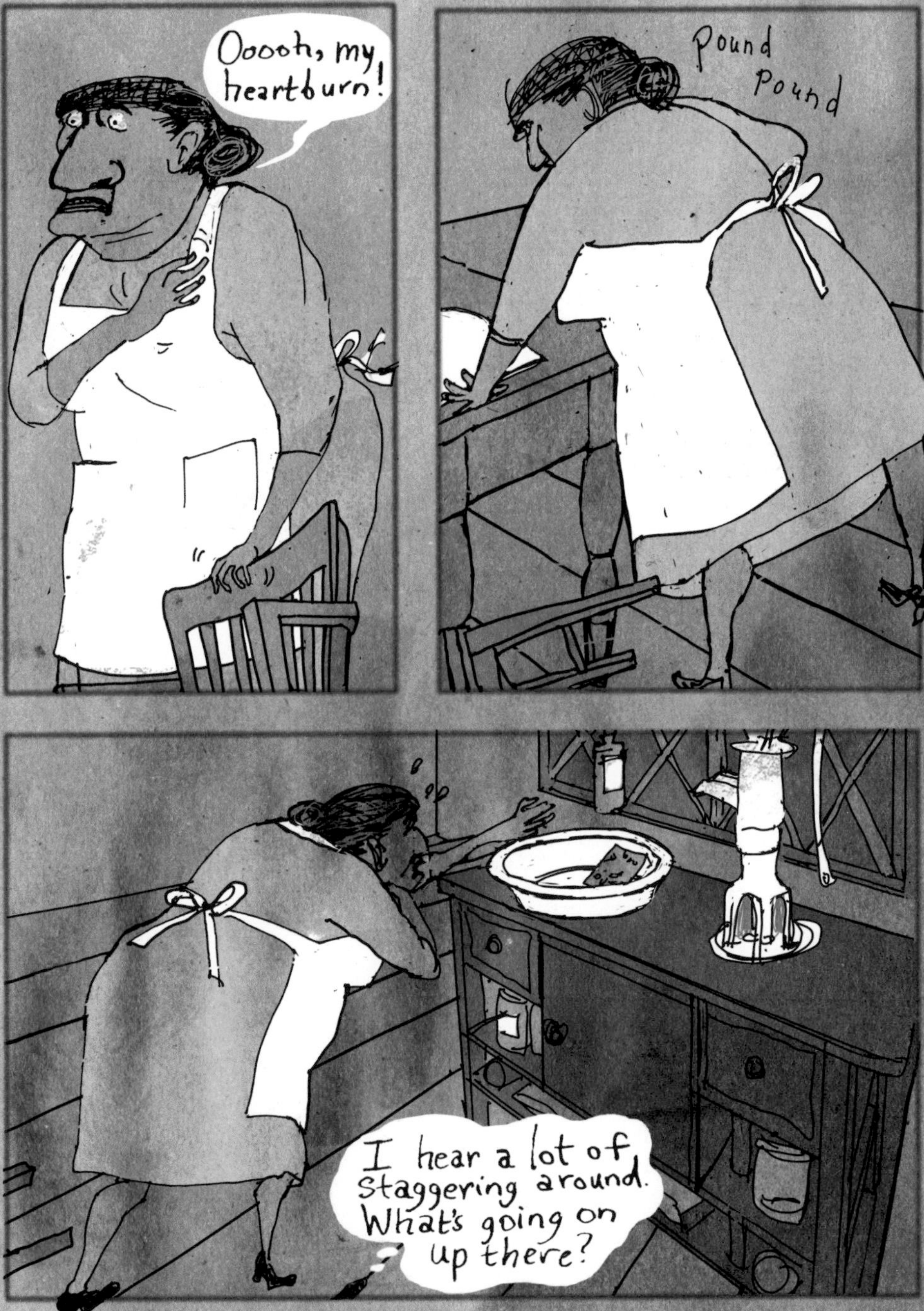
Ooooh, my heartburn!
Pound pound
I hear a lot of staggering around. What's going on up there?

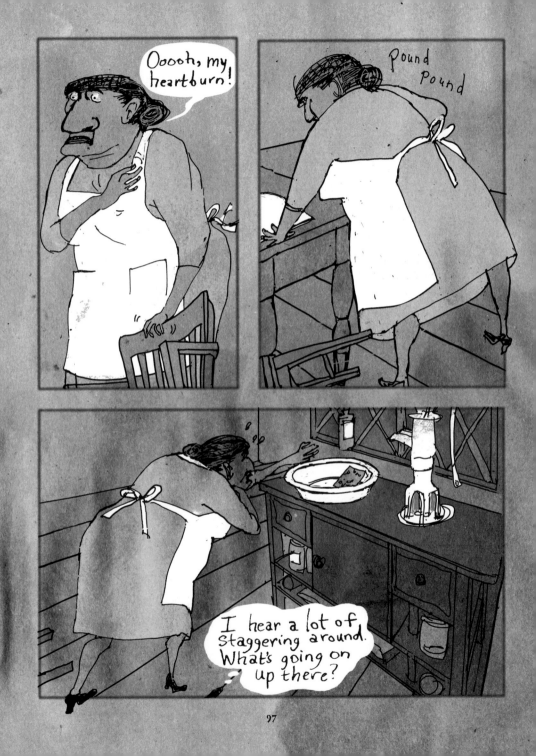

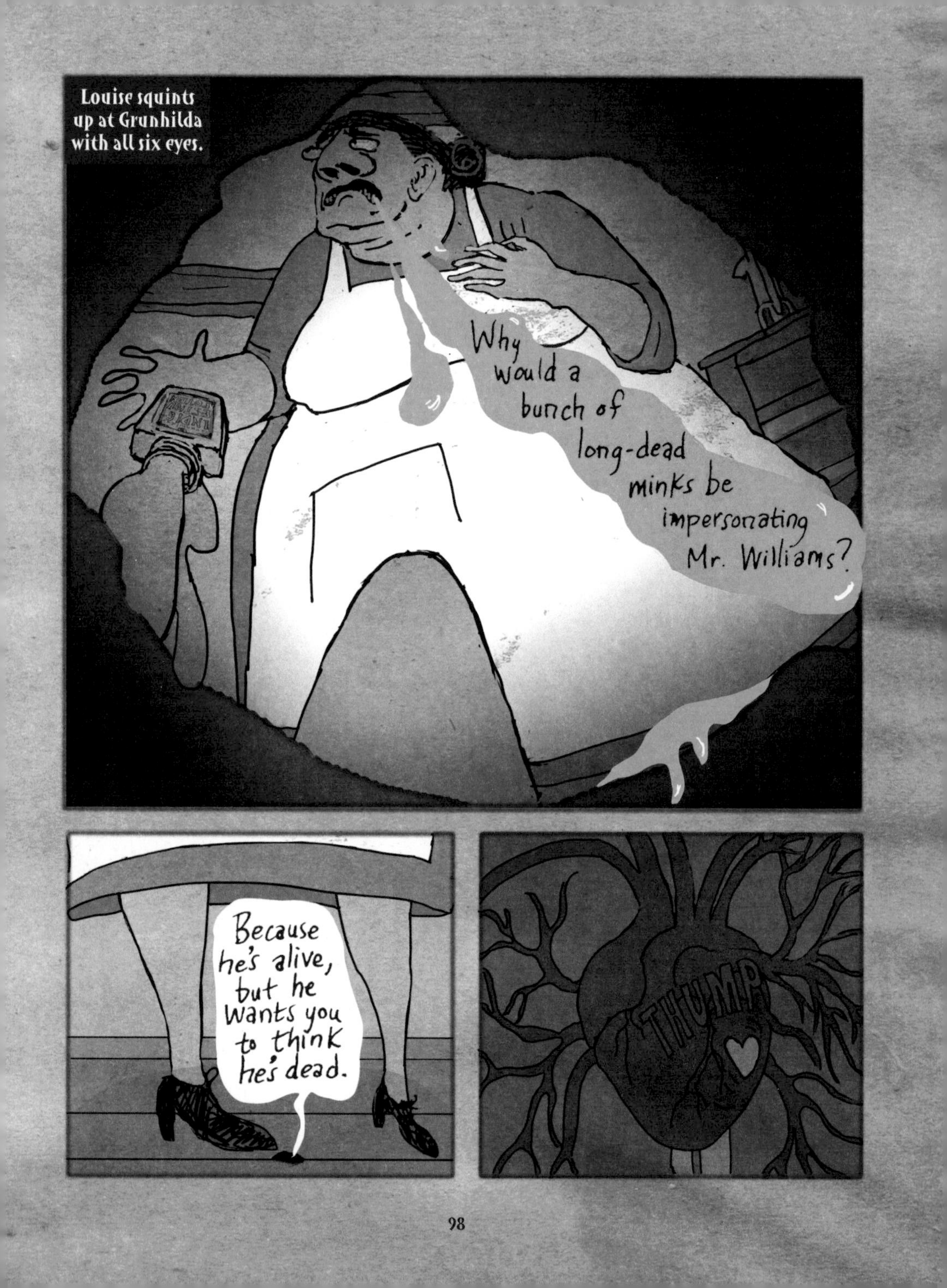
Louise squints up at Grunhilda with all six eyes.
Why would a bunch of long-dead minks be impersonating Mr. Williams?
Because he's alive, but he wants you to think he's dead.
THUMP

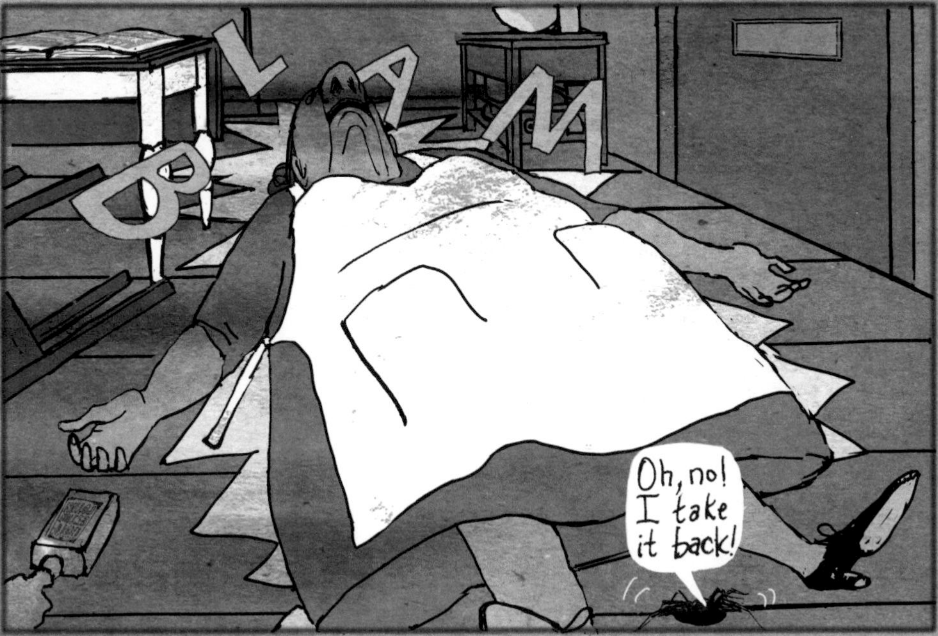
BLAM
Oh, no! I take it back!

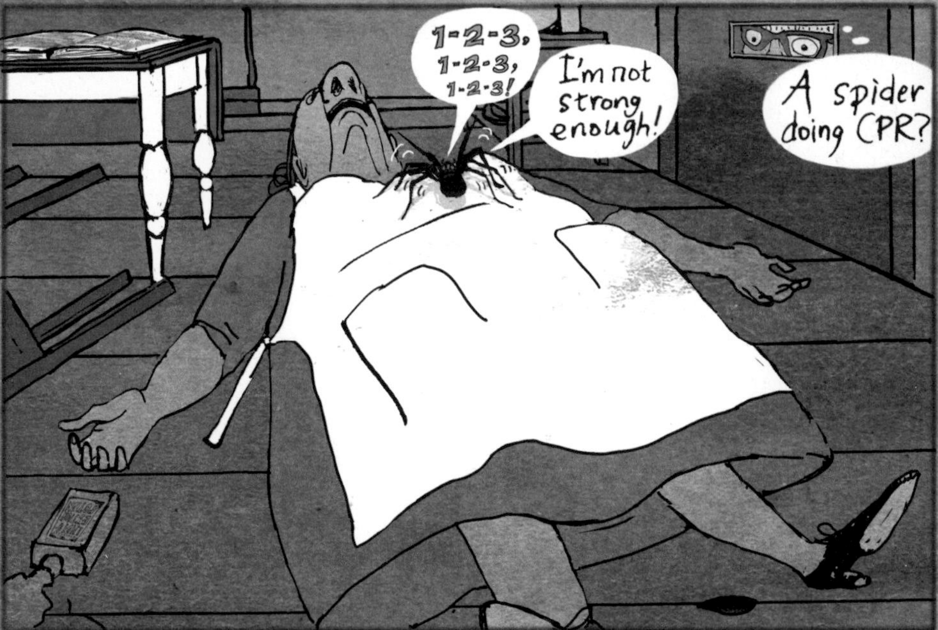
1-2-3, 1-2-3, 1-2-3!
I'm not strong enough!
A spider doing CPR?

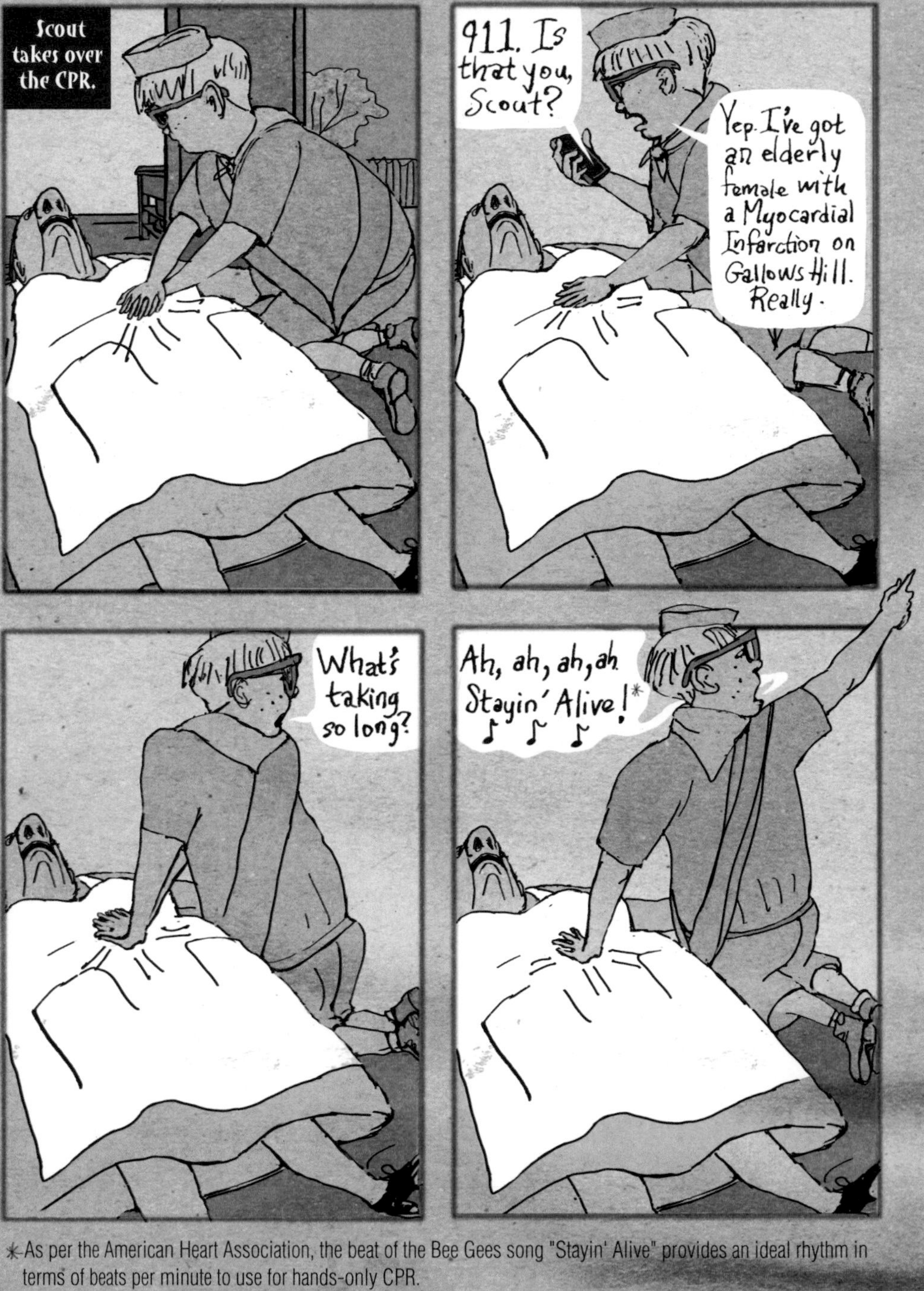
Scout takes over the CPR.
911. Is that you, Scout?
Yep. I've got an elderly female with a Myocardial Infarction on Gallows Hill. Really.
What's taking so long?
Ah, ah, ah, ah Stayin' Alive!*

*As per the American Heart Association, the beat of the Bee Gees song "Stayin' Alive" provides an ideal rhythm in terms of beats per minute to use for hands-only CPR.

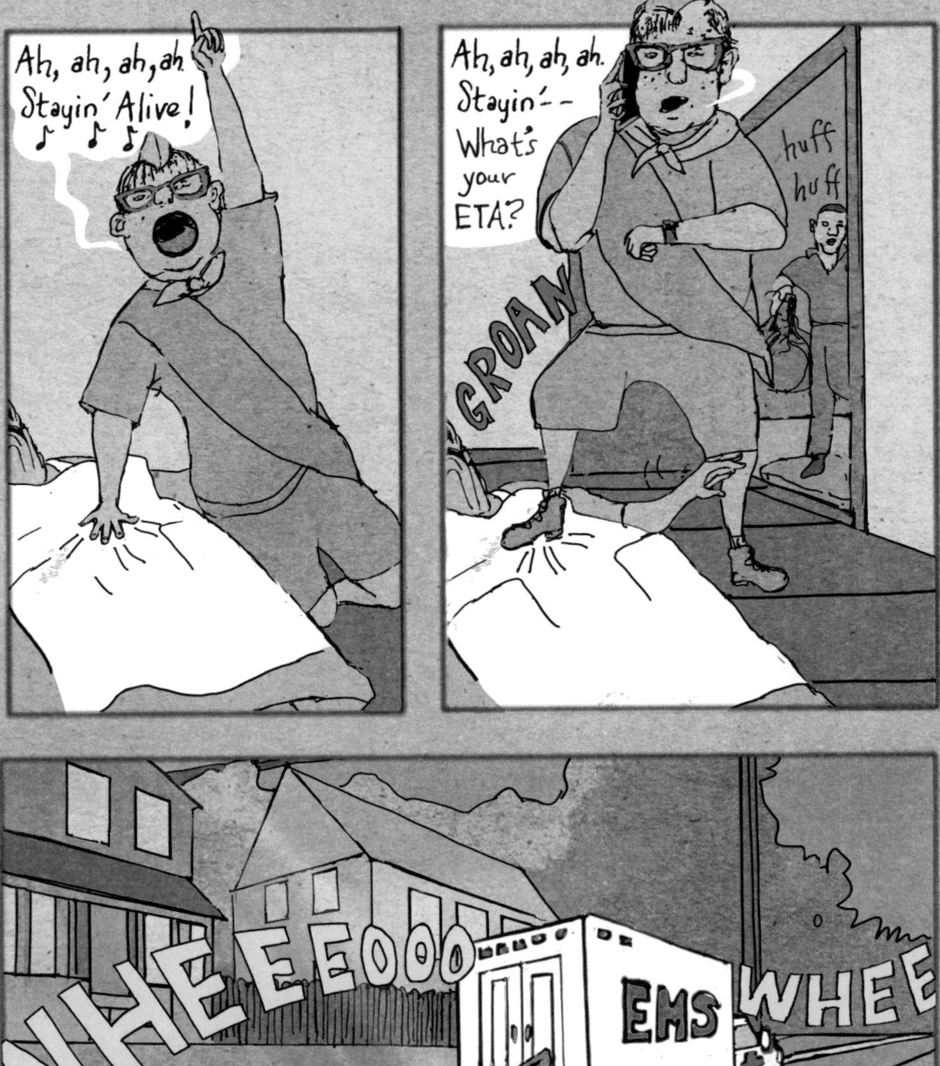
Ah, ah, ah, ah.
Stayin' Alive!
Ah, ah, ah, ah.
Stayin'-- What's your ETA?
huff huff
GROAN
WHEEEOOO
EMS
WHEE
Ah, ah, ah, ah.
Stayin' Alive!

8th

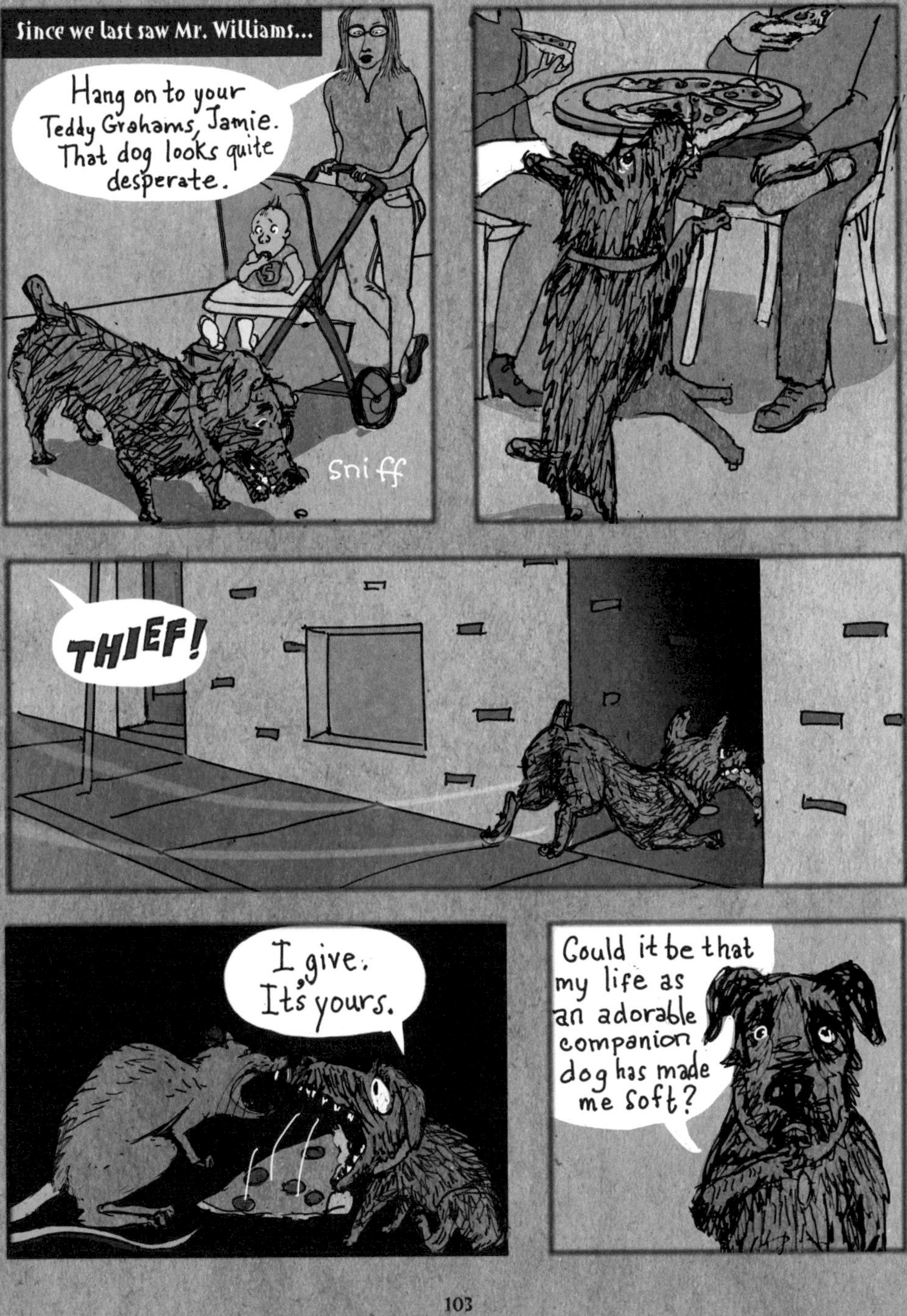
Since we last saw Mr. Williams...
Hang on to your Teddy Grahams, Jamie. That dog looks quite desperate.
sniff
THIEF!
I give. It's yours.
Could it be that my life as an adorable companion dog has made me soft?

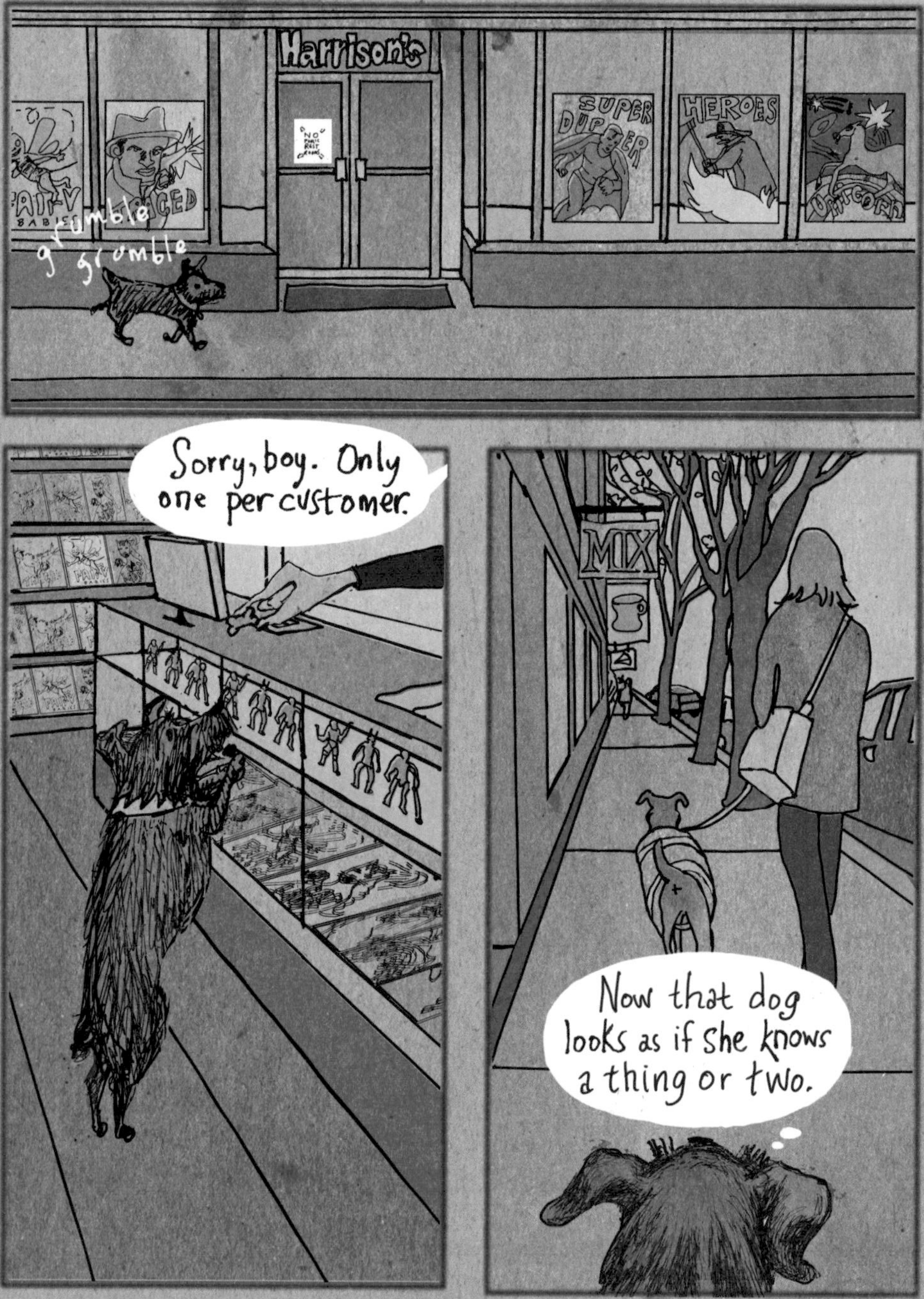
Harrison's
SUPER DUPER
HEROES
grumble grumble
Sorry, boy. Only one per customer.
MIX
Now that dog looks as if she knows a thing or two.

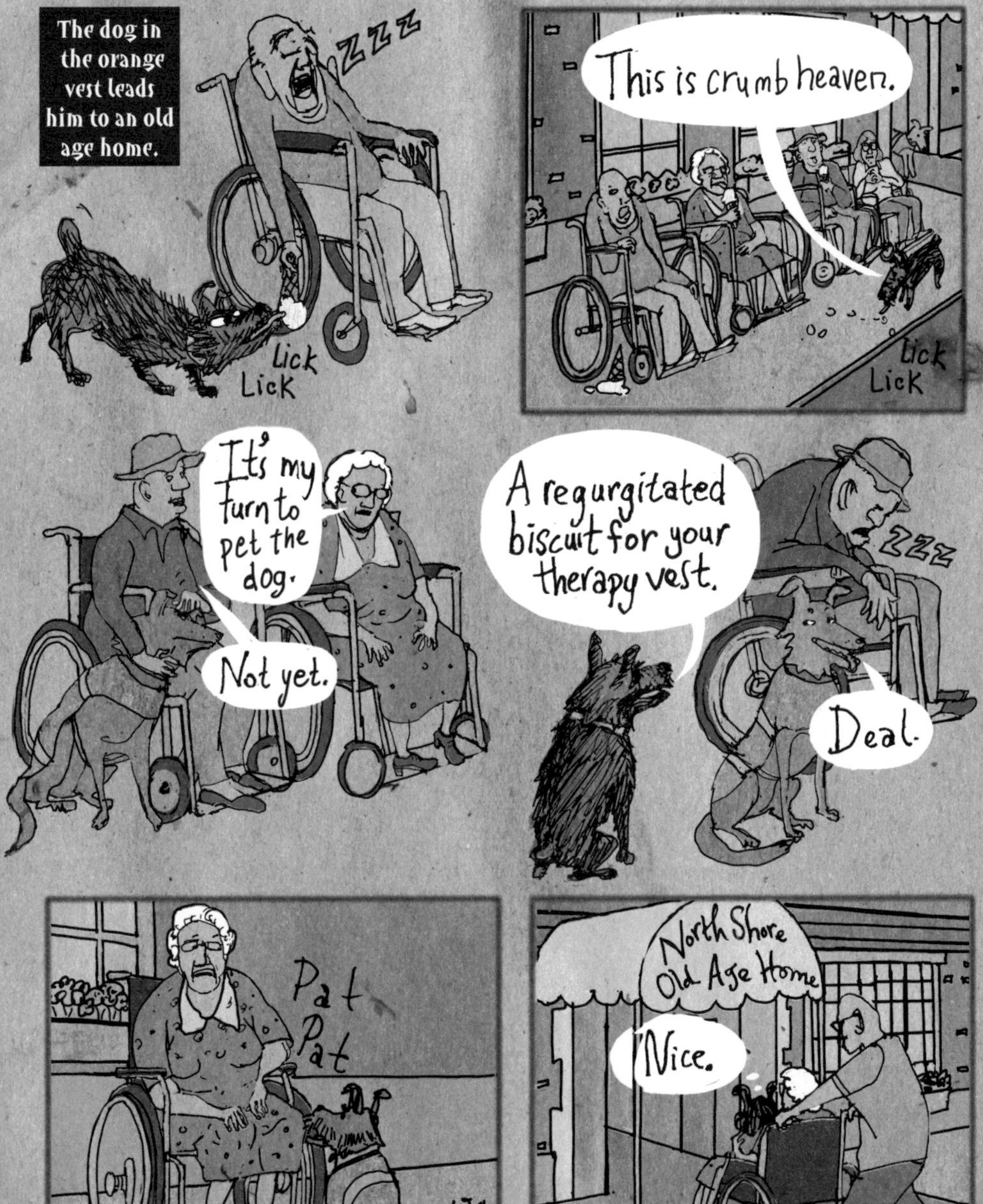
The dog in the orange vest leads him to an old age home.
ZZZ
Lick
Lick
This is crumb heaven.
Lick
Lick
It's my turn to pet the dog.
Not yet.
A regurgitated biscuit for your therapy vest.
ZZZ
Deal.
Pat
Pat
wag
wag
North Shore Old Age Home
Nice.

9th

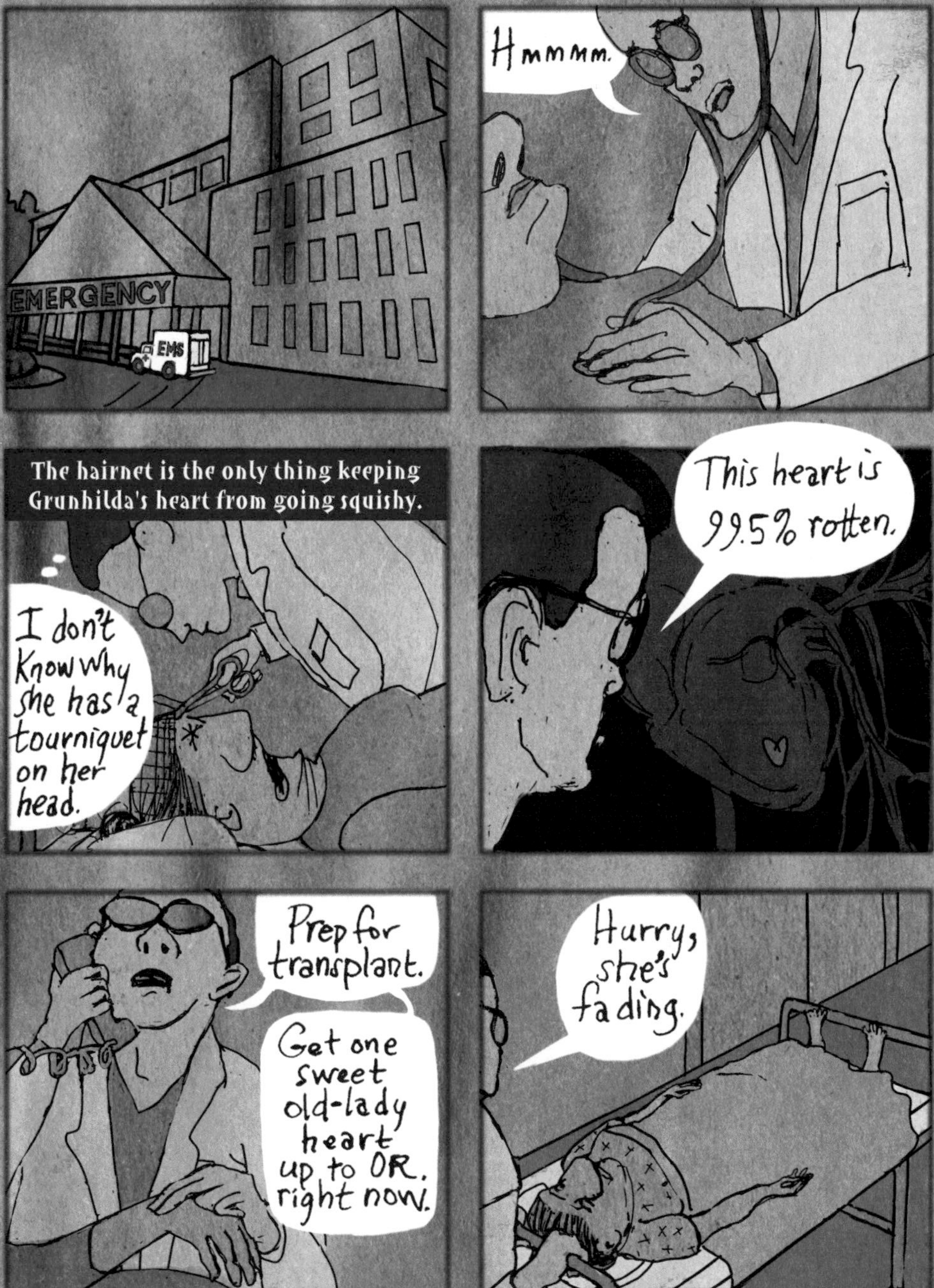

EMERGENCY
EMS
Hmmmm.
The hairnet is the only thing keeping Grunhilda's heart from going squishy.
I don't know why she has a tourniquet on her head.
This heart is 99.5% rotten.
Prep for transplant.
Get one sweet old-lady heart up to OR right now.
Hurry, she's fading.

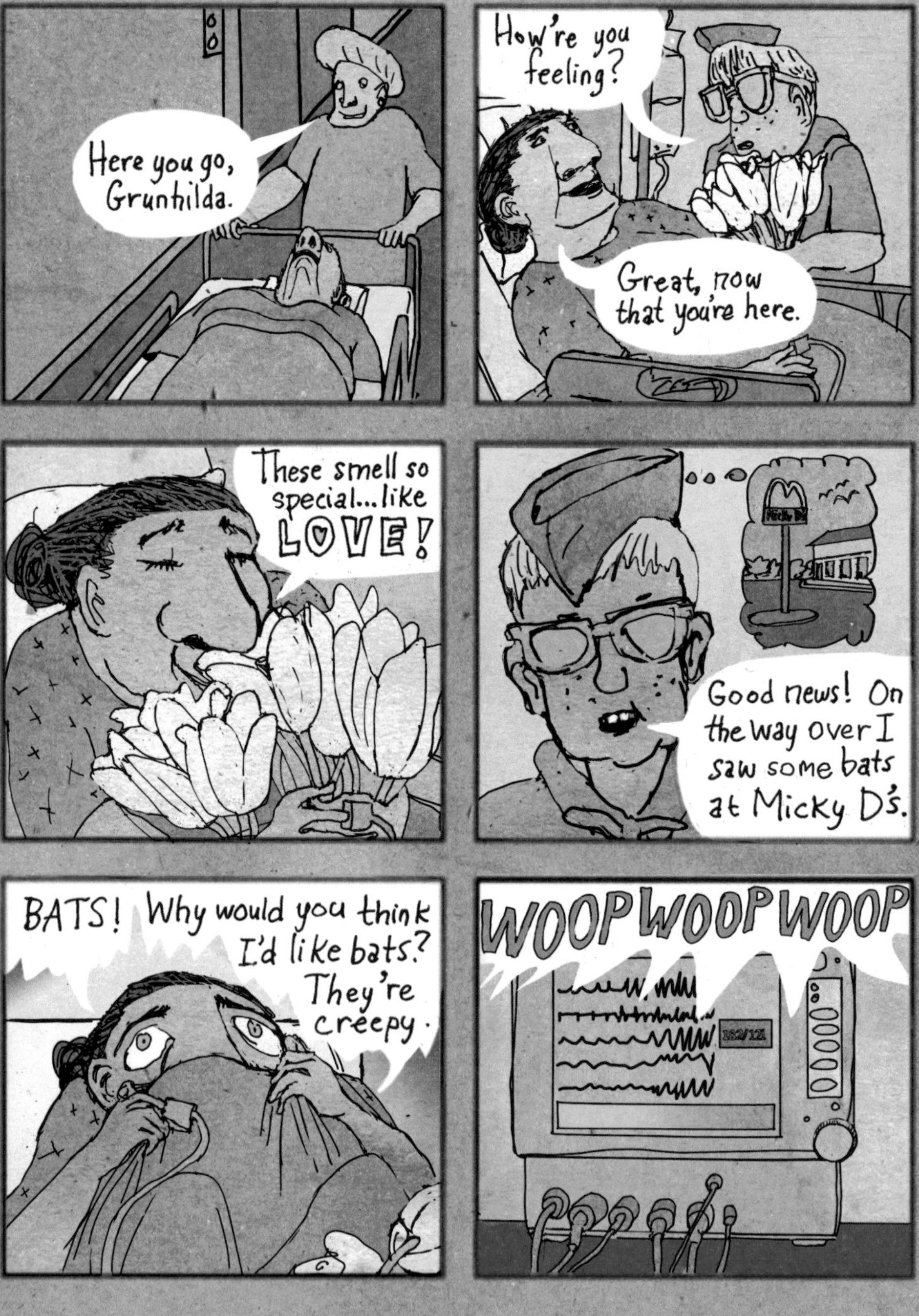

Here you go, Grunhilda.
How're you feeling?
Great, now that you're here.
These smell so special...like LOVE!
Good news! On the way over I saw some bats at Micky D's.
BATS! Why would you think I'd like bats? They're creepy.
WOOP WOOP WOOP
182/121

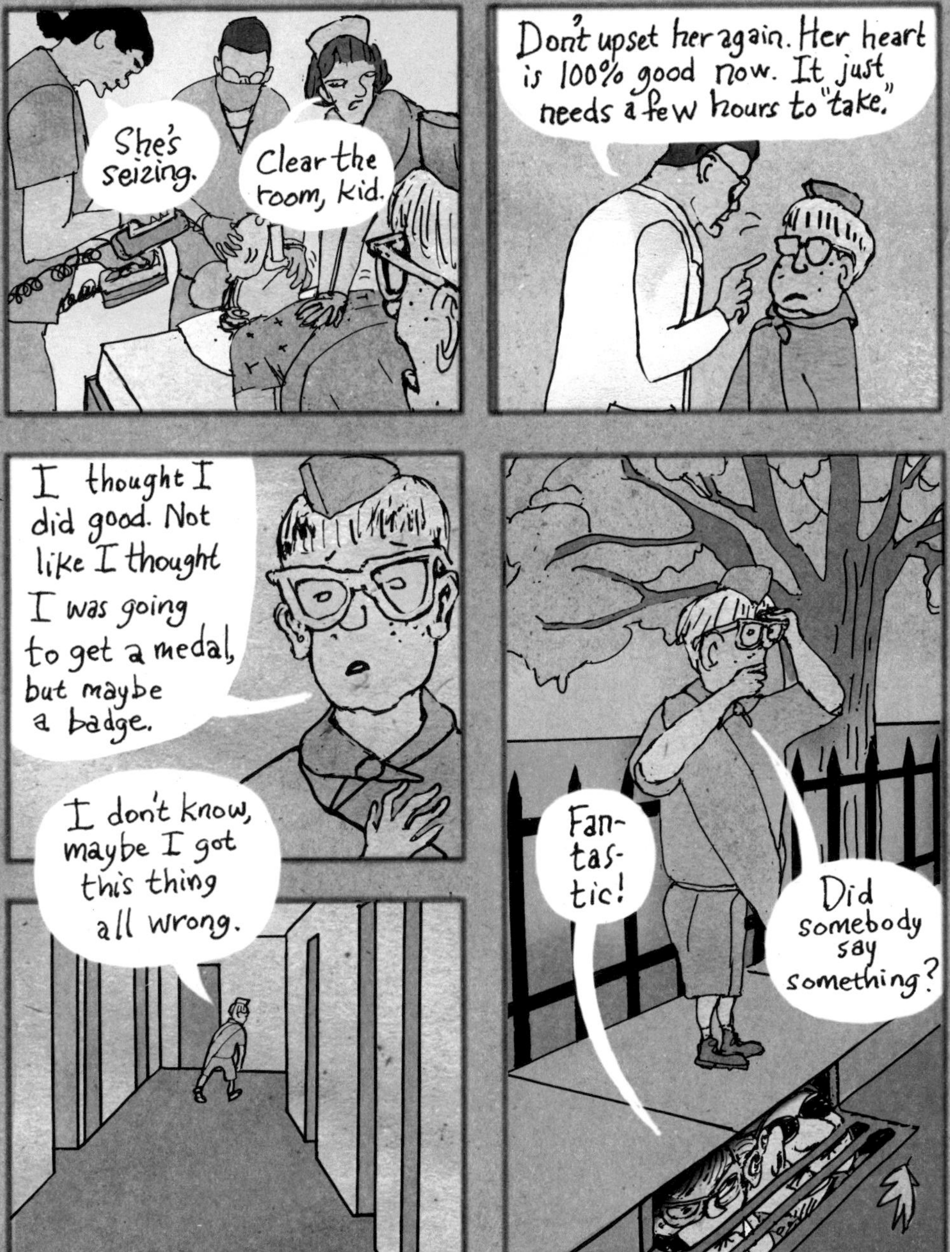
She's seizing.
Clear the room, kid.
Don't upset her again. Her heart is 100% good now. It just needs a few hours to "take."
I thought I did good. Not like I thought I was going to get a medal, but maybe a badge.
I don't know, maybe I got this thing all wrong.
Fan-tas-tic!
Did somebody say something?

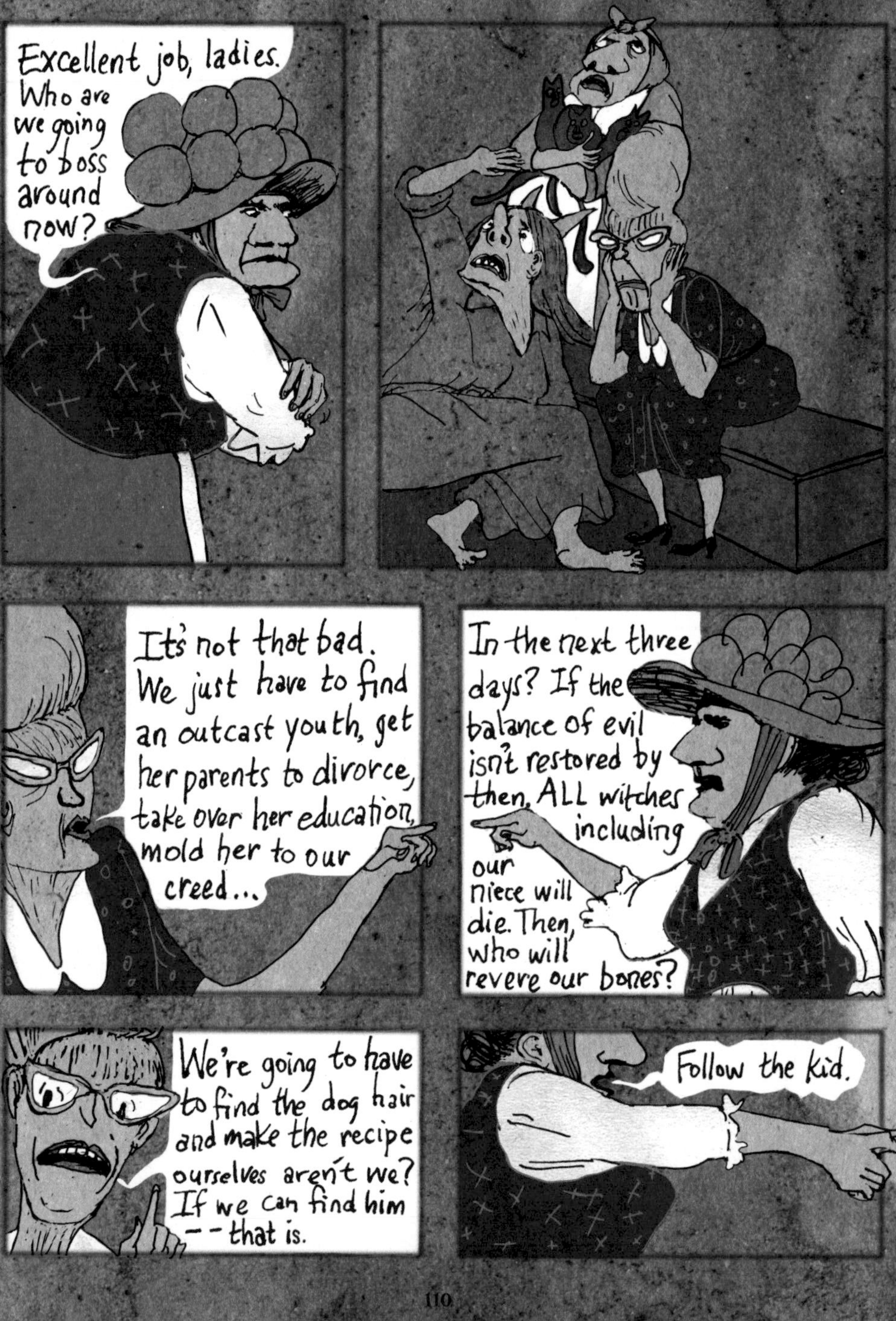
Excellent job, ladies. Who are we going to boss around now?
It's not that bad. We just have to find an outcast youth, get her parents to divorce, take over her education, mold her to our creed...
In the next three days? If the balance of evil isn't restored by then, ALL witches including our niece will die. Then, who will revere our bones?
We're going to have to find the dog hair and make the recipe ourselves aren't we? If we can find him -- that is.
Follow the kid.

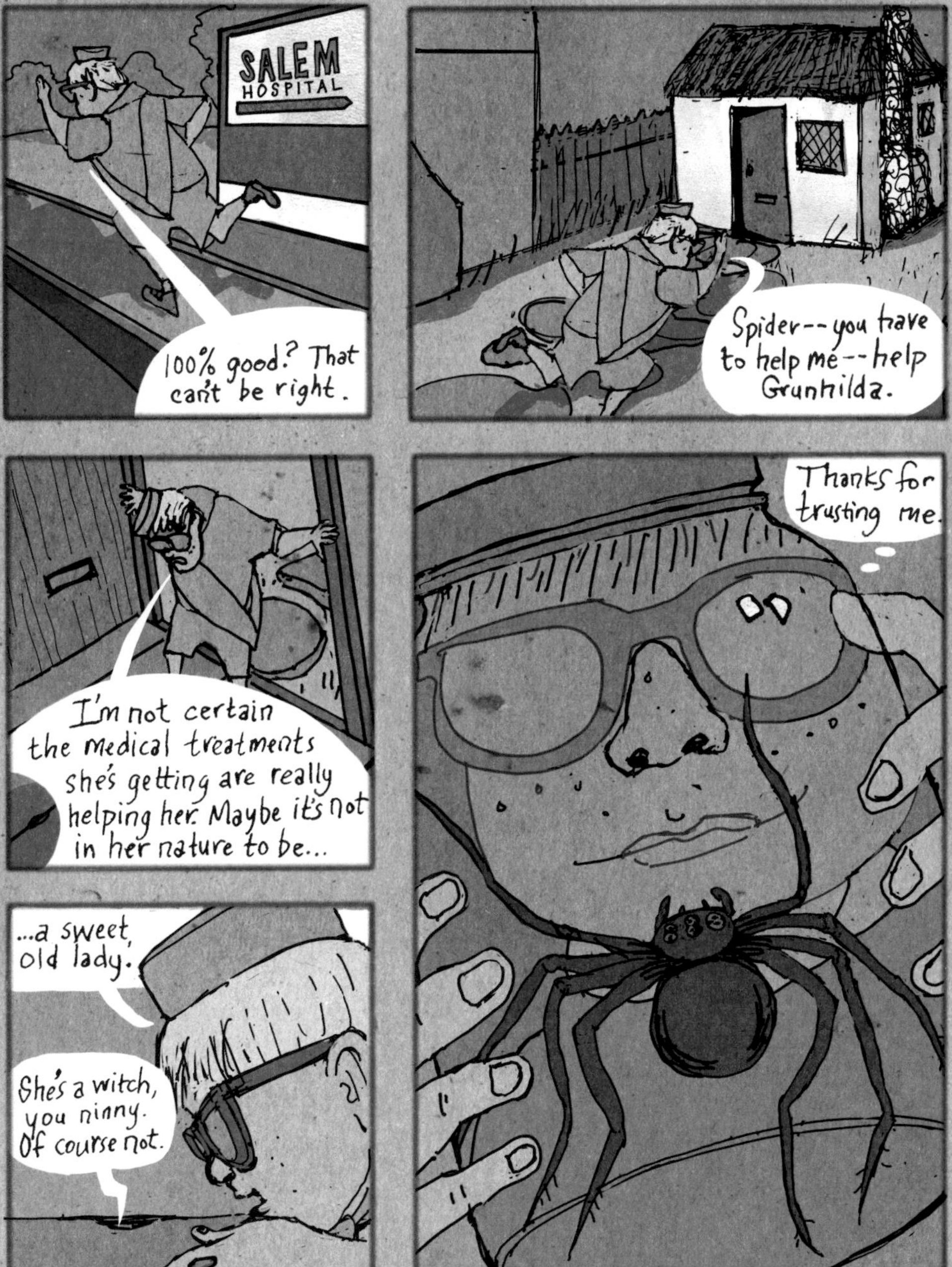
SALEM
HOSPITAL
100% good? That can't be right.
Spider--you have to help me--help Grunhilda.
I'm not certain the medical treatments she's getting are really helping her. Maybe it's not in her nature to be...
...a sweet, old lady.
She's a witch, you ninny. Of course not.
Thanks for trusting me.

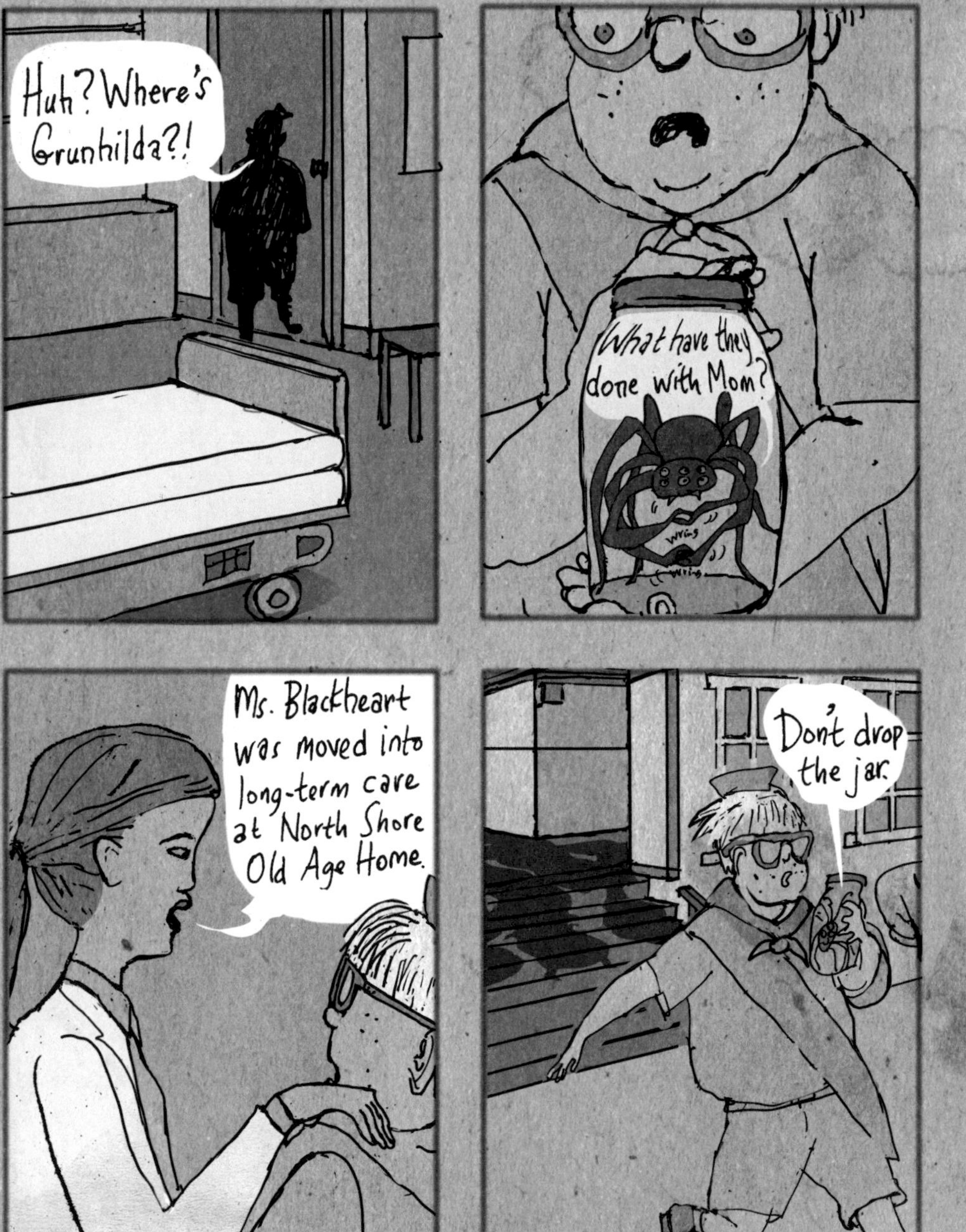
Huh? Where's Grunhilda?!
What have they done with Mom?
Ms. Blackheart was moved into long-term care at North Shore Old Age Home.
Don't drop the jar.

10th

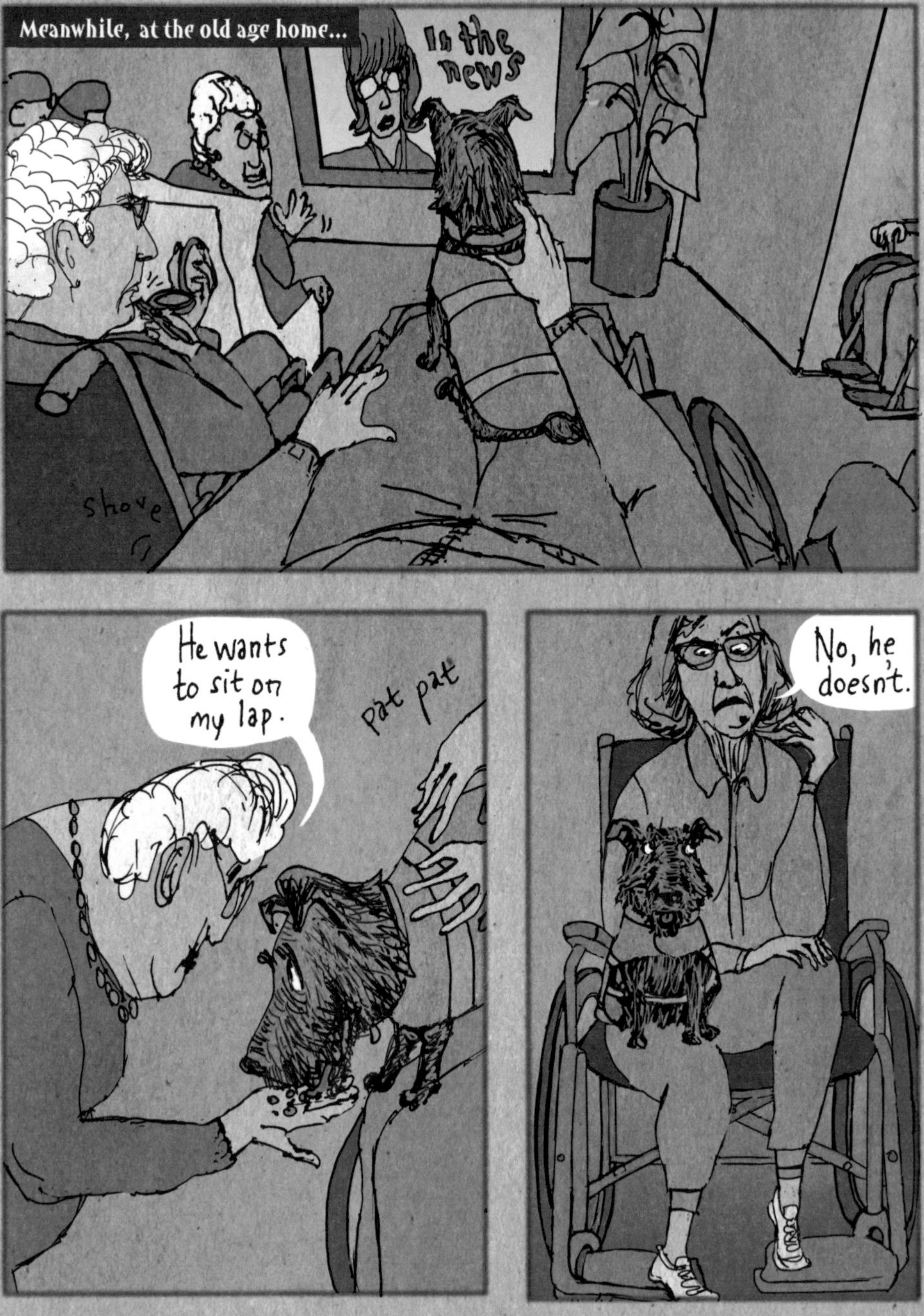
Meanwhile, at the old age home...
In the news
shove
He wants to sit on my lap.
pat pat
No, he doesn't.

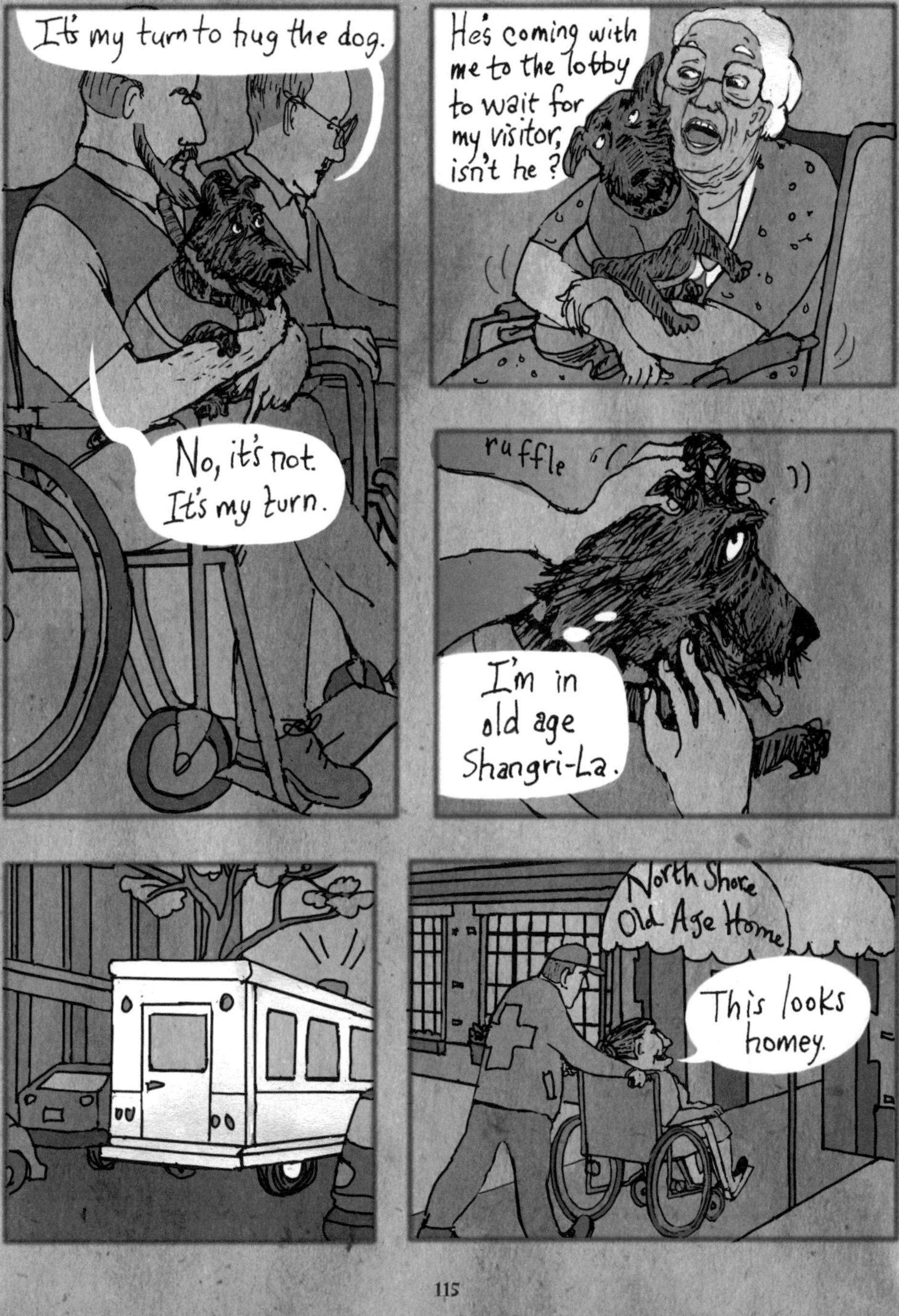
It's my turn to hug the dog.
No, it's not. It's my turn.
He's coming with me to the lobby to wait for my visitor, isn't he?
ruffle
I'm in old age Shangri-La.
North Shore Old Age Home
This looks homey.

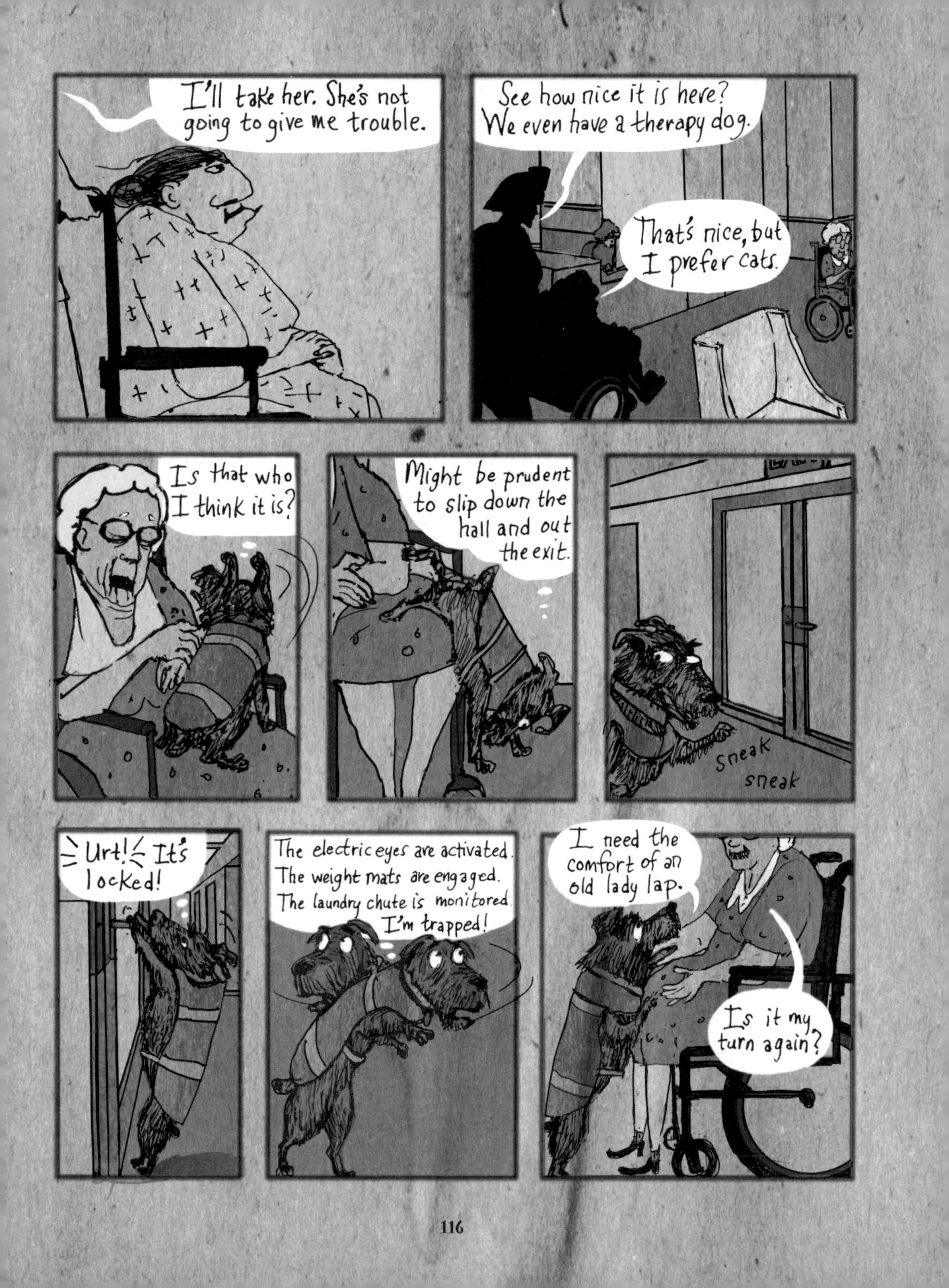
I'll take her. She's not going to give me trouble.
See how nice it is here? We even have a therapy dog.
That's nice, but I prefer cats.
Is that who I think it is?
Might be prudent to slip down the hall and out the exit.
sneak
sneak
Urt! It's locked!
The electric eyes are activated. The weight mats are engaged. The laundry chute is monitored. I'm trapped!
I need the comfort of an old lady lap.
Is it my turn again?

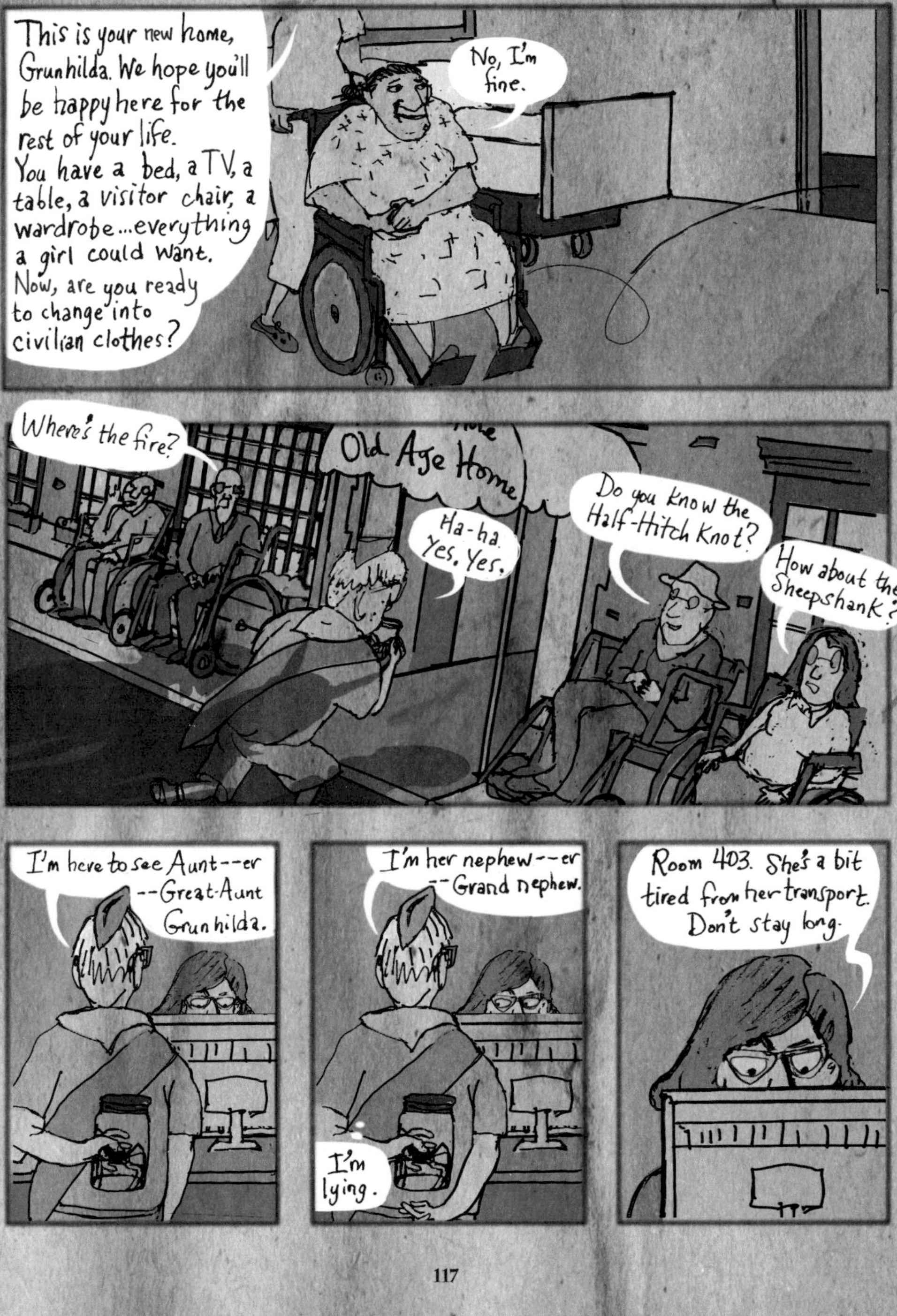
This is your new home, Grunhilda. We hope you'll be happy here for the rest of your life. You have a bed, a TV, a table, a visitor chair, a wardrobe...everything a girl could want. Now, are you ready to change into civilian clothes?
No, I'm fine.
Where's the fire?
Old Age Home
Ha-ha. Yes, Yes.
Do you know the Half-Hitch Knot?
How about the Sheepshank?
I'm here to see Aunt--er --Great-Aunt Grunhilda.
I'm her nephew--er --Grand nephew.
I'm lying.
Room 403. She's a bit tired from her transport. Don't stay long.

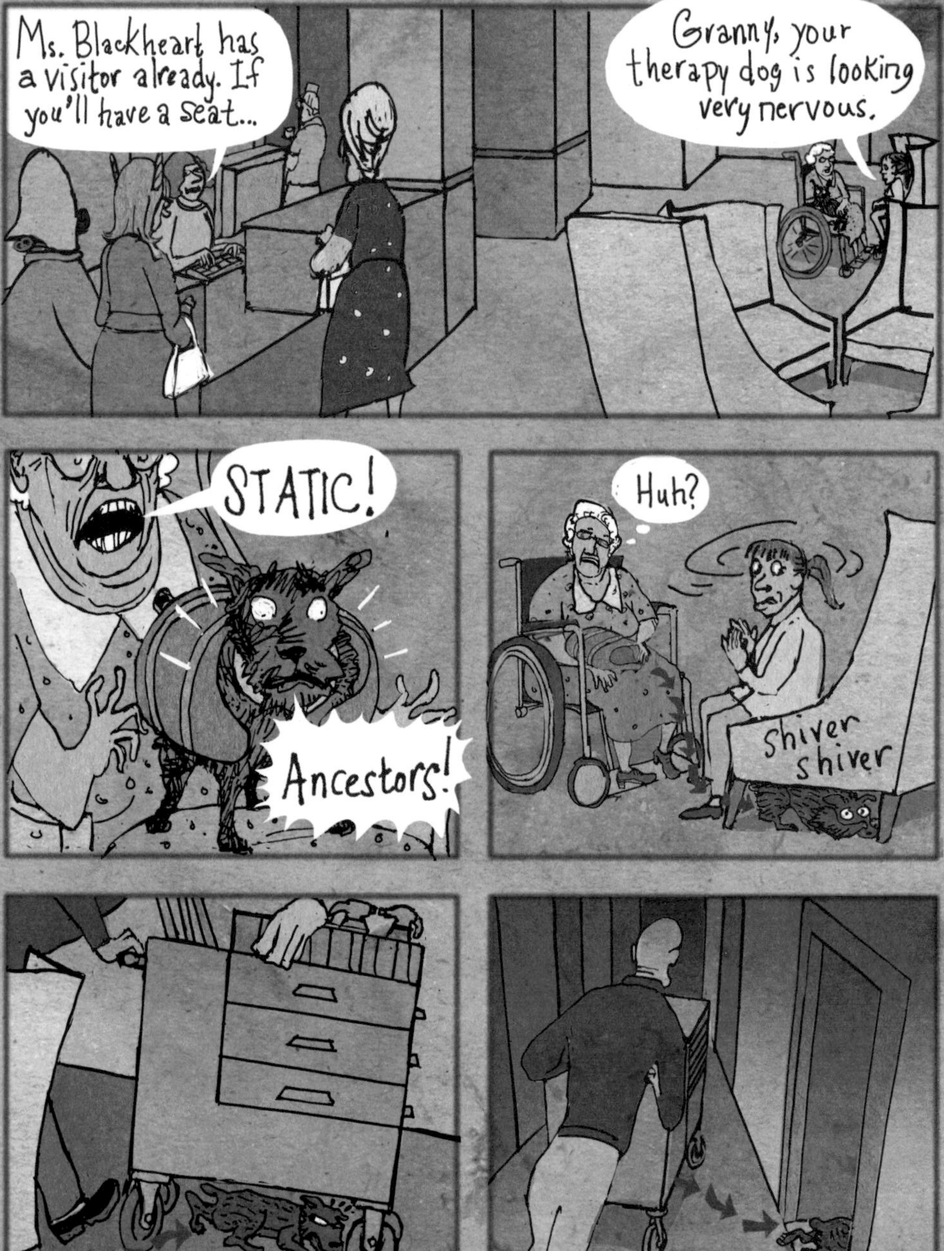
Ms. Blackheart has a visitor already. If you'll have a seat...
Granny, your therapy dog is looking very nervous.
STATIC!
Ancestors!
Huh?
shiver shiver

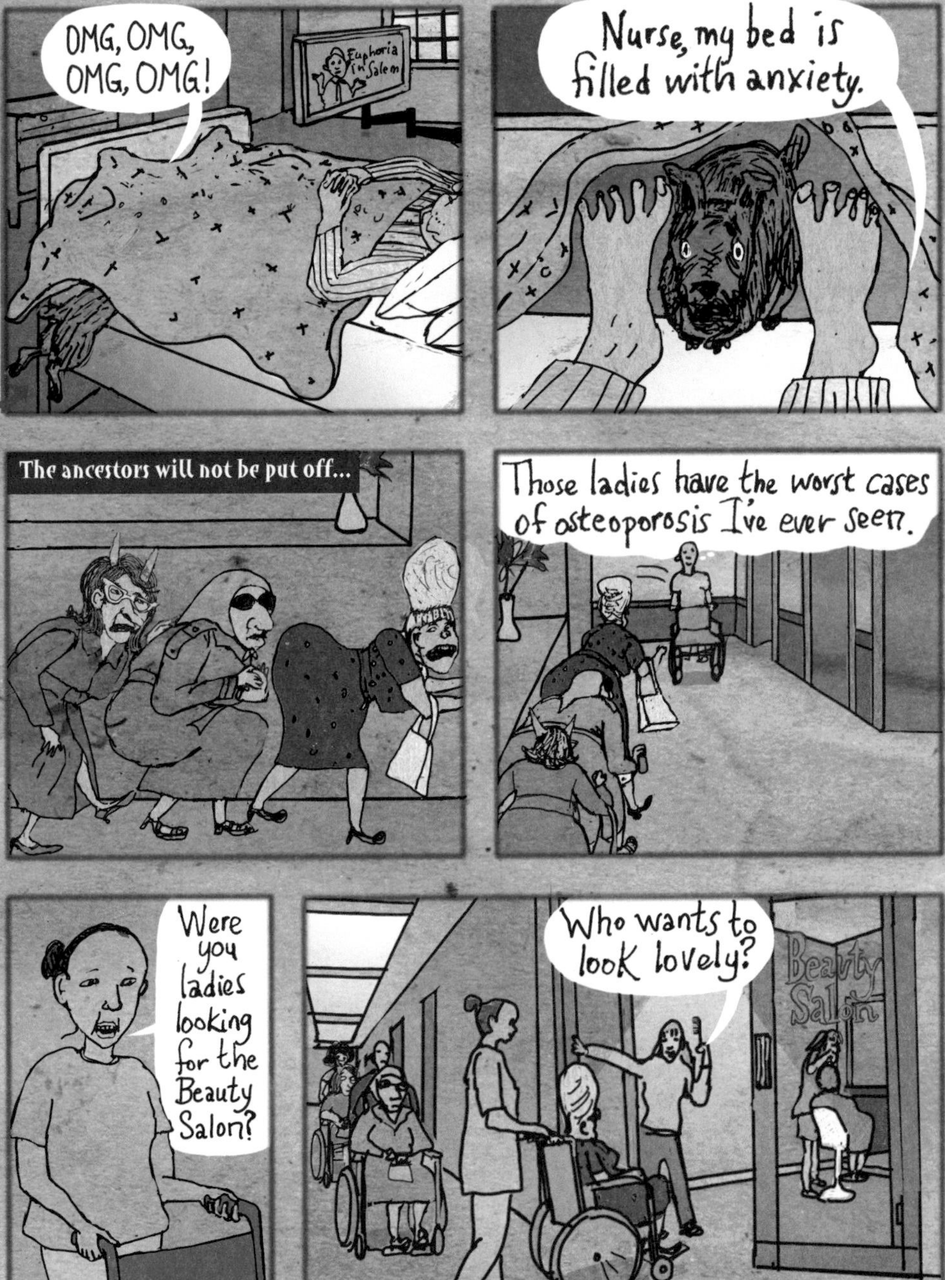
OMG, OMG, OMG, OMG!
Euphoria in Salem
Nurse, my bed is filled with anxiety.
The ancestors will not be put off...
Those ladies have the worst cases of osteoporosis I've ever seen.
Were you ladies looking for the Beauty Salon?
Who wants to look lovely?
Beauty Salon

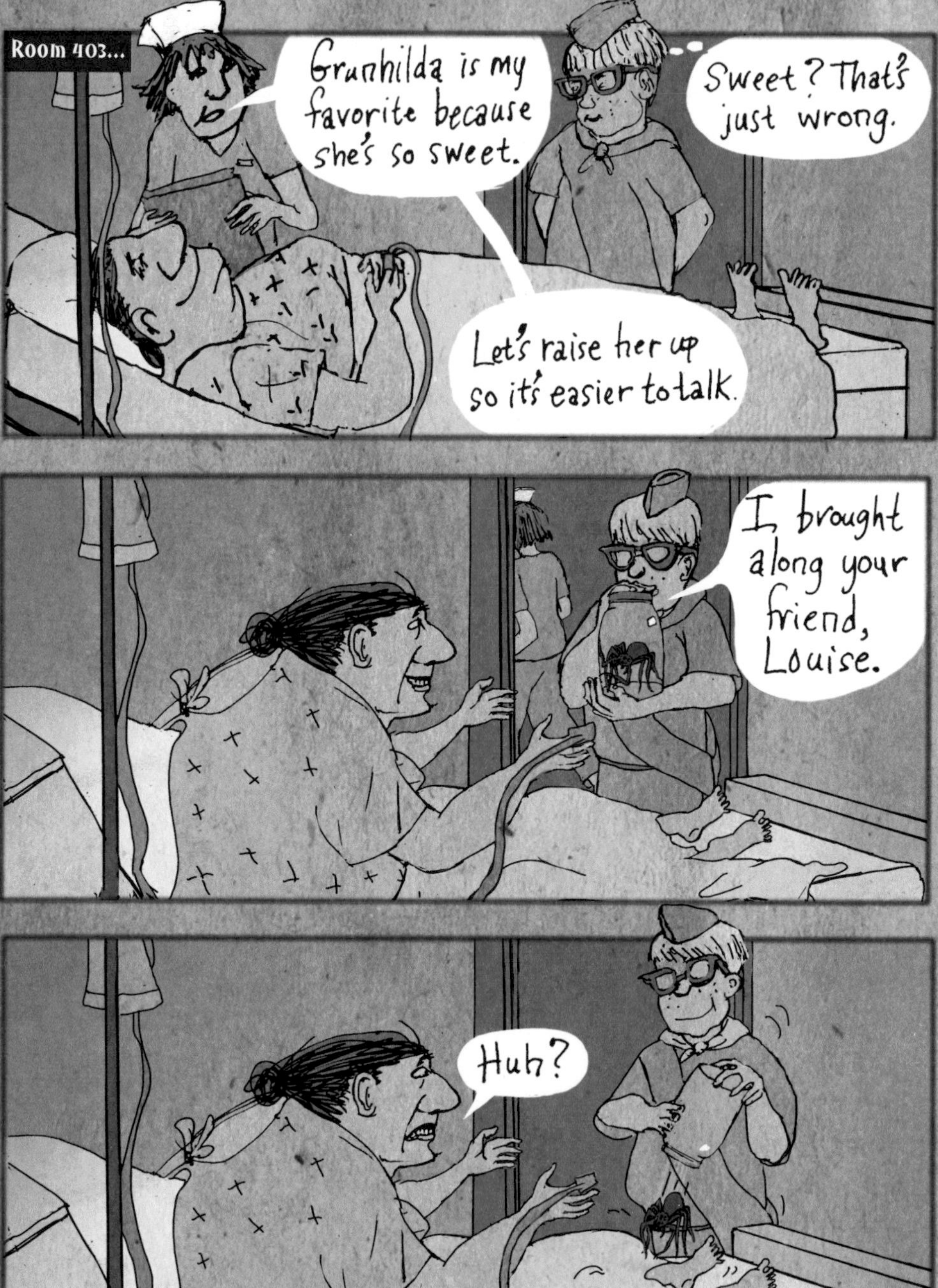
Room 403...
Grunhilda is my favorite because she's so sweet.
Sweet? That's just wrong.
Let's raise her up so it's easier to talk.
I brought along your friend, Louise.
Huh?

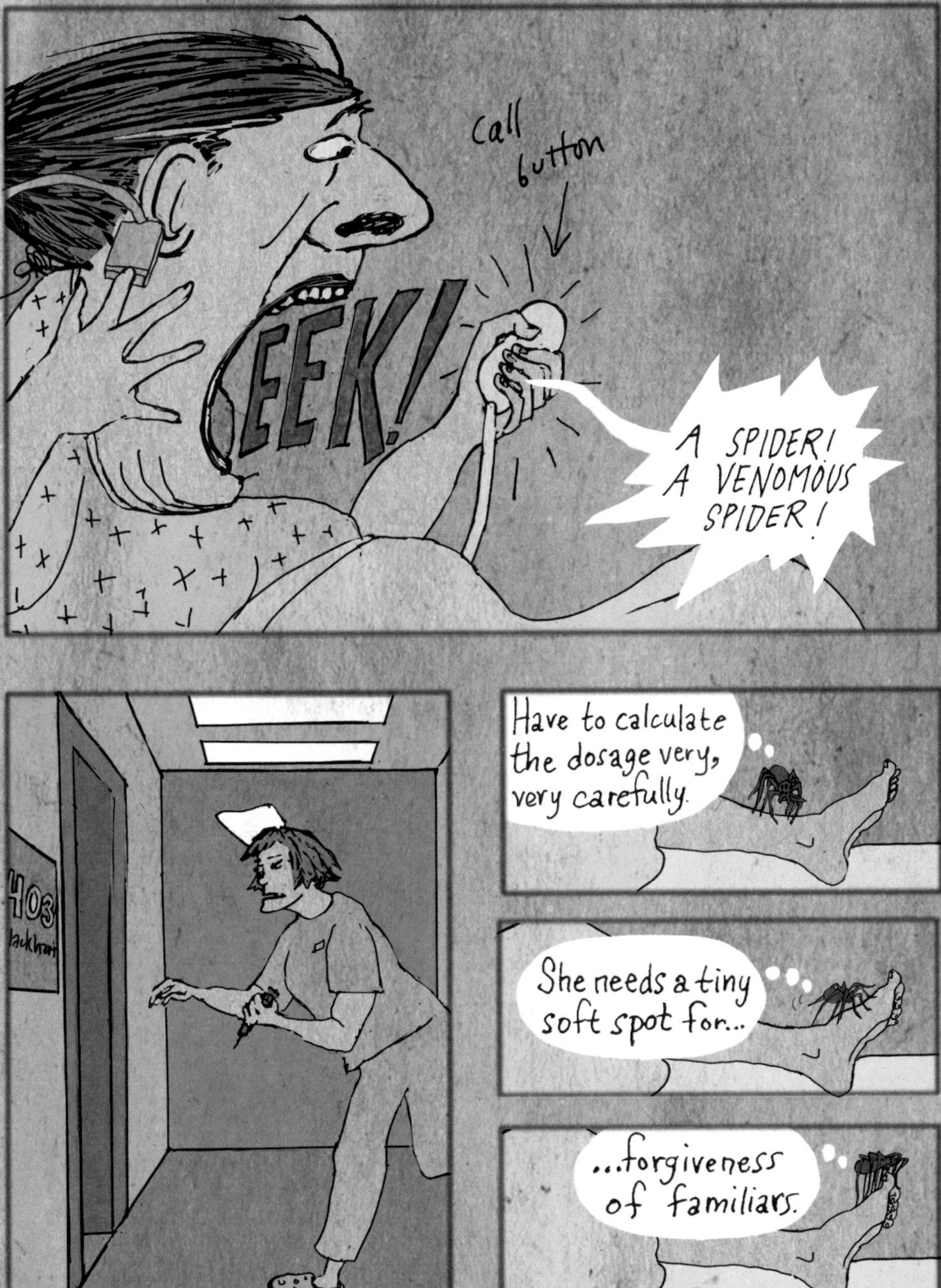
Call button
EEK!
A SPIDER! A VENOMOUS SPIDER!
Have to calculate the dosage very, very carefully.
She needs a tiny soft spot for...
...forgiveness of familiars.

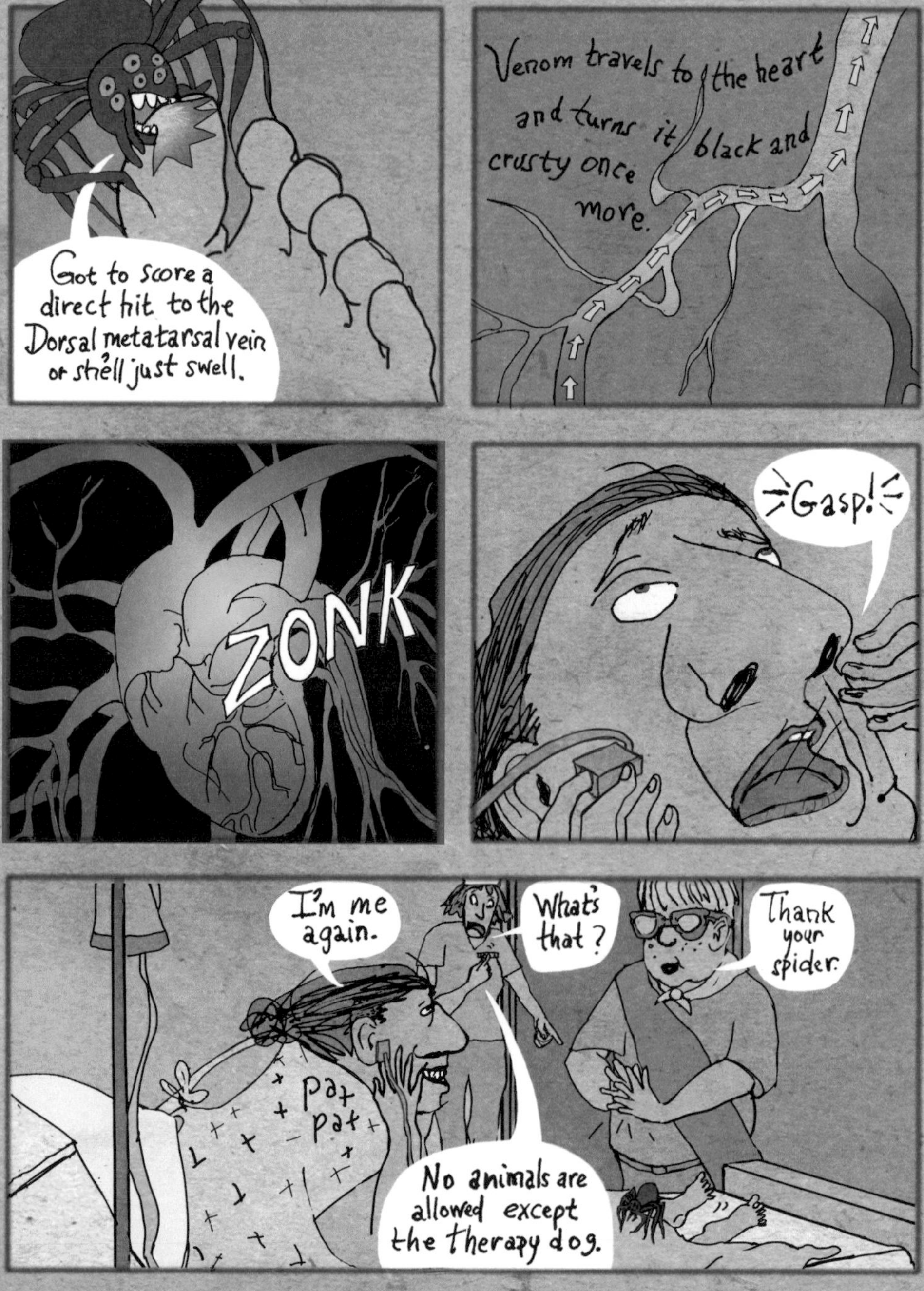

Got to score a direct hit to the Dorsal metatarsal vein or she'll just swell.
Venom travels to the heart and turns it black and crusty once more.
ZONK
Gasp!
I'm me again.
What's that?
Thank your spider.
pat pat
No animals are allowed except the therapy dog.

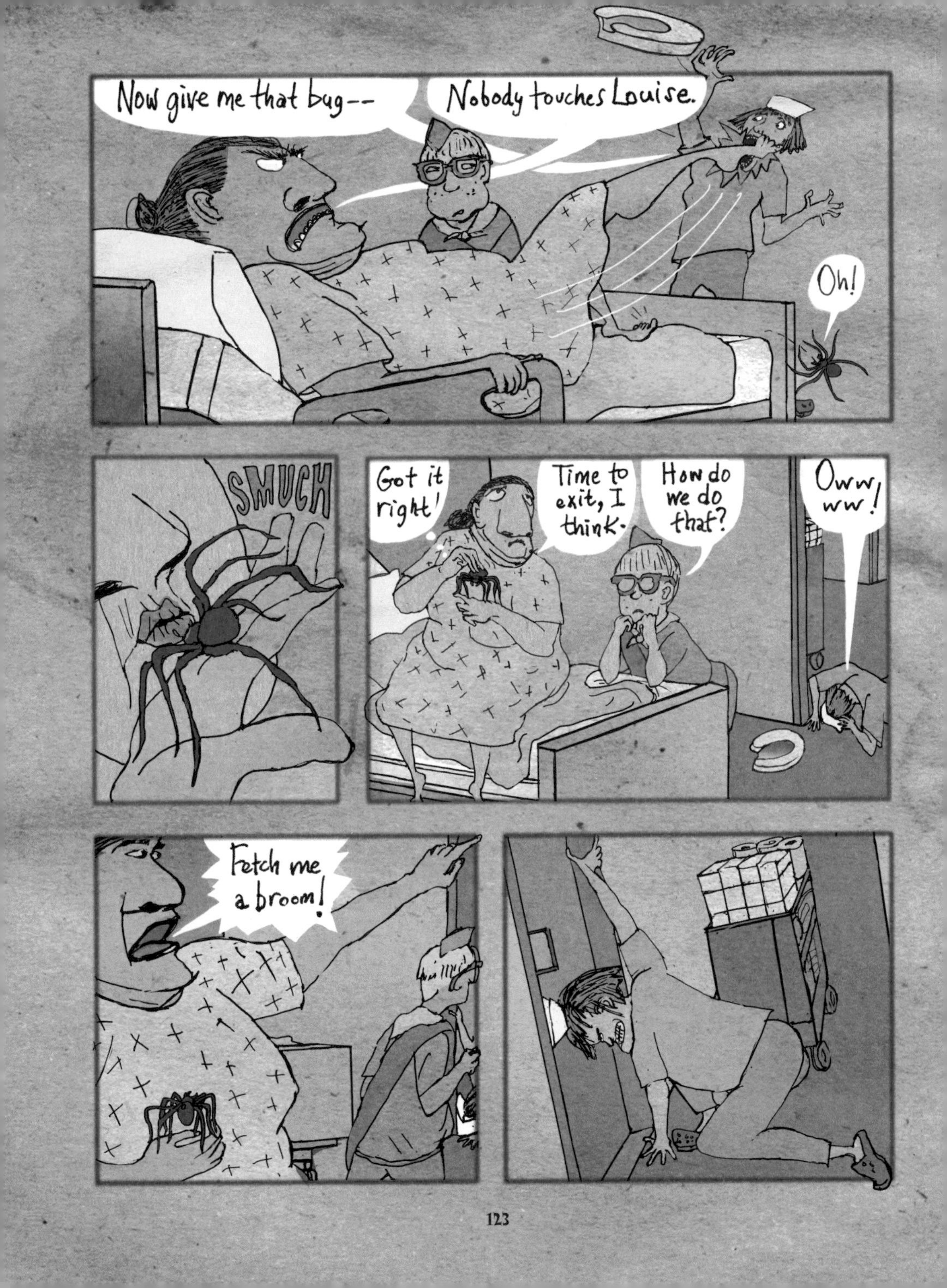
Now give me that bug--
Nobody touches Louise.
Oh!
SMUCH
Got it right!
Time to exit, I think.
How do we do that?
Owww ww!
Fetch me a broom!

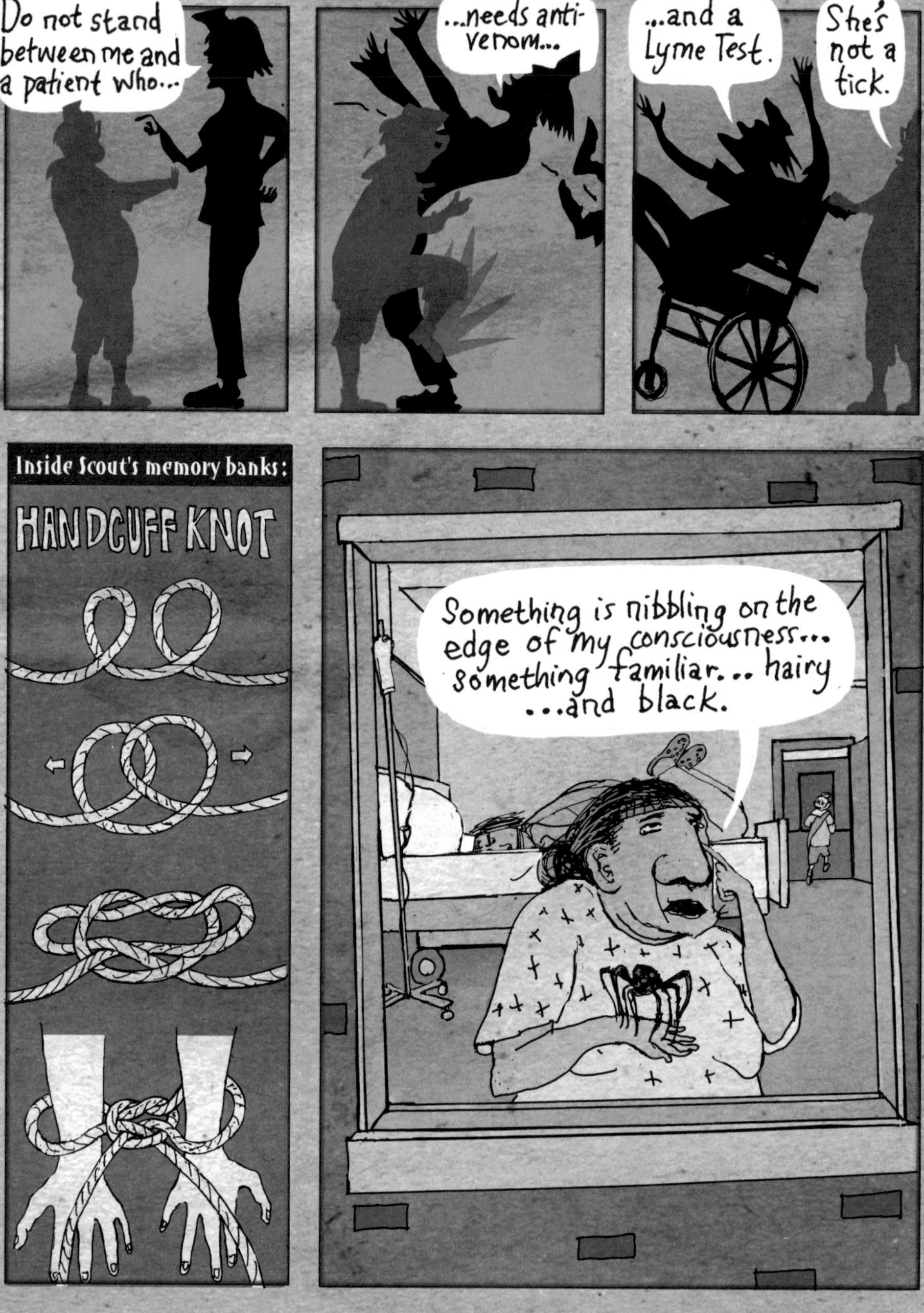

Do not stand between me and a patient who...
...needs anti-venom...
...and a Lyme Test.
She's not a tick.
Inside Scout's memory banks:
HANDCUFF KNOT
Something is nibbling on the edge of my consciousness... something familiar... hairy ...and black.

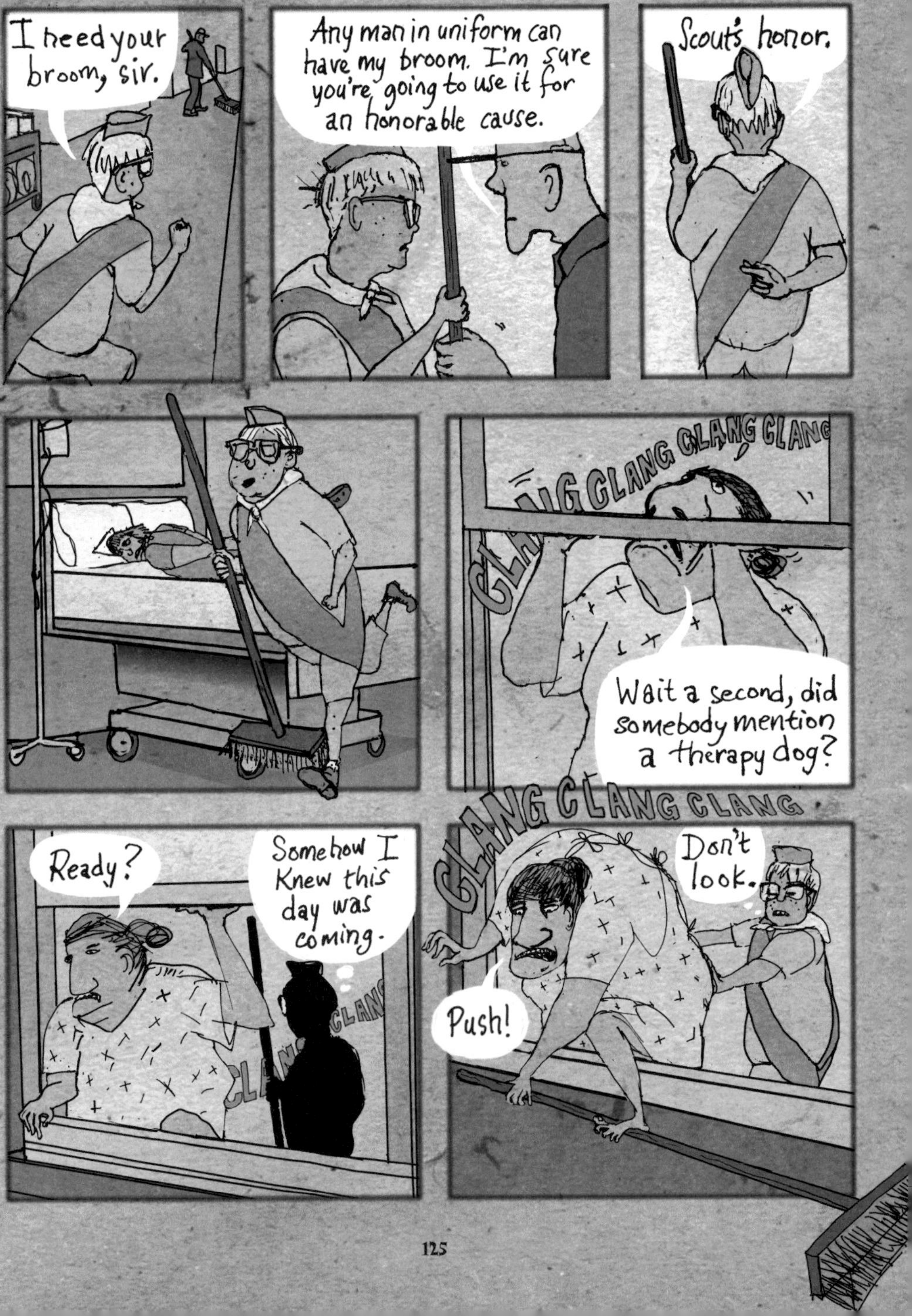
I need your broom, sir.
Any man in uniform can have my broom. I'm sure you're going to use it for an honorable cause.
Scout's honor.
CLANG CLANG CLANG CLANG CLANG
Wait a second, did somebody mention a therapy dog?
CLANG CLANG CLANG
Ready?
Somehow I Knew this day was coming.
CLANG
CLANG
Don't look.
Push!

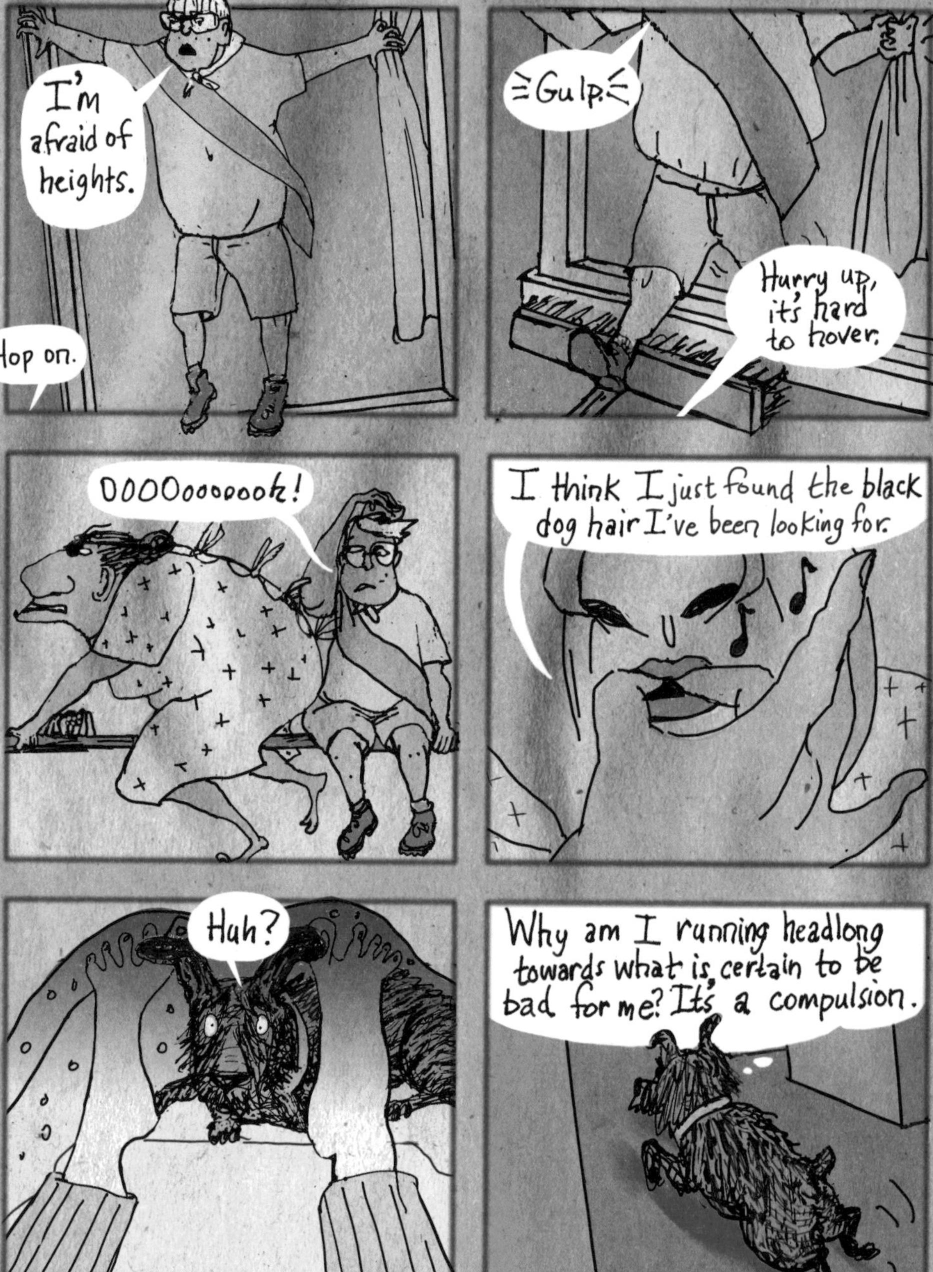

I'm afraid of heights.
Hop on.
Gulp.
Hurry up, it's hard to hover.
OOOOoooooooh!
I think I just found the black dog hair I've been looking for.
Huh?
Why am I running headlong towards what is certain to be bad for me? It's a compulsion.

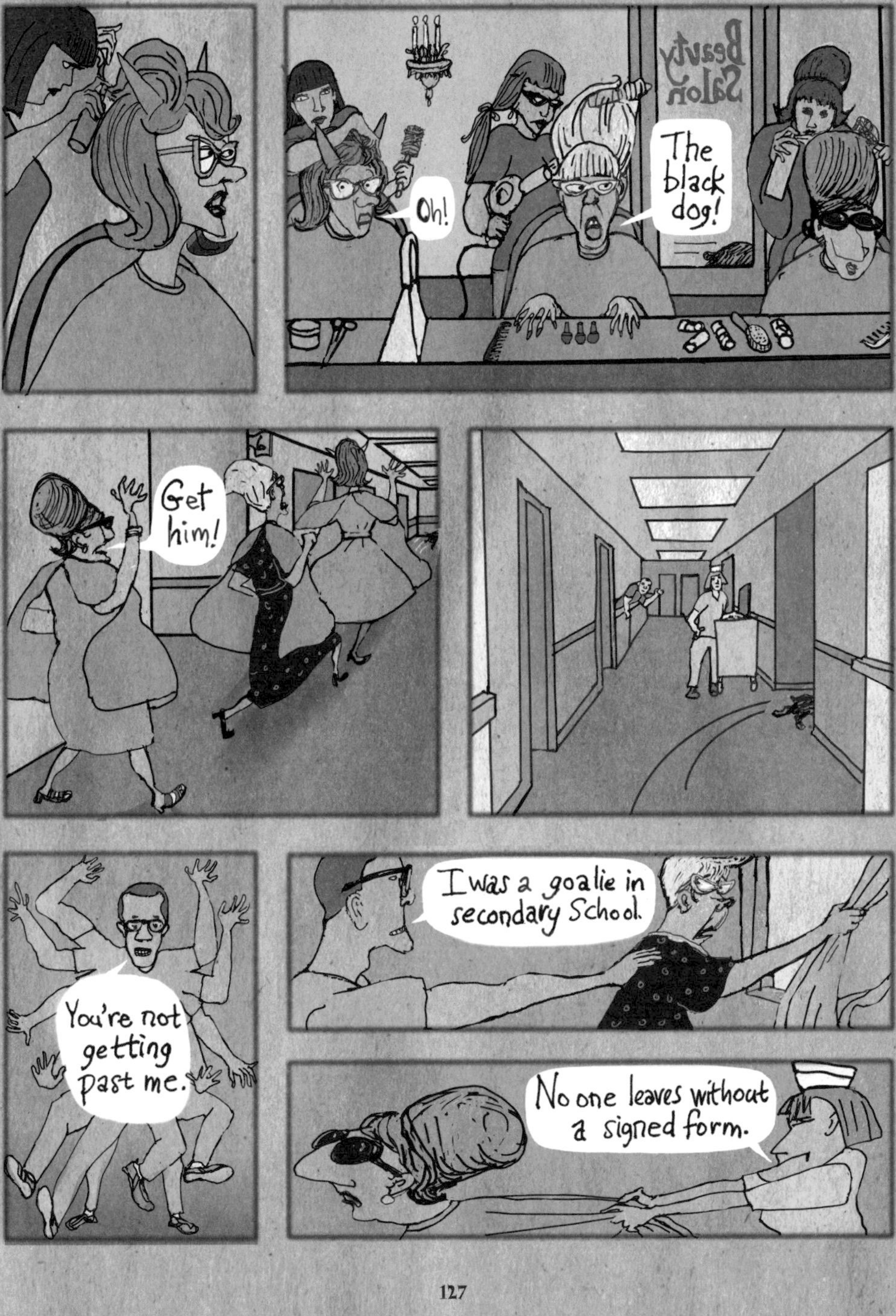
Beauty Salon
Oh!
The black dog!
Get him!
You're not getting past me.
I was a goalie in secondary School.
No one leaves without a signed form.

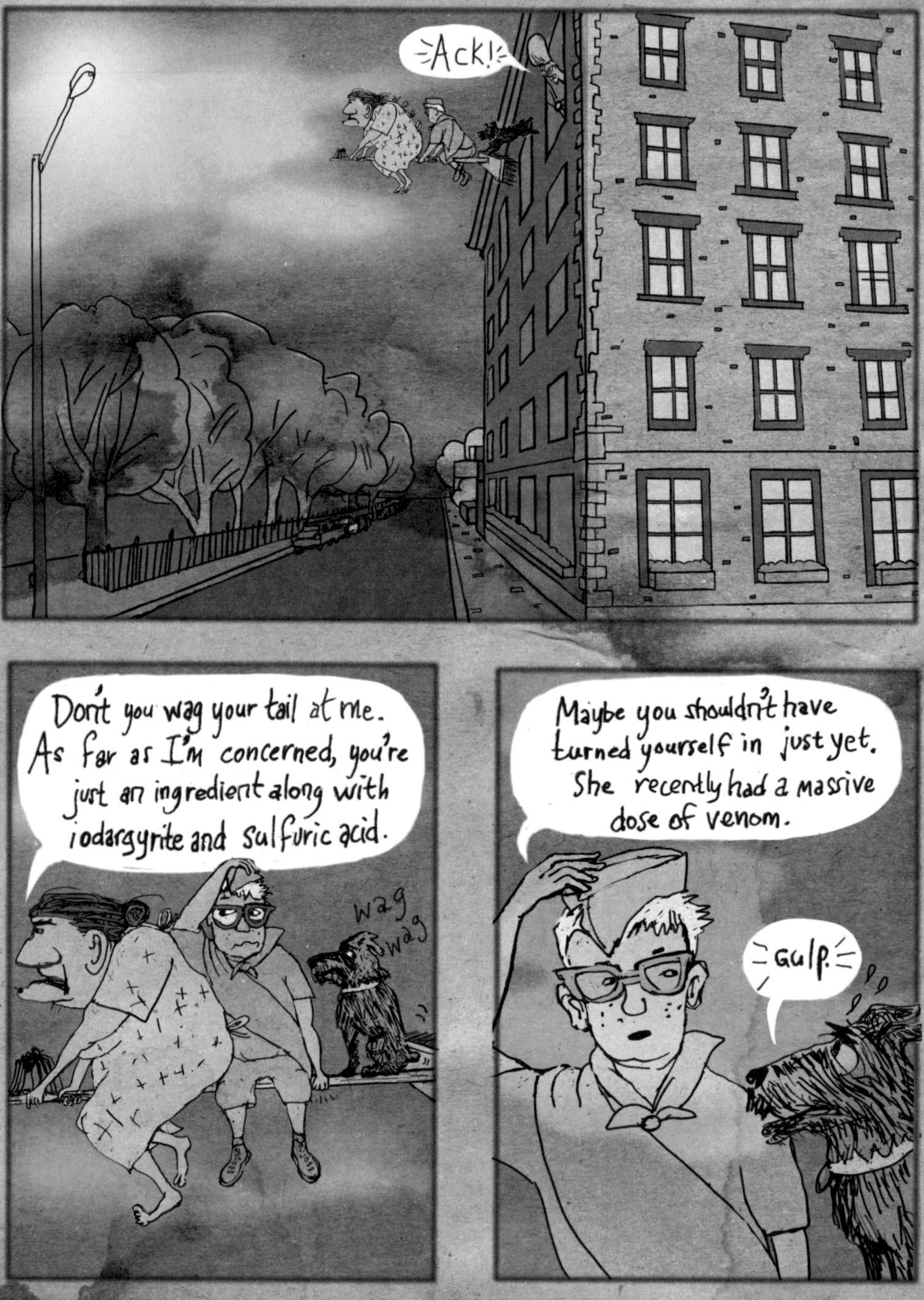
Ack!
Don't you wag your tail at me. As far as I'm concerned, you're just an ingredient along with iodargyrite and sulfuric acid.
wag wag
Maybe you shouldn't have turned yourself in just yet. She recently had a massive dose of venom.
Gulp.

11th

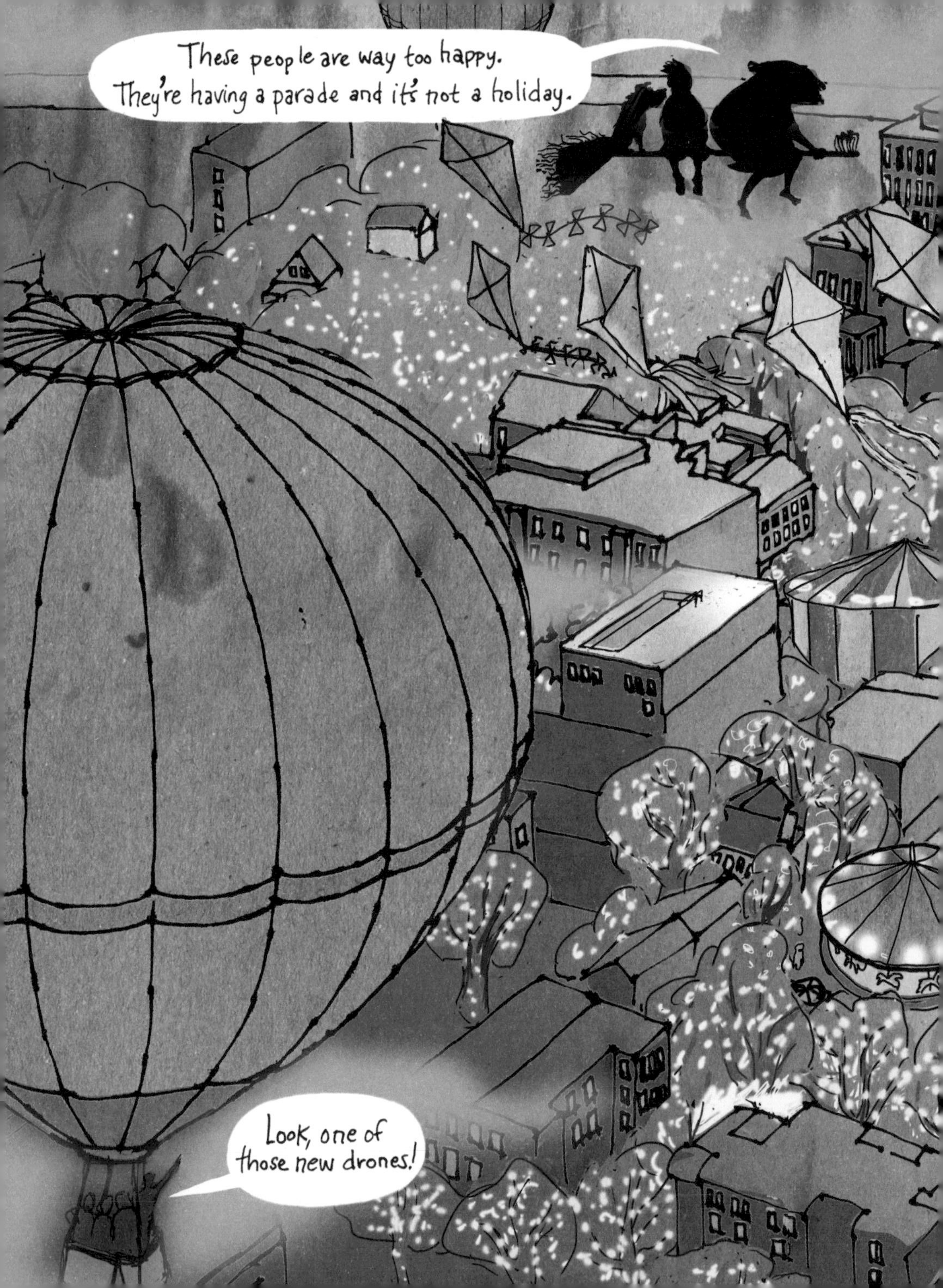
These people are way too happy. They're having a parade and it's not a holiday.
Look, one of those new drones!

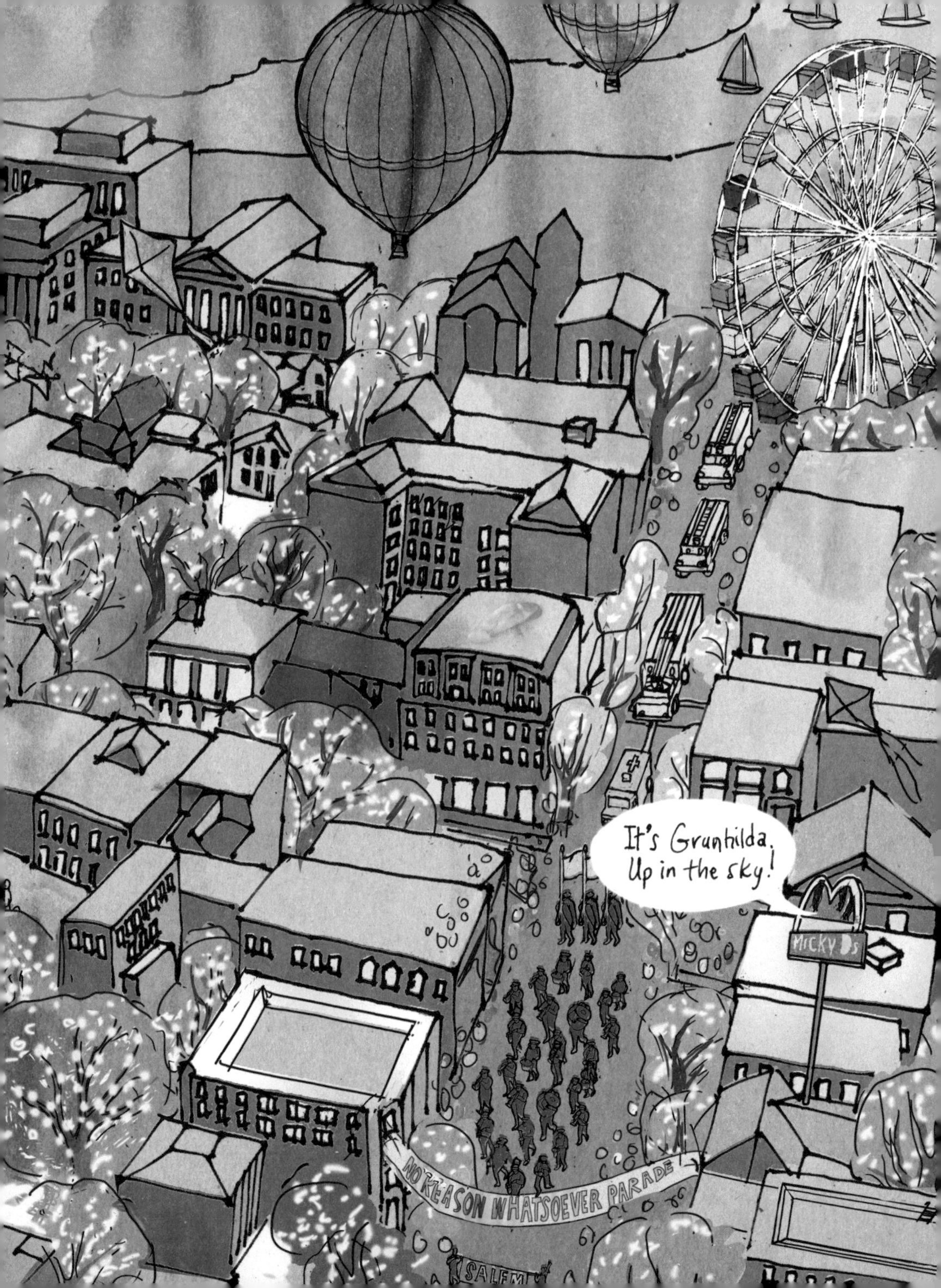
It's Grunhilda.
Up in the sky!
MICKY D's
NO REASON WHATSOEVER PARADE

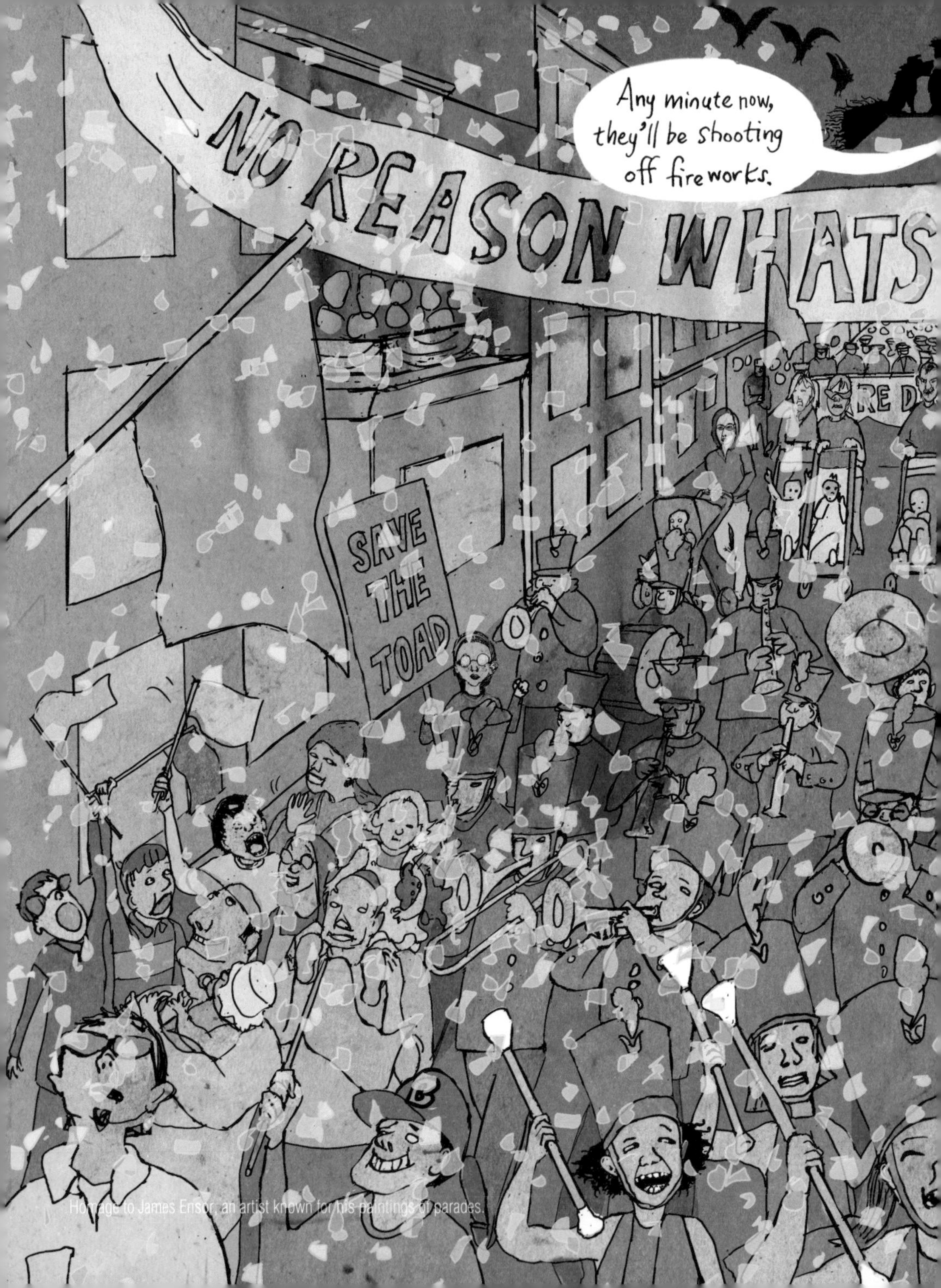
Any minute now, they'll be shooting off fireworks.
NO REASON WHATS
SAVE THE TOAD
Homage to James Ensor, an artist known for his paintings of parades.

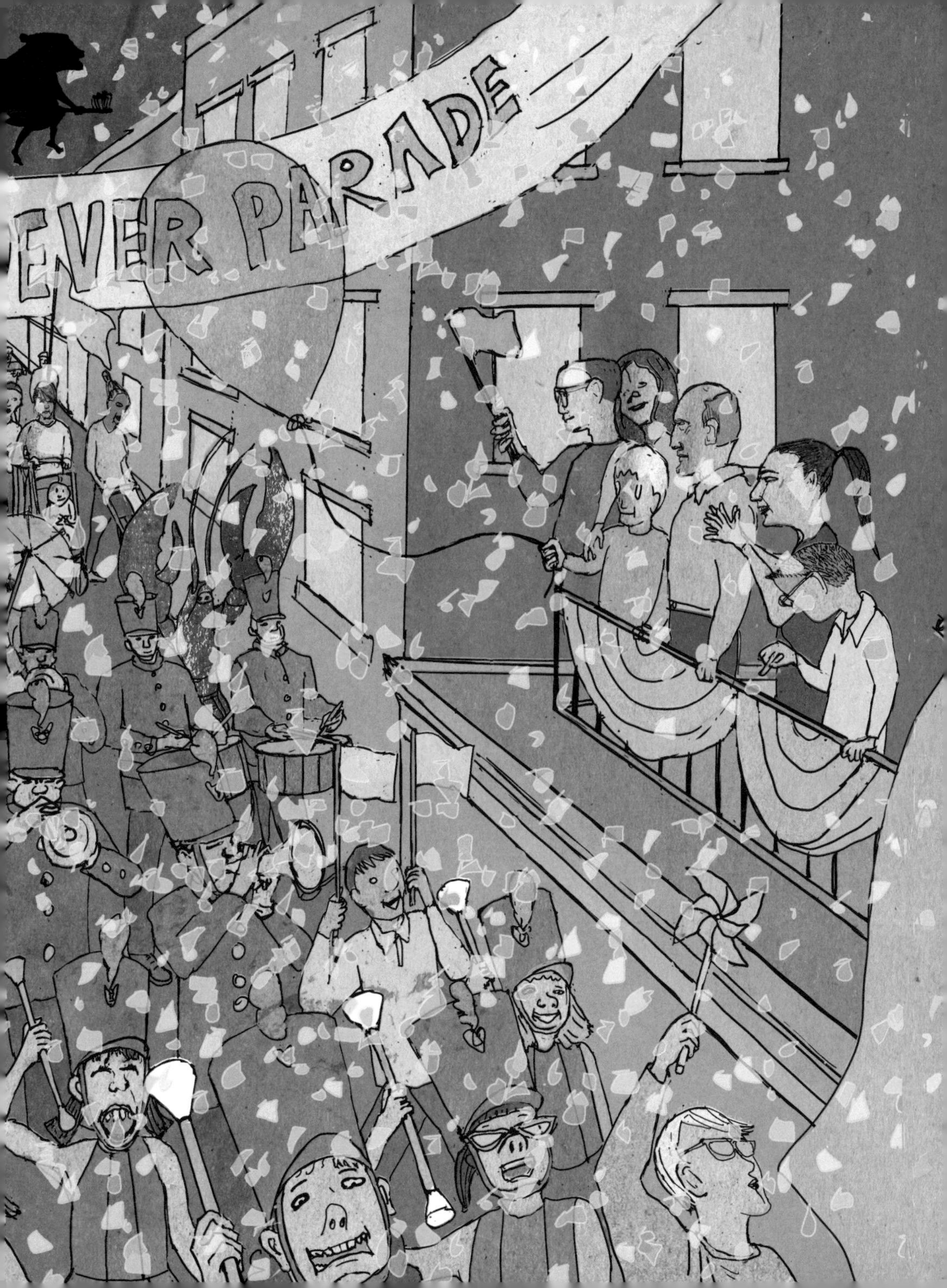
EVER PARADE

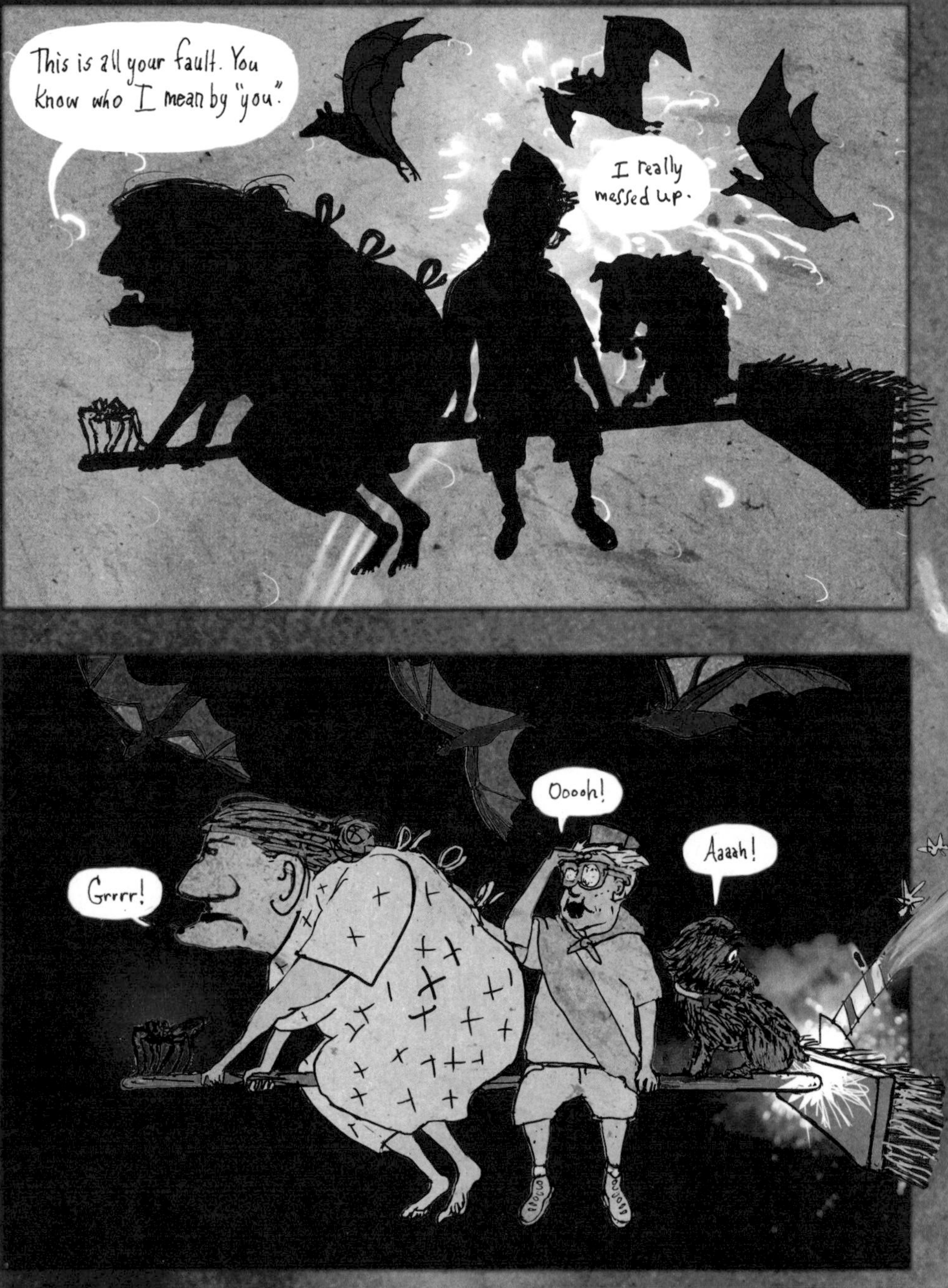

This is all your fault. You know who I mean by "you."
I really messed up.
Grrrr!
Ooooh!
Aaaah!

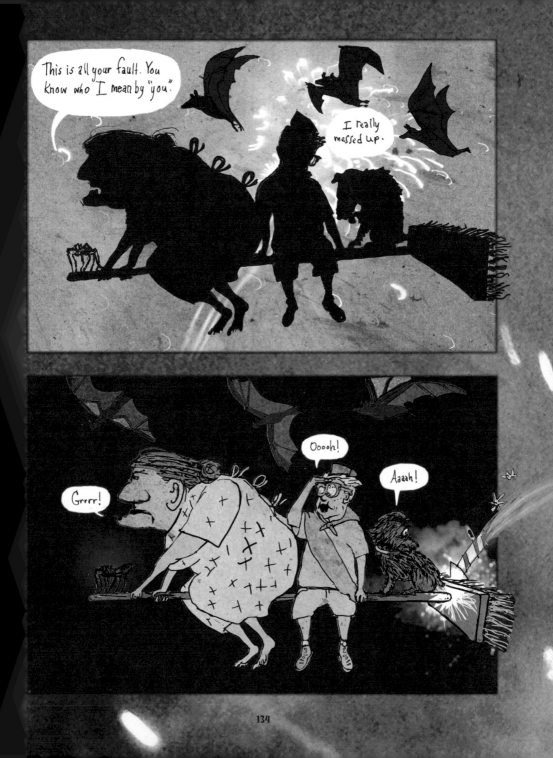

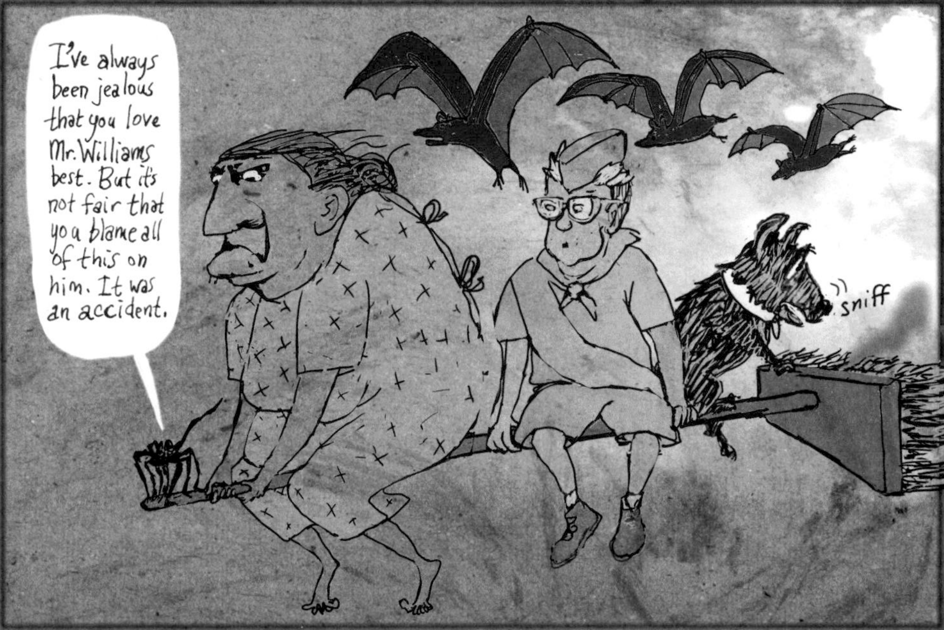
I've always been jealous that you love Mr. Williams best. But it's not fair that you blame all of this on him. It was an accident.
sniff

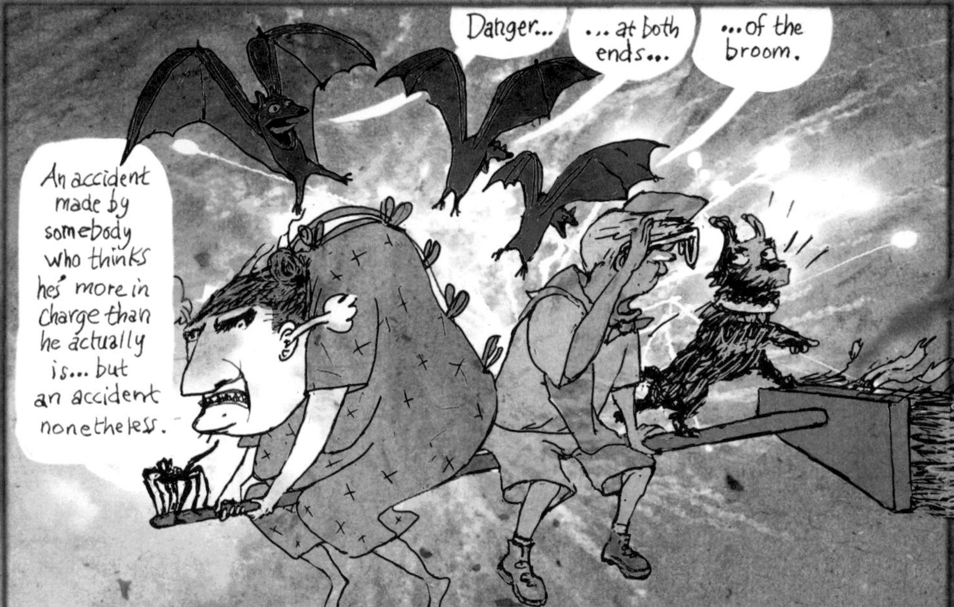
Danger...
... at both ends...
... of the broom.
An accident made by somebody who thinks he's more in charge than he actually is... but an accident nonetheless.

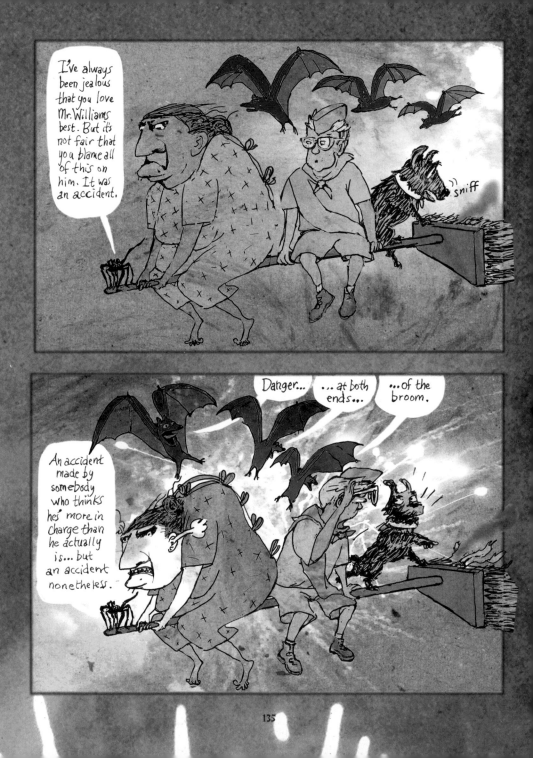

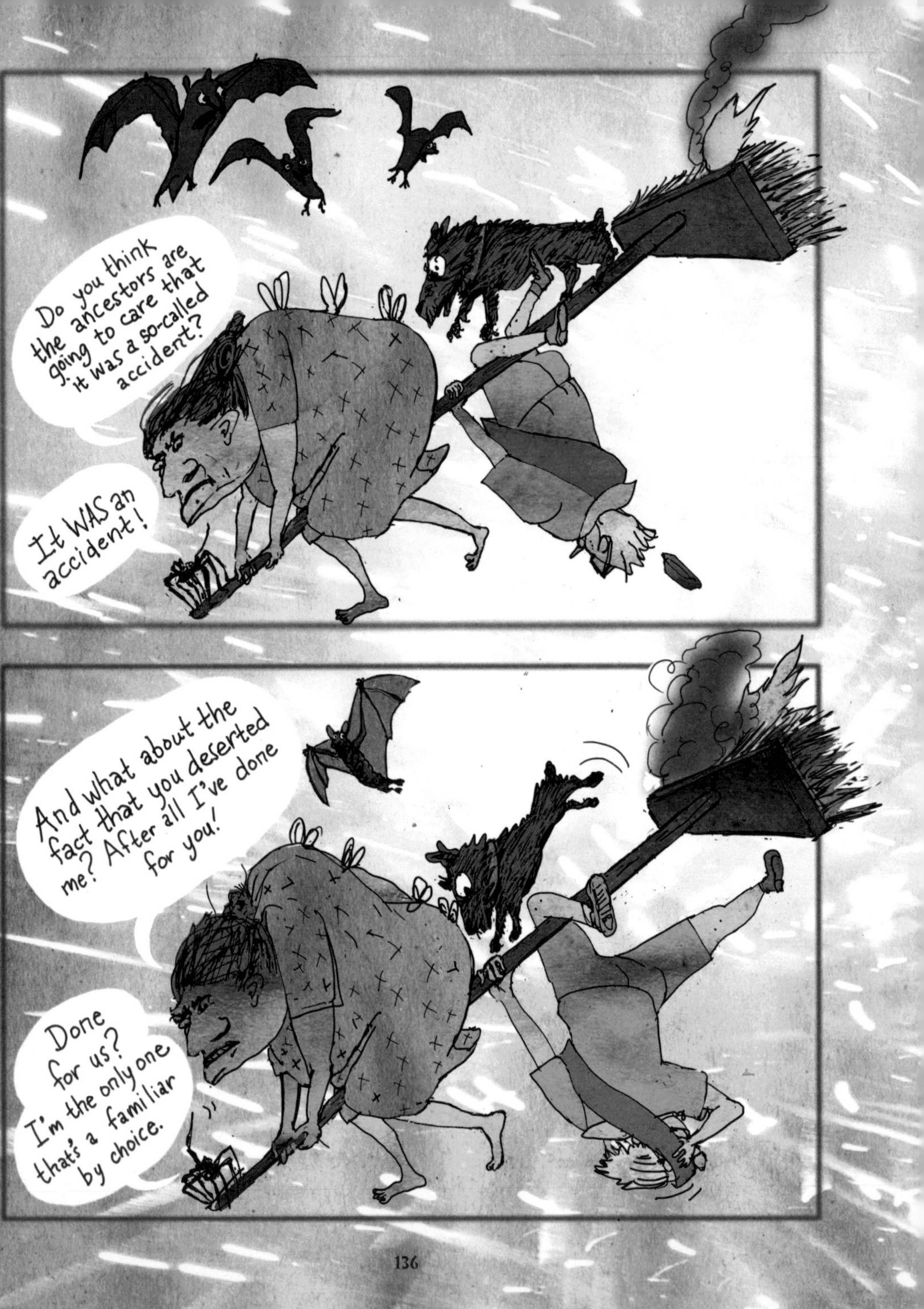
Do you think the ancestors are going to care that it was a so-called accident?
It WAS an accident!
And what about the fact that you deserted me? After all I've done for you!
Done for us? I'm the only one that's a familiar by choice.

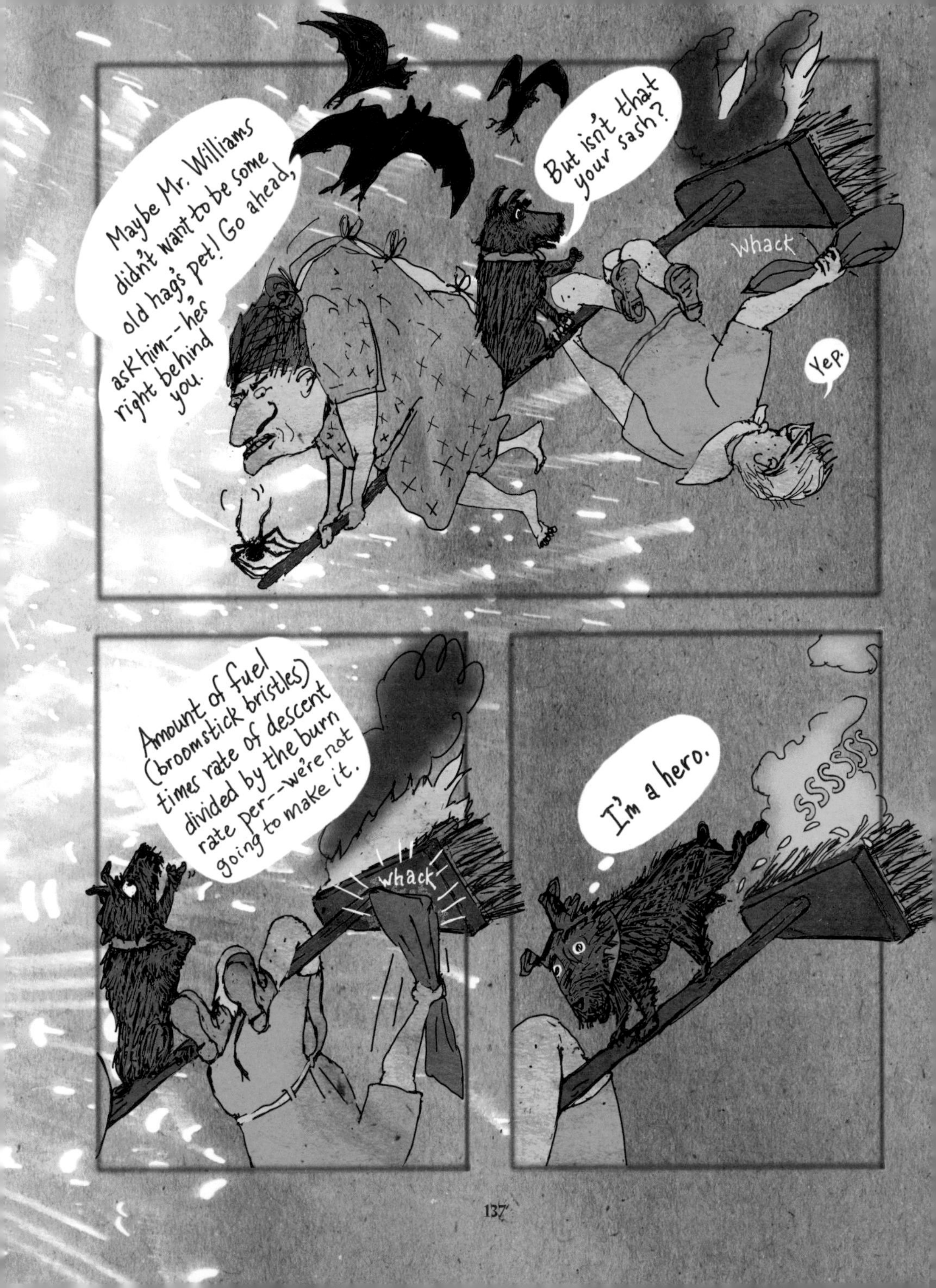
Maybe Mr. Williams didn't want to be some old hag's pet! Go ahead, ask him--he's right behind you.
But isn't that your sash?
Whack
Yep.
Amount of fuel (broomstick bristles) times rate of descent divided by the burn rate per--we're not going to make it.
whack
I'm a hero.
SSSSSS

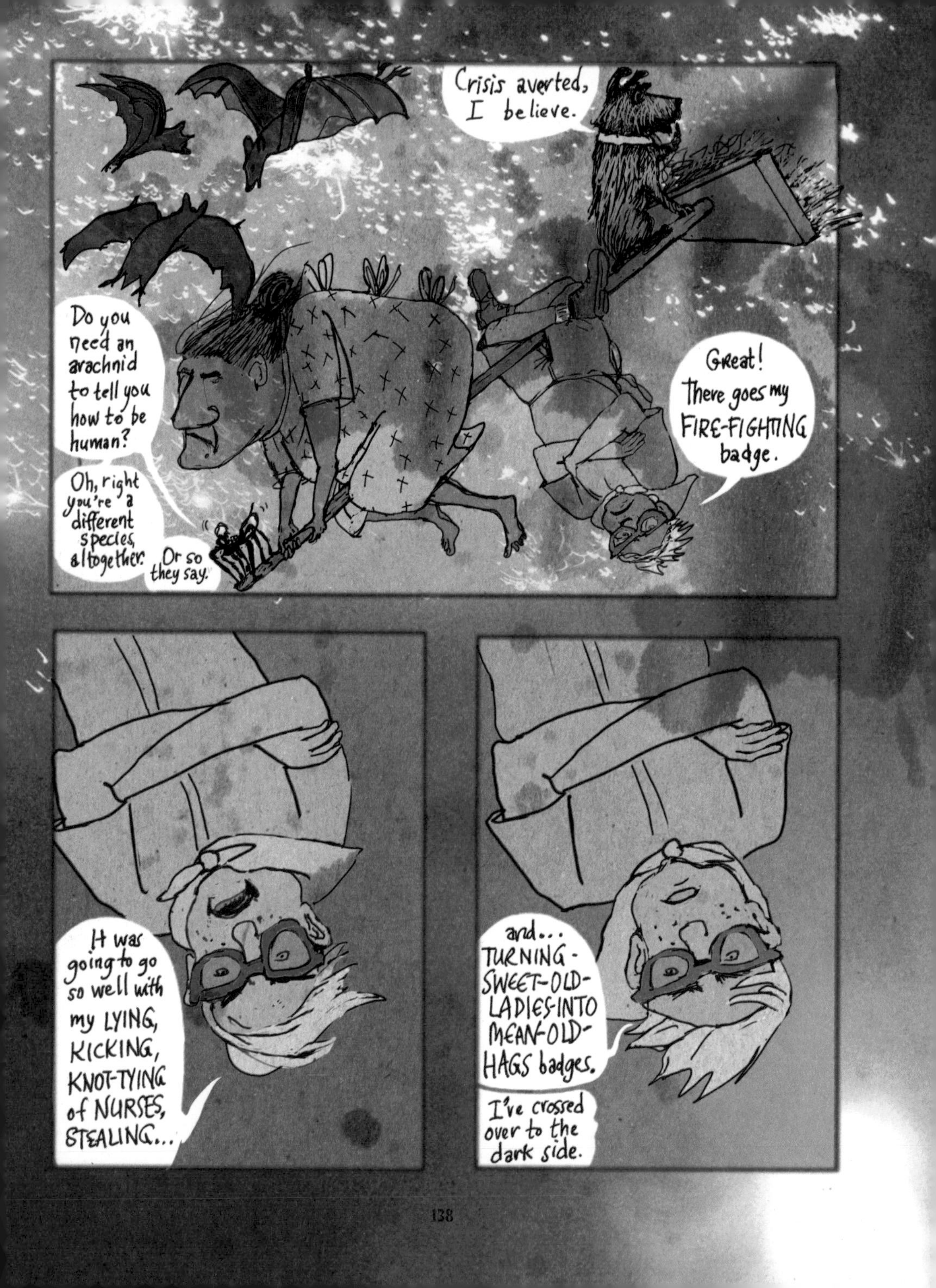
Crisis averted, I believe.
Do you need an arachnid to tell you how to be human?
Oh, right you're a different species, altogether.
Or so they say.
Great! There goes my FIRE-FIGHTING badge.
It was going to go so well with my LYING, KICKING, KNOT-TYING of NURSES, STEALING...
and... TURNING-SWEET-OLD-LADIES-INTO MEAN-OLD-HAGS badges.
I've crossed over to the dark side.

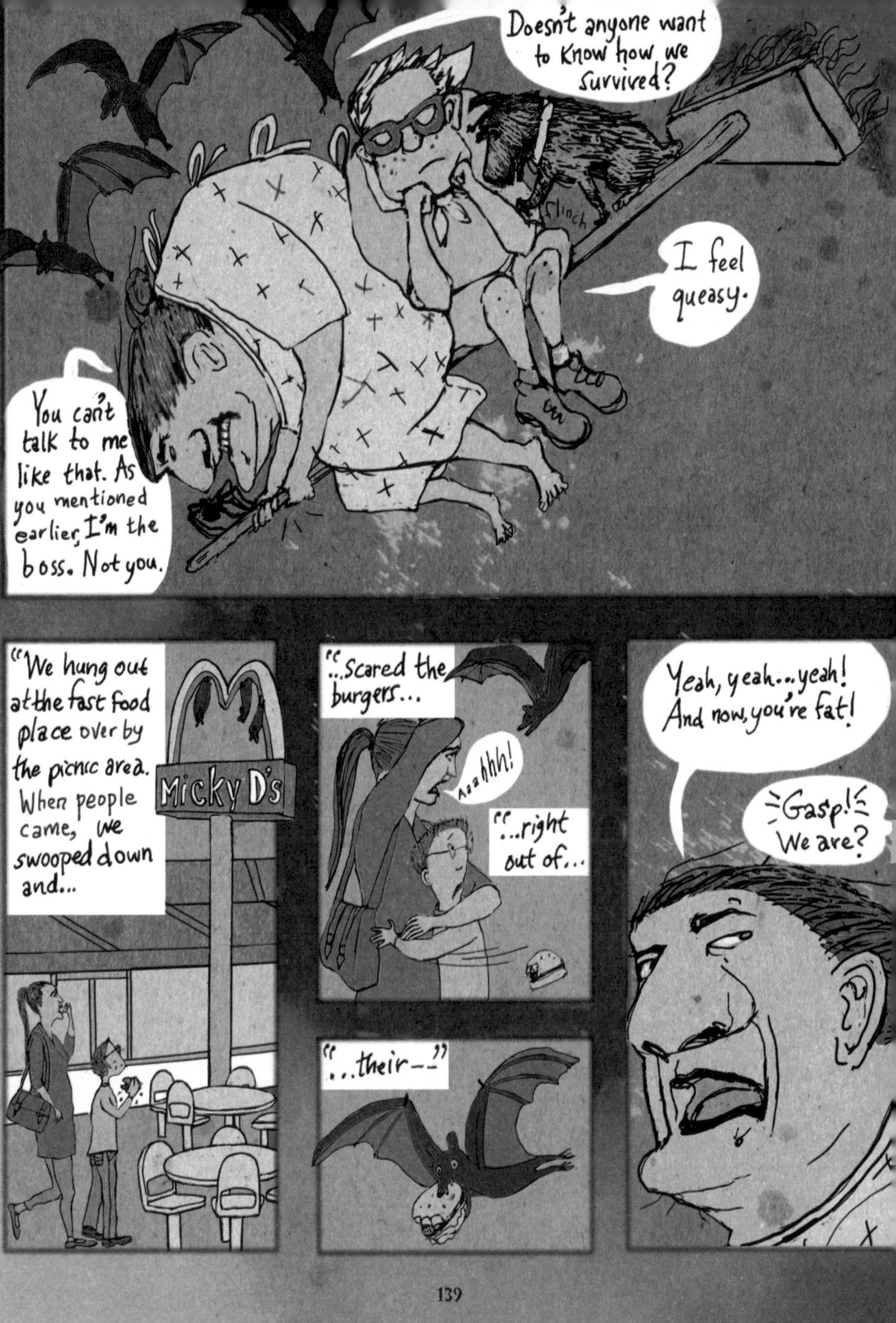

Doesn't anyone want to know how we survived?
flinch
I feel queasy.
You can't talk to me like that. As you mentioned earlier, I'm the boss. Not you.
"We hung out at the fast food place over by the picnic area. When people came, we swooped down and...
Micky D's
"...scared the burgers...
Aaahhh!
"...right out of...
"...their--"
Yeah, yeah...yeah! And now, you're fat!
Gasp! We are?

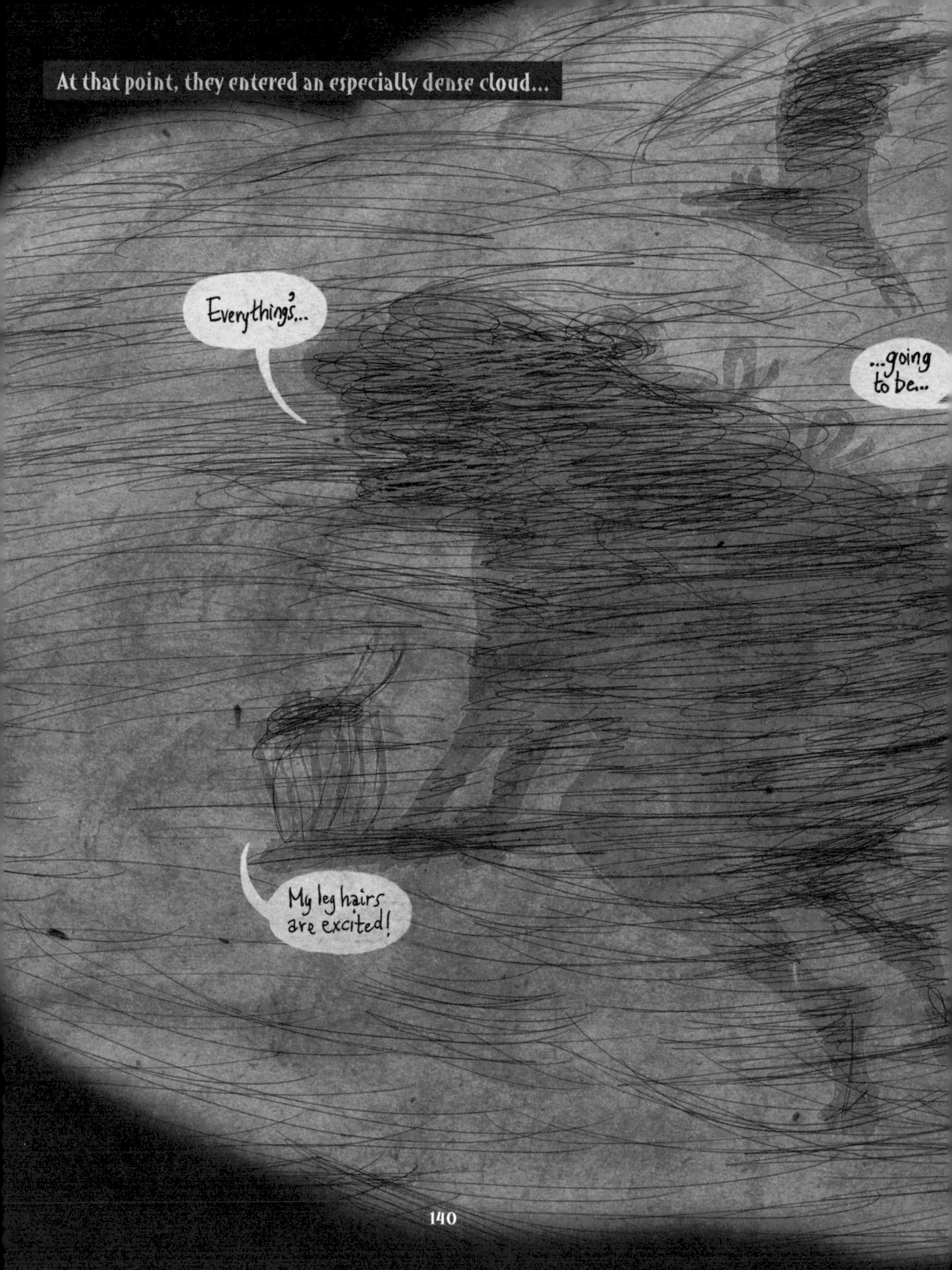
At that point, they entered an especially dense cloud...
Everything's...
...going to be...
My leg hairs are excited!

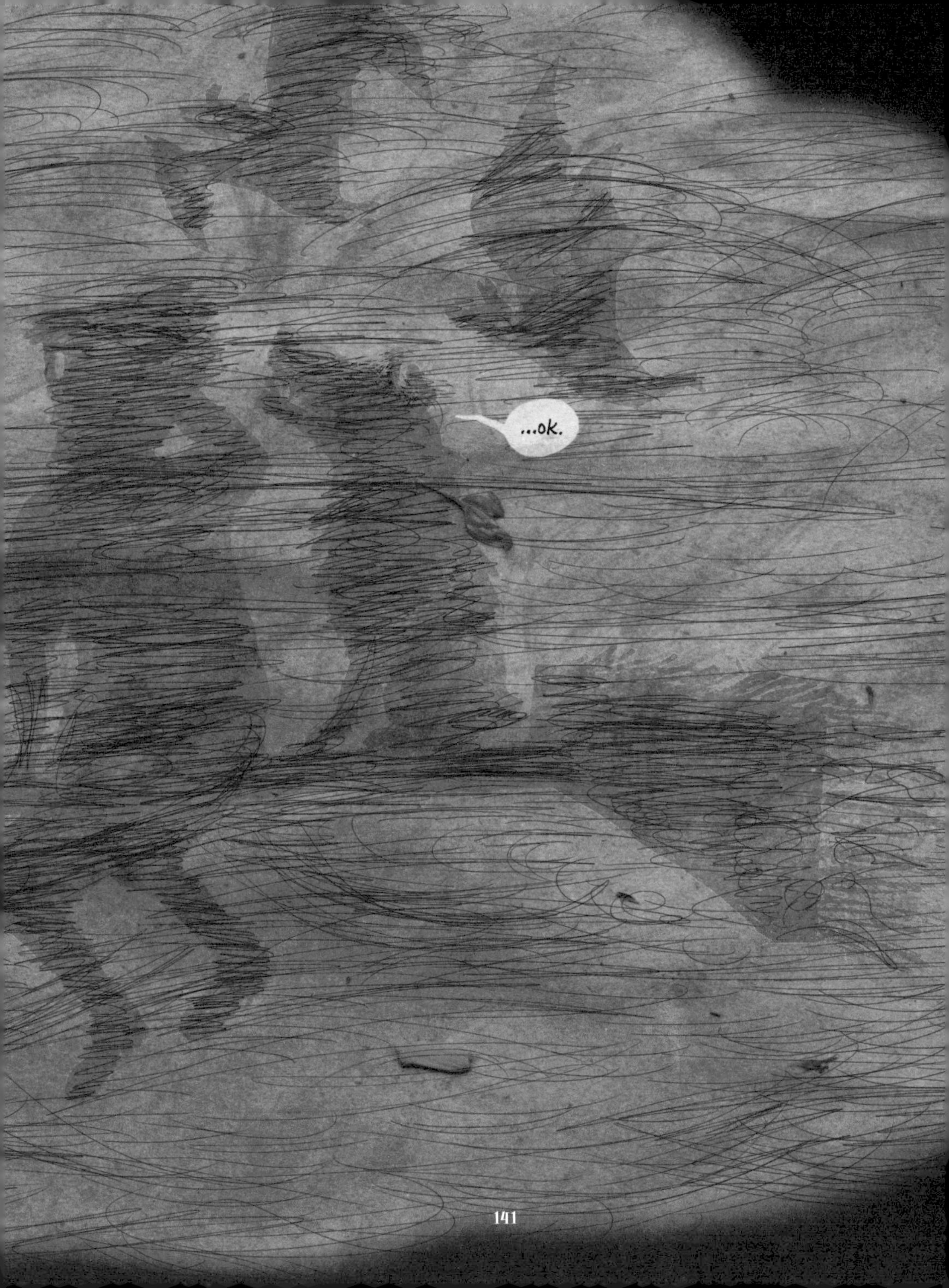
...ok.

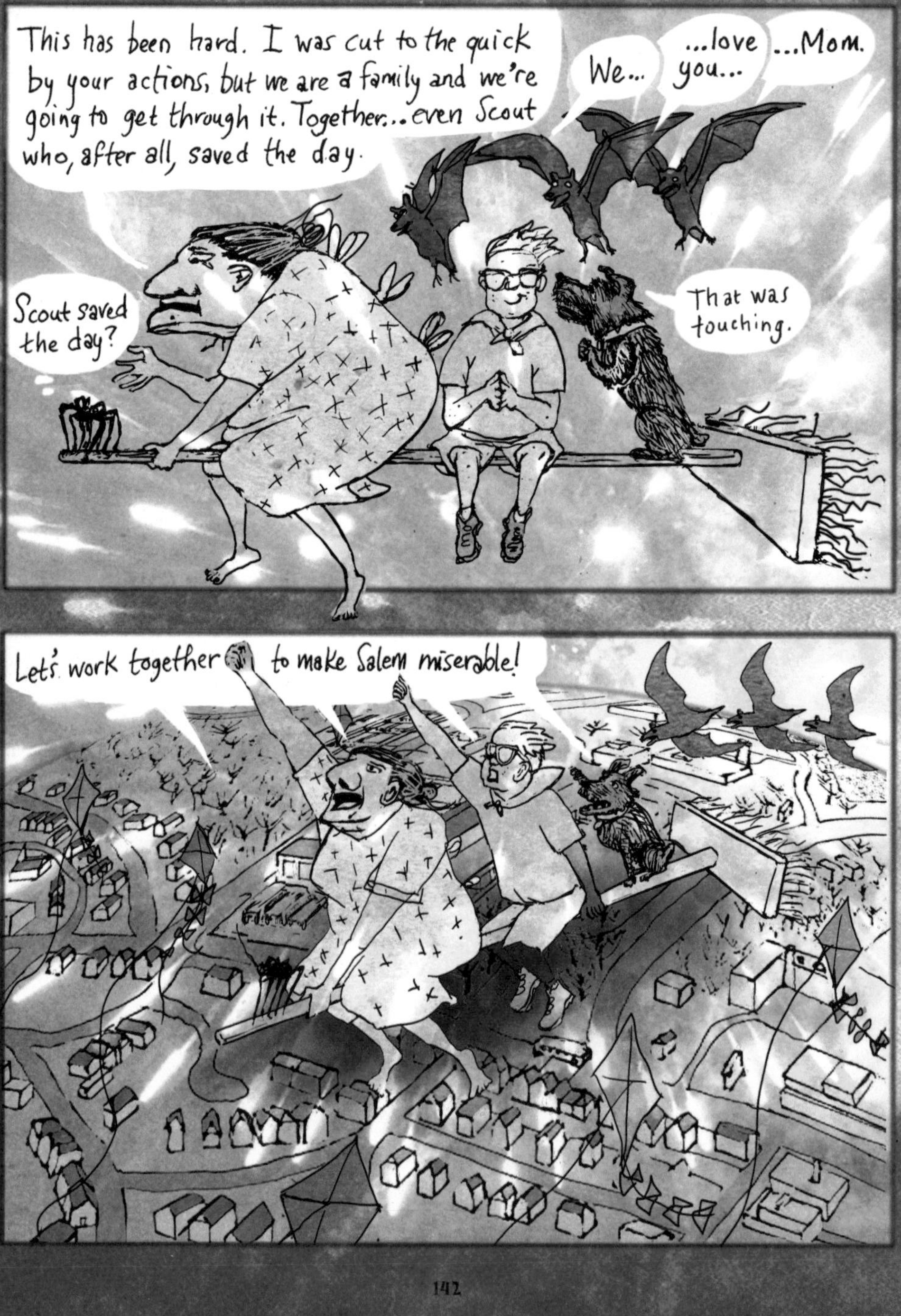
This has been hard. I was cut to the quick by your actions, but we are a family and we're going to get through it. Together...even Scout who, after all, saved the day.
We...
...love you...
...Mom.
Scout saved the day?
That was touching.
Let's work together to make Salem miserable!

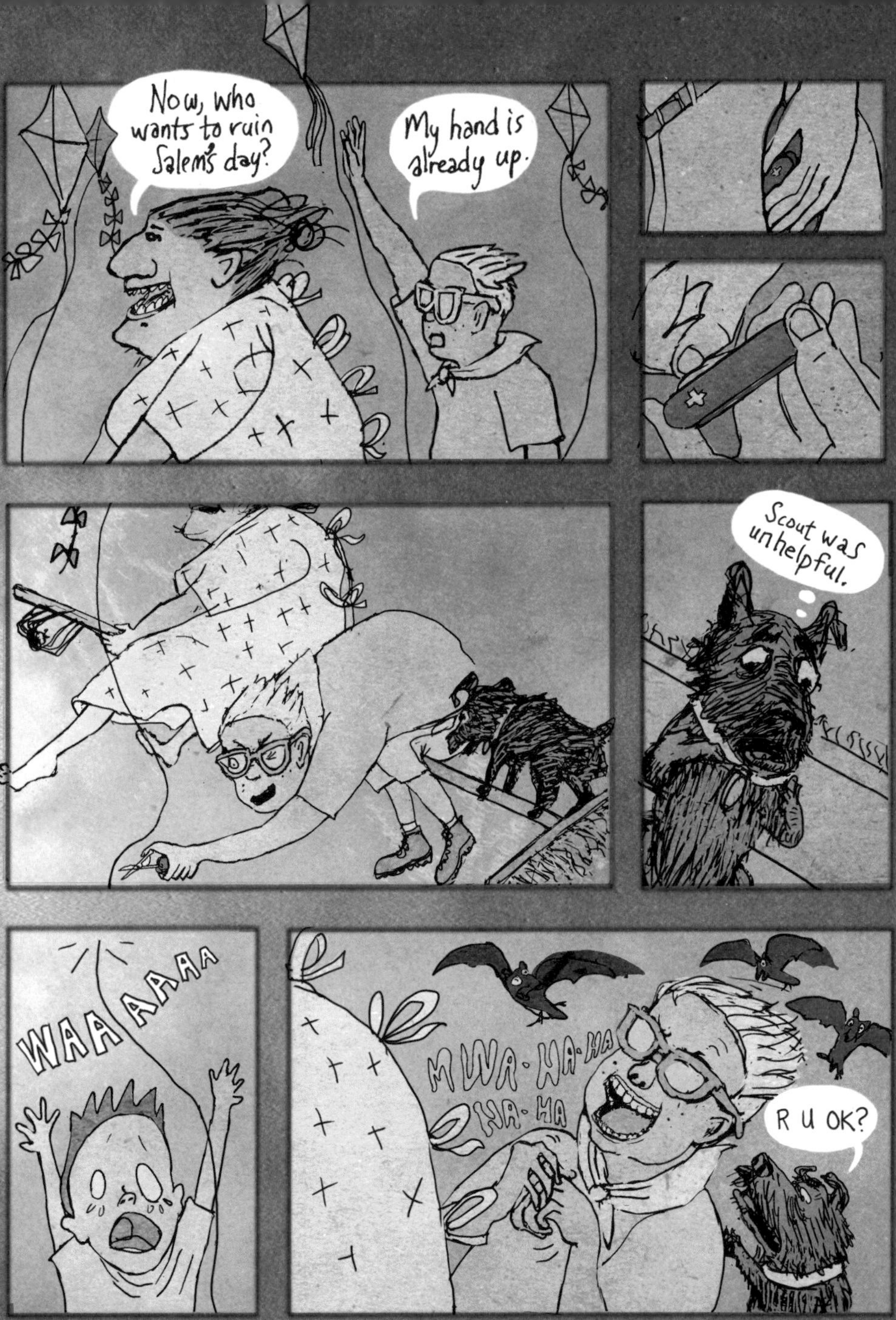
Now, who wants to ruin Salem's day?
My hand is already up.
Scout was unhelpful.
WAAAAAAA
MWA-HA-HA
HA-HA
R U OK?

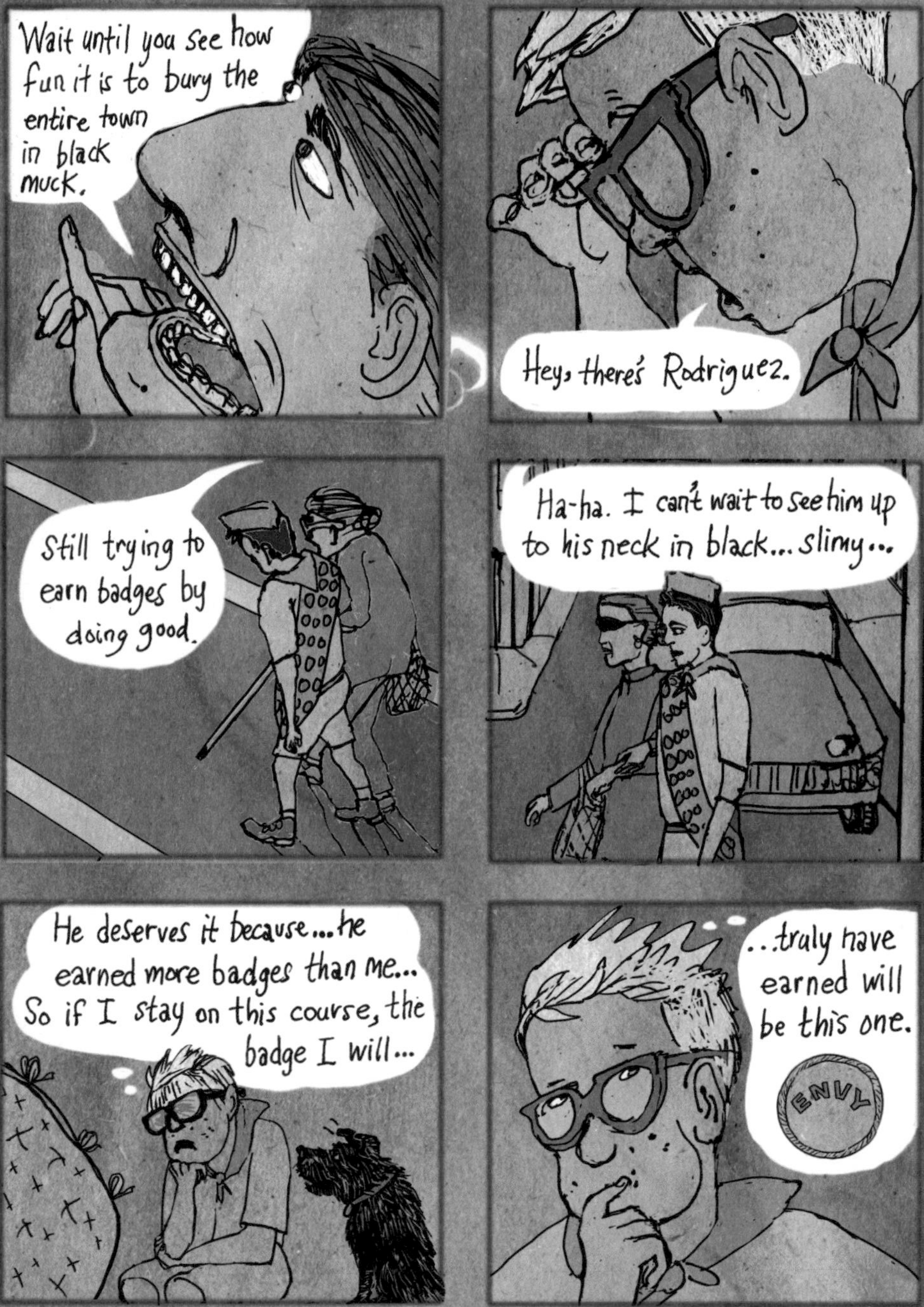
Wait until you see how fun it is to bury the entire town in black muck.
Hey, there's Rodriguez.
Still trying to earn badges by doing good.
Ha-ha. I can't wait to see him up to his neck in black... slimy...
He deserves it because... he earned more badges than me... So if I stay on this course, the badge I will...
...truly have earned will be this one.
ENVY

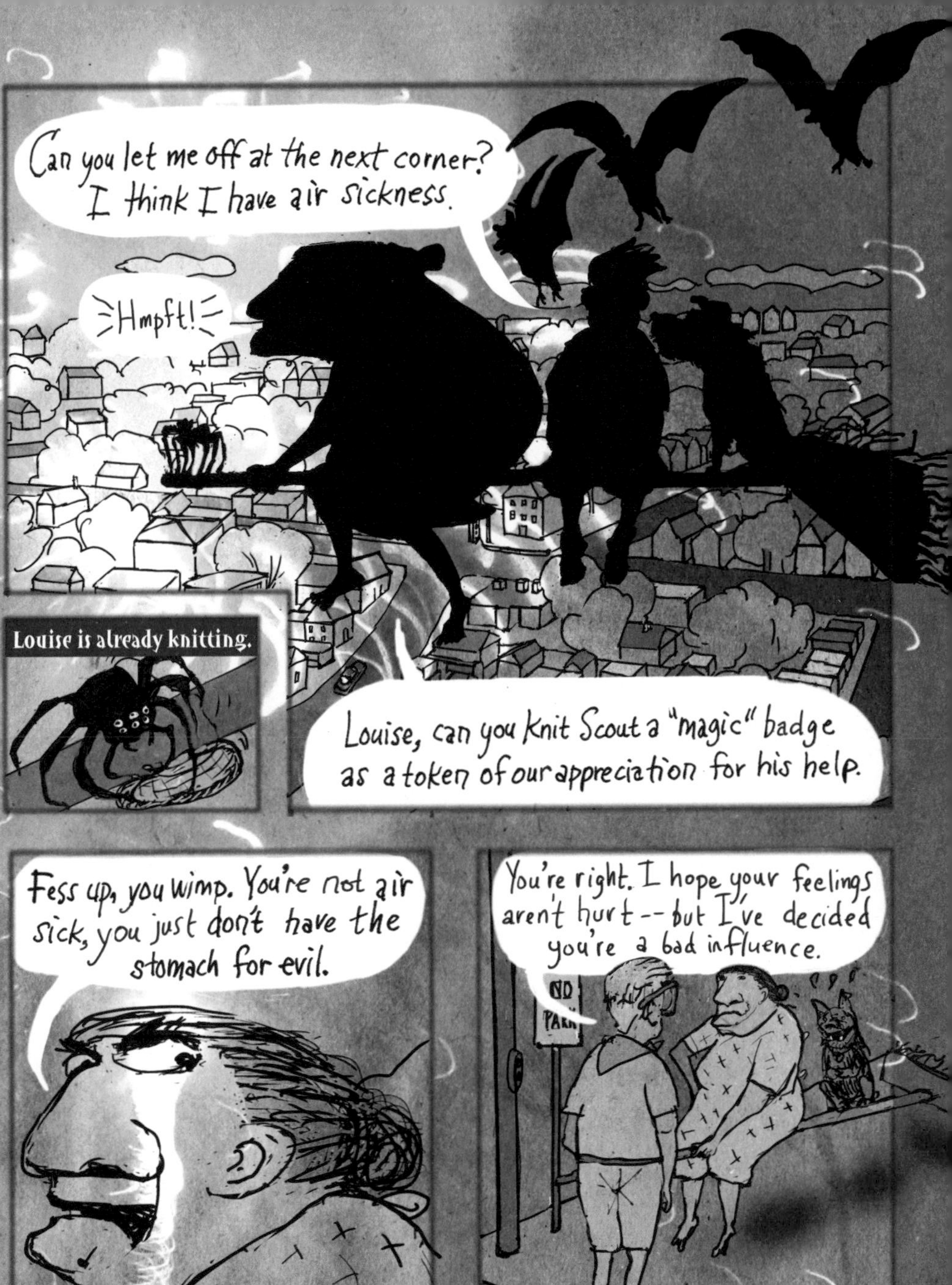

Can you let me off at the next corner? I think I have air sickness.
Hmpft!
Louise is already knitting.
Louise, can you knit Scout a "magic" badge as a token of our appreciation for his help.
Fess up, you wimp. You're not air sick, you just don't have the stomach for evil.
You're right. I hope your feelings aren't hurt -- but I've decided you're a bad influence.
NO PARK

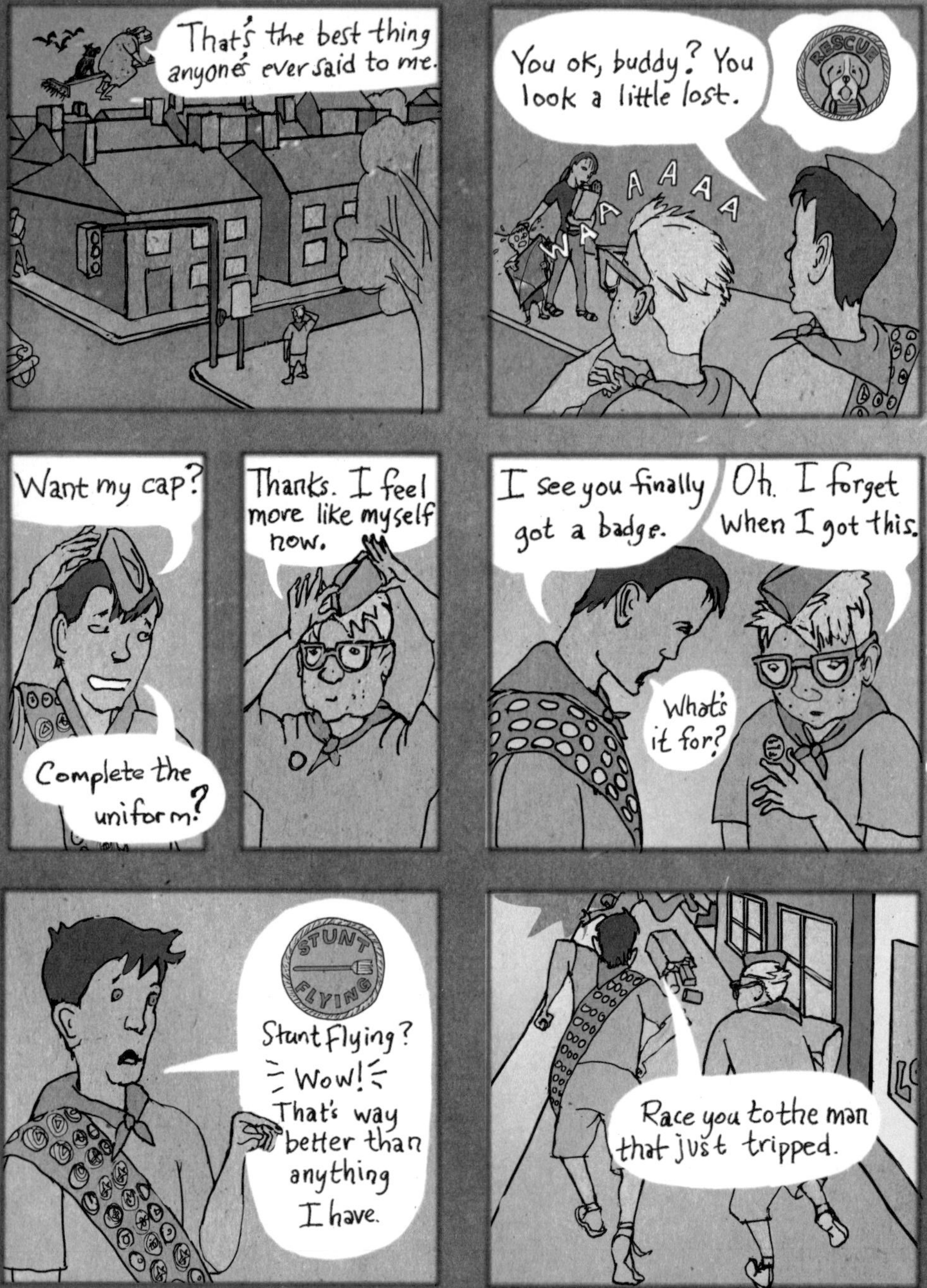
That's the best thing anyone's ever said to me.
You ok, buddy? You look a little lost.
RESCUE
WAAAAAAA
Want my cap?
Complete the uniform?
Thanks. I feel more like myself now.
I see you finally got a badge.
Oh. I forget when I got this.
What's it for?
STUNT FLYING
Stunt Flying? Wow! That's way better than anything I have.
Race you to the man that just tripped.

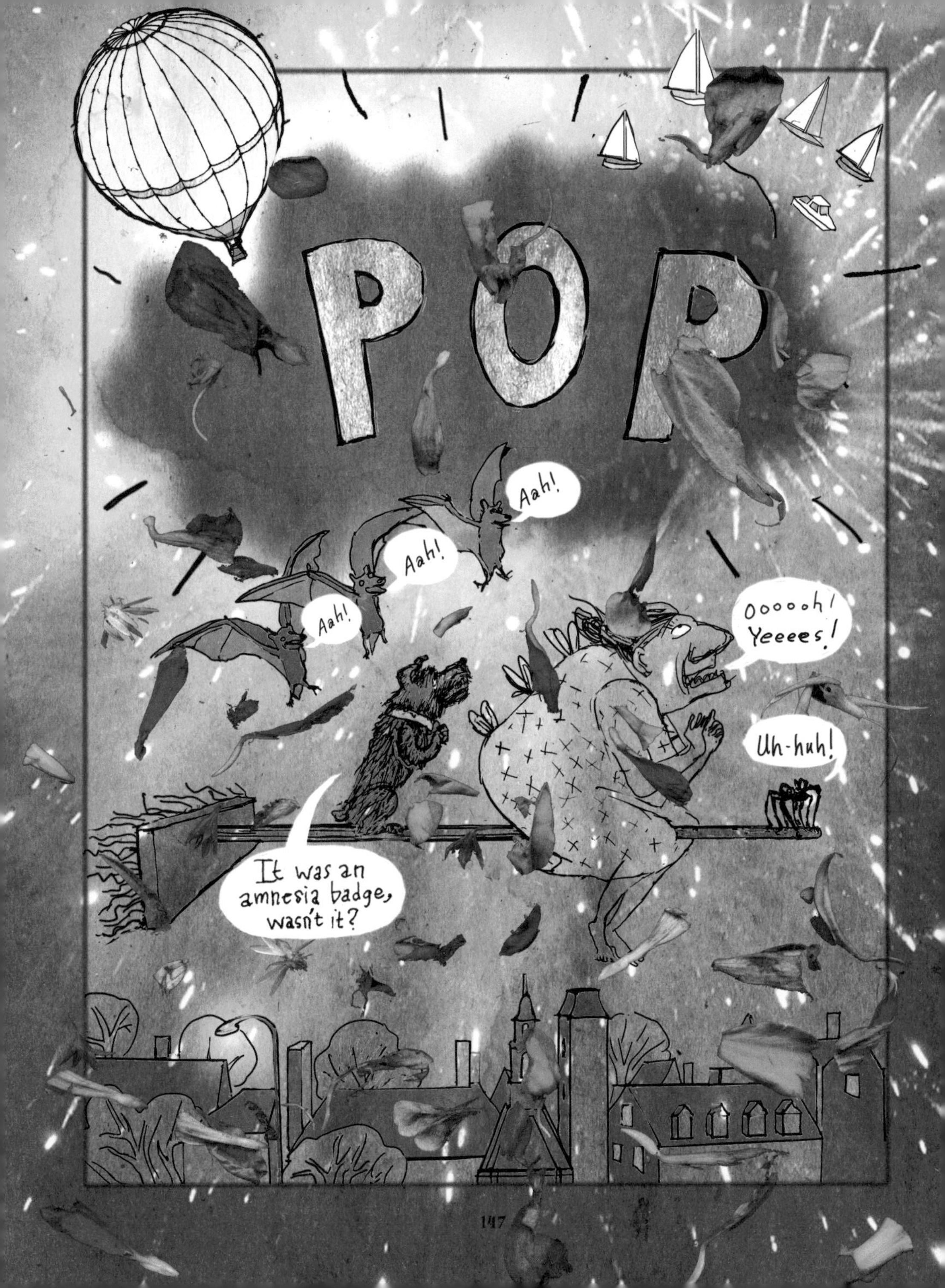
POP
Aah!
Aah!
Aah!
Oooooh! Yeeees!
Uh-huh!
It was an amnesia badge, wasn't it?

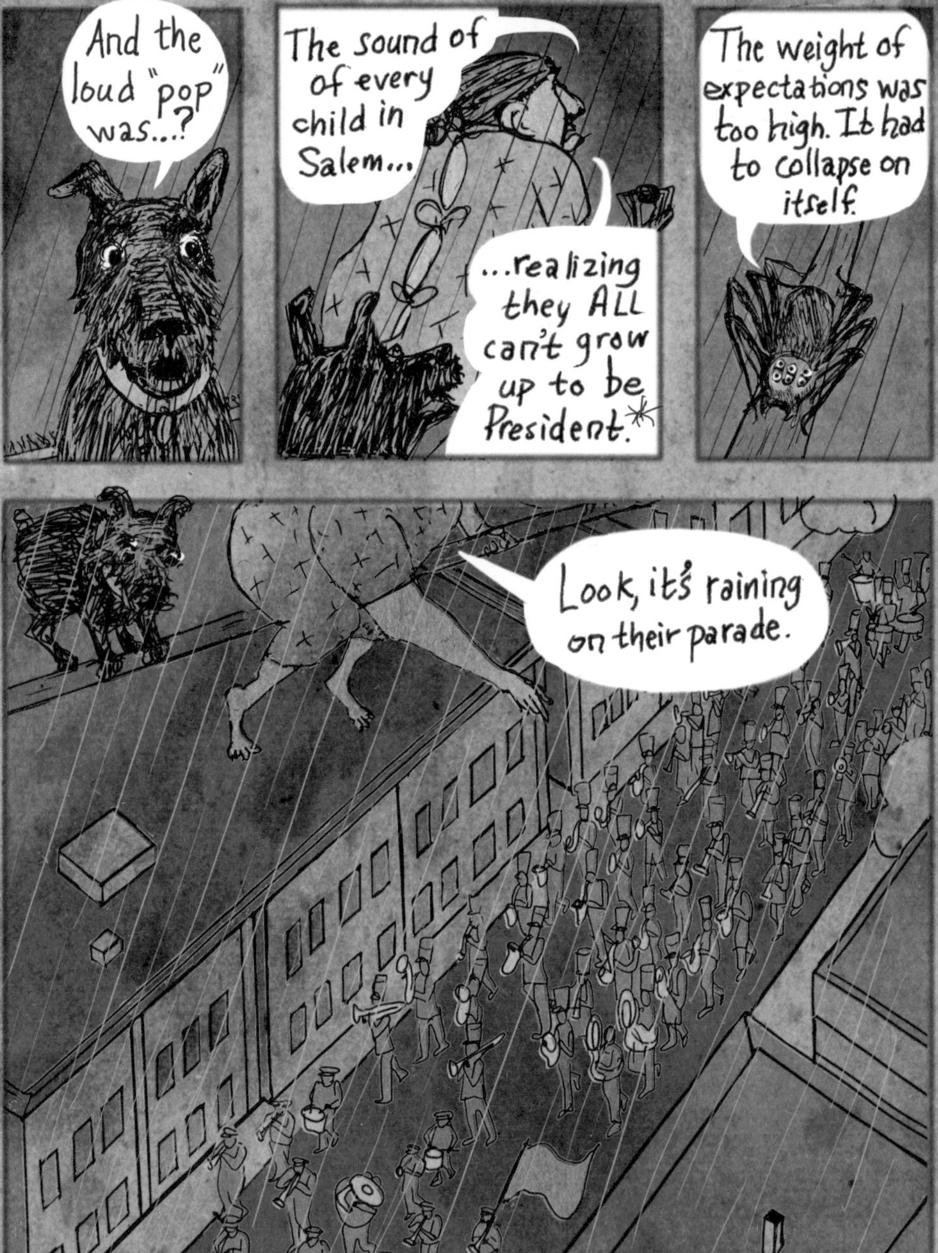
And the loud "pop" was...?
The sound of of every child in Salem...
...realizing they ALL can't grow up to be President.*
The weight of expectations was too high. It had to collapse on itself.
Look, it's raining on their parade.

*At the very least, they'd have to take turns.

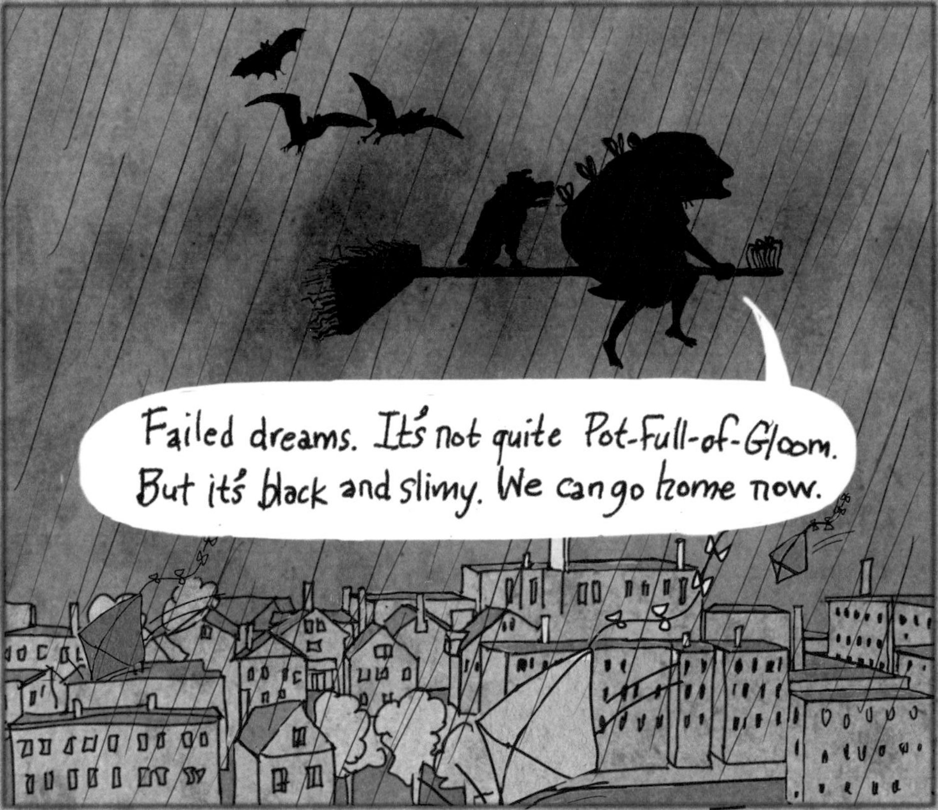
Failed dreams. It's not quite Pot-Full-of-Gloom. But it's black and slimy. We can go home now.

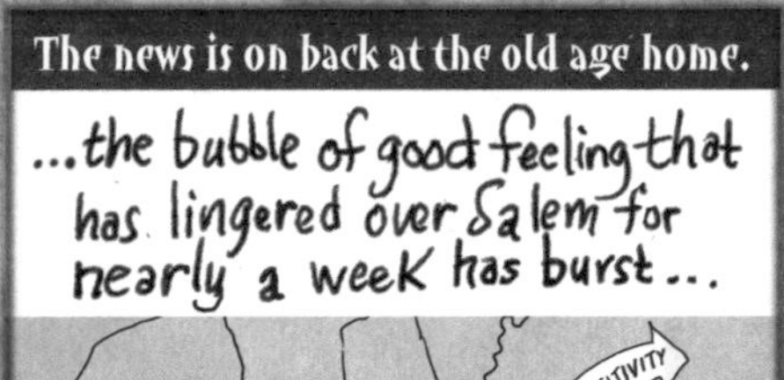
The news is on back at the old age home.
...the bubble of good feeling that has lingered over Salem for nearly a week has burst...
POSITIVITY
POSITIVITY
NEGATIVITY
NEGATIVITY
HALF-FULL
HALF-EMPTY

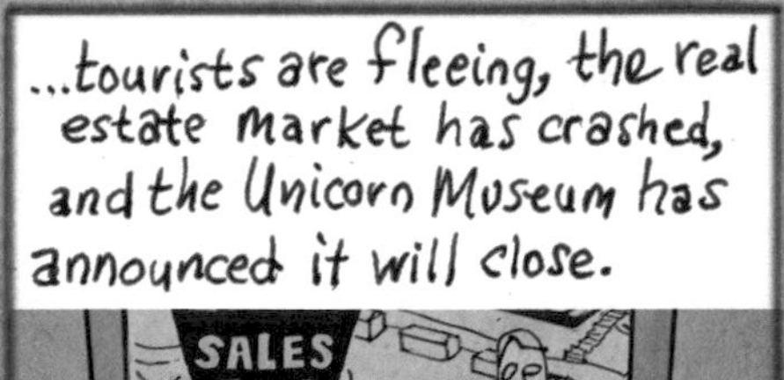
...tourists are fleeing, the real estate market has crashed, and the Unicorn Museum has announced it will close.
SALES FALL

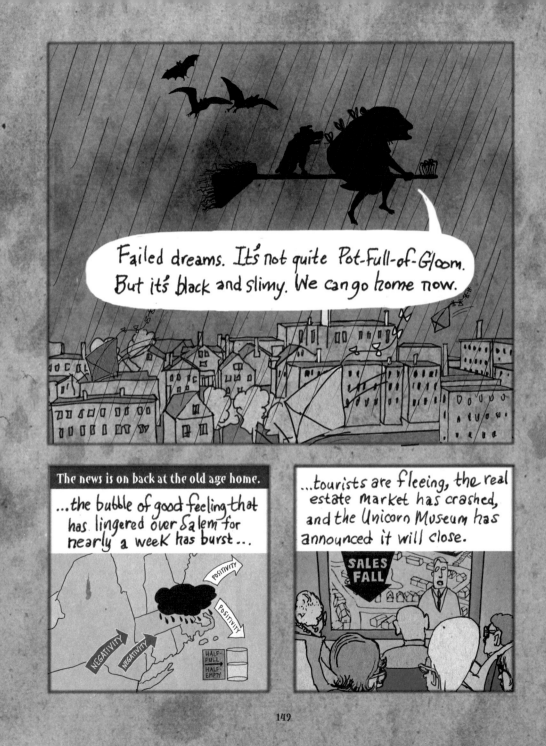

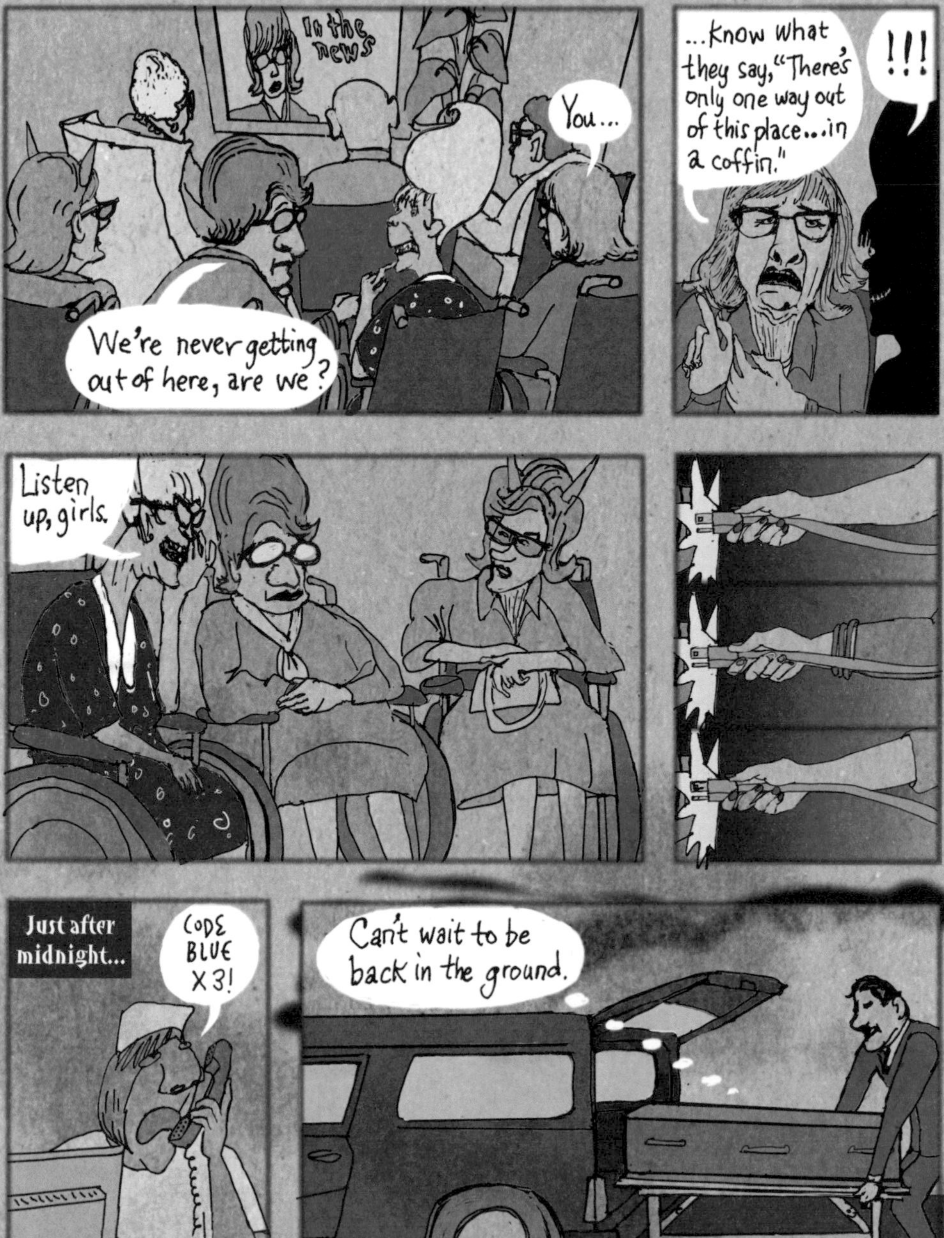
In the news
You...
We're never getting out of here, are we?
...know what they say, "There's only one way out of this place...in a coffin."
!!!
Listen up, girls.
Just after midnight...
CODE BLUE X 3!
Can't wait to be back in the ground.

12th

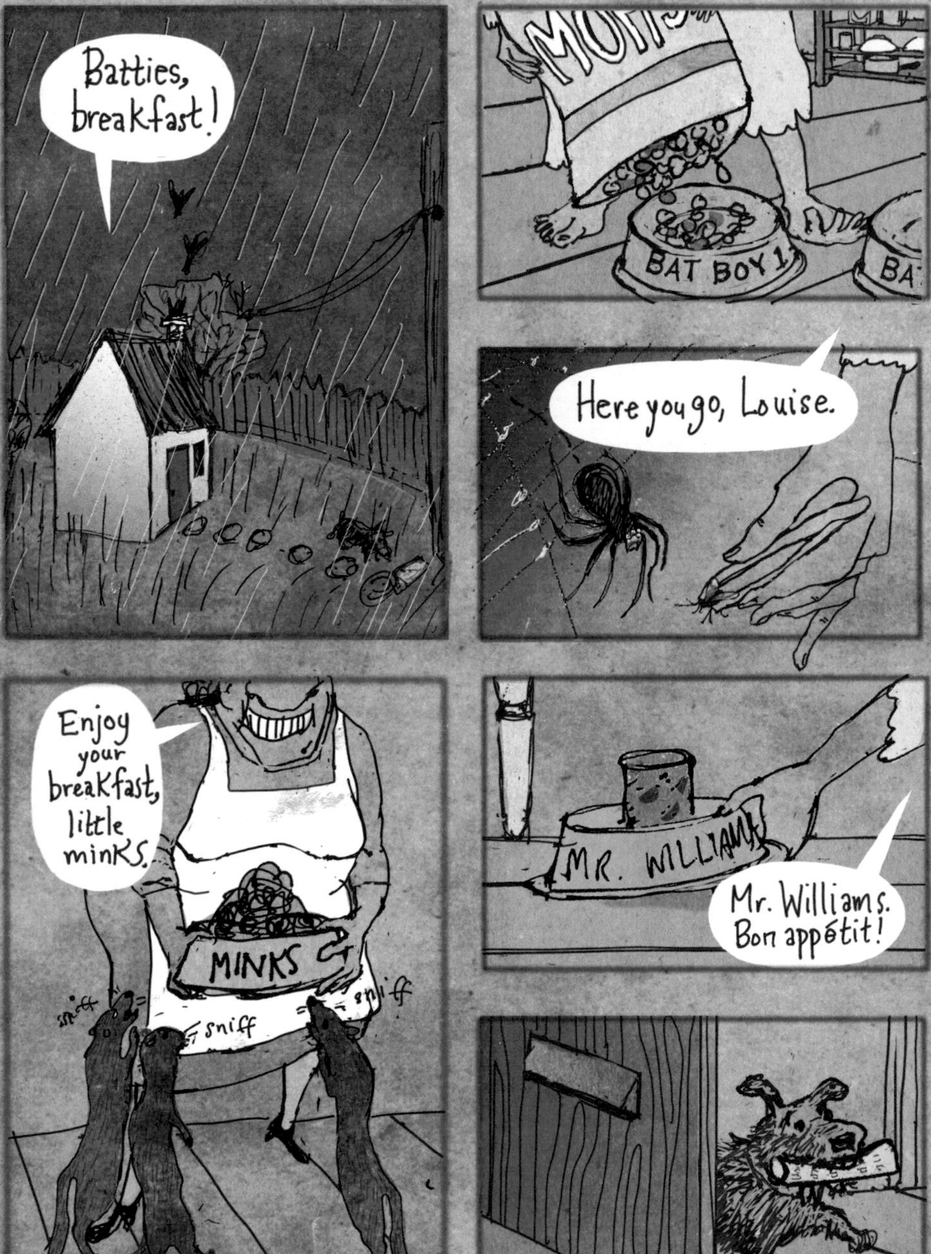
Batties, breakfast!
BAT BOY 1
Here you go, Louise.
Enjoy your breakfast, little minks.
MINKS
sniff
sniff
sniff
Mr. Williams. Bon appétit!

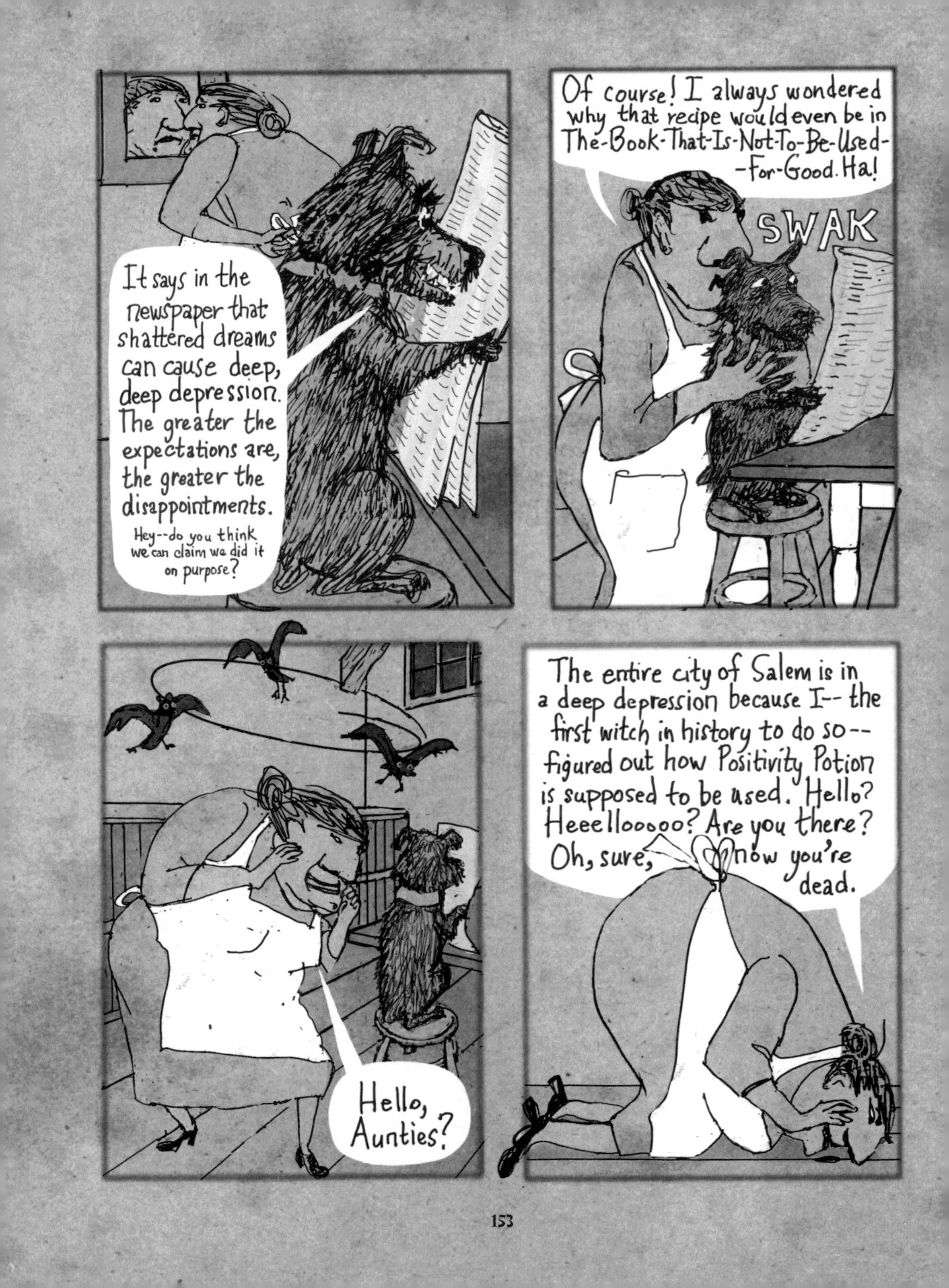
It says in the newspaper that shattered dreams can cause deep, deep depression. The greater the expectations are, the greater the disappointments.
Hey--do you think we can claim we did it on purpose?
Of course! I always wondered why that recipe would even be in The-Book-That-Is-Not-To-Be-Used--For-Good. Ha!
SWAK
Hello, Aunties?
The entire city of Salem is in a deep depression because I-- the first witch in history to do so-- figured out how Positivity Potion is supposed to be used. Hello? Heeellooooo? Are you there? Oh, sure, now you're dead.

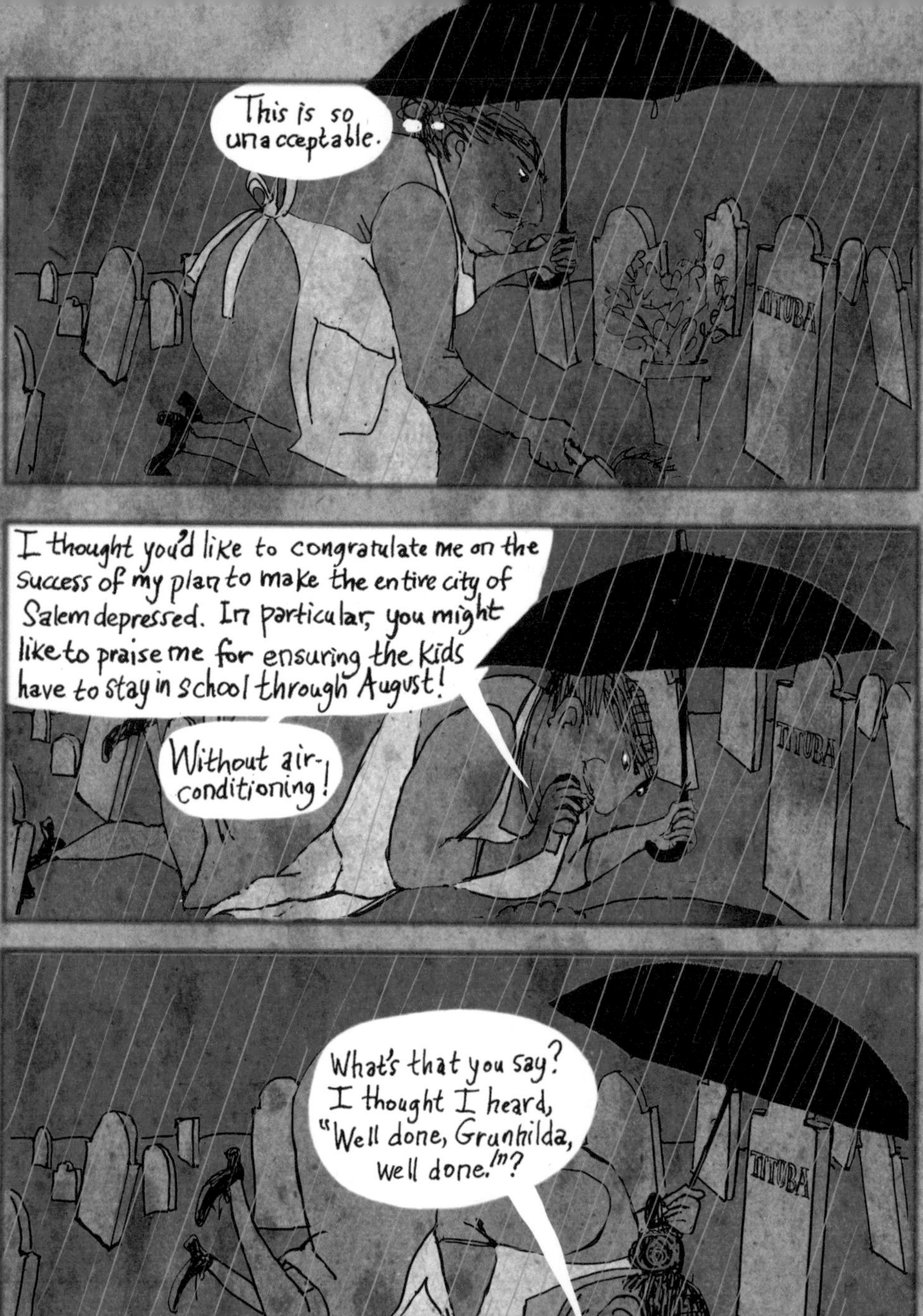
This is so unacceptable.
I thought you'd like to congratulate me on the success of my plan to make the entire city of Salem depressed. In particular, you might like to praise me for ensuring the kids have to stay in school through August!
Without air-conditioning!
What's that you say? I thought I heard, "Well done, Grunhilda, well done."?
TITUBA

last

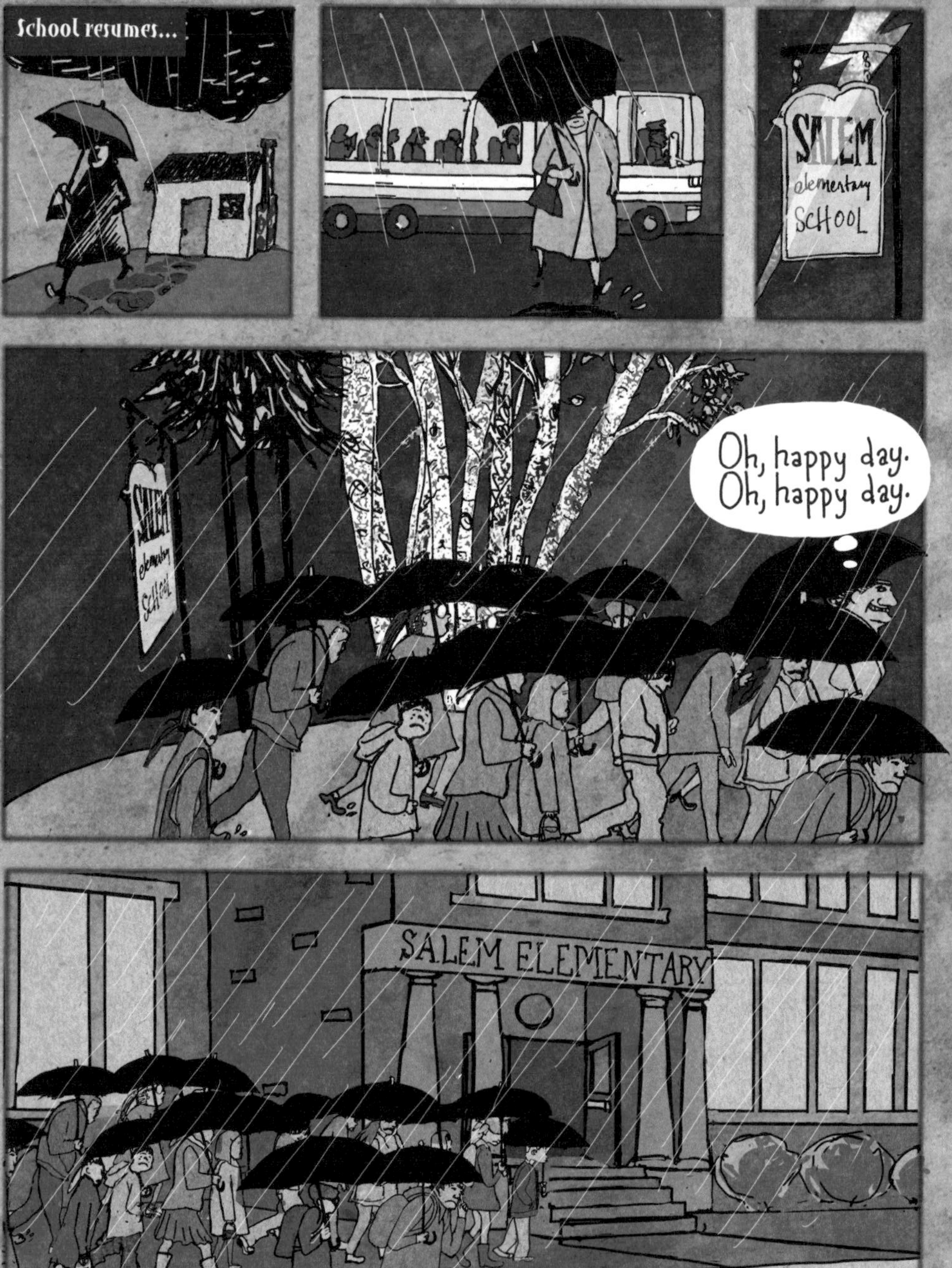
School resumes...
SALEM elementary SCHOOL
SALEM elementary SCHOOL
Oh, happy day. Oh, happy day.
SALEM ELEMENTARY

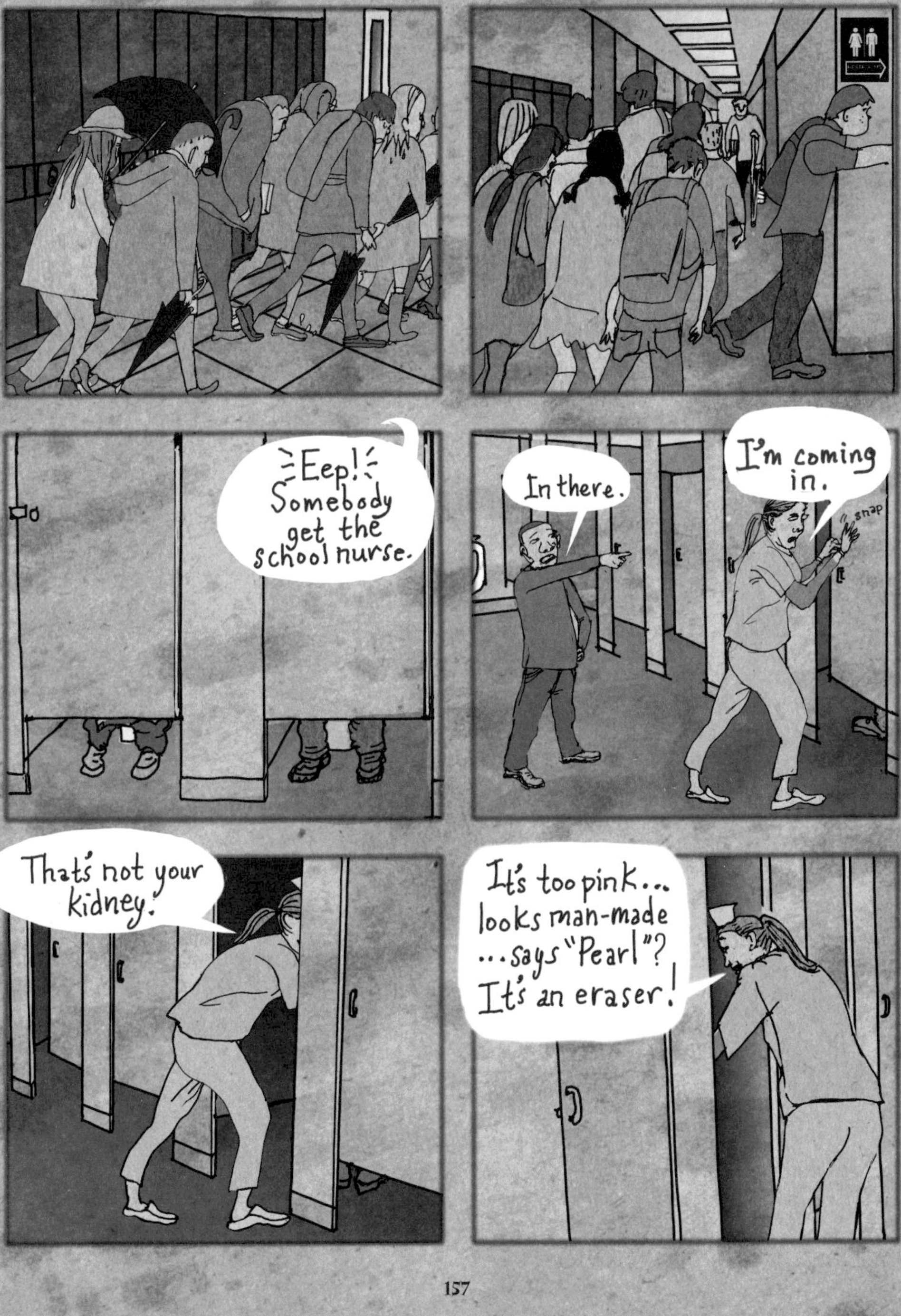
Eep! Somebody get the school nurse.
In there.
I'm coming in.
snap
That's not your kidney.
It's too pink... looks man-made ...says "Pearl"? It's an eraser!

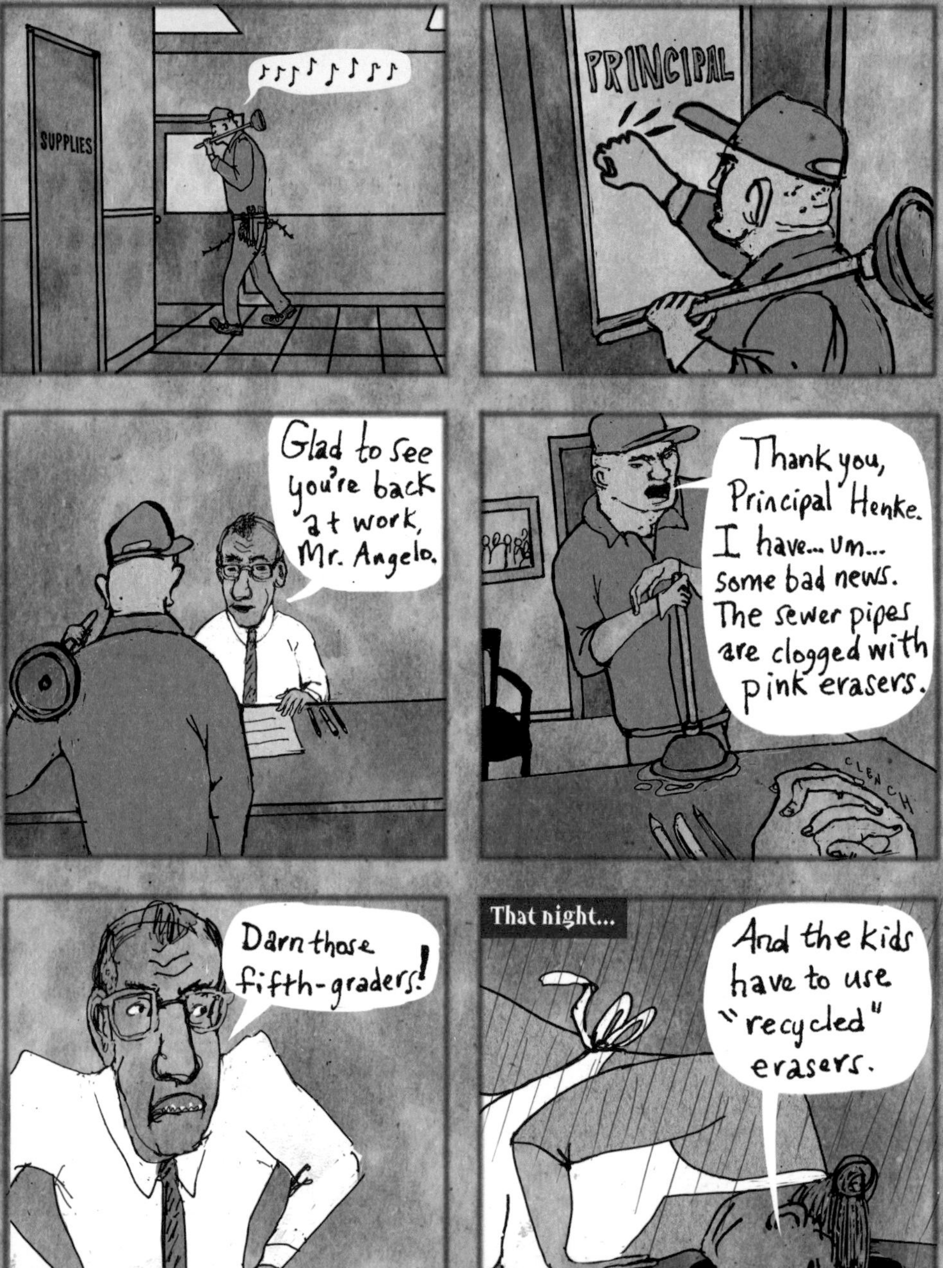
SUPPLIES
PRINCIPAL
Glad to see you're back at work, Mr. Angelo.
Thank you, Principal Henke. I have... um... some bad news. The sewer pipes are clogged with pink erasers.
CLENCH
Darn those fifth-graders!
That night...
And the kids have to use "recycled" erasers.

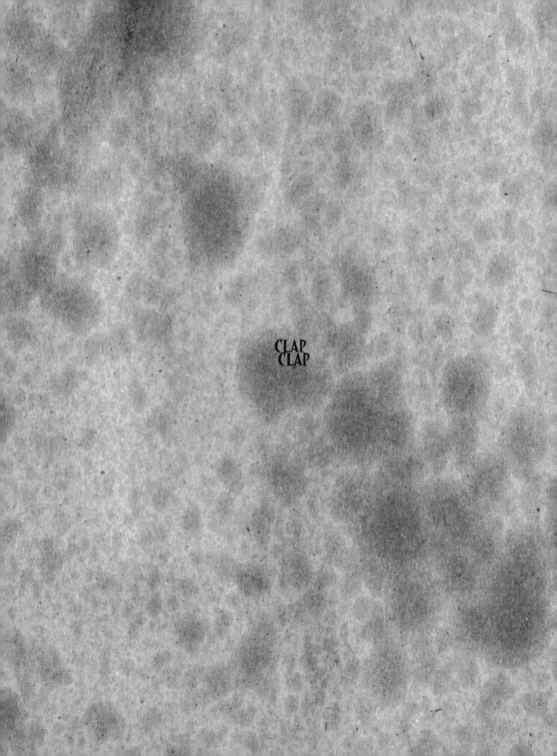

CLAP
CLAP

WATCH OUT FOR PAPERCUTZ

Welcome to the scary, yet super-nice, second LUNCH WITCH graphic novel, by Deb Lucke, from Papercutz, those lunch-loving lunatics dedicated to publishing great graphic novels for all ages. I'm Jim Salicrup, the Editor-in-Chief, and a big fan of witches. Here's proof, a pic of me in Salem, Massachusetts posing with one of my favorite witches…

Photo by Cherie Tieri

I wouldn't be surprised if many of you are unfamiliar with this particular witch, so allow me to introduce you to Samantha Stevens, the star of the popular 60s sitcom, Bewitched, which starred Elizabeth Montgomery as a good witch married to the advertising executive Darren Stevens. It was made into a movie in 2005 starring Nicole Kidman and Will Ferrell. One of the cute aspects of the TV series was that to cast her spells, Samantha would also wiggle her nose. As a fan of the show, I was surprised to learn very recently, that Ms. Montgomery wasn't actually wiggling her nose—it was trick photography! I'm sure Grunhilda Blackheart could wiggle her nose if she wanted to!

But speaking of witches, they seem to be everywhere these days. Just look at how many are appearing in the pages of various Papercutz publications. And just to help you tell which witch is which, we've assembled of few of them on the following pages. And this isn't even including the witches we mentioned in the first THE LUNCH WITCH graphic novel—the witch who lives in that gingerbread house can be found in CLASSICS ILLUSTRATED DELUXE #1 "Tales from the Brothers Grimm," in the adaptation of Hansel and Gretel," and Oz's infamous Wicked Witch of the West, whom we featured in a "Wicked" parody in TALES FROM THE CRYPT #9 "Wickeder."

On the following four pages, you'll meet a couple of interesting witches, and discover exactly what they're up to and in which Papercutz graphic novels they're doing their witchy stuff. But in the meantime, I think I might run out to get a bite to eat. For some strange reason I'm craving bacon…

Thanks,

JiM

STAY IN TOUCH!

EMAIL: salicrup@papercutz.com
WEB: papercutz.com
TWITTER: @papercutzgh
FACEBOOK: PAPERCUTZGRAPHICNOVELS
REGULAR MAIL: Papercutz, 160 Broadway, Suite 700, East Wing, New York, NY 10038

The WITCHES of PAPERCUTZ

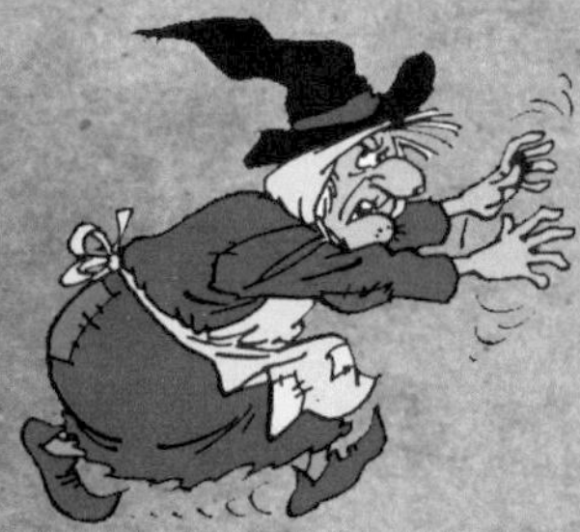

There are a few witches lurking about in the forest surrounding the Smurfs Village. There's Hogatha, who has appeared in the Smurfs cartoons, comics, and the super-popular Smurfs Village game. She looks kinda similar to Grunhilda Blackheart, except she wears a red wig to hide her baldness. There's also Brenda, a good little witch who appeared on a couple of animated TV episodes—"The Littlest Witch" and "Scruple's Sweetheart." But the witch we have to show you here appeared in THE SMURFS #10 "The Return of Smurfette," in the story entitled "Halloween." Here's a scene in which the Smurflings decided to spook the witch...

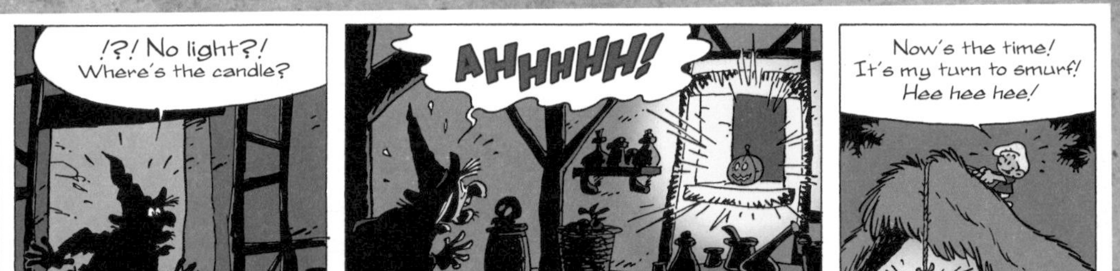
!?! No light?! Where's the candle?
AHHHHH!
Now's the time! It's my turn to smurf! Hee hee hee!
AHHHHH! Yet another head!
BOOOOOO!
Be gone, cursed ghosts!
SLAM
© Peyo

For the full story, pick up THE SMURFS #10 "The Return of the Smurfette."

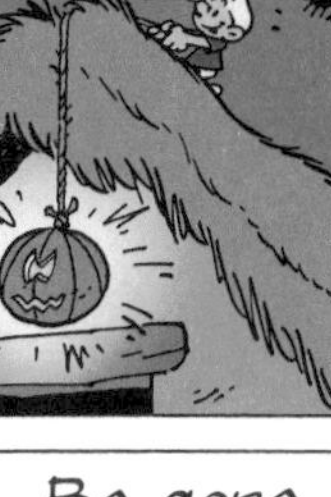
THE RETURN OF THE SMURFETTE
PAPERCUTZ

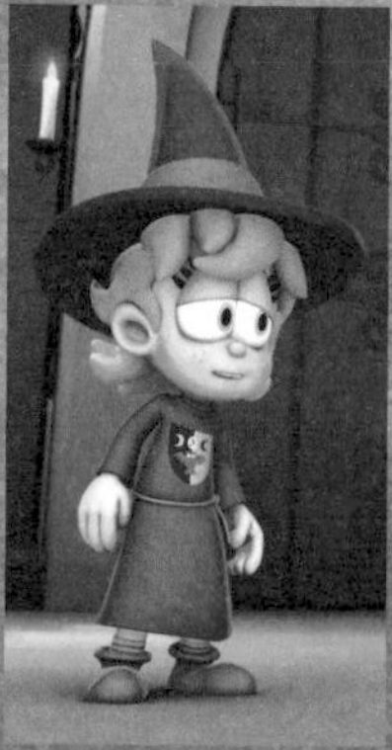

Who would've guessed that living right next door to Jon Arbuckle and his pets Garfield and Odie is a family of witches? Fortunately for Garfield and friends, their neighbors are all good witches. The youngest is Abigail, who accidentally unleashes a bad witch who had been trapped for a thousand years in a book. Gee, what is it with witches and books? Anyway, Abigail needed an animal to turn into her familiar—you know, what Mr. Williams, the batboys, and Louise are to Grunhilda Blacheart—for her witching class and decided to use poor hapless Odie. Against his own better judgment, Garfield decides to rescue Odie...

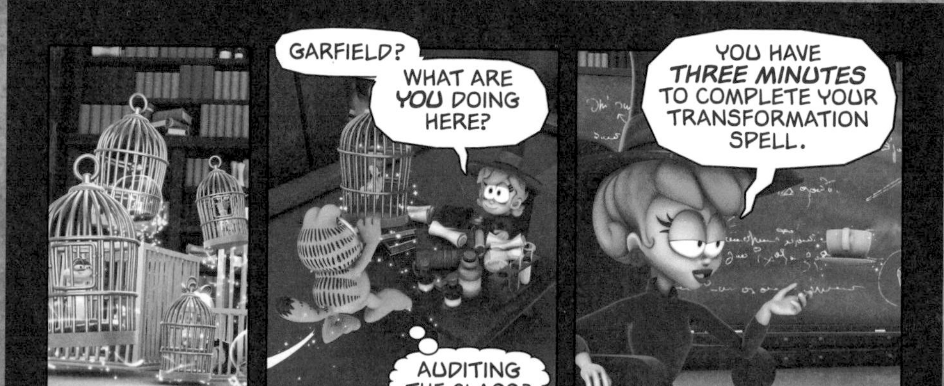

GARFIELD?
WHAT ARE *YOU* DOING HERE?
AUDITING THE CLASS?
YOU HAVE *THREE MINUTES* TO COMPLETE YOUR TRANSFORMATION SPELL.
I SHOULD GET EXTRA CREDIT FOR *TWO* TEACUPS!
COULD WE DISCUSS THIS?
RAZZLE FRAZZLE FREEN!

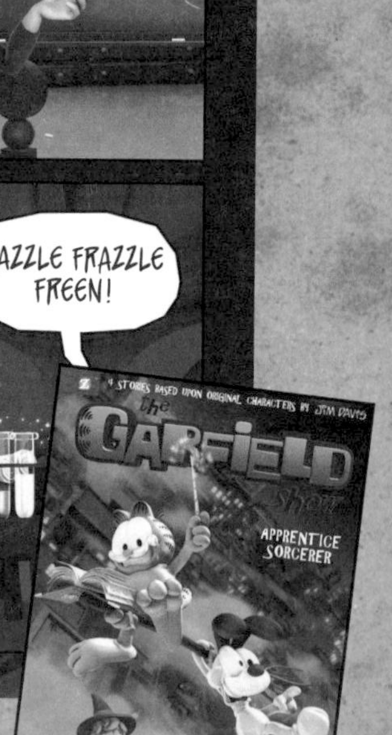

STORIES BASED UPON ORIGINAL CHARACTERS BY JIM DAVIS
The GARFIELD Show
APPRENTICE SORCERER
PAPERCUTZ

To see how it all played out, be sure to see THE GARFIELD SHOW #6 "Apprentice Sorcerer."

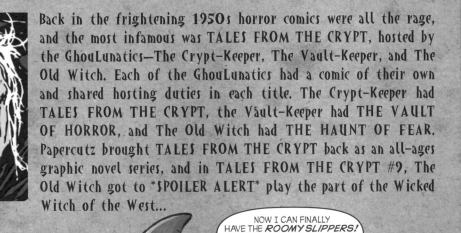

Back in the frightening 1950s horror comics were all the rage, and the most infamous was TALES FROM THE CRYPT, hosted by the GhouLunatics—The Crypt-Keeper, The Vault-Keeper, and The Old Witch. Each of the GhouLunatics had a comic of their own and shared hosting duties in each title. The Crypt-Keeper had TALES FROM THE CRYPT, the Vault-Keeper had THE VAULT OF HORROR, and The Old Witch had THE HAUNT OF FEAR. Papercutz brought TALES FROM THE CRYPT back as an all-ages graphic novel series, and in TALES FROM THE CRYPT #9, The Old Witch got to *SPOILER ALERT* play the part of the Wicked Witch of the West...

NOW I CAN FINALLY HAVE THE *ROOMY SLIPPERS!* THE MOST *COMFORTABLE* IN THE WORLD! AND THEY'RE ALL MINE!

FINE. JUST DON'T ASK *WHERE* IT CAME FROM!

© EC 2016

⌐WHOA⌐, MY FEET FEEL GREAT!

For the rest of the story and several other scary tales with a twisted sense of humor, try to track down TALES FROM THE CRYPT #9 "Wickeder," not to be confused with the all-new revival of TALES FROM THE CRYPT coming from Super Genius, the Papercutz imprint for older audiences.

TALES CRYPT
PARODY
PRESENTS A SICK, UNAUTHORIZED, WICKED PARODY
The Stinky Dead Kid is Back!
WICKEDER
Now Playing!
...and his little dog, too!
PAPERCUTZ

And last, and certainty not least, there's the Lunch Witch herself, Grunhilda Blackheart. Believe it or not, she wasn't always a High School lunch lady. Before she got the lunch lady gig she was simply an old witch struggling to survive. But just when things were looking their worst Mr. Willaims found a listing in the Help Wanted section of the local newspaper that would change Grunhilda's life forever...

I'm afraid the world has no use for me and my ilk.

ARF! I mean— LOOK!

LUNCH LADY
ELEMENTARY SCHOOL
CAFETERIA
978 555-1300
GOOD COOKS
NEED NOT APPLY

As you might've guessed, Grunhilda nailed the interview and got the job. But that didn't mean it was smooth sailing for the newly appointed Lunch Lady. One young girl, Madison Caruso, suspected that Grunhilda was hiding a secret—or did she? It's hard to tell with Madison, but Grunhilda really thought Madison could get her into real hot water and had to take action to make sure that didn't happen. But you probably already know all this if this graphic novel is on your shelf!

The Lunch Witch
By Deb Lucke
PAPERCUTZ